Snowballs!
Winter Fun
on the Slopes

Fliss Chester

ORION

First published in Great Britain in 2018 by Orion Books,
an imprint of The Orion Publishing Group Ltd
Carmelite House, 50 Victoria Embankment,
London EC4Y 0DZ

An Hachette UK company

1 3 5 7 9 10 8 6 4 2

A CIP catalogue record for this book is
available from the British Library.

ISBN 978 1 4091 7861 3

Typeset by Born Group

Printed and bound in Great Britain by Clays Ltd, St Ives plc

MIX
Paper from
responsible sources
FSC® C104740

www.orionbooks.co.uk

Snowballs!
Winter Fun
on the Slopes

Fliss Chester spent ten years working on magazines, writing about lifestyle and interiors, sampling the offerings in London's bars and restaurants and enjoying press junkets and parties. An early adopter of the 'portfolio career', her other varied jobs have included being an interior designer, a brief foray into finance, and Head of Gin (yes, that's a real job). Now she lives and works in the beautiful Surrey Hills with her husband and cat, who are both very supportive of her writing — although the cat may just like having The Lap at home more often.

To Mum
(sorry about the naughty bits)

and Rupert
(you are the naughty bits)

Prologue

From: Jenna Jenkins
Cc: Max, Angus Linklater, SalPal, Hugo, Bertie
Subject: Bon ski!

Guys – can't believe we're off tomorrow! Apparently, the snow is falling and I feel the vin chaud calling! Thanks again Bertie for inviting us all.

Get a good night's sleep and see you all sparkly eyed at Gatwick at 10!

Bon ski!
Jenna Xxx

From: Max Finch
Cc: Jenksy, Gus, Sally Jones, Hdog, Berts
Subject: RE: Bon ski!

Sleeping's cheating. Like the vin chaud idea though – might start early. Anyone out tonight? H-boss? Gus?

M

From: Hugo Portman
Cc: Finchy, Jenks, Sal, Big Gus, Roberta Mason-Hoare
Subject: RE: Bon ski!

Excellent notion old man. Rising Sun 8ish?

From: Sally Jones
Cc: Huggie Bear, Jenna, Angus, Bertie, Max
Subject: RE: Bon ski!

Excuse me Hugo! But YOU have packing to do and there's no way I'm travelling next to a hungover grump all day tomorrow!

Ladies – back me up here! Also, I think I'm coming down with something, might not be the craziest week for me, soz.

xSx

From: Roberta Mason-Hoare
Cc: Maxie, Hugo P, Sally J, Jenna, Angus L
Subject: RE: Bon ski!

Sorry darlings, have massive party tonight at Hix's new place as otherwise would have loved to have joined you . . .

Sally, sweetie – if you can't run with the big dogs stay on the porch ;o)

Bertie x

From: Sally Jones
To: Jenna
Subject: WTF??

I can't believe her!!!! What a b1tch! What do you think she meant 'run with the big dogs'? She's such a man-grabber. Hoare by name, whore by nature! God – please save me – and Hugo – from her all holiday? Who bloody invited her anyway?? xxxxx

From: Jenna Jenkins
To: SalPal
Subject: RE: WTF??

Umm – I think she invited us, sweetie! Don't let her worry you, Hugo totally loves YOU and wouldn't spare her a thought. Max on the other hand . . .

Anyway, love you, can't wait til tomo!! Eeks! Xxxxx

From: Angus Linklater
Cc: Jenna, Hugo, Max, Sal, Bertie
Subject: RE: Bon ski!

Can't leave work before 9 guys, so see you tomorrow.

A

From: Jenna Jenks
Cc: Max, Angus Linklater, SalPal, Hugo, Bertie
Subject: RE: Bon ski!

I find it hard to leave work before '9 guys' too . . . but then, that's working in a private art gallery for you . . .

From: Roberta Mason-Hoare
Cc: Maxie, Hugo P, Sally J, Jenna J, Angus L
Subject: RE: Bon ski!

What time are we meeting again Jenna? And flight number? My Add Lee Exec app needs these things apparently, but like, who knows why!!!!!!?

And, purleease can we get some champagne at the airport? Will the first-class lounge be open do you think? Am so going bonkers for Bolly at the moment!

From: Max Finch
To: Berts
Subject: Dirty Bertie?

I bet you are, you dirty thing. Love it.

M

From: Roberta Mason-Hoare
To: Maxie
Subject: RE: Dirty Bertie?

I know you do handsome. I think it's up to you and me to liven up these drears. I didn't go down on Dubious Dominic to get his lush pad to just stay in and eat fondue all week!! Got to dash. Looking forward to seeing YOU though ;o)

Mwah!

From: Jenna Jenkins
Cc: Max, Angus Linklater, SalPal, Hugo, Bertie
Subject: RE: Bon ski!

10am!!!! At NORTH terminal! BA2719 to GVA. That's Geneva by the way . . .

Sally's right – have packing to do tonight after rather large week and not exactly expecting a calm and restful holiday ;o) – but see you guys tomo! Xx

---

From: Angus Linklater
To: Jenna
Subject: RE: Bon ski!

Thanks so much for organising us all Jenna. Hitting the slopes was definitely one of the reasons I came back from Singapore. Looking forward to it.

A.x.

Saturday

1

Jenna took a long sip from her mochafrappolattecino and appreciated the hot foamy liquid on her parched throat. As someone who was ridiculously early for everything, she had managed to get to Gatwick at 9.30 a.m., a good half an hour before the slightly-earlier-than-needed-anyway meeting time of 10 a.m. But she just knew Sally and Hugo would be pushing it to the last minute and she wanted to make sure she had enough time to mooch around the shops in Duty Free. Not that she could afford the Rolex watches and Mulberry handbags, even if they were tax free. Anyway, there was no point being in a rush and getting all hot and bothered and ruining her carefully planned outfit of skinny jeans, soft grey cashmere cardigan and Uggs. OK, she thought, not fashion's wildest frontier exactly, but it was hard planning what to wear when you were invited to go skiing with London's hardest, most label-wearing partygoer, especially when you weren't exactly Kate Moss yourself. Jenna thought she would work the simple, casual look and anyway, leaving Clapham Junction this morning she would have looked bloody stupid dressed in what that girl over there was wearing . . .

It only took half a second, however, for Jenna to realise that 'that girl over there', swanning through the milling airport crowds towards her, was the label-wearing party-goer herself, Roberta — Bertie to her friends (last count, 2,358 on Facebook not to mention the 10,000+ Instagram followers) — and dear God, what was she wearing? Surely only the likes of Liz Hurley could pull off a Chanel ski suit, but no, here was living proof that ordinary folk, if you could call Bertie that, could do it too. The salopettes were skin tight, black and picked out with a white vertical line down the side seam. The ski jacket was tight, black and fitted, the hood rimmed with the realest of fur that perfectly set off her golden highlights. And of course, shielding her eyes from the fluorescent airport lights were the biggest sunglasses one could possibly fit on a face. Chanel, too, Jenna assumed — hoping her second-hand eBay ones would pass muster under Bertie's scrutiny.

'Darling!' shouted Bertie, making that first syllable last for about three seconds. 'Morning! Bet you didn't think I would be first!'

'Well, technically *I* was here first, but yes, well done! You look . . . um, amazing! Are you wearing that on the slopes too?'

'Of course not, silly, this is just my après-ski outfit; I have the Dior down jacket for chillier days on the slopes and the lovely PRs at Selfridges practically forced some super-warm pink Versace salopettes onto me, so I am totally kitted out for the slopes of Val d'Argent!'

'Wow — yeah, totally! Where's your suitcase?' Jenna said as she looked around, slightly bewildered as ever by Bertie, who was just starting to rattle off the list of other designer ski wear she'd felt it 'abso nesso' to bring.

'Oh, the man is bringing it over. Limo driver, you know. Couldn't lift it myself but he was so kind he said he'd bring it. Oh, there he is now.'

Looking beyond the growing queues of passengers checking in, craning their necks to read departure boards and leaning heavily on luggage trolleys, Jenna saw a small man coming towards them. Very slowly. He was obviously more used to sitting in a comfortable luxury saloon car for eight hours a day and was almost collapsing under the weight of — Jenna couldn't believe it — a trunk. A Louis Vuitton trunk.

'Oh. My. God . . .' Jenna felt a little bit nauseated, fear of how this behemoth would fit on a mere passenger airliner almost overwhelming her, not to mention the damage it must be causing that poor man's back.

'I know,' explained Bertie, furrowing her brow just the merest amount and nodding thoughtfully, 'a little excessive.' She paused, then obviously decided that this wasn't worth risking wrinkles over. 'But I just love the space it gives you for all your things, and it's really practical because, like, nothing gets squashed.' While she explained this to Jenna she slipped two crisp fifty pound notes into the driver's shirt pocket and, with a wave of her hand, dismissed the almost-crippled man back to his car.

'But you can't actually carry it.'

'No, but there are people to do this, yes?'

'Will it get on the plane?'

'Oh, yes, I think so,' said Bertie as she indicated the bulging purse in her handbag. 'Always pays to pay, as it were!' At that she screeched at her own joke, only stopping when she paused suddenly to pout and admire herself in the reflective surface of the plate glass window next to them. She gave her hair an idle flick and started tapping away on her phone.

Jenna was unbelievably relieved when her old friend Max turned up. Years of playing rugby for the Cambridge blues had made Max strong and incredibly muscly, which he had worked into a leaner look during his years as a City banker. Six feet tall and with the sort of deep brown eyes you'd want to stare into and believe anything he said, Max was certainly a catch, and Jenna's heart made a little leap as soon as she saw him. But Max was not a catch to be trusted. Flirting and flitting from one girl to the next, with conquests such as the impossibly glamorous and well-connected, not to mention well-endowed, Bertie behind him, Jenna knew Max was a super-charming bad boy . . .

but boy, she would let him be bad and super-charming all over her any day.

Looking at him now in his casual but expensive designer jeans, Gant T-shirt and cashmere jumper under a Napapijri ski jacket, she allowed herself to remember what it had felt like to have him touch her — a memory she hardly needed to dredge up from the past, bearing in mind it was only a few months ago and it floated so close to the surface of her consciousness any passing net could snare it. She closed her eyes and was instantly there again, standing up against the wall of the nightclub, swaying along with the music, taking a pause from the dance floor while her heart still thudded along with the beat. He'd come towards her, drinks in hand, raising them out of her reach as he pressed his body against her. But with the lowering of his head — and the brushing of his lips against hers she'd had to allow in a tiny moment of doubt during her growing euphoria. The overpowering smell of booze on him told her one thing — and she was right the next morning when no text had come, no dinner invitation issued, nothing. She opened her eyes. Knowing that her love was as unrequited as ever, she put her little heart's leap into the emotional box with all the other little leaps and closed the lid.

'Morning, Jenksy.' Max dropped his head down to kiss Jenna on each cheek. Almost instinctively Jenna inhaled — Max always smelt so good and his aftershave was like a memory stick of flashbacks: snapshots of college balls, evenings in the pub, days out together, picnics by the Cam, drinks in the City and late night dancing — *that* night from a couple of months ago. Breathing out as he pulled away, she saw Max look towards Bertie before conspiratorially saying to her, 'You look, um, completely normal this morning.'

'Oh, Max. She's in Chanel, don't you know — and the trunk . . . Louis Vuitton!'

'Blimey, does she have Sherpa Tensing with her?'

'Uh-uh, I think it might be you boys at the other end . . .'

'Jeez.' He paused, rolled his eyes slightly, then headed over to say hello to his old flame Bertie. Jenna looked at him as he strode over to the super-slim, super-rich and super-breastie Bertie, while a burning envy that had never quite been quashed rattled inside her. Jenna knew they had an off and sometimes very on relationship, and she hated how it made it her feel. Not for the first time, recently, she seriously questioned why she had agreed to come on this trip of Bertie's — only last week she'd almost backed out. They'd all been drinking in the City after work — a glass of wine had become a bottle of wine and Jenna felt sure Max was flirting with her again. She'd almost melted when his hand had rested on her thigh. But when last orders came it was Jenna that was popped into a cab on her own — kiss on the cheek goodbye — as Max carefully handed Bertie into hers, following her in. To stop herself from cancelling the ski trip there and then she had dwelt instead on that lingering hand, the warmth of it on her thigh . . . The thought of it now zinged around her, sending electric pulses up her spine. Yes, she thought, maybe, just maybe, this would be her week, her shared cab home, her chance to finally get together with the man of her dreams.

Jenna was shaken from her reverie when Angus appeared in front of her. She didn't know him that well, although they'd bumped into each other several times over the years at parties and nights out — and to Jenna's shame, she might not have been entirely sober for most of those 'bumps'. In fact, last time she saw him, didn't she burst into tears after too many white wine spritzers? Well, he had seemed a good shoulder to cry on at the time. He was Max's old friend from school, so he'd been up to see them all at Cambridge once or twice during their years there while he had studied architecture in London. After graduating he'd worked abroad for a few years but was now back in town, working long hours and putting his heart into his designs at his London-based firm. Blond and fair-skinned, he had the physique of an ex-rower and the height of, well, a near giant. His Atlantic-blue eyes had found Jenna in the general melee of the checking-in area and, as he loped towards her, his naturally serious-looking face broke into a wide smile. Jenna noticed that his collar was half sticking up, escaping from his highly technical ski jacket, which along with his rather bushy gingery beard made him look like a Cornish fisherman. Jenna returned his smile, her mind racing back to their last encounter, trying desperately to remember if Angus had been at all judgemental about either her drunkenness or her desperate crush on Max. But no, her mind was blank (damn those spritzers!) and she just had to hope for the best as the bristly ginger beard came down towards her, scratching against her face as Angus planted a perfunctory peck on her cheek.

As Angus and Jenna said their hellos, Max came and joined them, leaving Bertie to speak very loudly into her diamante iPhone to someone called Sebastian, who was obviously not playing ball.

'I see the hipster beard is still a "thing", mate.' Max stood back and pretended to admire the bushiness of Angus's facial fuzz. 'Couldn't get away with that in a proper job, you know . . .' He winked as he said it and then joshed his friend with a play-fighting fist into his chest.

'Helps me fit in with my new tribe − I couldn't be an architect, work in Old Street, *and* rock a Savile Row suit now, could I?' Angus, however, sub-consciously rubbed a hand along his bearded left cheek and Jenna noticed for the first time the very old school, and not at all hipster, gold signet ring on his little finger.

Leaving the men to catch up, Jenna looked up at the departure board. Flights to St Lucia, Barbados, Grenada and other dream Caribbean locations filled the screens and Jenna imagined what it would be like to be here just with Max, the two of them in executive style passing through the hordes to the First Class lounge on their way to some glamorous tropical island. She'd be thinner, of course, by this point, and still be tanned from their last jaunt, and sporting something very shiny on her left hand . . .

'You're dozing off, Jenksy — too early a start for you art world types?' Max wrapped his arms around her from behind as she sat on Bertie's trunk — well, it had to be useful for something — and gave her a raspberry on her neck.

'Eew!' Jenna cried. She relished having Max's arms around her, but her internal panic was rising — what if he sensed she was desperately enjoying this? How much should she lean in to him? Should she pretend she was not enjoying it? *Oh, but he's touching me . . . just like the other night . . .* The panic rising more and more, Jenna reacted by shrugging Max off her, although her 'shrug' became more of a shove (was caffeine to her like spinach was to Popeye?) and she managed to land an errant elbow straight into some poor, unsuspecting man's crotch.

'Ooof. Morning, Jenksy!' the poor unsuspecting man bellowed. 'If I'd wanted castrating I'd have let you know . . .'

Nothing about Hugo could be called discreet: from his confident, booming voice to his bright red ski jacket, he was a force of nature. When Jenna had first met Hugo Portman he'd been the golden boy of their college. A naturally gifted scholar who had spent as much time in the bar as the library, he'd done well — so well that now, as a successful banker, the good times had started to show around the waistline, and Hugo was as huggable as a big bear. Hugo was engaged to Sally Jones, Jenna's best friend. Sally, like Jenna, had followed a more 'creative' path, although thanks to her pure ambition and talent at just getting on the phone and getting things done, was now features editor of one of Britain's largest magazines. Working as many hours as Hugo did, though for a fraction of the pay, Sally had probably subconsciously thought, if you can't beat 'em . . . well, you can marry them. Lovely Sally swooped on Jenna, kissing her hello and giving her a squeeze. Amid the sound of the tannoy announcing the check-in desks open for their flight, she filled Jenna in on their horrendous journey to the airport and how if darling Huggy Bear hadn't been such a wonderful driver that silly little Renault Clio would have nicked their spot and who knows when they might have got here. Love her she might, but Jenna couldn't help sometimes tuning out as Sally wittered on. And at times like this she could become mesmerised by the three-carat love token on Sally's left hand as it caught the glaring lights of the departure hall on its perfectly cut facets. Jenna became like a rabbit caught in the headlights of a diamond-encrusted truck. 'One day,' she sighed to herself, as she pulled her suitcase towards to the airline's specified desks, '*one day* . . .'

2

Snow crunched under the tyres of the private minibus transfer as it wound up the mountain to Val d'Argent. Val d'Argent — colloquially called Val d'Angleterre due to its popularity among the Sloaney skiing set — was a picturesque, almost Disneyfied village. One of the first purpose-built ski resorts, it still maintained some of its Alpine charm, but you didn't need to scratch far below the surface to see the subtly hidden steaming spa baths of the five-star hotels and private chalets, or the Prada skis propped against the carefully constructed 'rustique' wooden ski racks. And a first for France: under-pavement heating that kept the paths clear of ice.

'Jolly good, too,' snorted Bertie as Sally read this last fact out loud from the info leaflet she'd picked up at the airport. 'I've got my Louboutins with the killer heels — so gorgeous, but I'd hate to ruin them on slushy paths and end up, like, practically ice skating everywhere!'

'You brought Louboutins? What else have you got in that massive trunk?' Sally said, raising an eyebrow. She was still smarting from Bertie's comment on the email chain yesterday and her constant one-upmanship — Sally's rather modest North Face barrel bag was not a patch on the two-tonne-trunk.

Leaving Bertie and Sally to continue verbally poking each other, Jenna thought about Max. Where had all these hugs and thigh squeezes come from recently? The other night he'd had his arm around her too as they sat in the wine bar in Paternoster Square. She'd felt sky high just pretending to herself that they were a couple — imagine how she would feel if it really happened? He'd made it clear, however, over all the years she'd known him, that she wasn't the one for him. As clear as 'shagging-just-about-every-other-girl-he-knew-and-not-her' could make it. And for ages she'd torn her heart out about it — so much so that it almost just seemed a habit now to fantasise and dream about a life with Max. He was her default fantasy, as it were, the Richard Gere to her not-so-pretty woman. On the face of it, they were the best of friends, and that was always her problem. Friends. The bloody 'friend zone'. And Jenna just couldn't find the courage to break out of it. She opened her eyes. She was getting herself worked up and it didn't help that she had been screwing her face up in an incredibly unattractive way, biting the inside of her lips as she tended to do when stressed or thinking. This hadn't been lost on Max, whom she was sitting next to in the minibus (thank you, travel gods!), and who was now doing an impression of her to a very much-amused Bertie.

'Oh, piss off, Max,' Jenna laughed, then stuck her tongue out at him, happy to have caught his attention, even if it wasn't for the right reason.

'What were you doing, Jenksy? Trying very hard to work out exactly how many positions in a one night stand?'

'That one isn't hard to work out, Max, it's easy: position one is leaning against the bar, position two holding out your hand to accept the large gin and tonic and three is on your back, thinking of England and wondering if you set *EastEnders* to record . . .'

'And there speaks a lady of experience?'

'Only repeating what your past conquests tell me.' Jenna felt a frisson of excitement flow through her body — was Max flirting with her again?

'Touché, Jenksy.' And with a wink, then a very exaggerated downturn of the mouth, 'You owe me a beer for that though, mean girl.'

'I shall buy you a lady beer, Max — I don't think my drinking budget will stretch to much around these parts!'

'It doesn't stretch much back home either. When was the last time it was your round?'

'Oh, shut up — I *am* a lady; we don't buy drinks, we just look attractive and have champagne on tap.' Jenna hoped she'd recovered from Max's dig at her — she felt terrible that it was always the boys who bought the drinks, but her job in a private art gallery meant she could barely afford her rates and rent, never mind nights out in super-hip bars and members-only clubs. Jenna closed her eyes again, but this time she was smiling.

Five minutes later and Bertie was cursing herself for not *insisting* on chartering a helicopter. She had allowed Sally to book the Ice Bus, which was, to Bertie's mind, definitely not the 'coolest way to arrive in the resort' as the website link had promised. 'Cool . . .' she'd said to herself, as she'd begrudgingly emailed her OK across to Sally, 'would be like, a Sikorsky twin engine with those gorgeous cream leather seats like the Blake-Howards had at Cheltenham last year. God, Monty B-H had been full of total BS, but *he* and *that* had been so cool. The Ice *bloody* Bus is not cool.'

Still, never one not to try to make the best of a bad situation, when they were getting into the — actually quite slick — black minibus at Geneva airport, her carefully timed 'accidental' dropping of her silk Hermes scarf had been meant to ensure that Max would bend down to pick it up for her, letting odd, hipster-bearded Angus and loopy Jenna get into the bloody van first and end up sitting together, leaving her next to the only man she really wanted on this trip: Max. But Angus, in his weirdly tall way, had contorted himself into almost Peter Crouch-style robotics to pick it up for her, bloody gentleman, leaving Max just one step behind Jenna and now annoyingly settled in next to her. Foiled again. Still, she thought to herself, better to be next to Angus than boring old Sally and bloody Hugo — and nothing wrong with getting Max's attention with a little bit of harmless flirting with the big A. Bertie had always been a bit jealous of Jenna's friendship with Max, but had contented herself with knowing that she was too plain to interest him in anything naughtier. Wondering now at what on earth Jenna could be saying to Max to make him laugh so much stirred up Bertie's curiosity and, by no small means, her libido. Angus dozed next to her, so she popped her hand on his (to her surprise) very pleasantly taut thigh and rubbed it up and down. His eyes popped open and he sat up with a start.

'I'm bored, Angus, you're no fun to sit next to,' Bertie half whined, half purred — a voice that usually got her anything she damn well wanted.

'Um, well, I think I have Travel Scrabble somewhere.'

'Travel Scrabble?' This was going to be harder than she thought, like squeezing blood from a frigging stone. Frigid stone more like. 'Now tell me, why would I want to spell out dirty words when I'd far rather be doing them? Perhaps that makes me a charades kinda girl?'

'And what exactly would you like to act out for me?' replied Angus. *Oi oi*, this is more like it, thought Bertie, though she barely had time to think now whether she really wanted to go down this track with Angus. She tilted her head, letting her long blonde hair tumble over her shoulder. Charles Worthington really was worthington every penny, she thought, as she noticed Max turn to look at her across the minibus's aisle.

'Well, Gus, I fake a very good orgasm, although of course I rarely have to, especially not when the man I take to my bedroom — heck, not even bedroom, sometimes it's the deck of a yacht, a private jet, a deserted beach . . .'

'I get the message!'

'Let me finish — men so rarely do! As I was saying, there's no need to fake it when a man really knows what he's doing. Do you, Angus?'

Angus was floored. He opened and closed his mouth a couple of times but by the time he'd thought of anything vaguely witty to say back, Bertie had turned to face the other way, plugged her Swarovski crystal-covered headphones into her equally blinging phone and produced a pout Mrs Beckham herself would be proud of.

Jenna, eyes still closed, had perked up her ears at what was going on. Bertie and Angus? Now that would be an odd match, she thought to herself. But wasn't he still going out with that Amazonian New York model? She remembered him telling her the last time they met (must have been before the memory-addling seventh spritzer) about Diane Blane, the half-Ugandan, half-American, six-foot-tall catwalk star who he'd met through friends while she was walking at Singapore Fashion Week. It had all sounded rather full-on, with flights booked on both sides to see each other again once she was back in the States. Jenna noted to herself to ask Angus about her, as even knowing a girl friend of a friend of a friend who was an international catwalk model was quite cool . . . She opened her eyes and looked over to Max next to her. He was just turning back to face the front, a smile on his lips and a sparkle in his now just closing eyes. Her gaze followed his ridiculously handsome jawline up to his cheeks and from there to his dark lashes. Pulling her eyes away from him she turned to look out of the window at the beautiful Alpine scenery beyond, the trees dusted with a light smattering of snow and the vast ravines that punctuated the jagged mountains, and tried to shake the slight uneasiness that for some reason had crept up from her stomach and into her heart.

The Ice Bus continued its death-defying journey round the snaking mountain road, the windscreen wipers swishing off the occasional white flake while its occupants continued to snooze or generally chat about the state of the snow; if there really had been a 'dump' last week or if the glacier would be the only place worth hiking up to get any decent skiing in.

'Damn this global warming,' said Hugo. 'Don't mind Rock being a bit sunnier and all that in the summer, but if me not recycling the old Bombay Sapphire bottles Sally gets through means I only get some rotten slush to skid through every winter then get me to the bottle bank on time!'

There was no point in Sally arguing with her betrothed. The girl did like gin.

3

About thirty minutes later, and about thirty crisp ten-euro notes later, Bertie's trunk and the rest of the Ice Bus passengers were deposited outside the chalet. Jenna noticed that the driver, who had been goggle-eyed at the size of the Louis Vuitton megalith, and then equally goggle-eyed as Bertie flashed him a winning smile — with her boobs — had taken only a bit of financial greasing to help unload the luggage. Jenna, still incredibly embarrassed by Bertie's extravagance, had had to wander away from the group to stop her from cringing terribly at what was going on. When she turned back she saw the minibus drive away, bouncing on its newly lightened axles, and she also took in the sight of their chalet. However, chalet wasn't really the word; Bertie had managed to score them an uber-slick, floor-to-ceiling glass, alpine shag pad. Jenna whistled under her breath as she shifted her boot bag from one shoulder to the other.

'Wow, Berts, kudos,' said Hugo as he put his arm around her, not noticing Sally's — or Bertie's — slight prickling as he did so. The others all chimed in — Sally included, to give her her due — congratulating Bertie on getting them the swishest-looking place in town. And its location was pretty awesome too. Jenna looked along the road that ran along the front of the chalet. There were a few other residences like this one, then the road dipped and fell into the main centre of town, only a five-minute walk to the ski lifts and, more importantly, Jenna thought, to the bars. Ooh, the bars! The prospects! The excitements! Jenna's thoughts instantly turned to Max: would this be the trip where they finally got together over too many Jägerbombs? Or would someone even better come along and pull her out of this sinking pit of Max-like quicksand? She couldn't help but wince when she thought of the years — and romances — she'd potentially wasted by always hoping she'd one day get together with Max. Surely all this love for all these years couldn't end up being for nothing, could it? Startled by another minibus hurtling down the road, Jenna turned around and finally noticed the view from the chalet: talk about wow factor — it was bloody awe-inspiring. The side of the chalet looked straight out onto the Bête Noir, one of France's most notorious black runs, known for claiming a few broken bones in its time but no less breathtaking to look at because of it.

Bertie tapped a six-digit code into a box by the entrance, then pushed open the glass and oak door into the boot room. Before she let everyone in, she slowly and deliberately recited the code for them all to learn.

'It's 9-9-0-5-4-9,' she intoned. 'Totally simple to remember, as it's Dominic's yearly salary, right? So funny! He said it was totally why he never pushed for a pay rise as seven digits just wouldn't work in the codey thingy!' Bertie snorted with laughter as she finally let everyone into the gloriously warm, and amazingly fitted out, boot room.

'Hashtag first world problem eh?' Angus whispered to Jenna as he held the door open for her.

'My salary barely goes above my pin number,' she replied, looking up at him and rolling her eyes as she ducked under his arm and followed her friends inside.

Bertie reminded them, although they'd all met Dominic at various parties, that he was *so* in love with her, hence the free chalet, and that 'if it wasn't for Gigi — I mean he's devoted to the woman, bizarre-looking as she is — then he would totally be with *moi*, I'm sure. Oh, chalet girl — hiya!' Bertie greeted the sulky-looking girl leaning against the handrail of the stairs that lead into the chalet proper. 'Roberta Mason-Hoare, *howjado*. I'm sure Dominic's briefed you. These are, like, my friends and we're here all week. I've got, like, a list of things I *must* not eat. Definitely no tap water over dinner, ya? I don't eat carbs and whatever happens don't let me have anything dairy after midnight. OK?'

'Blimey, she sounds like a Mogwai,' whispered Angus to Jenna, who had to suppress a giggle for the second time in about thirty seconds, this time at the thought of Bertie becoming a violent Gremlin if she went near anything so dangerous as a yoghurt after hours. *He's funny*, Jenna thought to herself, *I'd forgotten that*.

Not long after and bedrooms had been assigned — Sally and Hugo taking the parental-style double with a cute little en suite and balcony leading off full-height windows over-looking the pistes. 'It's only fair,' as Sally had tried to say seriously to Jenna. 'If I have to put up with sleeping with Mr P and his snoring then I should at least have some creature comforts!' She winked indulgently at her fiancé, who'd been the first to crack open a biere d'Alsace and was already barking at the other chaps to 'get one down' and then get straight out to the après-ski bars. Jenna was sharing with Bertie. And Bertie's trunk, which, once unpacked, meant that Jenna had approximately three inches of hanging space left and a small patch of floor to call her own.

'But darling,' Bertie had purred at her as she hung up yet another sequined gown, 'you've only brought one ski jacket anyway, so I just don't see the problem and, like, why you think you need more space? I mean, it's not like you even have any real evening wear.' At this Bertie had pulled from the trunk another dazzling dress, this one a mini, a pair of satin black skinny trousers and three different clutch bags because 'you never know, darling, how you might feel and what goes with what!'

Izzy, the chalet girl, quietly closed the door of her bedroom and rested against it, her head leaning back into her dressing gown that was hanging there. She let out a long sigh. Between dietary demands and boozing blokes she didn't reckon she'd have as easy a ride this week as Dominic had promised her. 'They'll be no trouble, Iz,' he'd said on the phone the other day as he briefed her on his calendar. 'Sorry, it completely escaped my mind to tell you.' Yeah, thanks Dominic, she thought. There go my plans for the next week. 'They'll be good tippers I'm sure — be nice to them and I bet you'll get some hefty wodge at the end of the week.' Hefty wodge or not, Izzy couldn't fail but notice how incredibly handsome one of the guys was — tall and dark with deep brown eyes. He'd smiled at her as she'd shown him and his bearded mate their room, and those chocolate eyes had been the ones melting her like a dropped Malteser down a cleavage. He can tip me any way he likes, she thought as she crossed the room to her dressing table, grabbing her hairbrush off the bed on the way.

'Mate, this place is awesome.' Angus tossed his bag on his larger-than-average single bed as Max happily claimed the other one, closer to the small-but-chic en-suite shower room.

'What's awesome, my friend, is that rather cute little chalet girl — Izzy, was it? Tell you what, she has already got my alpine horn tooting.' Max peered into the shower room as he spoke, checking out the state-of-the-art fixtures, and then turned back to smirk at Angus.

'Ha, yeah.' Angus raised a corner of his mouth into a half-smile and nodded at his friend, who was already heading for the door and raising his hand to his mouth in a 'let's go drinking' action.

4

Casper's Alpine bar was bustling with the usual crowd. Long picnic tables out on the terrace were piled with discarded goggles, hats and gloves, while chilled hands warmed up around glasses of vin chaud and half-pints of beer were quickly chucked down the throats of the après-skiers. A stream trickled alongside the terrace and a rickety-looking wooden bridge led back onto the road, where a mix of little beat-up Peugeots and Renaults were parked alongside mammoth 4×4s and quad bikes.

Jenna looked around her and smiled at the ski resort stereotypes: gap-year seasonnaires with their boards, beanies and cute plaits; trendy types masking their home counties accents with estuary English that came from too many nights trying to be cool in Hoxton; the braying types more used to the Admiral Cod in Chelsea and here to seriously party; plus the Scandinavians, the elite skiers, there for the kickers, the jumps, the adrenalin . . . Jenna, nearing thirty and feeling less and less the need for speed, or to be thought of as cool like those 'gap-yah dudes', mused on her own personal style: pearl earrings, nice hair, sensible shoes — not exactly a la mode. Some of her friends had trust funds brimming with cash and others were all arty and looked awfully cool in hand-made, market-bought clothes, but even though she didn't have the credit limit available to splash out on designer gear she still couldn't quite get her head around the thrift-store stuff. It was something she'd laughed about with Max once — how very Hackney they were not, he with his Church's brogues and she with her Kate Middleton-esque nude LK Bennetts

— and she looked across at him, standing at the bar, a small wrinkle appearing at the corner of his eye as he grinned at something the barman said. Dragging her eyes away from Max, Jenna caught sight of the other kind of ski resort client — especially here in the beautiful village of Val d'Argent, a place with more Michelin stars than Paris, it seemed: the über-rich. It hadn't taken Bertie long to notice them either. A few very beautiful women together with a dour-looking man — definitely Slavic, or most probably Russian — his lips curled into a cruel smile as he poured Cristal champagne into the waiting flute of a slight but seriously pretty brunette next to him. Jenna noticed a lot more hair tossing and lip pouting from Bertie, who had also spotted the wealthy Russians and was looking longingly at their table, which seemed to be dripping in Bollinger Grande Année as well as the Cristal among other tipples. 'Champagne super-nouveux riche,' Jenna said as much to herself as anyone as Max came back from the bar with a round of drinks.

'Right, three half-size "lady beers" and three proper man beers.'

Max was greeted with general approval by all except Bertie.

'Beer it is, I guess, but Maxie, darling, I thought we were going to be upping the stakes . . .?'

'Bolly all the way, you mean?' replied Max, having followed her stare over to the neighbouring table, and, in a hushed tone to only her, 'Later, babe — think I'd waste my money buying bubbles for these, shall we say, less sophisticated palates?'

Whether he meant it or not, Bertie giggled and tossed her golden locks again. She had organised this whole ski trip with the sole intention of getting together — for real this time — with Max. She knew he still had her in his little black book as Dirty Bertie — some girls might be affronted by that, but not her. If it's hot and dirty sex that will win him over, that's what he'll get, she thought to herself. As she flooffed her hair again and tried to take an elegant sip from the half-pint of lager in front of her she wondered why Jenna kept insisting on calling it a 'lady beer': there was nothing lady-like about drinking lager, full stop. Navigating the thin foam on top of the glass, trying not to get it on her perfectly applied lipstick, she thought back to her and Max's off-and-on relationships. Back at uni they'd courted throughout the final year, though that might be too chivalrous a term for the bonk-fest that was their coupling. She remembered their sheer bloody chemistry when they used to romp in the haystacks back at her parents' farm in Suffolk during weekends away from college — 'Anatomy 101', wasn't that how Max had apparently described it to Hugo when talking about their 'study breaks'? Ugh, Hugo.

She could even put up with Max being best mates with someone she really had no time for, if it meant being with Max — hence inviting Hugo and simpering Sally on this bloody holiday. And she could tolerate his fondness of Jenna — even if she was prone to the odd unexplained weep on nights out and couldn't carry off a Hermes Birkin, let alone afford to carry one at all. As for his old school friend, Angus, well at least he was halfway presentable, if only he'd stop insisting on growing that terrible beard and actually design something iconic rather than just talking about bloody architraves and columns the whole bloody time. It was funny how, even after she'd inherited a share in her grandfather's fortune, and gone from being Pony Club to private members' club, and could really probably score any London socialite she wanted, she still wanted the Max package, even if that included his friends.

*

Shuffling, slipping, giggling and overspilling with laughter, the gang wove their way through the streets of Val d'Argent in breathy, beery happiness. The tang of diesel hung in the air as a chill wind swept snow off the roofs and onto the street below. Hugo had his big arms around Jenna and Sally, singing his old school song heartily and loudly.

'Come on, girls, join in the chorus.' An overexcited Hugo pushed on, his booming voice echoing down the street, the warm air from his mouth turning to dragon's breath as he galumphed on.

Bertie, not one to let her glossed-up lips utter such a trifle, lurked at the back of the group with Max, and before he could join in with the chorus one more time, she stroked her manicured hand over his denim-clad butt. He turned to face her, reading the look of lust in her eyes as clearly as she meant it. Calling out to the others that he was just going to pop back to the ski hire shop with Bertie to 'adjust her poles', he took her hand in his and pulled her off the main road into a small alley, lined either side with exquisite designer shops.

'Far more my sort of place than conjuring up the memory of some crap minor public school,' purred Bertie, looking into the window of a high-class fashion boutique, the display showing an elegantly posed mannequin, stylishly naked except for a fur-rim of a hat and a tiny white thong.

'I thought you wouldn't mind taking the opportunity to see what other pole might be on offer, Berts — I fear the ones we got you loaded up with earlier aren't really rigid enough for you.' Encircling Bertie's tiny waist with his hands, he leaned down and kissed her neck, sending a ripple of pleasure down her alert — and pert — body.

'A more rigid pole, hmm, yes,' she whispered. 'I can't tell you how much I want something hard and powerful right now . . .'

Max, more than happy to give her something of his that was incredibly hard, moved his lips to meet hers and crushed her mouth to his in a deep kiss. One of his hands, already seeking the warmth of her skin, slid under her tight, white T-shirt and caressed her back, working its way to where he thought he'd find some sort of lingerie. But no, he realised as a small groan of pleasure escaped from the back of Bertie's throat, there was no bra to be found.

As much as Bertie was desperate to have Max and fulfil his notion of her being Dirty Bertie, sex in an alley way wasn't exactly her idea of a high-class venture. She'd wanted to subtly turn his mind to naughty thoughts and harvest her rewards under the goose down later, not have her back shoved up against a cold glass door while he pawed at her and shamelessly fucked her in an alleyway. No, a poke in the doorway of Pucci was not her thing.

Pushing him slightly away from her, Bertie looked Max in the eye, a long, lingering, eyelash-fluttering gaze that turned the tables from quick shag to something much more powerful. With her back still against the door of the shop, she used its icy glassiness to slide down it, stroking her hands down past Max's hips and the length of his strong thighs as she lowered herself. Giving blow jobs in doorways wasn't technically her 'thing', but Bertie knew how to play the long game, and if she was a saint in the kitchen (or at least, if her private chef was) then she sure as hell had to make sure Max knew she could be a sinner in the bedroom, or alleyway or wherever, if she was finally going to snag him for the long haul.

Despite the chill in the air, Bertie was delighted by Max's hardness and started Operation Maximum Max with a few deft moves of her tongue.

Sunday

5

Sunlight streamed through a chink in the curtains, illuminating Jenna and Bertie's bedroom in an ethereal, hazy light. Although Bertie's rather dubious friend Dominic, literally nicknamed Dubious Dominic, had lent them his chic shack for the week, it still gnawed at Jenna that she would be sharing *all week* with Bertie. And yes, their room was certainly a step up from the usual tongue-and-groove-clad horror with door-less shower cubicle and cardboard towels. And yes, the generous-sized twin beds and luxury en suite with all sorts of tricks in the shower — side jets and what not — was totally amazing. And yes, it was an exemplar of style, but anyone walking in now could have mistaken the place for the aftermath of the first day of the Harrods sale. The polished wood floor was hidden under strewn lingerie, designer skiwear, and the odd telltale nail-polish-red sole of a Louboutin shoe. Slinky silk dresses were draped over a plush armchair and the Louis Vuitton trunk was all but pillaged of its contents, as if fashion terrorists had exploded it all over the room. Jenna's smaller — positively tiny by comparison — suitcase was sitting neatly by the side of her bed, occupying the only tranche of land clear of knickers and hair straighteners. But the light, in all its hazy glory, started to do its inevitable work and Jenna blinked into consciousness.

Next to her, Bertie slept on, unaware of the daylight thanks to a pink sateen eye mask, embroidered with the words *fabulous fuck buddy*, that ruffled up her Jemima Goldsmith-glorious hair. Jenna reached up from the comfort of the Egyptian cotton sheets and felt her own mop. Last night came back to her slowly as she remembered the boisterous Hugo scooping her up on the way home and dropping her into an all-too-welcoming snowdrift. Of course, Hugo hadn't realised that the snowdrift was less a smooshy cloud of powder than a few inches of snow over a particularly hard bit of concrete. Her arse now really hurt and she hadn't even got near a red run yet. Angus had been the one to help her up, but not before a victorious Hugo had seen fit to shake the tree above the 'snow drift', covering her totally in ice-cold snow. Her squeals soon turned into fits of drunken giggles, especially when moments later Sally was perfunctorily dumped in next to her by her doting fiancé.

What had happened to Max and Bertie, though, wondered Jenna as she tested the water of wakefulness. After a less-than-gallant Hugo — and a slightly more gentlemanly Angus — had helped the girls out of the drift-come-concrete lump (with Sally getting an exaggerated 'helping to dust you down' groping from Hugo added in as a special treat), they'd all weaved their way home, ready to raid the fridge — no doubt to the despair of Izzy, who still hadn't quite lost her initial frostiness at having her rather cushy winter job disturbed. Seeing a six-foot rugger bugger being told in no uncertain terms to leave the pâté de fois gras right where he found it by someone who only a few months ago was languishing in the dorms of Cheltenham Ladies College had been a sight to behold. Afterwards, Hugo was heard to mumble something about how he preferred the Benenden lot anyway as Cheltenham were always 'bitches on the pitch' with nothing ladylike about them *whatsoever* — especially once when his little sister got knocked unconscious in a particularly nasty lacrosse U15s final. At some point during the midnight feasting (or lack of) Max had sauntered in, winked at Izzy — which had turned permafrost into glowing smiles, Jenna remembered bitterly — and sprawled himself across the calfskin leather sofa in the vaulted-ceilinged sitting room of the chalet. Pausing only to crack open a beer, he'd slipped his arm around Jenna (less bitterly remembered) and rested his still-cold-from-the-outdoors cheek on her shoulder (oh joy!). Jenna thought back to their conversation, nuzzling her pillow as she remembered what he'd said to her last night.

'What's important, Jenksy,' he'd turned to her, a look of mischief in his deep brown eyes as he deflected a question on Bertie's whereabouts, 'isn't where Bertie is right now, but how you're going to escape from the French love dungeon your bound-to-be-super-hot ski instructor will have you enslaved in in no time . . .'

'At least in a love dungeon I'll be on solid ground, and not making a complete arse of myself in front of some arrogant French ski bum. Anyway, you'd come and rescue me, right?'

'Jenna, I would see it as my duty and would happily face any red room of pain to help you out of a pickle.' Max winked at her, while pulling his arm back from around her shoulders.

Jenna had forgotten whatever banter had followed, thinking at the time that she was more worried that whoever had the lousy job of teaching her would realise it was more than a refresher course she needed, especially if she was going to keep up with the rest of her friends. Sally was a regular on the slopes and, as to Hugo's capabilities . . . well, she knew he was just one to throw his not insubstantial weight downhill and hope no small children got in the way. Bertie was more about the slinkiness of the salopettes than the severity of the slalom. In fact, it was doubtful if Bertie — who had slipped in just after Max had been teasing Jenna over her instructor — would ever actually see any on-piste action the whole holiday. She had declared last night to a very drunk Jenna that she was 'quite *literally* fucked if I'm going out in that cold again'.

Memory assessment complete, Jenna swept her messy hair into a quick ponytail, slipped a hoody over her PJs and crept out of the room. 'Let a sleeping Bertie lie' was definitely her motto, plus Jenna didn't think her throbbing head could take any decibel higher than 'warble' and Bertie tended to operate on 'screech' quite a lot. In the corridor, she heard voices from Sally and Hugo's room, and found herself slightly disappointed to see that Max and Angus's door was closed. She shuffled in her overly long PJ bums down the wide, glossily wooden stairs straight into the sitting room, where they'd all chatted and drunk far too much last night, and then into the open-plan dining area. Angus was already down there, sitting at the long refectory table where, if Jenna remembered rightly, they'd tried to play ping-pong with Mini Babybels at 1 a.m. He was fully kitted out, ready to ski (bar the goggles, although even those were being worn as some sort of ocular arm band) and eating a hearty breakfast on his own.

'Morning, Gus,' croaked Jenna.

'Suffering? What will Jean-Paul say?' replied Angus, looking up from his foot-long baguette filled with cheese and ham, the remains of two boiled eggs evident on his plate.

'I don't know how you manage it, Angus. How can you look so, well, *healthy* this morning? I'm sure I saw you neck at least five beers once we were back last night.'

'Credit must go to the strong constitution of the Linklaters,' Angus replied. 'My great-grandfather was renowned for holding the Western Front on a sturdy diet of moonshine and Fry's chocolate.'

'Eew! Don't mention food — or drink — I don't know how you can bear it. Plus, you've put Izzy to work this morning — how much have you troughed already?'

'All essential fuel for the system, Jenna . . . and I made it all myself, actually.' Angus looked back down at his plate.

'Where's Izzy, then? I thought she was our handmaiden on tap for all our foodie and bed-making needs? Don't tell me she took offence to Hugo so much last night she's done a runner, via the Headmistresses' Conference?'

'Perhaps,' nodded Angus, starting to colour.

'Angus, you're blushing,' said Jenna as she slipped onto the bench seat next to him, flicking off a suspect piece of squished red wax as she did do. 'What is it?'

Angus, feeling like a total tool, clammed up. Finally, he came up with, 'No, I'm just overheating. I'm wearing three climate-controlled T-shirts, plus a very manly pair of long johns.' He recovered himself — making Jenna chuckle at the thought of Angus dressed like Compo from *Last of the Summer Wine*. And with that ghastly beard to match, too, she thought to herself rather uncharitably. Remembering that Angus had agreed last night to walk her to her lesson, she felt chastened and hastily piped up, 'Sorry, I'll go and get ready straight away — if I can find a pathway through Bertie's debris in our room, that is. Would you wait for me? I'm a bit nervous about looking like a prat waiting for Jean-Paul with all the French three-year-olds taking *ze peese* out of me.'

'Of course, Jenna, get your kit on and, if you're really lucky, I'll even carry your skis for you.' Jenna smiled at him and turned back towards the stairs. Her smile faded, though, when she noticed the sofa cushions all awry and a couple of blankets scrunched up in the corner of the 'L' shape. She frowned as she recognised Angus's watch on the side table and turned back in the direction of the dining table to question him. He wasn't there, though, and Jenna caught sight of the door down to the boot room swinging slightly on its hinge. Left alone then with her theories as to why Angus might have kipped on the sofa, she turned back towards to the stairs and was halfway up them when she was greeted by a very dishevelled Izzy, naked as the day she was born — though, by the looks of things, now considerably less innocent.

'Oh God, um, sorry.' Jenna averted her gaze and let the lithe young chalet girl whizz past her, clutching her clothes to her.

'Shit,' was all Izzy could come up with, and then, 'Sorry. Um, breakfast in ten mins?'

Jenna was speechless and kept her head down as she hurried up the stairs, mumbling some sort of 'OK' to the departing bottom. She reached the landing, her brain in overdrive, realising to her horror that there was only one possible room from which the naked chalet girl could have emerged.

6

About ten minutes before Jenna had seen Izzy's all-too-naked ambition, Bertie had woken up. She'd wanted to wake to the smell of brewing coffee, freshly baked croissants and sizzling bacon. Not that she'd actually *eat* the last two — it had taken three years to convince personal trainer to the 'slebs, Tracy Anderson, to come up with a regime for her and she was blowed if she was going to lose her Paltrowesque figure over a bit of pig, however deliciously it sizzled. Bertie, instead, woke up to the unmistakeable noise of two people having sex. Wrenching her eye mask off and instantly grizzling at the bright sunshine Jenna had foolishly allowed into the room — she must have a word about that; thoughtless of the ninny to practically blind her — Bertie started to tune in more to the noise. Yes, it was definitely sexual, she decided. Where was it coming from? A shudder passed through her as she toyed with the idea that she was listening to Hugo and Sally. Bertie, still feeling a bit icky over hearing the rutting noises of the greater and lesser heffasloanes, slipped out of bed, stopped to fling on a silky kimono that barely covered her own modesty, and sashayed to her bedroom door. Opening it a crack she saw Sally and Hugo's door open. *Eew*, she thought. *Double eew*. Couldn't they even close their bloody bedroom door before subjecting us all to their mating cry? She stopped, though, to listen as a guttural moan started its crescendo. It wasn't coming from Sally and Hugo's room at all. In fact, upon closer inspection it was clear that they had obviously hit the slopes, leaving their room rather annoyingly tidy. Or perhaps the chalet slave has been in to do the tidying, thought Bertie, wondering if she'd get round to doing hers too. Hang on a minute — Bertie's thoughts took a U-turn as she got back on subject — if Jenna's gone (she could hear her downstairs talking to someone), Sally and Hugo are gone, then unless either Angus or Max have become particularly effeminate in the last twelve hours — and she knew for certain Max was all man after last night's little alleyway adventure — *then who the hell is making all that noise?*

Bertie crossed the landing to stand outside Max and Angus's door. Hearing the moans and 'yeah, come on baby' orders coming from inside she acted on impulse and threw open the door to see Max humping up and down on top of Izzy, chalet girl Izzy, who was in rapturous delight as Max wielded his full power over her.

'What the—'

Max stopped suddenly at the sound of Bertie's voice and snapped his head round to see her standing in the doorway, her arms petulantly crossed.

'—fuck!' Bertie finished her own sentence, yet the words seemed to hang in the air painfully. A pause and then she continued, 'I think we all know you're the fuck, don't we, Max?' And at that she turned on her heel, leaving the rigid Max and red-faced Izzy alone, to glean whatever pleasure they still could from the affair.

Slamming her bedroom door shut and flinging off her kimono, Bertie went straight into the en suite and turned the shower on full blast. The side jets pulsed into action and she stepped in, letting the water drench her completely. The jizzing bastard, she thought to herself. *The jizzing, sexual, bloody-hot, nerve-tingling bastard*. 'Damn it!' she yelled into the steam. 'Damn him!' What was worse, she thought, was not that she was angry, or felt cheapened or betrayed; it was that she still wanted him. Even though he was obviously out for everything he could get, from anyone. 'Argh, damn!' she let out one last exasperated yell before getting down to the much more serious business of conditioning her hair. As she stroked the softening crème through her long locks, she hit on a plan. There was only one thing to do and it was age old. Bertie wanted Max. Hell, he was the only thing that kept her hanging around with this dull old uni set and their pedestrian ways. She wanted him so very much. He already earned a fortune and had the guile to make it as big as her old grandpa and darling daddy had. And there was this needling little fact that, money and status aside, Bertie actually *really liked* Max. She fancied the D&G pants off him and she got so un-coolly excited whenever she knew she was about to see him. Once, she even ate a chip in front of him, just because he offered her one (not the one covered in mayo, there are limits). It was certain: Max was meant for her and together they could be *real* society's answer to Posh and Becks, just a lot more, well, posh. So, the plan would be to make him as jealous as hell and realise exactly what he was missing.

With that thought in mind, Bertie stepped out of the shower and took control of the situation, delving into the cavernous trunk for her Jo Malone body cream and most tight-fitting ski wear. If anyone was going to look like a billion dollars at that mountain restaurant this lunchtime, it would be her. And if some Russian oligarch liked what he saw, so much the better.

Still reeling from seeing a completely naked woman running down the stairs, Jenna slowly pushed open her bedroom door. Bertie barely glanced up as she entered, but the wafts of Pomegranate Noir greeted Jenna in a more civilised way than Bertie could ever muster. Jenna looked at the long sleek limbs being gently massaged by the expensive moisturiser and sighed as she looked down at her own short, PJ-bum-covered, probably-quite-hairy-underneath-all-that-brushed-cotton, legs. If Max was going to be interested in anyone this holiday, then Jenna could pretty much put herself to the end of the queue — and with that thought in mind she shuffled into the bathroom and closed the door.

7

'Right, off you go,' said Angus, about fifteen minutes later, loading both his and Jenna's pairs of skis onto his shoulders. Jenna took the poles and, as they walked towards the ski lifts, Angus was relieved that he'd managed to steer the earlier conversation away from Max and his night-time antics. He knew Jenna had more than just a passing crush on Max and he didn't want to see her hurt. She seemed different, though, this holiday — different from the blotchy-eyed mess that he'd last seen a few years ago. He hoped, for her sake, that she wasn't still as obsessed by Max as she was then. What suddenly struck him as odd, though, was how much he hoped for *his* sake too that she wasn't.

'Gus . . . Angus!' Jenna was calling his name now and Angus saw that they'd arrived at the entrance to the funicular. 'Welcome back to the real world, buddy,' she joked as he handed over her skis and swapped them for his poles that she'd been carrying. 'I thought I was meant to be the zoned-out, hungover one? You, the skiing man of steel!' Her finger jabbed both their chests in a 'me Tarzan, you Jane' style. He looked down at her. Her plaits tamed her wayward hair, but didn't quite restrain the strands that curled down around her face. She looked sad, though, beneath the jokes, Angus thought.

'Shall we meet up after your lesson?' he blurted out.

'Yes, that'd be cool, but I'll still be so much slower than you — so blast yourself off this morning and use up all that baguette fuel so you're not too quick this arvo!'

'Blast off yourself, Jenksy,' Angus winked, and with a quick look at the map to ascertain which mountainside restaurant they'd meet up in, he left her to the fate of the French ski instructor, Jean-Paul.

'Bend ze kneez, Zhenna, you must take ze bend wiz more gutz, you know?' Jean-Paul was proving to be a bit of a tyrant, thought Jenna, who didn't mind so much because he was as beautiful as the Alps themselves. Rugged jaw, icy blue eyes, a face that had been seasoned with sunshine and wind, and ruffled white-blond hair that swept up and followed the breeze, like the little drifts of snow caught on the edge of the mountain. But she was finding the lesson hard. Having never really taken to skiing, she'd always gone on holidays for the après, sometimes spending as little as half an hour a day on the piste — just to ski to lunch, ski home again, disco nap, out for beers later. Now everyone was a bit older, it seemed they could all ski perfectly and she was still reverting to snow plough whenever the going got tough.

'Zhenna.' God, even his complete inability to pronounce her name didn't rankle; it just made him more Frenchily sexy. 'Zhenna, you are not leestening, I zink. Peut etre eets time for a leetle chocolat chaud zo we ave a leetle rest and maybe zee what ozzer good skiers look like when ze whizz past, oui?'

'Oui, Jean-Paul, bon idee,' sighed Jenna as she followed his snake-like hips down the mountain and towards a welcoming-looking restaurant. But instead of stopping outside by the racks of designer skis, Jean-Paul beckoned Jenna to follow him along a bit.

'Zer ees a much better place . . . Voila!' gestured Jean-Paul as he showed Jenna the most awesome view. Just under the main terrace of the restaurant there were a few deckchairs, each positioned to catch the glistening Argent Glacier at its most spectacular. The sun shimmered on the icy slopes as its width drove through the mountains, carving out the most stunning, snow-covered passageway. Jean-Paul found Jenna a deckchair and crunched through the hardened days' old snow to buy them a couple of hot chocolates from the café bar. Jenna settled herself into the rickety deckchair — no small feat in itself, bearing in mind the way her legs felt after just an hour or so of lesson — and watched as the expert skiers slalomed their way down the pistes. One tall, dark-haired chap caught her eye: was it Max? He'd been so lovely to her so far this holiday. That hug at the airport, sitting next to her on the minibus . . . and last night he'd bought all her drinks, chatted away to her, and reminisced about all the old times at university. But she was just so confused. He'd obviously slept with Izzy last night — one more notch on his bedpost, one more nail in her love coffin.

'Who are you zinking of?' asked Jean-Paul as he walked over, looking about as stylish as anyone can in ski boots, carrying two steaming mugs of chocolat chaud, generously topped with Chantilly cream. 'I zink it was a man as you were looking so sexy, oui?'

Tickled by his forwardness, Jenna replied, 'Oui, bien sur — of course it's a man. Can you guess who?'

'I zink it was me,' said Jean-Paul, shrugging and winking at her, oozing Gallic charm. As he put the mugs down on the table between their two chairs he knelt and looked her in the eyes. Never flinching in his gaze he slipped his hand into his ski jacket and felt for something in his pocket. Just for the slightest of moments, Jenna thought he was about to pull out a ring and propose. When his hand came back into view holding a hip flask, her giggle was two-fold: relief and amusement.

'You zought I was gonna propoze, oui?' chuckled Jean-Paul. 'Mais non, I prefer to get to know my wife a leetle better before zen. And ze one way I know to get to reconnaitre un femme deliciouse is to loosen zem up a beet.

Avec le rum!' At that he sloshed a generous amount of the dark liquid into the mugs, handed one to Jenna, clinked his with hers and laughed in such a free and unfettered way she couldn't help giggling again.

'Salut!' chirped Jenna. 'Salut, Jean-Paul. You know, at home my friends call having sex, having jiggery pokery. And then we shorten it to JP. Like your initials!'

'Ah — zo I am JP. Zhiggery pokery . . .' Jean-Paul nodded. 'And you, Zhenna, do you like your JP?' Winking again, he took a swig from his mug and looked at her, his handsome face humorously covered in cream.

'Yes,' laughed Jenna, 'I like JP a lot. I like his cream-covered nose, it's like Mont Blanc, except . . .'

'Except zat you cannot lick ze snow off Mont Blanc, ha?'

'No — I was going to say, it's smaller. You are naughty, Jean-Paul,' flirted Jenna, right back at him. Her inner voice was gabbling away along the lines of *Oh god. He's so handsome. And he's flirting with me. And I'm nearing thirty and it would be so nice to join the list of ladies who look back and say they've slept with sexy ski instructors . . . But he's not Max. Oh – why did I think of Max? Especially after this morning. Oh.* That all passed through her mind in the time it took for Jean-Paul to lean across the table and kiss her — just softly, and hardly a kiss at all, more of a transferral of cream from his nose to hers. *Wow*, the inner voice was well and truly silenced.

'Zer you go, maintenant you av Mont Blanc nose aussi.'

'Merci,' whispered Jenna, who without further internal commentary let her playful, flirty instincts take over as she dipped her finger into her own whirl of cream and dobbed a bit on Jean-Paul's chin.

'Ah, I zee, we are playing a game, ma cherie. Eet is a guessing game. I zink.'

'Hmm, see if you can guess where I'm going to put cream on you next . . .?'

'Maybe eet ees you who should guess where I am zinking of putting some crème, and eet ees not on your beautiful face . . .'

Leaning towards her again he kissed her, and this time it was deeper and far more sensuous, as his tongue parted her lips. Not quite able to conceive this was happening, Jenna fell into the kiss before her mind could catch up with her and tell her in a slightly prissy way that this was territory that she really shouldn't be in. *How many other girls has he romanced all season? Will he expect a quickie in the loos?* Before she could work herself up any more, Jean-Paul pulled away and, as if it was his calling card, winked again.

'I zink zat ees enough for today, oui? We don't want you zinking I am ze arrogant French man and I zink eet ees also time for zome more parallel turns!'

Jenna exhaled and smiled. 'Oui, Jean-Paul, you're right, this is what I am paying for!'

Jean-Paul looked at her seriously for a second. 'Alzough I would not charge you extra, ma cherie, you know, like I charge ze older laydees for my "love lessons" — you know?' At that, he launched himself from his deckchair and took Jenna's hand to pull her up. Giggling, she followed him back to where their skis were and, whether it was the kiss, the rum or the fun, she felt much better about getting out there and hammering a few more pistes before lunch.

Angus watched as Jenna and Jean-Paul left, flirting and chatting. He wrestled with his binding that had unclipped itself just metres from where that sleazy Frenchman had kissed her. That she had not seemed to mind this 'French exchange' annoyed him: and not being able to pinpoint why it annoyed him, annoyed him even more. His binding fixed, he skied off in a swoosh of powder, his mind suddenly racing as fast as his skis.

8

With Jean-Paul not far behind her, Jenna parallel-turned into the ski rack area outside the Auberge Montagne, the alpine restaurant that she and Angus had agreed to meet at before they'd said goodbye that morning.

'Zat ees excellent, Zhenna!' boomed Jean-Paul from behind. 'You ave ze making of a total ski bunny, ma cherie!' At that he swished up behind her, ever the show-off, patted her on the bum and placed a lingering kiss on her cheek. 'I zink you ave learned much about JP, aussi, oui?'

Jenna blushed about seven different shades of pink as indeed, after the hot choc stop, Jean-Paul had helped her to overcome her fear of one particularly vertiginous chairlift by gently stroking her inner thigh all the way to the summit. Even through her salopettes he'd made her feel incredibly turned on, which was aided in part by the shuddering of the chair as it reached its own snow-station climax. The fact that a small French child was sitting the other side of Jean-Paul didn't put him off, but Jenna put that down to the French attitude: they let their children drink wine from a young age, so sitting next to a man who is gently stimulating a woman is mother's milk to them, surely?

Wishing that she could have stretched to more lessons, Jenna bade farewell to Jean-Paul with a couple more kisses on each cheek and the promise that she would see him for some après and another session mid-week. Turning to leave him she saw Angus swerve into the ski racks, narrowly missing Jean-Paul, but leaving him covered in the powder from his perfectly executed stop.

Jean-Paul, who had a begrudging admiration for anyone who was as good a skier as him and as equal an attraction to handsome men as pretty laydees, just shrugged it off in a nonchalant way and carried on, pausing to pout Jenna a kiss before he took off into the freshly bashed powder of the piste.

Jenna watched his cute bottom go as she waited for Angus to join her, and was slightly surprised by the small peck on the cheek he gave her as a hello.

'Hello,' said Jenna, as she watched him undo his jacket, revealing one of his many Lycra layers.

'Good lesson?' Angus steamed slightly as he kept peeling off more micro fleeces and T-shirts.

Jenna coloured a bit. 'Yes, very instructional, but you know these Frenchies — so up themselves, um, yes. Up to something. Yes.'

'Right, well, glad I've got you firing on all cylinders this arvo, Jenksy — food?'

They headed into the unsurprisingly alpine-themed restaurant, one of those ones where the interior designer obviously looked no further than the inside of a sauna and said, 'that'll do', and aimed for the cheese-and-potato-fest of the self-service buffet. They stopped in their ski-boot tracks as a very red-faced Hugo caught their attention on the other side of the restaurant.

'Whoa, someone forgot the factor thirty this morning,' whispered Jenna to Angus as they changed direction and headed over to join Hugo and a considerably less sunburned Sally, who was waving at them vigorously from a small booth in the corner of the main restaurant.

'Darlings! Thought we'd catch you here. So lovely to see you two together.' Sally, as embarrassing as she was adorable, winked at Jenna and made room for them both while issuing Hugo with orders to 'pop to the bar, darling, and get two more of those lovely vin chauds'. Settling themselves in,

Jenna and Angus heard all about Sally and Hugo's morning, from the annoyingness of Izzy being nowhere to be seen to make breakfast, to the glorious — if horrendously early by Jenna's standards — first run of the day ('You really missed out, darlings, it was just superb, best snow I've ever had'), to Hugo face-planting into an unforeseen drift ('Well, to be honest, sweetie, I think he needed it to cool that sunburn, silly sausage'), and then back to the curiosity surrounding quite where Izzy was. Jenna was about to tell Sally what she'd seen that morning when Hugo returned with the small glass mugs of the deliciously spiced and sweet hot wine. The foursome chatted away happily before tucking into huge plates of spaghetti Bolognese covered in cheese ('Honestly, darling, at ten euros a pop it's ridiculous'). Vital leg fuel, as Angus pointed out, patting Jenna rather enthusiastically on her already over-stimulated thigh, causing a red-hot poker of lust to fire just where she didn't need it right now. They finished up and decided to soak up the unseasonal sunshine on the restaurant's terrace for one more drink ('Not that Huggie needs any more Vitamin B for Burn today!'). As they found a table and some stools, and got into the groove of the saxophonist who was playing from a first-floor balcony to a hyped-up jazz backing track, Jenna caught sight of the Russians again. Done out in jet black skiwear, the obvious alpha male must be some sort of oligarch, she thought to herself, as no one born into a country renowned for its Siberian front could be that tanned without the aid of a yacht and several months of the year in Monte Carlo, Cannes and possibly the Caribbean. Looking at him more closely than she had the day before, she saw that he was a shortish man, but powerfully built, with mousey-blond hair and piercing blue eyes. His lips were thin and, to Jenna's mind, his mouth looked cruel, as if he'd as soon order an assassin's hit as bite into a caviar-topped blini. He wore a tight black T-shirt with a discreet logo, and Jenna only noticed it as the logo bobbed up and down occasionally as he flexed his pectoral muscles. What it took Jenna about five seconds more to notice was the gorgeous blonde sitting next to him, hidden behind a huge pair of Chanel sun glasses and tossing her hair in all sorts of flirtatious ways. Bertie.

Pointing out their friend's new choice of playmate to the others, Jenna couldn't help but be a tiny bit — actually, more than a tiny bit — jealous of Bertie's confidence and determination. It'd been obvious last night that Bertie had noticed the cool, seemingly impenetrable group of mega-rich Russians. And here she was, infiltrating them like an MI6 pro.

'I don't know why she bothered inviting all of us along, really,' mumbled Jenna, to no one in particular. 'I mean, Sally, you guys have never really got on, and I'm sure she looks at all of us with a certain amount of disdain.'

'Hmm,' agreed Sally, pausing to take a sip from another, new steaming glass of vin chaud. 'She is a cold fish at times. Never worked out why she took against me suddenly halfway through uni, yet sort of *frenemied* me, if that's the right word. Weird, sweetie, weird.'

'It's a fall back, isn't it,' said Angus matter-of-factly. 'Of course there's Max — she's still, you know, into him,' he glanced at Jenna, 'and through him she's kind of tied to the rest of us.'

'Whereas it's only Max she really wants tying to,' interrupted Hugo with a rather unsubtle wink. 'Though Angus, she'd probably let you into her coterie — that model girlfriend of yours must pass muster in Bertie's book, don't you think?'

'I think you guys are probably the closest thing to real friends she has,' Angus replied, looking over to Jenna.

'That's a bit sad, really. If she wasn't so disgustingly rich and horribly pretty . . .' Jenna raised an eyebrow as she spoke to show she wasn't really being a total bitch, 'I'd feel quite sorry for her. Proves you can have all the money in the world, but it doesn't buy you friends.'

'Oh, I don't know,' contradicted Sally. 'We're only here because she got us that gorgeous chalet for zilch and because we still remember the old Bertie who would be a good egg and have a giggle with us. Fine horsewoman too, wasn't she, Hugo? Ever since she inherited that fortune it's terribly changed her. As the pounds rolled in, the morals and manners rolled off. But I suppose when you're mega rich you get used to having what you want and suddenly everyone wanting to be your "friend".' Sally made little quotation marks with her fingers. 'Makes me a little glad really that we're only moderately well off.'

'Unspoilt by worldly wealth!' agreed Jenna, who, earning far less than Sally and a fraction of Hugo's banker's salary, had to bite her lip slightly at Sally's comparison.

'Don't worry, Jenksy, lunch is on us,' bellowed Hugo as he fished around in his jacket pockets for his wallet.

'Oh Hugo, you honestly don't have to,' Jenna said as she eyed his fingers pulling out only a couple of the many fifty-euro notes he had stashed in the folds of his wallet. Her words belied the fact that she really would very much like him to pay for her lunch.

'Don't you worry,' Hugo luckily continued, 'I know us mere tradesmen have to pay into the greater good that is the Arts . . .' he pronounced this last word as if he were Olivier himself. 'Besides, without you manning that little desk in your little gallery, how would I ever know when the next Hockney was about to come along? I'm relying on you to find us all grand investment pieces, Jenksy, so we can retire early and play golf.'

'I promise, Hugo, that as soon as Hockney Junior comes knocking, you'll be the first to know and you can thank me from the deck of your super yacht, but for now, ta muchly from me.' She leaned over and gave Hugo a kiss on the cheek, much to his red-faced pleasure and an indulgent grin from Sally.

Bertie lowered her sunglasses down the bridge of her exquisitely sculpted nose — no one had realised she'd had it 'done' in Harley Street soon after her twenty-third birthday, which was surely a hallmark of an excellent surgeon — and peered over to where her friends were sitting. As she sipped champagne, delicately holding the glass as she sat ramrod straight with perfect posture, she watched Jenna and Sally joyfully delve into pasta and pints of beer — totally relaxed and laughing at Angus and Hugo and themselves. She pressed her glasses back into position and turned to face the powerful man next to her who had just slipped his hand onto her thigh.

'You want to join your friends?' He leaned over towards her, his thick Russian accent making it sound more like a threat than an offer.

'No,' replied Bertie, who couldn't fail but notice there was one friend in particular missing from that group. 'There's nothing for me over there.'

9

The gentlest of flakes began to fall just as Jenna was nearing the end of what was, she thought, a rather long and arduous piste. The others had all bombed down it, carving snakes of snow into the soft powder, looking like pros. Sally had skied carefully, but fast, hoping the lagging Jenna would be able to keep up and follow her path, but Jenna had had to stop so many times to demist her goggles or catch her breath, that she'd lost Sally's trail half a piste back and was veering around all over the place, trying to keep her balance on the steep bits and make the most of the fantastic powder. She was not a fan, however, of this falling snow business. Snow, she pondered, was all very well when it had fallen and had made these lovely-ish pistes and created a fairy-tale town, but this blizzarding nonsense? No. And how quickly it changed from being super sunny to horribly hazy! The mountains baffled her and delighted her in equal pleasure. With those thoughts occupying her enough to stop her from over-thinking her technique and route down she finally reached the bottom of the piste and her friends. Seeing them leaning over, resting on their poles or mucking around skiing backwards and throwing snow up into the air with the tips of their skis, made her feel both guilty for making them wait and jealous that she constantly missed out on these fun moments. Sure enough, as soon as she arrived, Hugo suggested they crack on.

'Hang on!' Jenna panicked, glove only just off as she delved in her pocket for some more lip balm. 'Let me get myself sorted — I'm really sorry I'm so slow . . .'

'Take your time, sweetie,' Sally interrupted her, realising that a tired and hungover Jenna could easily burst into tears with the slightest provocation. She glared back at Hugo, who had rolled his eyes.

'I'm really sorry, guys. Look, why don't you go on and I'll just pootle at my own pace. No point holding you all up.'

'Makes sense,' Hugo mumbled, wary of another dirty look from Sally. Angus looked over at Jenna and she caught what she thought was a patronising glare. As soon as she met his eye though he smiled at her and flicked the tip of his ski in her direction, sending the snow on it flying towards her.

'I'll ski with you, Jenna,' he said, and went on to describe some problem with his binding that was far too technical for Jenna to understand, but apparently required him to see someone down at 'base camp' as he put it.

'If you don't mind?' Jenna was so relieved. Even as they'd been standing there the weather had got worse, with a slow mist descending from the summit of the mountain and the falling flakes now not so gentle and a little bit sharp as they dashed against her face and ungloved hands. It was agreed then, and Hugo and Sally took off, with Sally making Angus promise that he'd get Jenna down the mountain before she decided she'd never come on another ski trip again. With reassurances from both Angus and Jenna, they left. Angus then turned to her.

'Ready, champ?'

'Ready, Gus.'

As slowly as he could, he led her down the mountain. The pistes were busy in that languorous afternoon way, and Jenna was very aware that all her energy and focus was going on staying upright and trying to spot random icy patches in the otherwise perfect pistes, not looking out for zippy, arrogant skiers who would cut her up and throw her off balance with neither a wave nor an apology.

Angus, though, looked out for her all the way down and made sure she got to the bottom of the lifts unscathed and in one piece. The town was buzzing with the bars open and skiers milling around and Jenna thought she might be just as happy curled up on one of the soft outdoor sofas under a heater with a vin chaud as she would be up on the slopes. She hinted as much to Angus and he chuckled.

'Not one for actually doing the skiing bit of the ski holiday, are you, Jenks?'

'Nah, I'm more here for the holiday bit.' She looked up at him as he laughed at her. 'Thanks, though, Gus, for seeing me down.' She stood, looking at him.

'No probs, Jenks.' And at that he leaned down and gave her a very perfunctory kiss on the cheek. Slightly startled, she stood just sort of staring at him as he turned and headed back to the main cable car, joining the throng of afternoon skiers who were still piling up the mountain, despite the weather closing in. She watched until she saw the navy blue of his helmet disappear into the funicular building, then, with a deep sigh, Jenna turned around and headed back towards the chalet. It was only as she fiddled with her own skis, precariously balancing them both over one shoulder so that she could carry them, that she realised that Angus never did go and get his bindings checked.

Sally, meanwhile, was experiencing a totally different sort of afternoon.

'Perhaps one or two good deeds from him,' mused Sally, 'would do it. And we could finally get Jenna to lose this ridiculous crush on Max . . .'

'Whassat?' mumbled Hugo, less interested in his friends' love life than getting to the front of the cable car queue. If it had been Sally's idea to let Jenna and Angus ski together to give her friend some 'wake up and smell the Gus' time, then Hugo's motives might be said to be have been a little more selfish. Not only would Jenna have slowed them down (let's face it, he thought, her past experience of skiing amounted to about fifty-four minutes of actual skiing time, even though she had been on about five ski trips), but also Hugo had decided it was high time his future wife had a bit of, well, him. Edging closer to the front of the queue, Hugo did a bit of mental arithmetic and worked out that although the relatively 'commodious' little bubble cars could take four people, the group in front could take the next one, leaving him and Sally to one all by themselves if they were lucky. Although there were a few tuts from those behind them in the queue, one little bubble car to themselves they did get and clattered their skis and poles into the corrugated metal holder just beside the rubber-edged sliding door and hopped up into the little pod-like cable car seconds before the doors closed behind them. Sally, completely unaware of Hugo's tactics (one dropped ski and a bit of English bluster) to get the pod to themselves, started to relax into the seat, taking off her gloves and loosening her jacket by unzipping it a fraction. Using her newly freed hands to delve into her pocket for her lip balm, she noticed that Hugo, who by now had nestled himself rather snugly in next to her on the plastic bench seat of the pod, was using his freshly ungloved hands for something entirely different, undoing the zip down the front of her jacket more than just a 'fraction'.

'Darling . . .?' she started, a questioning though not too admonishing tone in her voice.

'I just thought my gorgeous wife-to-be, now we're alone, might like to warm my hands for me . . .' As Hugo said this, his right hand — chilly or not — found its way through the undone zip of her jacket and around one of her rather wonderful breasts. Before Sally could say much else, he had used his other hand to cup the side of her face and brought her in for a long deep kiss. As their lips met, Sally felt her body become more and more electrified by her fiancé, his hands now holding her in the firm embrace that she so loved. Her pulse was quickening and she knew what Hugo had in mind and moments later, anyone skiing on the piste below, who happened to look up at that moment, would have seen two or three little brightly coloured pods gently making their ascent up to the next cable car station. The wind obviously caught them occasionally and the tension in the cables themselves gave rise to the odd vibration, but one car in particular was noticeably more 'bouncy' than the others. A really keen observer, who might have stopped to watch, their attention grabbed by the extra motion in the air, might also have been treated to the sight of Hugo's naked arse, as he pulled down his salopettes ready to plunge his not inconsiderably sized member into his loving wife-to-be. Sally was flushed and exhilarated, having been thoroughly ravished by her fiancé in the ten minutes they knew they had between the cable car stations. Hugo, always the gent, had taken his time to get Sally to the very peak of climax, having slowly worked his kisses down from her now completely exposed breasts to her knicker line. Slowly undoing her fly, he tugged at her salopettes, inwardly chuckling to himself at her slight gasp as the chill of the plastic seat touched her bare skin. Without saying a word, though, he parted her legs and pulled her forward, nuzzling his way into her most private, and nerve-tinglingly sensitive, area. With his tongue darting in beside the white cotton of her knickers he brought her to a most excruciatingly wonderful peak – at that moment pulling back while he too rid himself of his ski wear so that he could cum inside her – finishing both their orgasms, with the resultant gasps and yells, just in time to reclothe themselves and rather red-facedly dismount from the bubble car as it pulled into the docking station.

'Darling, I'm really quite impressed,' whispered Sally as they lugged their skis and poles down the ramp from the cable car station and out onto the glistening white snow in bright sunlight above both the tree and cloud line.

'I like to think I can still surprise you, Sals,' Hugo said nonchalantly. 'Wouldn't like you to think that we're too old and boring now.'

'I said impressed, not surprised — something tells me you've been planning that little stunt in your head for a while.' Sally looked over at him, her mock censure completely given away by the broadest of smiles.

'Well, I suppose I did count the minutes to the last second when we first did that bubble this morning . . .'

'Yes, I wondered what all that stop clocking was about. But darling, should I be proud, or worried, that we can both be so utterly fuckingly brilliantly satisfied in nine minutes forty-seven seconds?'

'Efficiency, my love, efficiency. But I suppose best keep our saucy secret to ourselves.'

'Oh, I will, darling, absolutely.' And with that Sally lowered her goggles over her eyes and wrapped her ski pole leashes around her wrists, wondering to herself as she pushed off against the crisp, crunchy snow exactly how she was going to describe the whole sordid affair to Jenna.

Max paused on the side of the piste, waiting for Izzy to catch up. As he looked back up the mountain the familiar noise of the cable cars overhead caught his attention. His gaze followed the perpendicular height of one of the massive pylons, its monumental size making an impression on him for perhaps the first time. Something else was making an impression too — the sight of a rather large arse pressing against the full-length window of the sliding double doors. Good work, thought Max, mentally tipping his hat to which-ever total legend was up there right now. It reminded him of his morning's rumpy pumpy, so brutally interrupted by Bertie. If only she'd come flouncing into his room in such alluring undies when he wasn't already doing the dirty with another hottie — or perhaps, if only she'd stayed . . . Surely it was basic economics to know that, when it comes to lovemaking, three was better than two. Izzy, who brought her skis round to a perfect parallel turn to stop right next to him, interrupted his internal dialogue.

'Sorry, Max, I totally got caught chatting to Ginny — she's having an absolute ball as she's meant to be working in this super-swish chalet, but it's been taken over by Russians for the fortnight and they brought, like, ALL their own staff, so she's off the hook and having so much fun — it's so unfair.'

Max, who did his best to feign interest in the ups and downs of chalet girl life, was a bit miffed that an 'unfair down' was being in a chalet with him. Especially as, after this morning's intrusion on their lovemaking, not to mention the 'services rendered' the night before, *twice*, he had treated her to the most sumptuous brunch at the Château Marmotte, the slickest hotel in town. They'd found out from one of her Cheltenham chums, also seasonnairing and working on the reception at the hotel, that the penthouse was empty and begging to be seen to be believed. So they'd spent a very enjoyable few hours of total uninterrupted carnal bliss in the Jacuzzi bath, emperor-size bed, leopard-skin rug and outdoor hot tub — or sex pond as it was now christened.

After a moment or two's light-hearted banter Max suggested that they get off home, knowing full well that Hugo and Angus would never forgive him if freshly made cakes and afternoon sandwiches were absent thanks to his lusty desires.

Izzy nodded and breathed in a lungful of the fresh mountain air. Days didn't get much better than this in chalet girl world, and for now Dominic and his last-minute 'forgot to tell you they were coming' call were all forgiven. Effortlessly gliding off from standstill, she followed Max down the piste, unable to hide her enormous Cheshire Cat grin.

10

Jenna had never been so happy to slip into a hot bath. Her legs ached, each muscle putting itself forward for the Most Abused Muscle of the Day Award. As she lay there, she could feel her thighs and knees still in motion, as if she were still using them to cling onto the edge of the mountain, braced and ready to take on any turn. All that effort had exhausted her, and the final yomp back to the chalet with her skis over her shoulder had almost finished her off. 'Must do more exercise, must do more exercise' had been her chant as she'd puffed her way to the boot room door, so relieved to be in that she'd almost dumped all her kit on the floor. Somehow, she knew that Angus would take a very dim view of that behaviour and so she had patiently re-clipped her boots firmly and placed them over the bar heaters. All that had been only minutes ago and she was so pleased to have found the chalet deserted so that she could just sink, undisturbed, into a hot bath. The only tub was in the en suite for Sally and Hugo's room, so, double checking that they hadn't raced her back and weren't catching a quick, er, nap, she'd let herself in and started to run the bath. The chalet came with some deliciously scented toiletries, so Jenna didn't stint on pouring in lots of lovely bubble bath, swirling her hand through the hot water to disperse it through and get those bubbles going. Once in, she sank down low, letting the warm, soapy water seep over her sore shoulders. She blew a few bubbles off the peaks that formed near her chin and luxuriated in finally feeling relaxed. She hadn't been joking earlier when she said she really did relish the 'holiday' part of ski holidays.

As she soaked, her mind wandered over the events of the day. JP being quite so full on — in a nice way — well, it made her feel a bit good about herself. Better than when she found out this morning that Max had been up to his usual shenanigans with the chalet girl already. And where had he been all day? She was almost tired of caring, and it had been so many years now with not so much as a hint in her direction that he felt the same way about her as she did about him. As she thought of Max she subconsciously moved her hand down her stomach and between her thighs. One last fantasy, she thought to herself, for old time's sake. Gently rubbing herself she began to allow her body to rock to the motion, feeling the bath water rise and fall against the back of her neck as her ministrations became more rhythmic and started to build to the climax that she knew she could easily give herself. But then it didn't seem to happen — she couldn't orgasm. She took a deep breath and imagined Max again, pretending he was with her. She kept imagining one face, one torso, one smile. His dark chocolate eyes, his muscled arms . . . then suddenly a different image sprang to mind. Someone taller, sandy haired, not dark . . . that bloody beard. As if a switch had been turned on inside her it was the thought of *his* touch, as she moved her free hand over her soapy nipples, caressing and squeezing them, and brought herself to the most heavenly rush of pleasure. A final slap of water sploshed over the side of the bath and she lay back, breathless, the instantaneous pleasure suddenly gone as she chastised herself for coming over Angus. Angus, for God's sake. How? Why had he popped into her mind? Bobbing her head under the water she drenched her hair, hoping to drench the confusion that was racing through her mind too. As she began the mundane task of washing her hair she became side-tracked, wondering if any pheromones in the water would react with the shampoo to make her desirable to all men. Or perhaps to just one . . .

'Jenna, sweetie,' Sally's voice broke Jenna's reverie as she called from the bedroom, 'are you in the bath?'

'Yes!' Fuck, Jenna thought, quickly calculating the time since her last 'splosh' and wondering if Sally would have been in the chalet long enough to hear any moans of pleasure that she might have let slip.

'Just checking! Thought I could see steam coming from the bathroom. Do hurry up — after this afternoon's, um, session, I could do with a soak myself!'

'I'll be five mins, hun,' Jenna replied, relieved that Sally seemed completely unaware of her little sub-aquatic fiddling. 'Come in, though, if you want to chat — I'm quite decent, well, if you count bubble bath as a chaste form of cover up!'

'Does that count for me too, Jenks?' laughed Hugo, his (hopefully) obvious jest met with shrieks from both girls. Checking the door was actually closed, Jenna pulled herself out of the bath and wrapped herself up in a wonderfully soft white towel. She rubbed her long hair on another towel, and as demurely as possible entered her friends' room. By then, Hugo had gone, pushed from the room no doubt by the very apologetic Sally.

'Just ignore him, sweetie, I do,' she said, stripping down out of her skiwear to her undies. 'Now I hope you didn't let all that lovely bath water go: waste not want not and all that.'

'Sorry, Sals.' Jenna had to stop herself from not blurting out why her friend really wouldn't have wanted to share her bath water. Escaping the conversation, Jenna headed back to her own room, relieved to find that Bertie wasn't there. Her wonderings as to her whereabouts were short lived, though, as almost as soon as Jenna had dropped her towel and started dressing, she sauntered in.

'Gawd, sorry Jenna, Didn't realise it was pussy show time in here!'

'Er . . .?'

'Like Bangkok, sweetie. Honestly, the awkward shape you seem to be pulling trying to get those skinny jeans on — or are they actually straight leg? Anyway, you look like something one might see in a bar on the Pat Pong Road! If a little larger, perhaps, sweetie — no offence, know what I mean?'

Bertie's drivel, as always, left Jenna feeling perplexed and hurt in equal measure and she had no choice but to just carry on dressing and hope that Bertie could be distracted by some other subject. Jenna knew just the one to get her going. 'So, Bertie, your new friends? Do tell . . .'

'Oh yah. How did you know?'

'Well, we could hardly miss you all — talk about a black Russian cocktail; do they know how to dress in any other colour?'

'If you're referring to the very expensive skiwear, then no, why should they wear anything other than Bogner and Chanel? Why should anyone?' Bertie said looking over to Jenna's discarded pile of second-hand pass-me-downs with one of those 'judging' faces on. 'Anyway, turns out that Yuri — he's the head honcho really — did some deal with Daddy back when he was younger, so he welcomed me into the fold, so to speak.'

'Wow. Good for you.' Jenna was a bit miffed that it had taken barely twenty-four hours for Bertie to seemingly shake off her old pals and find some new shiny pennies.

'Are you seeing them again?' was about all she could muster.

'Oh yah, totes. Probs a party tomorrow night — I didn't think you guys would mind so I said I'd go along. It's just a small thing anyway — like twenty or thirty of his closest, er, well, I guess, friends. But I mean, poor Yuri — he's like me — you just never know if people are after you for your moolah, you know? Oh,' Bertie snorted at her own mistake, 'of course *you* wouldn't know.'

'There's always the safe harbour of old friends,' Jenna said through teeth so clenched she could have played Jaws in any Bond movie. Bertie paused, by now undressed and draped in not much except one of the chalet's white fluffy towels, then acquiesced to Jenna's suggestion.

'Yah, s'pose.' Of course, what Bertie meant to say was that she could hardly inspire raging, lustful jealousy in Max by cosying up to 'some old friend', but she still thought it best to keep her plan to herself. 'You guys are great and all that. You know, feet on the ground and all that shit, but I just don't think you understand.' With that she turned and went into the shower room, closing the door behind her and ending the conversation. Jenna, left gobsmacked as usual by Bertie, took her cue and finished putting on a quick bit of face powder and mascara and left the room, ready — as ever — for a big glass of wine and a gossip with a real friend.

11

As Jenna poured herself a generous glass of something very nice from the well-stocked fridge she heard the sound of chatter coming from the sitting room.

'Get us a beer while you're in there, Jenks!' yelled Hugo.

'I'll be two secs,' Jenna called back, and opened the fridge again for the beer.

Izzy, who was in the kitchen too, preparing the crudité for the traditional cheese fondue they were having that night, snorted in slight derision.

'What?' snapped Jenna, which really wasn't like her, but having seen Izzy leave Max's room that morning, and just having had Bertie's dressing down while she'd been, well, dressing down, Jenna really wasn't in the mood for any more snarky comments. Or snorts.

'Nothing!' Izzy pronounced almost every single letter, along with a roll of her eyes – and Jenna knew the public-school girl's lexicon well enough to know that meant 'Fuck off and mind your own business while I get on with this shitty job that is totally beneath me.'

'Fine,' mumbled Jenna, who popped as many beer bottles as she could under her arm and carried through her glass of wine along with another she'd poured for Sally, who'd be down any minute from her slightly less raunchy bath, she hoped. As she turned the corner into the sitting room she saw Angus had also come downstairs. A flashback to her own self-pleasuring almost stopped her in her tracks and she dared to glance at Angus as subtly as possible as she placed the glasses and beer bottles down on the coffee table. Why had he popped into her head at that embarrassingly vital moment? Heaven knew, the last thing she needed to do was to start crushing on another unattainable man. Max was bad enough, but someone supposedly going out with a model? Dream on. Hoping she wasn't blushing, or if she was she could pass it off as sunburn as bad as Hugo's, she sat down. Luckily, as distractions go, a freshly bathed Sally, half slipping, half tumbling down the last few steps into the sitting room meant no one noticed Jenna's slight blush at all. Finally, taking her place next to Jenna on the vast modular sofa, having batted off the usual banter of 'started drinking already?' from her beloved, Sally gratefully took the already poured glass and took a large gulp. Jenna smiled at her and decided a subject wholly unrelated to drinking or Angus was needed. Izzy — and her non-existent people skills — bore the brunt.

'She's a bit moody,' she whispered to Sally, hoping the boys wouldn't hear what might be construed as bitchiness towards to their young hostess. But of course they did, and Hugo butted in with, 'Agreed — she was like a dorm matron last night, protecting her sacred fridge from prying eyes . . . and stomachs.'

'I don't blame her!' retorted Sally, while smiling indulgently at her fiancé.

'Don't let it worry you.' Angus had appeared at Jenna's side. 'Let's face it, she's probably going to eclipse us all one day with some mega job and is probably quite rightly fed up to the nigh teeth of serving idiots like us all the time.'

'I think I might take offence at that,' Max said as he walked down the stairs and into the sitting room. Plonking himself down on the corner sofa and reaching over to the coffee table to where the spare beers were, he carried on, 'Forgive me if I'm wrong here, but we've got some shining lights of the professional classes among us . . . and then also you, Jenna.' At that he winked at her and ducked as a cushion was launched at his head.

'Ha bloody ha, Max'

'Well done, Jenna, use your words,' Max teased. Jenna sent him a withering smile and sank back into her now cushionless seat. She wasn't upset at all — it was par for the course that she would have the piss ripped out of her for her poor salary by her much more financially successful friends. And, sadly for her, it wasn't like she didn't need to work. A few nice heirlooms aside, Jenna knew that after mortgages and school fees had been paid, her darling parents didn't have much left for anything so decadent as an allowance for her. In fact, arriving at Cambridge all those years ago, she remembered feeling pretty bloody special and rather well-to-do . . . for about five seconds. There were the haves and have-yachts, the crème de la crème and the bloody double crème de la double crème. Still, she loved her toffy mates — and took their gentle ribbing over her financial situation (and a load of free lunches) in her stride.

Moody Izzy wafted in from the kitchen to start laying the table. Moody, Jenna noticed, until she spied Max, whereupon the English-rose complexion went a deeper shade of horticultural rouge and a certain swing seemed to be in her hips as she laid down the knives, forks, and devilish-looking fondue prongs.

Several bottles of decent Pinot Gris later, and the bubbling pots of cheese kept coming from the kitchen.

'Another one bites the dust, my love!' a roaring Hugo pointed out the all-too-obvious to Sally as she pushed her fondue prong around the pot of melted cheese, frantically trying to find the piece of baguette that had just fallen in. Muttering under her breath and concentrating on the task at hand so much she barely noticed Max creep up behind her and put one large, freezing ice cube down her back. The screech could probably have been heard the other side of Mont Blanc and may well have caused several avalanches.

'Oh, you brute!' she exclaimed once the offending ice cube had finally worked its way down her spine and fallen to the floor. 'I'll get you for that!'

'Only if I'm stupid enough to let my bread fall in the fondue . . .' retorted Max, referring to the set of the rules they'd come up with as the meal begun. Firstly, all food must be eaten with the ridiculous prongs (or with no hands at all, face first) and secondly, anyone who lost a piece of bread or a potato or whatever in the pot got a forfeit. Where these rules came from, no one could remember, but Hugo thought he'd read them in an Asterix book once. And everyone knows the Romans (and indomitable Gauls) loved a good orgy.

'Better rescue that ice cube from the floor, mate,' Hugo nudged Angus, implying he should pick it up. 'Bertie's looking at it hungrily.'

'Well, it's not my fault that there is nothing, I mean *nothing*, here on this table that I can eat,' moaned Bertie as the now dripping ice cube was deposited ceremoniously next to her empty plate.

'But Berts, it's delicious,' chipped in Jenna, hovering a piece of bread cautiously over the bubbling pot.

'Delicious does not come into it. What did darling Kate say once? "Nothing tastes as good as skinny feels" — well, a bloody pot of cheese does not a skinny tum make! Angus, your Diane would agree with me I bet.'

'She's not my . . .' Angus started, but Sally interrupted him in her attempt to stand up for Jenna, who was starting to navel gaze, feeling the full force of Bertie's stare at her not-so-slim midriff. 'I think it's perfectly delicious too,' she said, 'and certainly makes for a yummy tum in my book!'

High-fiving her friend meant Jenna lost concentration on her piece of bread, though, and she didn't notice when it was knocked off her prong by a flying piece of carrot, courtesy of Hugo.

'Whooooo — score!!! Forfeit for Jenna!'

'Hang on!! That's not fair!' Jenna yelped, less concerned now about her tummy than fighting her corner.

'Nothing in the rules about how the bread gets lost,' said Hugo, brimming with chuffedness over his incredibly lucky shot. 'So, what shall we make young Miss Jenkins do, team?'

Bertie shrugged her shoulders and looked like she couldn't care less, and just reached over Max to pick at another piece of celery, giving him an eyeful of her cleavage as she did so. Jenna, who decided fighting was useless, took a large swig from her glass to bolster herself for what lay ahead.

'Be nice, Hugo,' warned Sally, 'I'm already getting you back later for the ice cube — and am more than happy to add Jenna's debt of honour to my revenge too!'

'Angus, what do you think? Tie her down for a good tickling—'

'God no,' Jenna butted in, 'for the only reason that this chalet does not need redecorating in Cheesy Vom, the new colour from Farrow & Barf.'

'Fair enough, then,' continued Hugo, who seemed to be greatly enjoying his role as ringmaster. 'Angus, I say that Jenna's forfeit is that she has to kiss all the singles round the table — that includes you, Bertie.'

'Oh, for gawd's sake,' snapped Bertie. 'Just fill her glass, make her down it and be done with it.'

At that suggestion Jenna and Sally cheered, clinked glasses and Jenna proffered hers to Hugo for the mother of all refills. Although the thought of kissing Max had fleetingly been a good one, Jenna knew it would have only led to some terribly embarrassing awkwardness — she knew he'd baulk at the idea and it would turn into some terrible approximation of a third-year disco at school, where miss-kisses and unwanted lunges were the order of the day. She caught his glance though as she took a massive gulp of the white wine in her glass — his cheers, along with those of Sally and Hugo, filled her ears — but she noticed Angus was quiet, and looking rather concerned. *I wonder what his problem is*, thought Jenna as she finished off the glass and put it down, only to have it refilled almost to the brim again by an over-exuberant Hugo.

As it happened, Angus's problem was that he had just lost not one, but two pieces of bread into the fondue pot.

'Cheat!' yelled Hugo, pointing his prong at Angus, who was trying to retrieve his chunks of bread with no one noticing. 'That's surely double the forfeit for you my friend!'

'Plus extra for trying to conceal — oh, the skulduggery!' chipped in Jenna, highly amused and relieved that it was finally someone other than her and Sally that was in trouble.

'Angus, mate, they're right.' Max stood up from the table, as if to give his pronouncement more gravitas, and with his thumbs tucked into the top of his jeans in a mock Tudor pose he continued. 'This needs a serious forfeit. What say you all, my lords, ladies and gentlecheeses, to . . . off with his beard!'

'No fucking way,' Angus exclaimed, although to little effect as the chant had started up from the others of, 'Off with his beard, off with his beard.' Even Bertie showed a little enthusiasm and after the chant had died down she took the stage and said, 'Angus, darling, your people have spoken, and I'm afraid, as technical head of household here, I uphold their decision. Plus, that thing is ghastly and needs to come off, stat.'

'No *fucking* way,' was all Angus could say again, then, 'Guys, really, please. I'll drink, look . . .' At that he filled his glass to the brim and started to glug it down.

'Sorry, mate,' Max brought his fondue prong down on the table like a judge's gavel, 'the crowd has spoken.'

Jenna looked over to Angus and suddenly felt ashamed of herself for so verbally and enthusiastically joining in with the chanting. Angus looked haunted by this peer pressure, but she could see that his naturally good temperament and drummed-in manners were stopping him from retaliating. She stood back while Max held Angus down in his chair, the poor bearded victim helpless to defend himself as Sally plopped herself on his lap. Jenna knew enough of Angus to know that he would never hurt a lady, even if he was being bullied mercilessly. Jenna almost started forward, wanting to at least tell Sally to get off his lap, to give him a fair man-on-man fight with Max. But then it was too late. By now Hugo had been upstairs and got his own razor and a pair of Sally's nail scissors and had started to hack away at the sandy, gingery beard.

'Off with his beard,' Sally still tipsily chanted as Bertie, now seemingly bored by the stunt, pushed the end of the melting ice cube around her plate with the tip of her manicured nail, while she absent-mindedly checked her messages on her phone.

'Mate, this is coming off beautifully.' Max raised his eyebrows as if to make the point.

'Honestly, fuck you bastards, I mean not you Sally, but well . . .' Angus looked angry, but also, Jenna thought, a little sad — or was that something else? Embarrassment? Jenna noticed, as most of the beard was removed — not by the razor, as even Sally had seen sense to prise that from the very drunken Hugo's hands before it got too close to Angus's throat — that a large, pale scar was revealed across Angus's cheek. As more hair was snipped and the game became less new and fun, Max released his grip on Angus's arms and gradually Hugo stopped snipping too.

'Wow, mate,' Max stood back from Angus and took in the creeping white welt that travelled across his face from the corner of his mouth, up to about two inches from his eye socket. 'Nice scar.'

'I hate it,' was all Angus could say as he gently pushed Sally off his lap, swiped the razor blade off the table and quietly went upstairs to finish off what his braying friends had started.

'Oh, poor Angus,' Jenna whispered, her mind flooded with thoughts of how he could have sustained such a terrible injury. 'Did you know, Max? Is it from school?'

Max, subdued now, replied, 'I don't think so, no, I mean, definitely not. He didn't have that beard then.'

'Must have happened in Singapore or wherever it was he lived after uni,' Hugo suggested.

'Poor love, that must have hurt,' chimed in Sally, leaving Jenna to state the obvious.

'And we've just reminded him of it. And he must have been so desperate to hide it all these years and we've just bullied him into removing his beard. Oh, poor Angus.'

'He'll look better for it,' said Bertie matter-of-factly, never taking her eyes off her phone. 'However bad it is, that beard was worse.'

'True,' Max began to perk up at this get-out clause.

'Still, I'm going up to see if he's OK,' and at that Jenna left the table, wine glass still in hand, and wove her way up the staircase.

12

Jenna knocked softly on the closed door of the boys' room. She got no answer, so gingerly pushed it open, calling out Angus's name as she went. She could see the door to the little en suite was closed, so she tiptoed across the room and knocked on it too.

'Hang on.' Angus's voice was gruff and Jenna felt incredibly chastened. She then felt something quite, quite different as the door gradually opened and saw Angus standing there. He'd taken off his shirt to shave and she noticed for the first time that he was incredibly well toned. His torso was indeed that of a rower, or swimmer — his chest looked wider than it did when he was dressed, probably because loose shirts covered the trimness of his waist, the muscles of which were semi-covered, tantalisingly, by his jeans. She looked up to his face as he ran a towel over his freshly shaved jawline. The white scar stood out stark against his skin, though not as much as his natural tan line did above where his beard had been. Angus threw the towel down and grabbed his shirt from the bed, not ignoring Jenna exactly, but waiting perhaps for her to go first.

Jenna was confused. This had been happening a lot recently, she noted to herself. Naked torso-gazing aside, it was Angus's face that had most taken her aback, and not because of the scar or wonky tan. He just looked so different without the beard. Yes, she'd seen him fuzz-free when they were teens and just after uni, but now, years later, she could see just how handsome he was. She was mesmerised by his jawline and the fine pinkish outline of his lips, both things that had been sadly hidden, along with the scar, by the beard. She was also becoming quite aware of a rather fizzing sensation in her nether regions, not dissimilar to the one she'd given herself only an hour or two earlier.

'You look lovely,' was all she could say, before blurting out a 'sorry' too on behalf of everyone. 'But really, you don't need it. You look, well, so, um . . .'

'Like a monster? A street fighter? Take your pick.'

'No, Angus, I mean it's noticeable, yes, but it's not, well, I mean . . .'

'Let's go downstairs, Jenna. I might as well face the music, or screams, sooner rather than later.'

While Jenna and Angus were upstairs the rest of the group finished off the last slim pickings of the fondue, except Bertie, who shunned carbs with the same grace as a toddler shuns broccoli. As she pooh-poohed the last couple of cherry tomatoes ('full of natural sugars, you really shouldn't') she noticed Izzy come in with a tray to start the clearing up.

'Chalet girl, you really should wait until we're all finished before you charge in here with your paraphernalia,' Bertie flicked a piece of limp celery off her plate and onto the table as she got up. 'Now I'm done.'

Not caring what scene she left behind her, though imagining it would be full of eye-rolling and cringey apologies from her 'friends', she stalked over to the sofa and draped herself across it, leaning over briefly to pick up a magazine. As she glanced up — just the once — it was in time to catch Max, still sitting at the table with his back to her now, talking to Sally and Hugo, not missing a trick in the arts of seduction. As Izzy bent over to clear the table, he had stealthily slid his hand up her leg and under her short skirt, brushing his fingers over her stockinged thigh.

Master of subtlety though he was, Bertie had certainly noticed. Rather than make another scene, she slipped away upstairs just as Jenna and Angus were heading down.

'Bertie, where are you off to?' said Angus as they passed her on the stairs.

'Just the bathroom,' she said, followed by, 'nice face, by the way.'

Izzy pushed open the kitchen door with her bottom, edging through the doorway with the massive tray. Her 'paraphernalia', as that snobby bitch called it. Domestic chores did not agree with her and neither did being talked down to. Dominic had promised her an easy ride this season. 'Seems I was the easy ride,' she muttered as she vowed to herself never again to accept a job from a one-night stand — not even if they begged her. Her pride was ruffled, but more than that, she was feeling more than a little hot under her Ralph Lauren collar. Max was getting just as under her skin as he had been under her skirt a minute ago, and Izzy had to clench both hands around the edge of the worktop to steady herself as she thought about their amazing morning. Perhaps some domestic chores could be tolerated, if it meant getting anywhere near his sheets again she thought to herself.

Upstairs, Bertie fumed as she paced the bedroom she shared with Jenna. Flicking a pair of discarded knickers up with the pointed toe of her Jimmy Choo pump, she decided that it was time to take her plan up a notch. And in a moment of pure inspiration it came to her — she couldn't believe that she hadn't come up with this idea earlier: the party tomorrow night that Yuri had invited her to . . . there was no point going alone. Max wouldn't be able to see how popular, stylish and sexy she was from several chalets away. No, she'd have to invite him — and therefore the whole bloody lot of them — along too. She set about tapping out a message to Yuri on her bejewelled iPhone, putting her plan into action, before sashaying downstairs again.

'Deuce, chalet girl, and now Advantage Roberta,' she whispered to herself as she went.

13

Sally clapped her hands together as she saw Angus and Jenna come downstairs. Angus had, naturally, been rather wary in coming back down, but knew he would have to man up and show off his newly shaven face at some point. Jenna's reaction in his room had been encouraging, he thought, though she hadn't actually said he was handsome or anything. Perhaps she was too polite to say how terrible he looked. Max, *et tu Max*, he wouldn't hold back though.

'Mate, where did that cracker of a scar come from?' Angus had been right. Sally on the other hand was full of praise of how lovely it was to see his real face and wasn't it frightfully nice to have that itchy fashion accessory off now? He'd been tempted to reply that maybe she'd like to have her woollen twinset forcibly removed, as surely that was an itchy fashion accessory too, but he stopped short and in general they were all being remarkably positive. Except Jenna, who just kept staring at him, and Bertie, who once she'd come back downstairs, seemed more intent on admonishing Izzy.

'Shouldn't staff keep to their quarters?' Bertie queried rather loudly as she once again took up position on the large modular sofa.

Ignoring Bertie's rudeness, Izzy called over to the group in general, saying that, as they'd finished supper for the night, she was heading out to meet some chums.

'That's fine, sweetie,' Sally acknowledged. 'Thanks so much for a super supper, you are clever. Honestly, when you're done here this season, do contact us in London as we could get you loads of catering work among our friends.

They'd love you.' Hugo raised his eyebrows at Max, who in turn winked at Izzy on her way out, and after the door slammed behind her, Hugo, like a naughty schoolboy, leapt up from the sofa and headed towards the kitchen. 'Right,' he chuckled as he flung open the cupboard doors. 'We need to celebrate Angus's new look and without the Obergruppenführer of catering here. Let's see what she's got stashed away.'

'Oh Hugo,' sighed Sally, thinking his mind was on food, again. 'Honestly, sweetie, aren't you stuffed?'

'God yes,' he agreed. 'This has nothing to do with food. Gin, my girl, gin. That's what I'm looking for!' Sally beamed in the direction of her beloved, who knew her far too well.

To save the kitchen from being hit with a literal H-bomb, Bertie piped up with her most team-spirited comment yet, 'The booze is here in the sitting room, you idiot.' She gestured with her pointy-toed shoe towards the cabinet under the large plasma-screen TV. Max got to it before Hugo and opened it up to find a fine collection of artisan gins, plus a few bottles of vodka, rum and what looked like moonshine.

Jenna's eyes, which had been rather distracted by Angus's face for quite some time now, lit up at all the gins. 'Ooh look, Brighton Gin, I love that one! And Monkey 47 – wow, Dominic does know his stuff, doesn't he?' Hugo picked up the one unlabelled bottle and unscrewed the cap. Taking a sniff he recoiled. 'Blimey, I know why he gets called Dubious now.' Undeterred, he took a massive swig, thumping his chest with his fist as the fiery liquid went down. Letting out a noise somewhere between a cough and wheeze he then declared it a 'hate-filled bottle of Satan's urine' and took another swig before handing it over to a rather hesitant Angus and heading off to the kitchen to get some glasses and tonic so the girls could tuck into the gins.

'He's a silly old sod sometimes, but I do love him . . . Oh!' Sally exclaimed mid-sentence as Hugo re-emerged from the kitchen completely naked except for a rather short, if fetching, pinny. He was brandishing a paring knife in one hand and a lime in the other. The others creased up in laughter. Max whooped in appreciation of his friend's daring prank and Sally coloured somewhat, blushing at the embarrassment, while secretly being rather proud of her flamboyantly hilarious betrothed. 'So, who's for one of my extra special G & Ts?' asked Hugo of his chortling audience.

'I think gin is meant to go with lemon, Hugo, not plums . . .' Jenna started laughing at her own joke almost before she could get the line out. Max slumped himself down next to her, the bottle of Brighton Gin in his hand. 'Or a nice stick of Brighton rock — or is that what Sally calls Little Hugo these days?'

'You can see if you like, mate . . .' Hugo started backing onto Max, bum first, who automatically covered his face with his arms in an X-like cross. 'Urgh, get off you big homo,' he retorted as Hugo's scantily clad body loomed closer.

'We may as well be in Brighton,' remarked Sally, as she prised the knife and lime out of Hugo's hands, muttered something about an accidental vasectomy, and clumsily started cutting wedges of it on the coffee table.

'Fill 'em up, Sals,' laughed Jenna as she squeezed herself out from next to Max, who still had a semi-naked Hugo sitting on top of him, and knelt down next to her on the floor by the coffee table. Bertie just sighed again and this time got up and declared to all that she was off to get her beauty sleep, as she for one didn't want to waste the day tomorrow being tired and hungover — she glared pointedly at Hugo when she said that — and then bade them all good-night. She raised one well-plucked eyebrow at Max as she turned to leave and, with that, elegantly went up the stairs.

'She's probably not far off the right idea,' said Angus, checking his watch and giving into a slight yawn, 'as enlivening as it always is seeing you in the buff, Hugo.'

'Thank you, sir,' replied Hugo, who doffed an imaginary cap and let out a sneaky fart — causing Max to finally throw him off his lap along with a few choice words before heading up to bed.

'So, I think I might call it a day,' continued Angus, getting up from the sofa. 'Night all.' He bowed his head slightly and, although tempted to stay by Hugo's cajoling, he resisted and instead headed towards the stairs. Jenna looked up at his departing figure and, without really thinking, leapt up and grabbed him, catching his arm as he was about to mount the first stair.

'Goodnight, Angus,' she said, waiting for him to turn around. She suddenly felt incredibly self-conscious, holding onto his arm with no real place to go from there. It must have only been seconds but it felt like, well, lots of seconds, before he turned and she suddenly let go of him.

'Goodnight, Jenna, sleep well,' he leaned down to kiss her on the cheek, but at that moment she looked up and his chin caught her across her nose.

'Oww, oh, ah . . .' A kiss had been the last thing she expected.

'Oh Jenna, sorry, um, you OK?'

'Yes, fine.' She checked her nose with her fingers, 'Not broken! All fine, goodnight.' She dashed upstairs, not even looking behind her as Sally and the still aproned Hugo called out their goodnights too, along with calls that they were all pussies and that they were going to stay downstairs and play 'Mistress and Parlourmaid' — a game no doubt made up on the spot, but highly entertaining to them both and to the sounds of screeches and laughter from the sitting room as naughty parlour maid Hugo was disciplined by his harsh mistress (a visual image that Jenna was desperate to get out of her booze-addled head before bed), she opened the door to her bedroom.

'Oh, it's you,' Bertie sounded as if Jenna had been the last person she'd expected to see. 'I thought you might stay down longer with Sally and the boys?'

'Nah, it's just Sally and Hugo, you know, doing their thing now — Max and Angus came up a minute ago.'

'Oh, did they?' At the mention of the boys' names Bertie perked up. 'Both of them, straight to bed?'

'Um, I think so. Why?'

'No reason. Just wondering.'

Jenna tried desperately to see the relevance of the conversation, but at more than a bottle of wine and a rather strong G & T down she was in no place to decipher the inner workings of Bertie's thoughts. 'Finished in the loo?' she asked instead.

Bertie nodded and moved out of the way of the door.

By the time Jenna had finished scrubbing her make-up off and had hopped around the bathroom a bit trying to get out of her jeans, and finally opened the door back to the bedroom, Bertie had gone.

14

Izzy heard nothing except the sound of snoring as she climbed the stairs from the boot room to the internal door that led into the hall and sitting room area of the chalet. Gingerly opening the door, she saw in front of her the naked, hairy legs of an unconscious male sticking out in front of the sofa. As she came into the room fully she could see the complete scale of the nakedness, and the horror that — apart from Sally doing her best to protect Hugo's modesty by wrapping her legs around him in her slumber — the only thing stopping his meat and two veg from being on display to the world was her grandmother's apron, given to her by her mother on her first day at cookery school. Screwing up her eyes in disgust, she swore under her breath, cursed the fat idiot and bloody Dominic for letting them stay, and vowed to put on a boil wash first thing in the morning.

Izzy let herself into her room, just along the corridor from the boot room door. She almost yelped in surprise when she walked in to find Bertie sitting on her bed, long silky smooth legs crossed, and with nothing much on save a matching silk negligee and robe. At the sound of the door opening, the golden-haired Bertie looked up from her phone, and took in the sight of the still-peeved chalet girl, behind her the scene of chaos in the sitting room. Smirking, she said, 'Yah, I know — horrible sight isn't it. I would apologise, but I, like, had nothing whatsoever to do with those two — hands washed of them, if you know what I mean.'

Not to be outdone in the rah stakes, Izzy countered with, 'Yah — I don't blame you. But, um, what are you doing in my room?'

'Oh — see, chalet girl . . .'

'My name's Izzy. Isabella Horatia Glaston-Smythe, to be precise.'

Cutting her off with a dismissive wave of her manicured hand, Bertie carried on. 'Yah, whatevs, still, what I was saying, if you just let me finish, is that I've noticed you may have developed a sort of soft spot for my friend Max. Thing is, that has got to stop.'

Still utterly shocked by Bertie's presence in her room in the first place and now utterly pissed off at being told what to do, Izzy started to defend herself. 'Um, excuse me,' she began, 'but what right do you have to tell me who I can and can't sleep with. I mean it's . . , Well, it's downright . . .'

'Rude, yah, I know. Thing is, sweetie, you're not part of the plan. You're a little distraction, and fair play, I respect the fact that you're obviously a nice gel from an all right part of town, so to speak, but you're not in the final cast list, get my drift?'

'Not exactly, no.'

'Max and I, well, we go way back. He's definitely in the cast list — capiche?'

'What makes you think he wants you now, though?' a thoroughly annoyed and hackles-upped Izzy retorted. 'Why aren't you in bed with him now if he's so much in your bloody *cast list*?' Izzy flung her handbag down on the bed as if to punctuate her point.

'He's getting there, and like I said, you're a distraction, so this flirting or whatever it is you're doing has to stop.'

'You can't make me.'

'Yes, I can.' The steel within Bertie's voice was almost tangible. 'But I won't *make* you. I will *pay* you.' At that she unfolded her legs and gracefully raised herself off the bed, revealing an almost perfect fan of fifty-pound notes that had been stealthily hiding under her bottom.

'Look, Roberta, I'm not that sort of girl, and I don't need your money . . .'

'No, but you would like it, though, wouldn't you? Think of it as a handbag upgrade from that old thing.' Bertie eyeballed the rather nice little Mulberry tote that had been swung onto the bed just a minute ago. 'Just think about it, sweetie. Not too hard, because, as I said, I can *make* you . . .' Bertie didn't wait for an answer and pushed past Izzy to the door, pausing briefly to once again send a withering look to the old leather bag on the bed, then gently closed the door behind her. Izzy — beyond mad with Bertie — thrashed her fist down on the bed, grabbed the notes and flung them at the back of the now closed bedroom door. It was only in seeing them flutter to the floor that she realised quite how many Bertie had left: a thousand pounds, fifteen hundred, maybe more. Indignation slowly turned to wonderment and she realised quite what a little bonus this actually was. She had just about picked up the last of the fifties from the floor when there was a knock at her door. Cautiously opening it, careful not to reveal the wodge of notes now grasped in her left hand, she was only a little surprised to see Max standing there.

Monday

15

Morning broke over the mountains of Val d'Argent, and to many it was just like any other wintry morning in the resort. The chairlifts swung into action, taking with them the keenest early birds. Wafts of coffee and freshly baked bread and pastries filled the streets of the small town, as skiers hobbled along the pavements in their bulky plastic boots, browsing the boutiques as they collected breakfast or headed for the lifts. A light dusting of snow had fallen overnight and given the place the most romantic of looks. Guttering held sumptuous little pillows of fresh snow and the ornamental pine trees looked picture-postcard perfect, topped off with a shimmering coating of snowflakes. All of this in the outside world passed Jenna by as she slept on, well into the morning. She was woken, not by the smell of freshly baked bread or the gentle hum of the lift motors, but by the banging of her door as Sally accidentally swung it closed a little too hard.

'Bloody hell!' she not very quietly whispered. 'Sorry, Jenna, did I wake you?'

Jenna didn't even need to respond. 'Still, rise and shine sleepy head, it's almost lunchtime!' Sally carried on, fussing around Jenna's bed trying to find her salopettes and jacket.

'Schtop ith,' Jenna mumbled as she turned her seriously aching head into the pillow.

'Nope.' Sally sat herself down on Bertie's vacant bed next to Jenna's rather more full one. 'If I can get up and get ready with my banging head, so can you. Plus,' she continued, pleased to see that Jenna had started to turn around under the duvet to face her, 'at least you actually slept most of the night in a bed! I was gasping for water at about 4 a.m. and woke up only to find myself, and Hugo, only about three steps from the kitchen!'

'Did you really fall asleep on the sofa?' Jenna was more awake now, her in-built gossip sensor having been alerted.

'Yes, Hugo and I wore ourselves out a little bit with the slipper . . .'

'Ooouch, no! TMI! I do not want to know what you did to Hugo's bare bottom with anything, let alone a slipper!'

'Yes, it was a bit dorm-room. I think he called me "matron" at one point.' Sally giggled to herself. 'Anyway, he's showering now and we're going to get up and get going. I think the weather will get worse later, so you may as well get out now, and knowing you, you'll give up at the first sign of a less-than-perfectly-fluffy cloud. So, lickety-split, sweetie, coffee downstairs in five.'

Jenna got up, feeling her way across the room as she blinked into the daylight. In the bathroom she squinted into the mirror and bemoaned the blotchy face with hair crinkled around it. Gradually, though, she managed to piece together her ski wear and pull on a clean polo shirt, hoping it — plus a liberal spray of deodorant — would mask the fact that she wasn't going to shower. Finally she headed down to the long, refectory-style table, that still had the remnants of breakfast laid out on it.

'Morning, Jenks!' boomed Hugo, in a voice that Jenna thought should be censored at times such as this. 'How's the head?' As if to emphasise his point he knocked his own with his breakfast cereal spoon, an action he soon regretted as everyone round the table winced at the resounding 'bonk'. 'Ow' was the only thing he could say as he then slowly put the spoon back to its proper use.

'Twit,' said Angus as he tucked into a large piece of baguette layered with Emmental cheese and slices of ham.

Jenna looked at him, almost as surprised that he wasn't up and out already as she was to see him again, so clean-shaven and, if possible, even better looking this morning than he had been last night when he'd first revealed his scar to them all. She sat down next to him and bade a quick good morning, still slightly ashamed of her behaviour the night before. Poor Angus, she thought, he must be worried that I'm about to lunge at any point and start waving my nose at his face again. Involuntarily her hand came up to touch said nose, and she felt that it was still the slightest bit tender. Angus noticed this straight away and began his apology.

'Sorry, Jenna, was that my idiot chin?'

'Um, yeah . . . but honestly, my fault, don't worry.' A blush crossed her still pillow-crumpled face. She hated the thought of her lunge actually being spoken of out loud. She reached across and away from him, fetching herself a now-cold croissant. Who knows how long they'd been sitting on the table: two, three hours? What was it now? Elevenish?

Hugo chimed in again, his head obviously now recovered for the second time in one morning. 'Late starts all round, but bloody fun night last night, chaps.' There were general nods from the others. 'Any sign of Max or Bertie, though?'

Jenna had a sudden memory flash. 'I think Bertie was up early. I seem to remember a hairdryer going off at some ungodly time. Trust Bertie to still need to be catwalk perfect when the rest of us are more hangdog hungover!'

'I went out with her, actually,' Angus quietly interjected, then took another massive bite of his open sandwich.

'What? Why?' asked Sally, licking croissant crumbs and sticky jam off her fingers.

'Well, I was up, and she was up, and there was no sign of you lot . . .'

'But weren't you horribly hungover? And where was Max?' Jenna fired off the questions in between mouthfuls of croissant.

'You know me, I never really get hangovers and the pistes looked great — how could I not!?'

'Urgh, you're so annoying,' Sally said with more vehemence than she meant. 'Sorry, Angus, darling, I didn't mean it quite so judgementally!'

'Yesterday you were the one up and out early!' he retorted.

'I kept her busy last night,' admitted Hugo, earning himself another bash around the head, this time with Sally's napkin.

'TMI again, you two!' exclaimed Jenna, covering her ears. 'La la la la,' she intoned, making sure she'd made her point.

'We are young and in love!' Sally triumphantly stated, waving her napkin around, as if that would make it less awkward for her friends to hear about her love life.

'Bringing the subject back to more breakfast-table-friendly themes,' chipped in Jenna, before Sally could go into any more detail, sotto voce at least, about how her pinny-wearing parlourmaid had given her a right good cleaning out. 'So, what happened to Max? And why are you back here, Gus?'

'I haven't seen him.'

'What, he was up before you? No way!' Jenna and Sally exchanged looks.

'Not exactly. Well, maybe. But when I got up at sevenish . . .'

'Sevenish?! Bloody hell!'

'Yeah, anyway, he wasn't there. So he might have got up earlier, or . . .'

' . . . or he might have never been in your room in the first place,' sleuthed Sally.

'Good man.' Hugo winked at no one in particular.

'That poor chalet girl,' bemoaned Sally, leaping to the obvious conclusion while looking across at Jenna.

'But why did you come back here?' Jenna surprised even herself. She'd just had Max's philandering spelt out to her again, yet for the first time in years it pained her a little less.

'Well,' he began, chewing as he spoke, 'I got to the lift with Bertie and we went up to the top of La Glace, which was awesome by the way, mate.' He looked across at Hugo as he spoke, as if the girls wouldn't have been interested. An 'ahem' from Sally brought him back to the point. 'And we skied down to Robespierre, then across to . . . well, it's hard to explain without a map, but anyway, we skied for about half an hour and I was wondering about you guys, as Bertie barely uttered a word to me, and then after about three more runs she bolted.'

Jenna wondered out loud, 'How odd. Where did she go?'

'No idea! But I thought, "what the hell" and decided to come back here for a free brekkie and see if you guys were up.'

'Sounds legit.' Hugo nodded his blessing to Angus's explanation and made a point by spreading some more butter onto another ripped-off chunk of fresh baguette. Jenna couldn't help wondering, to herself this time, though, where Bertie had gone. And why she had made use of Angus as a ski buddy for a bit, and then ditched him? Who would ditch Angus?! She looked at him, his freshly shaved face devoid of any sign of the night before − not a dark circle in sight. His scar, so new to her, yet oddly already so familiar, caught the light. He never had got round to telling them all last night how he'd got it and her mind raced over various scenarios: an Indiana Jones-style whip accident, perhaps, or dashing into a collapsing building to save some puppies . . . Her reverie was broken, as was the light conversation going on between the others, when the sound of a door opening just along the corridor alerted them all to Max, who was carefully closing Izzy's bedroom door while trying to hold all his clothes in the other hand and not let his towel slip from his waist. A whoop from Hugo, followed by an 'oi, oi, lover boy', meant that he definitely couldn't get past them all and up the stairs unseen. Instead he gave into the ribbing and dramatically bowed to the foursome, letting the towel fall off completely, to more whoops from Hugo and Angus and shocked screeches from the girls. Sweeping low to pick up the fallen towel, he then righted himself and covered his todger with his bundle of clothes and dashed upstairs, his rather taut bottom giving the girls a special treat.

Jenna looked at his departing figure, emotions so mixed inside her that she didn't know whether to laugh along with the others or gulp down air to hold in the years of hurt that suddenly bubbled to the surface. If hearing about his philandering hadn't hurt, then seeing it sure as hell did. She looked across at Angus and caught him looking at her too. His cool blue eyes seemed to search her face, as if he was trying to read her. It was almost too much for her sore head and confused heart to take.

'Well, that's put me off my pastry,' she managed to get the words out before a sob almost broke free. 'Off to dress.' She finished her sentence and dashed upstairs, managing to get into her room before the first tears — grief? confusion? — rolled down her cheeks.

16

All five finally made it onto the slopes just before lunch, and so did the only sensible thing and headed straight for the Auberge Montagne — which was not only ramping up the sound system ready for the lunch trade and party faithful, but was mercifully only a few metres' ski down from the top of one of the main lifts. Jenna unclicked her skis from her boots with the sort of relief and exhaustion that should have followed about three hours' worth of skiing, not three minutes, and she hoped her fatigue and rather bad hangover wasn't as obvious to her friends as it was to her.

'You look terrible, Jenna.' Angus destroyed that possibility.

'I still don't know how you do it, Gus,' Jenna retorted.

'I cheat,' he winked at her. 'I don't go to bed without downing about two pints of water, then when I have to go pee in the middle of the night, I down another two. And so on. I end up so bloody hydrated I'm like a kids' water bomb!'

Jenna couldn't help but smile and took his hand as she navigated the metal steps and slippery wooden deck of the restaurant. Would he realise that her shaky steps weren't just hangover induced, but that it was his supposedly steadying hand that was actually making her tremble? Thank God he's got sunglasses on, she thought to herself, as another piercing look from those blue eyes might just cause the trembles to become a full-on magnitude eight earthquake.

Darker clouds than Jenna would have liked were lurking behind the tops of the mountains, but for now a wonderful beam of sunshine was hitting the deck just at the place where she plonked herself down. Within minutes a steaming latte was placed in front of her and Jenna said thank you, along with a silent prayer of gratitude.

'Thought this might help,' said Sally as she edged in along the bench next to Jenna. 'The boys have popped into the bar and we won't stay long, but you can just chill here for a bit if you want to? I'm very impressed, sweetie, that we got you this far to be honest . . .'

'Thanks — I think.' Jenna decided not to take the ribbing personally and instead rested her head temporarily on her friend's shoulder. Just as she was about to close her eyes and bask in the sun for a little while, she noticed a familiar swish of golden highlights and the svelte figure of Bertie. Blinking more awake and raising herself upright on the bench again, she pointed her out to Sally.

'Oh yes. Shall I call her over? Coooo-eeeee, Bertie!!' Sally made a noise like someone's mother at their most embarrassing and Jenna cringed as Bertie slowly turned around to see them and let her professional smile drop as she realised she'd just been hailed down by two hungover trolls. At least, that's how Jenna felt in comparison to the vision of chic, thin, glamorous womanhood that she saw before her.

'Shit,' said Sally. 'She's seen us!'

'Um, wasn't that the point of yelling at her?' Jenna replied, confused.

'Er, yes, well, um — oh, I sort of did it on instinct,' explained Sally, 'forgetting that she's a bit of a pain now. I keep remembering old Bertie — the fun, nice one.'

'I know what you mean. I used to really like her. It's like you said yesterday, as soon as she got all that inheritance it was like, out with the old, in with the nouveau riche. It's almost like she's trading on it too — it's all about the perception of her and "Brand Bertie". It's exhausting!'

Brand Bertie at that point had turned away from looking towards Sally and Jenna, having given the friends a weak wave, and back to her little posse. It included, of course, the ice-cold oligarch and his cohort, all like Bertie wearing slim-fit black ski suits with fur-lined hoods, the glint of Rolexes and Cartier diamonds flashing occasionally as their champagne-flute-holding hands were raised to their mouths every so often.

'Looks like she is willing to drink when it's with the right people,' Jenna noted, as she wiped her hand over her still slightly sweaty, hungover brow.

'Yeah,' agreed Sally, 'though I never got the message that Grand Crus were the only calorie-free drinks out there.' The girls smirked to themselves and kept watching the spectacle until Bertie prised herself away from her new friends and sauntered over to intercept Hugo, Angus and Max as they headed out of the bar. A few minutes later and the guys had bade goodbye to Bertie and sat down with Jenna and Sally. Jenna noticed how Bertie's gaze lingered after the group. The old, unshakeable fear that Bertie was after Max took hold of Jenna again and she hid her face in the giant mug that her latte had come in as she pulled herself together. You're over it, she said, like a mantra to herself. It didn't help that Angus had just squeezed into the bench seat next to her, letting Hugo and Max with their slightly beefier frames take the opposite side of the table. Jenna felt her thigh against his. His, even through the layers of thermals and salopettes, was firm, muscly, and through no fault of its own, sending a terribly-hard-to-cope-with electric whizz up Jenna's leg and straight to her core. She braced herself and tried not to turn the ninety degrees that would reward her with a sight of his aquiline profile. He's like a Nordic god, she thought to herself, scarred in the Viking wars. God-like he might be, but she was starting to think of lots of ways to sin against him.

However, coffee break was soon over and Jenna had to face the fact that in mere moments she would be clipped back into those skis and hurtling uncontrollably down mountains again. Angus, to her bemusement, had offered to ski with her, much to the combined relief of the other three.

'You are a star, Gus.' Sally had tucked her arm through Angus's, but Jenna had wondered why she had winked at her. Trying to avoid looking at or thinking about Angus, Jenna let herself gaze once more out across the wide, man-made pistes that carved their way down the mountains to the village below. Skiing, she thought, is basically man's total, arrogant dominance over nature. It's like we saw the mountains, thought we'd like a new playground, and just bossed them. Well, some of us, anyway.

17

About twenty minutes later and Jenna was definitely not bossing the slope. She was barely middle-managering it. She was, in fact, the slope's intern — metaphorically making it tea and writing its presentations for it. The mountain's total dominance over her wasn't being helped by the fact that Angus had taken her poles off her.

'It's the best way to learn, Jenksy,' he yelled from the bottom of the slope. The very steep and painfully icy-looking slope.

'I was learning all yesterday,' she shouted back, through gritted teeth, arms wobbling as she tried to keep her balance while making turns without a nice steadying pole either side of her. Starting to lose control, *oh shit oh shit oh shit*, she slid her way around the last traverse and careered towards the stationary, and now rather vulnerable, Angus. His expression changed from all-knowing teacher smugness to mouth-open horror as Jenna picked up speed, hitting an ice patch just metres from him, *oh God oh God oh God*, and was completely unable to stop.

'Slow down, Jenks!' he yelled, though there wasn't a snowball's chance in hell of her hearing him.

'Fuuuuuuuuu . . .' and then a muffled 'eek' as she bombed straight into him, her face firmly planted into his chest and her legs going straight around his, knocking them both backwards as their skis clattered together into an undignified knot. Lying there perfectly still for a moment or two, it was Angus who moved first, gently raising his head from the gritty snow of the piste to survey the damage.

'Right, well,' he mumbled, spitting out some snow and the bobble of Jenna's hat, 'maybe you're right, maybe poles next run, Jenks.'

'Told you so — and what do you mean, "next run"?' Jenna tensed as she tried to work out if anything was hurt. Noticing, Angus stopped smiling,

'You OK?'

'I think so, but I've definitely had enough for one day . . .' She shook her head slightly and reached up gingerly, her hand following the line of Angus's chest, lingering slightly, to find her recently spat-out bobble hat on the piste next to his shoulder.

'I won't allow it — what would Pony Club have said? Straight back on your horse, young lady . . .'

'I wasn't in *bloody* Pony Club,' Jenna seethed through gritted teeth, suddenly properly annoyed with Angus for getting her into this mess of legs, skis, bobble hats and sexual tension. 'And with a horse, at least you know how *bloody* straddled your *bloody* legs are going to be and they don't just *bloody* run away with you and get wider and wider and—'

'OK, OK, sorry!' chuckled Angus, flinging his arms back in a mock surrender and flailing them on the piste. 'Heaven forbid your legs got carried away with getting wider and wider apart!'

Being in such close proximity, with the chat heading towards spread legs and all that, made Jenna suddenly clam up. Angus was still too, and after an unbelievably awkward few seconds, which felt more like an ice-cap melting millennia, he gently removed himself from underneath her, and with no more talk of Pony Club or spread legs, encouraged her to stand up. As he dusted her down she couldn't help but think again of all the times she would have killed to have Max rub his large, manly hands all over her body, but now she was standing here with his best mate and it all seemed so . . . so . . . oh, she didn't know. But let's face it, one friend or the other, she was usually unlucky in love and he'd been pretty quick to get out from underneath her. She closed her eyes rather than see what must be a blank and unemotional look on his face. Angus lightly brushed some snow from her hair and murmured something about goggles. Jenna opened her eyes in time to just catch him turn away from her in order to find the poles and other equipment victims of the crash. Was that a frown? With a little more dusting down and checking that each other were both all right, Jenna took back her poles from an unresisting Angus and tested the icy snow with them before sliding away, relieved the awkward situation had ended.

But as they waited in line for the final chairlift that would take them just high enough so they could easily ski straight down one piste to the main ski station of the village, Jenna decided that she needed to break the ice. It was all very well falling dramatically into someone's arms (or legs), but the traditional way of getting to know someone was by having 'deep and meaningfuls', as the girls at school used to call those searching conversations. And more and more, Jenna really did want to get to know Angus better. And find out if he was still with the strikingly beautiful Diane — a name she'd heard mentioned a couple of times by the boys but hadn't been able to clock Angus's response. Trouble was, those sorts of heart-to-hearts were so much easier after a bottle of wine. And when you hadn't spent most of your adult life crying over this guy's best friend.

'Gus, you're so good at skiing. When did you start?' As ice-breakers went, not bad, she thought — though deep it was not.

'God, years ago — my family all go every year, so practically since I could walk.'

'Lucky you. It's so much easier as a nipper. I'm just too aware of quite how breakable I am.'

'Sorry again about earlier. Making you ski without poles, I mean.'

'Christ, no, sorry Angus, I didn't mean to bring that up.' *Last thing I wanted to bring up, actually*, she thought to herself.

'I hope I haven't broken you, anyway,' Angus said as he gently pressed his gloved hand against the small of her back to help her move forward in the ever-pressing crowd-like queue for the chairlift. 'Sorry again about your nose last night too,' he continued.

Jenna interrupted him, wanting to change the subject. 'So, speaking of apologies . . . I'm so sorry we made you shave your beard off last night. But you really do look better without it. Honest.'

Angus stayed quiet, staring ahead. Jenna pushed it a little further. 'How did you get it?'

'Well, there are these things called follicles . . .'

'No, the scar, I mean.'

'I don't really want to talk about it, Jenna.' So here it was, the 'deep stuff' that Jenna had wanted. She looked up at him, squinting into the sunlight that was reflected off the brilliantly white snow all around them. She shivered as an icy wind suddenly whipped through the queue, and waited to see who would break the silence first. Impatient to find out more, it was, of course, her.

'You might have to get used to people asking now, what with the beard gone and all.'

'It'll grow back and then everyone can go back to minding their own business.' Angus's words were abrupt and Jenna told him as much as they shuffled forwards, keeping pace with the queue. They got themselves in line with the mini automatic gates that swung open onto the chairlift launch pad.

'I don't see why you're so private about it,' Jenna continued as she shuffled forward and got into position next to Angus as the chairlift swooshed around and scooped them both up.

'You wouldn't.' Angus sighed as he lowered the safety bar over them both, making sure no legs or hands would get jammed against the seat. 'Look, Jenna, you're sweet for taking an interest, but please, just . . .'

'But you look fine,' Jenna interrupted him, 'and please don't grow that ghastly beard back just to cover up the scar. I'm sure Diane would agree.'

'For God's sake, Jenna, will you give it a rest?' Angus almost shouted at her, and she was relieved that it was just the two of them on the chairlift seat. She looked over at him. The offending scar was on the other side of his face but a scowl as dark as hell itself had settled over his features. Jenna stared hard at the white blankness below them, hoping that any tears that might be working their way out of the corners of her eyes could be attributed to the biting wind. That'll teach me to open a big old can of whoop-ass worms, she thought to herself and stayed quiet for the rest of the chairlift. The gentle swaying of the lift turned into a clattering shudder as it reached the top of the piste and they both slid off neatly and got themselves prepped for the descent to the village. And with Angus never skiing off very far away from her, Jenna rather shakily (still a bit tense after the little incident earlier, not to mention the chairlift queue chat) got herself down the mountain and bade Angus goodbye as he headed back up the main cable car to get a few more runs in. She heaved her skis over her shoulder and headed back on the short walk to the warmth and comfort of the chalet.

Angus was infuriated. With himself, with Jenna, with the bloody stupid scar — and Max for making it a 'thing' now.

How could he ever tell someone as beautiful as Jenna how it made him feel? Fine, she said he looked better without the beard, but surely he'd look a whole lot better without this white welt that carved through his left-hand cheek? He touched it sub-consciously, running the leathery tip of his ski glove along its length, from the edge of his mouth almost to his ear lobe. He had lost all feeling in his left cheek as the jagged blade had ripped through nerves and tendons; although the icy wind that had sprung up since he'd gone back up the mountain was doing its best to numb his face altogether. Angus looked out over the mountain and down the Bête Noir black run that he'd chosen to challenge himself on. The wind had brought needle-like snowflakes with it that flurried around him and the piste, making the hardest run in the resort that little bit harder. He didn't mind, though. He needed the adrenalin rush, needed to stop thinking about Jenna and how he'd been so rude to her when he realised now that all he wanted to do was make love to her. How could he ever tell her how he'd got his scar? Looks aside, she'd never want to lay her eyes on him again.

18

'It's so hard for Yuri,' mewed Bertie, curled up on the leather sofa in the sitting room of the chalet, a crystal-studded nail file casually being flicked over the perfectly manicured tips of her fingers. After Jenna had returned she'd gone back up to her room and gratefully fallen into bed. The others must have all met up again, she thought, although how anyone could enjoy skiing in this blizzard was beyond her. Bertie had obviously felt the same and she'd heard her come into their room just as Jenna was coming round, finally recovered from her hangover. With it being far too socially awkward to ignore each other, the girls had ended up seeking mutual companionship in the sitting room, flicking through recent copies of *Hello!* magazine and occasionally chatting.

'Why?' asked Jenna, already tired of hearing all about darling Yuri's yachts, château, Manhattan loft and totally unfair run-in with the nasty little men at customs and excise.

'It's just they're so small-, like teensy-minded — just because he is so amazingly rich they think he can just hand over billions of dollars, just like that, but it's, like, tied up in trusts and stuff, and his businesses and daughters own part shares or whatever. And they're only, like, teenagers. I mean, people see him as a target. You know, even me just hanging out with him, I could so be a target now to kidnappers.'

Jenna almost choked on her tea at that last suggestion, but Bertie carried on obliviously, dropping her voice to a conspiratorial whisper.

'I actually think I saw the flash of a pap camera when we were at the Auberge Montagne earlier — it was, like, so intrusive. That's why he's sending his guards over to pick us up tonight. Oh!' Bertie's tone leapt up a gear, 'I totally forgot to tell you, sweetie — you're all invited to the party at Yuri's chalet. I told him you guys probably wouldn't be interested, but he insisted. Said something about how he, like, needed to know my people or something. Whatever. He'll come and pick us up at ten. Or at least his driver will.'

Before Jenna could interject, Bertie immediately struck up again with, 'God, please tell me you have something half decent to wear!? I would maybe, like, lend you something but you are a bit, um, heavier than me — no offence, sweetie, but you know what I mean!' Bertie sniggered to herself, until she suddenly turned deadly serious again. 'No, really, honey — what will you wear?'

'Um, wow, well, er, I guess I'll come . . .'

'Of course you'll come! It's, like, possibly going to the best party of the season! You'll have to bring your bikini too as there's bound to be some hot tub action.'

'Hot tub!'

As Bertie smirked, Jenna's mind somersaulted and tried to land approximately at the time she'd last had a bikini wax. That being very many months ago, she brought her unwilling mind back into the present and smiled wanly at Bertie.

'I didn't think to bring one, Bertie; I mean, we're skiing. The whole point of a ski holiday is that you don't have to worry about getting your body out in public — let alone in front of a Russian gazillionaire who's used to supermodels.'

'Oh Jenna, that's so sweet,' whined Bertie. 'I mean, you've like, just said I'm like a supermodel. Which one do you think? Kate? Lily? Oh, not Lily, she's way too pale. Um, maybe Giselle, yah, I think Giselle . . .'

Leaving Bertie to her own immodest musings, Jenna stretched her legs out, nuzzling her aching feet into a fluffy sheepskin throw, and thought about the pros and cons of going to the party tonight. It was sort of cool, being escorted by bodyguards to the party of a super-rich oligarch. No one at Roach & Hartley, the art gallery where she worked, which did only total about three people, would believe her. But that wouldn't matter as at least the telling of the story would have the new work experience girl rapt enough on Monday morning that she could probably get away without doing any work until at least 11 a.m. But the thought of the bikinis, and Max, or Angus, or anyone, really, seeing her very untoned and un-Brazilianed body . . . No, the thought was too ghastly, she just couldn't go. At that moment, with her mug begging for a refill of tea, Jenna heard Bertie's phone going and it wasn't without a little amusement that she noticed that Bertie answered it in her husky, pan-Atlantic voice, a far cry from the fields of Suffolk where her vowels had really been honed. The call was from Max — checking in on both the girls and the plans for later. Jenna listened as Bertie told him all about the invitation, the hot tub, the undoubted totty that would be around and, as Bertie's voice got huskier and huskier — and Max's responses on the other end seemed to get more and more positive — Jenna finally admitted to herself that it was time to find the flashing green cross of hope on the Rue d'Argent and get some razor blades and hot wax.

A few very painful hours later, Jenna stood looking at herself in the mirror. She was clad, as only something so very, very close to her body could be termed, in one of Bertie's bikinis. It was the largest and most modest of the ones on offer, yet still it prompted Jenna to think that she might as well just immerse herself in a vat of Veet to fully de-fuzz — this bikini was taking no prisoners and she had definitely been a jungle to wage war in. The bikini was black and gold, luckily not a thong but very high cut, with the top plunging about as far down her cleavage as one could sensibly go. Bertie trounced in, having been uncharacteristically nice to Sally, helping her into a small cocktail number she'd handily brought along. Bertie was in her swimmers, too — not a bikini, but a one-piece so drastically cutaway it looked like someone had just gaffer-taped Bertie's boobs onto her body. It was silver and neatly encrusted in rhinestones. Ouch, thought Jenna — if she sits on a seam that's going to leave a nasty mark.

Bertie kicked off the silver Jimmy Choos she'd been skipping around in and beamed at Jenna.

'There you go, sugar,' she purred, 'you'll do fine! I mean, it's not like you actually want any of these guys, so if they don't fancy you it's not a problem!' And in a hushed tone, 'And anyway, you're not so bad as porky back there,' indicating a really unporky Sally. 'I had to convince her NOT to wear a bikini in case she tried to get in, and all the water tried to get out!' Snorting almost obliterated the end of the sentence.

'Bertie, you're not nice, you know?' Jenna was finally appalled at her roommate. 'Sally's not fat, she's not even borderline overweight! If anything, I'm bigger than her! What have you got against her? Did she run you down on her pony once when you were both kids? Did she sabotage your gymkhana hopes?'

Jenna would have thrown example on example but Bertie's silence cut through her rant and lasted for what seemed like an age before Bertie said, 'Something like that. It doesn't matter.' And, slipping on a tight-fitting cashmere jumper-dress in a deep midnight blue, she fluffed her hair in a dignified manner and left.

Of course, Bertie didn't think to close the door behind her as she left Jenna standing in front of the mirror, still wearing her couple-of-triangles-and-a-pair-of-pants ensemble. Jenna was about six feet from the wide open door and was about to cross the room to slam it shut, muttering something about 'catching her death', but was mortified when Angus appeared in the corridor. *O sweet Jesus*, Jenna thought, breathing in and using every abdominal muscle God gave her to try to suck in her tummy.

Angus was speechless. Not so much due to the blonde goddess he now witnessed, standing there, semi-nude, stuff of fantasy and all that, but because just before he'd rounded the top of the stairs he'd shoved a four-inch-long piece of baguette, smeared with lovely French unsalted butter, into his gob. Jenna flailed around for a cover-up — anything — and chanced upon her ski jacket still lying on the bed from earlier, and wrapped it around her. Angus, distraught that his unintentional intrusion had caused Jenna so much anguish, and rather sad really that he hadn't had longer to relish the loveliness in front of him, felt even worse as at least two inches of the baguette was still unchewed and not at all safe to swallow, meaning he couldn't issue all the apologies and platitudes he so desperately wanted to. Caught in this impasse, Jenna broke first and regained composure enough to waddle towards the door, the toggles of her ski jacket swinging between her knees. Angus on the other hand could only watch, make odd grunts and strange hand gestures of apology, but also praise, before the door was roundly closed in his face.

Jenna dropped the jacket, hell with tidiness, and flung herself on the bed. In a moment she had jumped back up and hotfooted it to the bathroom to take a few deep breaths and strip out of the bikini, in total privacy. But as she was about to unhook the clasp she had a brief moment of rationality. Angus had seen her. In the bikini. He had looked slightly horrified, although that might have been due to the lack of oxygen being allowed through the dough-plug in his mouth. But horrified none the less. Thank the Lord it wasn't Max who'd been standing there. But still, the fact that it was Angus was oddly not much of a comfort. But he had already seen her, so what was the point of worrying now? She had planned to sink a few ice-cold neat vodkas before being confident enough to slip out of the Diane von Furstenberg Bertie was lending her ('Ruched, you see, darling, around the tum; so much more flattering on you') and into the hot tub. But at least the worst was over now. So, she thought, she may as well keep the damn thing on, do her face, pop on the dress, and head downstairs.

19

As Jenna teetered on the top step, the stacked heels on the borrowed Kurt Geigers ('Sturdier than the Louboutins, sweetie, probably better for you.') not quite what she was used to, she could hear the general sound of friends having fun coming from the sitting room. As she descended she could hear Bertie, recovered from her telling off, it seemed, and braying as usual to Max about something or other. Max, she could hear laughing and the deep tones of Angus and Hugo discussing something at depth. A high-pitched, sing-song trill, aimed at no one in particular, hinted that Sally was also there, and happily, totally unaware of Bertie's earlier barbed comments about her.

The wood-burning stove was lit and giving out a warm glow. Izzy, in a ridiculously short skirt that showed off her ridiculously long, slim legs, was handing around a few canapés, something Bertie had requested instead of a proper supper, the reasoning being that no one would want to hot tub on a full stomach. Only Bertie would use the term 'hot tub' as a verb. Or cancel a proper dinner in favour of mere nibbles. Of course the guys had had something to say about this and so poor Izzy was going to have to whip up a last-minute spag bol to keep the troops at bay. She, of course, was more than happy to do anything for Max, after yesterday's lovemaking at the Marmotte, not to mention the particular pleasure he'd given her last night. She felt a little bad about taking Bertie's money, but what was a couple of thousand compared to Max making her feel like a million dollars?

Bertie, oblivious to Izzy's motivations, began running her finger down the edge of Max's shirt buttons, telling him in serious detail the problem she, or at least her fund managers, had had in completing a few risky trades last quarter. Not that she really knew what she was talking about, but to her mind Max seemed impressed and was encouraging her with his chat about City finance, while subtly edging closer to her whenever Izzy was out of the room.

Jenna made herself a stiff gin and tonic aided by the contents of the cupboard that they had all raided last night (thank you Dubious Dominic!) and plonked herself down next to a strained Sally who was keeping her spine pencil-straight in the slightly tight sateen minidress Bertie had forced her into. Never one to admit an easy defeat, she instantly turned to Jenna and whispered, 'Roche Bobois, sweetie.'

'I'm sorry, what?' said Jenna, leaning in and borrowing Sally's hushed tones.

'The sofas. Roche Bobois. But you know you can get something quite similar in Dwell at Westfield. I noticed them when we first got here, but I had to wait until no one was looking so I could ferret around for a label. Just had to know.'

'Ah,' nodded Jenna, whose only thoughts of sofas in her shabby little flat were how best to position them to hide the much-scrubbed wine stains on the carpet. Before Sally could pass judgement on the provenance of the sheep-skin rugs, Jenna butted in with, 'Have you seen Angus? I thought I heard him talking to Hugo?' But, alas, Sally was already onto the bifold doors and telling Jenna how she and Hugo were definitely thinking of getting some for the extension as 'they simply bring the outside in, darling, and you know in a west-facing town garden like ours in Putney you need a nice lot of evening light'. Sighing to herself and nodding along gently, Jenna accepted that she was just going to have to deduce for herself where Angus was, as Sally was obviously not to be distracted. As a delightful plate of mini Yorkshire puddings ('So clever of little Izzy to find these in the Spar,' gushed Sally. 'I wouldn't be surprised if her clever mummy sent them from Ocado.') filled with horseradish and pastrami was passed around by Hugo, Jenna realised that neither Izzy nor Angus was in the sitting room. Separating herself from Sally and her chat about the difference between Peter Jones on Sloane Square and the larger John Lewis on Oxford Street, Jenna eased herself back into her high heels and headed for the kitchen, suddenly aware of a lot of chuckling and giggling coming from the open doorway. She glanced back briefly to her friends on the sofa and noticed Bertie pouring herself all over Max — and him not exactly refusing the refill. *Always the bridesmaid* she thought to herself as she turned back towards the kitchen, weighing up in her mind that it was less annoying to make conversation with Max's one-night-stand chalet girl than to stay and watch another episode of the *Max and Bertie Show*. Plus, after the horrors of bikini-gate a few moments ago she really needed to see Angus who was leaning sanguinely against the worktop, glass of red in hand as Izzy topped him up before sploshing a decent amount into some bolognese sauce.

'Jenks,' said Angus warmly, 'come and join the only two people in this chalet talking any sense at the moment.' Jenna, finding it hard to look Angus in the eye, struggled to mimic his relaxed stance as she too leant against a countertop.

'If by sense you mean gossip,' snickered Izzy, 'the word on the street, you see, is that Yuri Popacokkov is definitely some arms-runner or a drugs lord billionaire or something. Apparently, some of his group only have breakfast at teatime, and spend the next few hours on the Internet, browsing for prozzies, then they meet up with them at après-ski time and, like, literally go at it all night.'

'Blimey,' said Jenna, taking a massive slug of her G&T, glad that for all Izzy's faults (Jenna had to admit, except for being posh and moody, Izzy's only real fault in her book was shagging Max) she was at least a good source of gossip and an excellent distraction from the total awkwardness she was feeling towards Angus. She further perked up as Izzy continued.

'I know — amazeballs, isn't it? My old BFF from school, Ginny, is one of the chalet hostesses in that mansion they've taken over and she's been, like, released for the fortnight as Popacokkov has brought his own chef, maid, butler, and, er, "other" staff, it seems.'

'You mean mistresses?' said Angus, eyes wide at the thought of a man who had the stamina to cope with more than one woman at a time.

'A gentlemanly way of putting it, Gus,' deadpanned Jenna, 'but you've completely ignored the most important bit of info Izzy's just told us. He's called Pop A Cock Off!'

Amid the giggles and a wry grin from Angus, Jenna continued, 'Please, please Lord in heaven, let Bertie marry him. She can be Mrs Popacokkov — all men will fear her!' Jenna raised her arms to the ceiling and swung them low in a mock bow of deference.

'Oh God, like, I know, it's just too funny but if you're going to his place tonight — which, by the way, I am sooo jealous of, you mustn't make any jokes — he knows how funny his name sounds to us and apparently, Ginny said, he once got one of his henchmen or hired guards or whatever they are, to like totally do in someone who laughed at him.'

'Cripes, so no pops at Popa, ha?' said Jenna, making a mental note to seal her lips all night long.

Spag bol devoured and with spirits and voices high, the friends were having so much fun between themselves they were almost half-hoping that the Russian envoys wouldn't arrive to escort them to the chicest party in town. But at 10 p.m. precisely, the front door intercom buzzed.

'I told you!' said Bertie, as much to herself as anyone else. As they all began to find coats, scarves, gloves and ear muffs, Bertie glanced at Sally and in a horrified screech announced, 'Oh God, no — Sally, please don't say you're putting on Hugo's fleece? Are you *trying* to look ridiculous?'

'No, Bertie, but it's freezing out there and I for one am not in the mood for frostbite!'

'But Yuri has sent us a car — we'll not need to be outside for more than a second and I'm sure he'll provide us with furs and the like if there's a terrace.'

'Well, I'm taking something — you just never know, he might not have any dead mink lying around, and at that point I think you'll all be bloody jealous of my sensible fleece!'

'Sally, sweetie,' trying to ease the situation, Jenna whispered to her friend, 'I totally agree, but do you think the fleece is the best idea? It might not cause sartorial sparks but it sure as hell might cause static ones with that satin dress you're wearing . . .'

Sally just looked at her friend, a little hurt but not cowed, and flounced past Bertie and the boys into the waiting Hummer, glorious in the massive black and red fleece that almost reached her knees. She ignored the strange look from the chauffeur as she slowly turned pinker and pinker in the stretched car's near-tropical climate. Piling in next to her, Hugo didn't help by increasing her body temperature until she was almost at boiling point. Jenna wasn't having a much better journey. Grateful, after a belly full of pasta, for the ruches in the borrowed wrap dress, she was now awkwardly pressed up against Angus. His legs and arms were taut, like steel girders next to her, and even though their laughs in the kitchen earlier had broken the ice from bikini-gate, she still had ripples of anguish flowing through her. And she couldn't help but notice a certain tingle in her leg, the one so close to his. She was distracted, at least, by Bertie admonishing them all. 'I don't know why I bother with you all sometimes,' she started. 'I mean, to eat at all was pretty loathsome of you, and to indulge in that horrible garlic bread — I mean, how will you ever fit in with the beautiful people now? You'll scare them all off with your terrible breath!'

'What are they, vampires?' Hugo chuckled at his joke, causing Sally to sweat a little more as the fleece was rubbed up against her. 'Let's hope that hot tub is full of holy water, for all our sakes!'

'Maybe Pop-a-Cock is actually Vlad the impale-her,' giggled Jenna, before she was quickly silenced by a glare and 'ssshh' from Bertie, who indicated the silent menace of the driver.

20

The car park of the chalet, though spotlessly clean and devoid of any mess, was nonetheless dank. The bright neon lights weren't enough to fight back the darkness that shrouded and blurred the seemingly endless nature of this underground temple to automotive design. It wasn't helped that the lights were angled not to illuminate the area as a whole, but to spotlight the various cars and skidoos that were housed there. The driver, in words of one syllable or, if indeed possible, fewer, had unceremoniously dumped them out of the outrageously showy-offy Hummer next to a small lift and indicated that they should use it, before grunting some sort of affirmative into his walkie-talkie. He then carefully parked the massive vehicle in between a white state-of-the-art Range Rover with blacked-out windows and a gold Bugatti Chiron — the latest super car handily equipped with four-wheel drive. Not that Jenna had really taken any of this in — except for the skidoos, which looked great fun — but the running commentary from Max and Hugo kept her informed of their host's total amount of BHP and engine sizes, plus how long waiting lists would be for cars like that and how much he would have had to have paid to get to the top.

'I know a guy who waited months for one of those,' Max began, 'only to bump into a rock star who said he'd just been given one as part of his rider at the O2.'

'Gutting,' nodded Hugo in appreciation of the cruelty of the world.

'Yuri doesn't like to be kept waiting,' Bertie announced, glancing at the stony face of the chauffeur who was now holding open the lift door. 'Come on, people.' Bertie clicked her fingers a few times and then took Max's hand and led him into the lift, swiftly followed by everyone else. The chauffeur-cum-lift attendant barely checked to see if everyone was in safely before tapping in a code on the very high-tech-looking keypad beside the lift, causing the doors to abruptly close on the chattering group. The initial shudder of upwards motion unbalanced Bertie, in her vertiginous heels, enough to almost topple her into a very willing Max, something she would have made a very big deal out of, if she actually wasn't quite excited about her grand entrance into Russian high society.

Everything Jenna had imagined, except perhaps some towering pyramids of Ferrero Rocher, was in front of her. The lift had opened its doors into a wide reception hall, covered on floor, walls, and even ceiling with highly polished sand-coloured marble, and lit by the most impressive of gold chandeliers. Tiny crystals hung from its fifteen arms and glints of light sparkled off them, adding to the dazzling opulence of the hall. Staff held trays of champagne glasses, liberally filled, the bubbles racing to the top and demanding to be drunk. Jenna took one, trying to stop herself from shaking slightly. Nerves? Perhaps just anticipation of what the next room must be like, and she wasn't disappointed. The hallway led into a plushly carpeted, huge room, about twice the size of Jenna's entire flat back in London. It was like one of those scenes you see in posh magazines, the couture models draped elegantly over red velvet Rococo-style sofas and chairs, while louche young men flittered back and forth with magnums of Cristal and misted bottles of pure Russian vodka, straight from the freezers. A glistening ice sculpture of a horse's head, nose down as if drinking from a lake, dominated the centre of the room. A short, red-faced man was pouring vodka down through it, giggling whenever a girl underneath got a cold shower of almost pure alcohol, while other men looked on impressed as some girls caught a full shot in the mouth and swallowed it effortlessly. Jenna caught Sally's eye and raised her eyebrow before raising her glass to her friend.

'Here goes nothing, sweetie,' Sally whispered as she looked longingly at the petit fours being brought out on silver trays and placed near an ornate samovar, from which hot coffee was being poured. Jenna clinked Sally's glass and looked around for the others, expecting them all to be standing in shocked silence just like she was. Far from it. Bertie had taken Max by the hand and led him over to meet Yuri, instantly recognisable in his trademark black — this time a well-fitting suit over another tight black T-shirt. He was sitting, legs wide apart, on one of the red velvet upholstered sofas, its gold ornate woodwork complementing his sandy-blond hair and the massive gold chain around his neck. A beautiful, if sour-faced, brunette, at least twenty years his junior, was sitting beside him, pouting into thin air and looking terribly bored by the whole affair. She flicked her hair, fiddled with her phone and blew a pink bubble that burst just as Bertie approached them. Jenna looked on as Bertie made a fuss of the girl, complimenting her in a rather obsequious way. Ah, thought Jenna to herself, a daughter perhaps. Max had shaken hands with Yuri by now and still seemed to be flexing his fingers, bringing them back to life after the dominating crush of the Russian's handshake.

Angus had noticed this too and leaned into Jenna, saying, 'Blimey. Rather him than me.'

'I know, talk about killing them with kindness,' Jenna replied. 'If that's the warm welcome, I'd hate to see the cold shoulder of goodbye.'

Angus raised his already half-drunk champagne flute to her in a silent 'cheers' and, having checked that Jenna and Sally had enough to drink, joined Hugo, who had by now wandered over to another room, this one home to a full-size billiard table, which happened also to be host to a very attractive and very leggy redhead. Jenna frowned. Still, she thought, at least I'm in no way as attractive as most of the women here, so I reckon I'll be way down the creeping-on list. A firm hand on her bottom made her instantly re-evaluate that assumption and she quickly moved away from the bum-grabber, who she noticed had hidden his sleaziness in an attempt to pick up a cream-filled profiterole from the plate on the table behind her. Narrowing her eyes and shooting him a warning glare that she hoped conveyed exactly where he could stick that cream puff if he touched her again, she tiptoed as best she could on her high heels into the party. She smiled at the handsome men and mentally noted which of the women were definitely naughty ladies of the night, paid by the hour to hang out and have fun with these sleazes.

'Oh,' Sonia exclaimed in mock outrage, 'you English men are all the same.' She winked at Angus. 'You have put your balls in my pocket and now I am fucked.'

'Well, I took my cue from you.' Angus raised just one eyebrow at the stunning Russian playing some form of house-rules billiards with him. 'You seem to be playing hardball yourself.'

Sonia smiled at him, and slowly moved around the large baize table to stand next to him, seemingly to eye up her next shot. Her hip nudged him out of the way as she bent over the long wooden cue in her hand and expertly potted one of the coloured balls fast and straight into a far corner pocket. It made a satisfying clonk and then a purr as it found its way out of the netting and down under the table. Angus subconsciously winced. She stood up, slowly, as if she was a ballet dancer or Pilates teacher, her back slowly straightening one vertebra at a time, a controlled movement that best showed Angus how lean and strong her figure was. Angus had met Sonia as soon as he'd followed Hugo into the billiards room — she had locked eyes with him as she ran her hand up and down her cue, and he would be the first to admit that for just a minute his trouser-brain was doing the thinking. Sonia was stunning. Soft red curls fell about her naked shoulders, the finest threads of straps held up a wisp of fabric that just about covered her extremely pert breasts, but left her back and its toned muscles on full view. Slim fit jeans and rhinestone-studded cowboy boots finished off her outfit — she could have walked off the set of an *American Dream*-style film. But her thick, accented English gave away the fact that she was as Russian as a fur-lined Fabergé egg filled with vodka. Hugo, noticing the look of pure carnality Sonia had given Angus, left him to it with a not-so-subtle nudge and mention of 'Slavic salivation'.

'Hardball, you said?' she looked at Angus. 'I'll give you hard balls.'

Angus found it hard to concentrate on his next shot, but luckily saved face and managed to get a tricky cushion-bound ball into the pocket next to it. As he stood up he briefly caught sight of Jenna batting off some sleazy old git in the next room. His hand clenched his cue a little tighter, and then tighter again as Sonia started to stroke one of her perfectly manicured hands down his back.

'Tell me, Englishman, how did you get that nasty scar on your handsome face? If I didn't think otherwise, I'd say you fit right in here with these gangsters and mercenaries.'

'I'd rather not say.' It was his default position, now the scar had been revealed. Although maybe someone like Sonia wouldn't give two hoots about how he'd got it. If her moral fibre was as thin as her silky top, she'd understand the position he'd been in. 'It was when I was in Singapore.'

She raised an already arched eyebrow. 'Are architects renowned for bar brawls or street fights?' She ran her hand down his arm, feeling his muscle as he clenched his fist around the cue, tighter now as he felt the old memories that he'd tried so hard to conceal come ripping their way to the surface. When he'd admitted to Diane how he'd got the scar she'd made her all-too-obvious excuses and he never saw her again — but there would be no wasted flights or faked tears if he told this stranger.

21

'Straight from the horse's mouth, quite literally darling,' Sally squealed in excitement as she watched Jenna expertly gulp down at least two shots from underneath the icy horse. Jenna stood up and wobbled a bit, 'Any more Belvedere might lead to Belve-oh-dear later!' she giggled as she righted herself. Fresh air was needed. Leaving Sally with a refilled glass of fizz and dangerously close to the champagne truffles, she slid open the terrace door and shivered suddenly as the chill of the winter weather hit her. And of course, there it was, the hot tub. Sheltered from the snowflakes that fell all around it, it bubbled and steamed away, looking invitingly warm and large enough for almost half the party to slip into, it seemed. Jenna decided that now was the time to release the kraken and have a dip herself. Carpe diem was one thing though, she thought, but carpe-ing your death of cold for not taking a towel out with you for afters was quite another. She slid the heavy door closed and twisted her way back into the party until she found Bertie, entwined on the plush sofa with Yuri, whispering sweet nothings into his oligarchical ear.

Interrupting them was awkward, but not without its rewards. Both Yuri and Bertie, and then Max, Angus and Sonia, were all keen to get all bubbled up too, and only minutes later the girls were ushered into a warm, marble bathroom, complete with sumptuous robes that were plush flannel against the skin and cream silk on the outside. Towels, fluffy and white, were neatly folded over the chrome radiators and the three of them were invited, by a Filipino maid who had appeared as if by magic, to strip off in the warm before using the towelling slippers and luxury robes to make their way to the hot tub. Luckily for Jenna the number of glasses of champagne — not to mention vodka shots — she'd had outweighed the feelings of inferiority while undressing in front of two Amazonian goddesses and, quick as you like, they were all in bikinis and snuggled into their deliciously comfortable robes and slippers.

'I may never want to leave here, you know, Bertie,' said Jenna as she wandered, glass still firmly in hand, down the wide corridor, which was decorated with the most beautiful paintings of the Alps — not those old-fashioned ones that lined every hotel designed in the vintage-Alpine-style, but obviously by a contemporary artist, one who knew how dark shadows could create a deep purple colour, while to the eye you knew it was still a crisp white snow, inviting you up into the peaks.

'Yes, I can see that it's been eye-opening for you, darling,' replied Bertie, 'and aren't you glad I made you wax?'

Jenna remembered the pain of earlier that evening, winced, and in the same moment remembered the look of shock on Angus's face when he had seen her in her room through the half-open door, wearing nothing but Bertie's skimpy bikini. Too late now, she thought as the girls made their entrance onto the terrace. Angus, Max and Yuri were already in the hot tub, with Max and Yuri puffing on stupidly fat cigars. Angus, she saw, was gazing out over the edge of the terrace looking at the amazing view, lit by the town's and pistes' floodlights.

Bertie slipped in right beside Yuri, with Max on the other side. Jenna noticed her looking incredibly smug, as if some sort of cosmic coming together was happening right in front of her. Sonia elegantly removed the soft robe and stepped into the steaming hot tub in between Yuri and Angus. Jenna noticed her speak a few words in Russian to their host before turning back to chat to Angus in her heavily accented English. Jenna, who was the last to slip off her warm and protective robe, made a slightly less elegant entrance, slightly slipping and splashing into the hot tub between Max and Angus, and didn't unclench her stomach muscles until she was well and truly immersed in the hot, steamy water.

Angus had definitely been enjoying the view. Having been introduced to Yuri at last, he'd declined a cigar and left Max and the oligarch talking international economics and puffing away. The mountains rose up majestically beyond the sheltered terrace, decorated with the lights of piste-bashers. He turned back towards the chalet in time to see the three girls approach, take off their robes and slip into the hot tub, and he felt something else rise up majestically too. He felt himself stiffen further, and not just in his trunks, as Jenna ended up next to him, splashing and giggling in the almost foamy froth around them. He was completely transfixed by her beautiful soft breasts as they bobbed up and down in the bubbly water and it was a monumental task to drag his eyes away from them. Desperately seeking something else to stare at, he focused on the soft tendrils of her hair, curling in the rising steam, and the smile on her face as she giggled with Max about the bubbles underneath them. As Angus watched her laugh and flirt with her old friend he tried to subtly move closer to her too, but was stopped in his tracks. In an instant he knew that the firm grip now around his very erect penis wasn't Jenna's, as both her hands were wildly gesticulating some story to Max, and with a feeling of disappointment that no man should have when he realises a girl who could do *that* with a billiard ball is fondling him, he turned to look at Sonia. It took him slightly by surprise that on the surface she was ignoring him while talking to Yuri and Bertie, but like the hand job version of a duck, underneath the water she was vigorously moving her hand up and down his considerable length, while above the surface she was serene as a swan. It was when she rubbed her thumb over the very tip of his dick that he let his pleasure be real. *Fuck it*, he thought as the surge of testosterone pumped around his body. When had Jenna ever been interested? She wasn't even looking at him.

Max was feeling less of the hot tub love. Having felt sure that a shag with Bertie would have been a dead cert tonight, he was feeling less and less like the odds-on favourite as he couldn't fail but notice the chemistry between his old sparring partner and Yuri the bloody oligarch. And what made it worse was that he wasn't just rich, or very, very rich, but ripped too. Max, for one of the first times since puberty, felt not a little inferior. Taking another puff of his ridiculously fat cigar, he decided there was only one thing for it. If Bertie was to have her fun, and she most certainly seemed to be having it with that Leningrad lothario (if the closeness of her chest to his head was anything to tell by), then he would make some hot tub memories of his own. And it's not like he'd never thought of Jenna in that way. Old friend and muckabout she might be and once a bit chubby and fresh-faced for him, but now, come to think of it, she was looking quite hot and that little black bikini was definitely helping her buoyancy aides become really quite bouncy. And hadn't she always had a bit of a soft spot for him? Slipping his arm around her even he was surprised at quite how quickly she melted into him, knocking back the last of her champagne and shakily placing the flute to the side of the tub.

'Hello, gorgeous,' he whispered into her ear. 'Looks like we've been rather thrown together in this sexual soup.'

'I thought it would be so much more fun,' she hiccupped, just as she realised that Max was fingering the straps of her bikini. 'Oh, I see . . .'

'No reason why it can't be fun,' replied Max, taking his wandering hand one step further and easing his strong, masculine fingers over her shoulder and down towards her bouncing, beautiful breast. 'I always thought we'd get together one day, Jenksy. I mean, in all these years we've known each other, neither of us has ever really had anyone special.'

Holding onto the last of her reserve, Jenna hesitated before saying, 'Well, I mean we have . . . don't you remember . . . I mean, but I've always liked . . .' But at that she couldn't say any more. Max started to nibble her ear while simultaneously sliding his adept fingers into the cup of her bikini top, finding her nipple, and gently starting to rub and squeeze it. Pulling her closely into him he whispered in her ear soothing words — that no one else right now mattered — and she believed him as the touch of his skin, the feel of pressing against his rigid torso was so exquisite after months and months of being alone, not to mention that this was Max, after all. Max, the university love god; Max, the City cad who could have any girl he wanted; Max, who just a minute ago had told Jenna that he'd always thought they should be together (hallelujah!) and that Bertie meant nothing to him (double hallelujah!). She pulled herself closer to him and as his mouth found hers she slipped onto his lap, letting the steamy, bubbling water be the only thing between them. Tracing his strong jawline with exploratory fingers, she deepened his kiss and felt that it wasn't just his torso that was hard. Letting him pull her closer so her legs were either side of him she felt the huge shaft of his penis rub against her stomach . . .

What Jenna didn't know at this point was that, although Bertie was unaware of Max's moves, happily occupied as she was being taught some very explicit Russian for parts of her body that Yuri was enjoying pointing out to her, it was Angus who now looked on, sick to the heart at what he saw. Sonia was still stroking his face and nibbling his ear, content in knowing she had given someone rather tasty the most amazing orgasm, and although he should have been revelling in the same semi-exhausted state as her, it had only taken a split second for all his feelings of well-being to be replaced with a jealous anger as he saw his best mate pull the girl he was starting to realise he loved onto his lap and start nuzzling her beautiful, bouncing breasts.

22

Just as Angus was flexing his fist, not really knowing how to react to what he saw in front of him, a very drunk and very upset Sally stumbled out onto the terrace, her face streaked with tears.

'Jenna! Jenna!' she yelled, half tripping and half sliding over the icy wetness of the veranda towards the tub.

'Watch the dress,' sneered Bertie as she disentangled herself from Yuri and for the first time noticed that Jenna was having more than just a friendly cuddle with Max. Before she could ask just what the hell was going on, Sally blurted out, 'He's kissed her! Hugo's kissed that bloody little girl. Oh, Jenna,' she sobbed as she fell to her knees. 'Please take me home.'

Angus was first out of the hot tub, pleased to have some action to perform other than bashing his best friend's face in or shaking the idiocy out of Jenna. He grabbed his towel from the edge of the balcony, wrapped it around himself as the steam rose off his body, and crouched by Sally's side.

Only an instant later, that instant having been well used in making sure all necessities were covered, Jenna had pulled herself out of the hot tub and grabbed her robe before also kneeling down next to her weeping friend. Trying to make sense of the situation through the heaving, snotty sobs, it was all Jenna could do to understand what Sally was trying to tell her. 'Hugo had what? Kissed Ulrika? Or was it Slavicka? Surely not, darling, he loves you, you're engaged . . .' Through the comforting and sobbing — with even Max and Angus helping the poor beleaguered Sally to her unsteady feet — Jenna tried to fathom what had actually happened. Far from being concerned for his guest, it all seemed rather distasteful to Yuri. And with a similarly withering look at Max, Bertie flung her own robe around her, flicked her hair out of the collar and let herself be led by her Russian lover along the chilled terrace, past the doors now open to the party inside, to his master bedroom suite, the other side of the chalet. As a security guard nodded them in, Jenna looked up to see Sonia breeze past the guard too. Usually this would have made Jenna wide-eyed with the thought of what could possibly be happening and who she could tell about it in hushed but excited whispers, but right now she couldn't give a monkey's what Bertie got up to with Yuri. Or Sonia. Or both of them. Her thoughts were all about getting Sally inside and sorted out, and getting herself out of this ridiculous bikini and off this fricking freezing terrace. With Angus's help (Max *had* been a little distracted watching the now be-robed and fur-hatted Sonia follow the lamé-ed Bertie into the boudoir), Jenna led Sally through the party throng. Some faces turned to stare, having seen the mad Englishwoman in the tight dress tearing through the room only moments earlier, others not at all interested due to the fact that their own lives were obviously of much more consequence and interest.

Out of the main reception hall and along the painting-hung corridor they walked, both Angus and Max by now helping the distraught — and quite drunk — Sally stay upright. Jenna stopped by the bathroom door. It was open and, as she glanced in to check that no one was in there, she thanked her slightly more sober self for hanging up her dress on the lovely warming rail.

'Sally, darling, I've got to get dressed and then we can find that lovely snugly fleece of yours.'

'It's Hugo's, the bastard,' Sally half-yelled through snot-filled sobs.

'Yes, but you so wisely brought it, darling, so let's get the boys to find it and I'll get dressed and we'll all go home, won't we, chaps?' Jenna looked up at Max and Angus — both standing there, still dripping wet, but no less handsome for the rash of goosebumps appearing across their broad chests. *Wow*, she thought, and added out loud to Sally, in an effort to defuse the situation, 'And look at these naked hunks next to you. Nice, huh?'

Jenna ducked into the bathroom and closed the door. She slipped the robe off, towelled down, and found her knickers and dress. Popping her clothes back on, her mind boggled. Only a few minutes ago she had been in a hot tub with Max telling her, kinda, that he loved her. Well, implying it really — he had after all said they were meant to be together, hadn't he? And then Sally — and Hugo — would he really cheat on her? Here? In front of her? Surely not, there must be an explanation, for if all was not right in Sally and Hugo's camp then Jenna's beliefs about true love and fidelity would be rocked forever.

With only a quick look in the mirror to check she wasn't looking too much like a drowned rat, and only pausing to let her hair down and run her fingers through it to detangle the worst of it, she opened the bathroom door to a still half-naked Angus.

'Took your time, Jenks,' he growled, as he stood, hugging the shuddering Sally. 'Max has gone to get changed. I need to. Stay with her.' Pointing to Sally wasn't necessary and Jenna harrumphed an 'of course' back at him, unsure where his sudden shit mood had come from and even more unsure of why its sudden nature bothered her so much. He continued, 'Max is phoning a cab because we can't go out in this weather, we'd all freeze by the time we got anywhere and I don't think Yuri will spare us the Hummer without Her Majesty with us.'

At that he turned on his heel and loped down the corridor towards the spare room he'd obviously used earlier to change in. More surprising to Jenna was the shoulder barge he gave Max as he pushed into the room he was leaving, iPhone in hand having spoken to the local taxis.

'Five mins,' he mouthed, holding his hand up to illustrate before pointing in the direction of the party and then mouthing 'Find Hugo' at the throng. Taking Jenna's nod as a go ahead, he disappeared back into the party, taking another full glass of fizz from a nearby waiter.

23

Twenty minutes later, Jenna was leaning over her friend as she tucked her into bed. Between dwindling sobs, Sally demanded, 'If he does dare to come back, then don't let him in, sweetie. I can't bear him — I don't want to see him!' A pause as she gathered breath. Jenna knew only too well how exhausting crying and talking could be. 'But do wake me, if he does come back. Oh, the rat! I want to be the first to scratch his lying, cheating eyes out! Oh Huggy, how could you!?' The sobs finally faded to whimpers and Sally switched from expressing violent thoughts to whispered heartbreak every second sentence. Jenna calmly stroked her forehead for another few minutes and eventually turned the bedside light off. She noticed Sally's engagement ring, reflecting first the bedside light and then the moonlight as it sat on the bedside table — the first time she'd ever seen it anywhere except on Sally's finger. Slipping away to the sound of ever decreasing sniffs, she quietly closed the door. She popped back into her room and found a large and comfortable old cashmere jumper that cosily covered the slinky dress she was feeling considerably less slinky in now that the party feeling had left them all. Jenna then quietly descended the stairs to where Angus was sitting, his head resting in his hands, his fingers scraped up into his sandy-blond hair. Looking up at her as she approached, she thought she saw a dash of anger in his eyes, but it was only a moment before they softened. It reminded her though of his shirty mood earlier, so plopping herself down next to him on the large squashy sofa she decided to ask.

'Here, drink this,' he offered a pint glass of water before she'd had time to open her mouth.

'Thanks, Gus.'

A moment of silence.

'Quite a night, huh?' Jenna said, before taking a long sip of the water.

'Yeah . . .' The word sounded like he was letting it seep out from closed teeth and a clenched jaw.

'You OK? I saw you had a bit of fun with Sonia, was it? Do you think you'll see her again?'

'No.' He turned towards her on the sofa. 'It was a mistake, I shouldn't have let her do that. And you shouldn't have got it on with Max either, what on earth were you thinking? You should know better, Jenks!' he blurted out. 'You're too good for him. You know what he's like!'

'What he's like? What *he's* like! You're the one who cheated on your girlfriend in a fucking hot tub tonight, for God's sake! And who are you to tell me who's good enough for me? You barely know me!' Jenna couldn't quite believe how angry she was at Angus's outburst. Nor did she really know why she was quite so pissed off with his opinion on her new-found relationship. 'He said he'd always thought we should be together, not that it's any of your business!' she hurled across at him. 'And why shouldn't I believe him? He's known me for years — he'd never screw *me* over. Although I think he'd be an excellent screw from what I felt in the hot tub!' Jenna was fuming now. Her hands were clenched into fists, her nails digging into her palms. Her eyes bore into Angus's face, demanding some sort of retort from him.

'For fuck's sake, Jenna. I don't want to know. I just want you to be careful. We both know he's a dick with women and I care about you too much to see you get hurt by him.'

'You have no right to tell me who is too good for me or who I can and can't shag. Leave me alone and go preach your double standards to someone else!'

Holding back the tears that threatened to dampen her vitriol, Jenna stood up abruptly and turned her back on the dumbfounded Angus.

'Jenna, wait . . .' His voice softer, all the confrontational anger gone. 'I'm not like that . . .' She paused. But afraid of the sobs that were about to rack her body, she couldn't turn around to look at him. She couldn't bear to see his face, feel his pity. He'd hit a nerve with what he'd said — a major one. She ran up the stairs and into her room, wishing she could lock the door and lock out the world, and fell onto her bed just as the first tears broke the surface.

24

Angus heaved a sigh and raised the pint of water to his lips. All he'd wanted to do was warn her off Max, to stop her from getting hurt like every other girl that Max had, quite literally, come across. Or if Max really did like her, then he was in trouble. How could he stay friends with them both when all he'd want to do was ravish his best mate's girlfriend? But then both Max and Jenna would have witnessed his and Sonia's antics in the hot tub — he was so stupid to have let that happen. As much as the bubbles can hide a lot of goings on, it's pretty hard to hide a sex face. Idiot, he thought. Complete idiot.

Suddenly his phone rang. Max. *Fuck him*. Angus turned the phone to silent. Typical of him to stay at the party on the pretence of finding Hugo. He was probably shagging someone new and phoning to brag; it wouldn't be the first time.

The vibrating started again. Almost more insistent in its low growl than any ring tone could be.

Angus answered.

'What?'

'Gus, mate — I need your help.' Angus lost any bitterness as he heard the desperate urgency in Max's voice.

'Christ, what is it?'

'It's Hugo — the guy's really badly beaten up. I've just found him.'

'Where are you?'

'By the stream, the one by the wooden bridge beside Casper's bar — mate, you've got to come now, he's unconscious.'

'Shit. I'm on my way — don't move, keep him warm, call an ambulance.'

At that Angus disconnected the call, grabbed his thick, down-filled jacket to protect him against the cold and dashed upstairs to where the spare blankets were kept in the airing cupboard. He paused, wondering if he should tell Jenna what he was doing, what had happened, but thought better of it as images of her angry face flooded his mind. Sally, though, she should know. He knocked softly on Sally's bedroom door and waited a brief moment before quietly opening it. With the lights off he couldn't make out much but could hear the quiet, repetitive snuffling of someone fast asleep. There was nothing Sally could do now, anyway, and Angus couldn't guarantee that she might just make things worse. He stealthily closed the door again and headed for the blanket cupboard.

Armed with four of the thickest blankets he could find and thankful for the hip flask he'd filled up before he left home and stashed in his jacket pocket in prep for the first morning on the piste, he dashed out of the chalet and ran along the treacherously icy roads, skidding and slipping over half-melted ice in his effort to get to Casper's bar as quickly as possible. Lights were still on in bars around the pretty town. Revellers were spilling out of doorways, laughing, hunched over cigarette lighters, sharing bottles of beer and hugging together in the cold night air. His boots crunched on the refreezing ice as he dodged the slippiest patches and hurried to where he knew Max and Hugo were. How could no one have seen — and stopped — an assault so close to a busy bar? Unless Hugo was beaten up and dumped there? *Jeez, that was almost professional in its viciousness*, and only one person who they'd just met could have done that . . .

Rounding the corner towards the stream he saw Max kneeling on the ground — Hugo's head in his lap, gently ministering lumps of compacted snow to his wounds.

Angus reached them at pace and skidded down next to Max.

'Careful, mate, he's really bad.' Max automatically defended Hugo with a flex of his arm, worried that Angus would skid right into them.

Small snowflakes glided through the air; a few had already settled on Max's hair and refused to melt as they gently covered Hugo's still body.

'Shit. Here, wrap him up.' Angus passed the blankets to Max who hurriedly laid them across the eerily still Hugo. Angus took in the effects of the beating. A gash across Hugo's forehead looked like the worst wound, the congealed blood showing where it had flowed down into his hairline, dark and matted against the usually fair, soft hair. His right eye was shrivelled closed, the fragile skin around it swollen and dark, purple and bloodied; his nose, bashed to one side, had blood oozing from it, and even after Max's attempts to wipe the worst away with the snowy first aid, it was clear where someone's fist had connected with the soft cartilage and blown it to bits. His lips were cut, on his own teeth maybe, and swollen to a garish clown grimace while his arm lay out on the snow at an odd angle.

'He's breathing,' said Max, as if to answer Angus's next question. 'Ambulance is on its way.'

A pause, Max's heaving shoulders giving way to the emotion of what they both saw in front of them. The snow continued to fall and carefully Angus brushed the cold flakes from Hugo's bruised face.

'Did they do this to him?' asked Angus, gripping Max's shoulder, all thoughts of romantic rivalry gone in the wake of this, and both knowing who 'they' meant.

Max stayed silent so Angus pressed on. 'What happened after we left? When did you find him?'

'Just now, when I phoned you.'

'So, that's what — no more than an hour since Sally saw him kissing someone else?'

'Yeah. Look, I know this is going to sound bad, but Sally can get hysterical when she's drunk, so I thought maybe Hugo was just being friendly with some other girl, bit of a bum pinch, or whatever. Don't judge, but I reckoned I'd find him at it and perhaps, er, take in the view on the way. Leave you to the snot-fest back home.'

'Not impressed, but yeah?'

'So that's what I did. I met a really nice gymnast actually.'

Angus looked at Max, a flash of anger crossed his face. 'I thought you were with Jenna now?' Max didn't respond, lost in his own thoughts, it seemed. Angus, frustrated though he was with his friend, realised his mind was on the here and now, so he pressed on.

'When did you drag yourself away to go looking for Hugo?' Max looked up at him quizzically; he'd made his point though, and Max knew it.

'When I found Slavicka crying on Yuri's shoulder, apologising. Bertie wasn't looking too impressed.' Max looked almost thoughtful. 'But then you can't blame her as she only had a silk sheet pulled up to hide her modesty. I'd followed the sound of weeping and shouting down the corridor to Yuri's room, you see.'

'What? Blimey.' Angus pulled his hip flask from his pocket and took a warming swig, before passing it over to Max and looking down at the beaten face of Hugo again.

'Thanks. Yeah, so basically, Slavicka is Yuri's daughter — obviously Mrs Yuri The First popped her out early doors, though she's not as old as she looks: she's only just legal, you know.'

'But why did Hugo kiss her?'

'He didn't! Or at least he didn't at first. He was hammered — you saw how much he and Sally were pouring down their throats at that luge thing — and apparently, not that we'd know this in the UK, but Hugo bears a striking resemblance to some Ukrainian YouTube star . . .'

'What. The. Fuck? You're kidding, right?' Taking his hip flask back, Angus took another welcome slug.

'No, that's Slavicka's story. It seems she'd had a few too many as well, and thinking her darling daddy had surprised her with her number-one crush at her party, had literally run up to Hugo and flung herself at him. At the only moment that Sally wasn't by his side. And when Sal came back from the loo . . . well, that was when she saw East meeting West as it were and she ran outside and we all found out about it. Yuri must have had a word with his — God, I suppose they're henchmen, aren't they? — anyway, he just thought his little girl had been compromised.'

'How did you get all this; do you speak Russian?'

'Bertie translated as we went along — did you know she could speak it? She's quite good, actually. And she was getting quite upset as she related it all to me — especially at the bit when she realised little Slavi had used the words "men" and "set on". So, I realised Hugo might have got in Slavi's daddy's bad books before anyone could explain the mistake. It was too late to call off the heavies by the time he'd realised. I must say, he's not the best apologiser, but then I'd run out to come and find Hugo as soon as I heard the outline of the "beat and dump" plan.'

Angus stared blankly into the sky, almost unable to comprehend what had happened. Before any more questions could be asked or answered the sound of sirens filled the air, breaking into their thoughts and a group of party-goers assembled as the paramedics set to work getting Hugo onto the stretcher. Craning their necks to see, blowing on cold hands and stamping Ugg-booted feet, they said things like, 'How that must have hurt', 'Will he be OK?' and other banalities. One nice old lady from the fondue place on the corner came out with hot, strong and sweet coffee for the two friends, pressing the mugs into their shaking hands and insisting they drink up. With Hugo loaded up into the ambulance and the paramedics keen to get him to the clinic as soon as possible, Angus and Max stayed to answer as many of the gendarmes' questions as possible. When they'd been through as much as they could piece together they began to walk home. Too exhausted now to even speak, Angus had lost the urge to punch Max after the evening's hot-tub shenanigans — too much blood had been spilt tonight already. It must have been the fondue lady's caffeine that was now getting them home, as they both concentrated on not slipping on the fresh snow that was settling on the pathway outside the chalet.

'So, who goes and tells Sally?' Max asked, almost rhetorically, as they slipped in as quietly as they could through the door.

'She was fast asleep when I left — and before that she was so angry with Hugo I wasn't sure if waking her was the sensible thing — she might have offered to finish him off,' Angus whispered back as they climbed the stairs towards the bedrooms.

'Look,' Max took control momentarily, 'the paramedics have both our numbers — they'll call if Hugo gets worse, so let's just get some kip and tell the girls in the morning. Sally's probably still hammered anyway and, like you say, probably not best disposed towards her beloved at the moment.'

Angus nodded a weary acceptance and opened the door to their room.

25

Twenty minutes or so later, Max lay awake listening to Angus breathing, deeply asleep, in his bed on the other side of the room. Tired as he was from the night's events he couldn't help but think how good it had actually felt to have Jenna in his arms in the hot tub. Even thinking about her soft body, so different to Bertie's pneumatic tits or Izzy's lean legs, made him start to feel a bit frisky. Not saying he didn't prefer Bertie's tits, pneumatic or otherwise, but having left her in the silken sheets of Yuri's bed, he thought Jenna would make as good a port as any in the sexual storm brewing in his privates. Slipping out of bed and not bothering to put anything on over his muscular torso, he adjusted himself in his boxers and quietly opened the door, peering back to check that he hadn't disturbed Angus. Assuming his old friend was probably happily skipping through dreamland with long-legged Russian models, he went to find his own brand of happy ending.

He knocked lightly on Jenna's door, unsurprisingly to no answer, and gently pushed it open. The light from the window cast the moon's glow over most of Bond Street on Bertie's side of the room, and under the eaves in an area of comparative calm, the silvery light fell on Jenna as she lay there asleep on her bed. Tiptoeing carefully over push-up bras, hairbrushes, and the enticing look of some silk panties, he gently sat down on Jenna's bed and, without really thinking about it, started to stroke her face. He pushed the soft curls of hair that had fallen over her eyes out of the way and began to trace the outline of her cheek down toward her mouth. She really isn't bad looking, he thought to himself, odd that I never noticed it, really. She stirred and very softly he said her name, then again a little louder while increasing the strokes over her cheek and down her neck.

Jenna walked slowly through the alpine forest, her feet sticky with mud, or was it wet leaves? For some very good reason that she couldn't put her finger on, she couldn't look down to check, she just had to keep walking forwards. Creepers from the trees swung down low and brushed up against her face, but they weren't all trees, some of them were Hugo — and then Angus was there! Angus . . . She felt warmed by his body close to hers. His arms were sweeping the creepers aside and then they were brushing her . . . With a start, she suddenly blinked herself awake.

'Whatssa . . .'

'Shhh,' whispered Max. 'It's me — Jenna, it's me, Max.'

'Oh,' and in a moment, her senses just about flowing back through the fug of half-slept off booze and that incredibly odd dream, remembered. 'What's wrong? Is it Hugo? Is he OK?'

'He's fine,' lied Max. 'Well, he's in hospital.' And thinking he might get more action from a sympathetic girl, he added, 'I found him, you know, beaten up. It was awful.'

She reached up and touched his face, still not quite believing what was happening. She thought of Sally and instinctively wanted to go to her, but just then a convenient draught caught Max's skin and made it goosebump in the moonlight. He shivered, and she saw his pained expression, reading into it just what he wanted her to.

'Oh, you poor thing, it must have been awful to see him like that,' she said as Max carried on with the description of Hugo's injuries and his heroics in stopping him from falling into the icy stream, which might have been slightly exaggerated for effect. Jenna, kind-hearted as ever, pulled on his shoulder and beckoned him to get under the duvet.

'You'll catch a chill and we can't have two of you in the hospital,' she said, easing herself onto her side so Max could rest his head squarely on the pillow.

'I wouldn't mind if you were my nurse.' Jenna looked at him. Could this really be happening? The events of earlier rushed through her mind, a mental pinch on the arm, reminding her that, yes, Max had said all those things to her. He did *really* want her, after all these years. Steeling herself for full-on fantasy fulfilment, she leant down and kissed him, letting her hand steady her by resting it on one of his well-formed pecs. 'I know all sorts of ways of keeping a man warm,' she whispered, sliding her left leg up his so she was straddling him, easily feeling the protruding length of his cock that had escaped from his boxers at the first sign of nooky. Just like in the hot tub earlier, she could tell he was ready, willing and able, and a bolt of excitement shot through her body. If only she could press pause and slip out of the bed and jump around the room, flinging knickers and bras in exhilarated excitement, shouting, 'He's mine, he's mine, he's finally mine,' as she punched the air and strummed a couple of power chords on her air guitar!

'Take your top off, babe,' he murmured, and Jenna was brought back to her very heightened senses. She tried to sexily take off the baggy T-shirt she'd bunged on after her fight with Angus. Angus — suddenly his face flashed in front of her, a flashback to her dream. Before she could analyse this mental intrusion into her real-life fantasy, Max had pulled her down and rolled her over so he was on top. Jenna needed no more help banishing Angus from her thoughts and braced herself for the ride of her life. Supporting his weight, Max slowly lowered himself down, kissing her lips and letting one hand slide down over one breast, down the soft curves of her body to where her knickers signalled the last line of defence. Jenna shivered with the excitement of his touch. He raised himself up to kneeling so he could pull down his boxers, and her knickers, and she saw how aroused he was. Max by name, max by nature. If nothing else happened tonight, she thought, she would treasure this moment. That now, after all these years, it was her who was in his bed, or at least him in hers. Max kissed her again. Jenna felt his cock pressing against her and opened her legs enough for him to know that she was willing. 'Are you sure?' he asked, suddenly sounding more serious. Jenna nodded, but eased him off her enough to reach her arm over to the bedside table where she had optimistically stashed a few condoms.

'Even doctors and nurses should be careful,' she whispered, liking the idea of keeping the naughty role play going. Max, though, just grunted and rolled over, taking the condom packet she'd found from her. He squinted while holding it up to the moonlight, finding some purchase on the foil to carefully rip it open. Jenna watched as he concentrated on fitting it over his not insubstantial cock, and felt mildly awkward, as if she should be entertaining him during this enforced interlude. She hummed a bit of Bon Jovi to herself, *'Ooh we're halfway there, oooh living on a prayer . . .'* before giggling about the aptness of the lyrics to her particular situation.

'I don't think that's what Jon and the boys were really singing about.' Max was ready to continue. 'Still, take my hand . . .'

'And we'll make it, I swear . . .' Jenna lay back down, her fingers interlaced with Max's as he lowered himself back down on top of her. This is it, she thought, this is it. It's perfect — he's already said we should be a couple, sort of; we're singing Bon Jovi together; this is finally happening and it's going to be amazing . . . Thank you, Bertie, for

making me wax! Jenna lay back and waited for Max to start pleasuring her — the anticipation of it had her fizzing with excitement as one of his hands unlocked from hers and lazily wandered over her breasts, stroking her skin as he made his way down to her most intimate area. As his fingers brushed the top of her legs she let out a small whimper of pleasure. He began to rhythmically rub her where he assumed her clit was and Jenna moved herself around underneath him, subtly trying to show him where she really, desperately, did want to be touched. He wasn't getting there, though, and Jenna began to feel sorry for him, thinking that she should really be orgasming by now out of some sort of respect for his hotness. Trying not to feel a little disappointed, she began to crescendo her own moans a bit, encouraging him, she hoped, with every false, ecstatic groan. Perhaps she'd get there soon, and at least he was trying, she thought to herself as she tried once more to guide his hand to the Holy Grail of orgasm territory. Max stopped and Jenna tensed. 'What is it, baby?' she asked, almost instantly regretting the 'baby' remark as it hung cloyingly in the air.

'Nothing.' He avoided her gaze and instead moved his hand and gave himself a bit of a tug. 'Just takes a bit of time with you, huh? Big Max is losing interest.'

Jenna, still slightly tensed, didn't really know how to take that. As if pleasuring her was a chore to be got through on a limited timescale before 'Big Max' deflated. Well, charming! But she did so want this to be perfect and surely Max was such a pro at this? Was there something wrong with her? She decided to take control and moved her own hand down to her clit and finally started to pleasure herself.

'You can watch, ba . . . Max, this should get you hard in no time.' With one hand caressing her own beautifully round breasts and the other gently, and then with more pressure, finding its own blissful rhythm, she brought herself to the brink of climax. She let Max climb on top of her again just as she was about to come, and his hard cock slipped inside her. She arched her back to get him in deeper and it was his turn to groan with pleasure — though it occurred to Jenna that his certainly weren't faked. She clasped his back as he rocked up and down, the concentration on his face almost comical. It was all about his pleasure now and although she was happy to give it, she felt, as he rhythmically pounded into her, a little underwhelmed at the whole thing. Her orgasm, which had been so preciously close, failed to materialise, and as much as she clenched her core and writhed underneath him she couldn't muster it back again. Her mind wandered back to the bath tub last night — hadn't she struggled then to come when thinking of Max? And hadn't it been a certain other man's face that had come to mind and finally elicited her pleasure? Before she could finish her thought, Max gave one last pump and shuddered, dropping his weight down on top of her. Still clasping his back, she felt the glistening sweat on it before slowly letting him roll off her.

'You OK?' he muttered, as he peeled off the condom and dropped it onto the floor.

'Yeah, fine, fine,' was all Jenna could muster as she wondered if that was really what all the fuss was about and why on earth all those girls had driven themselves silly over him. Perhaps he's a true romantic, she thought as she let him lie back down next to her, his head taking up most of the pillow. Having not had a kiss, or barely even an eye contact since they'd made love, she thought she would at least get a bit of a cuddle now, but before she could even wriggle out a corner of the pillow from under his head, he was gently snoring. Her rustling must have disturbed him as with a jolt he turned away from her, dragging most of the duvet with him.

Tuesday

26

The throbbing in Angus's head told him that, for once, his patented anti-hangover prevention routine had not magically undone the damage of the several bottles' worth of champagne he'd drunk last night, not to mention beers and vodka shots too. He tentatively stretched out his body to research the extent of his hangover, careful not to shock any part of the system too soon. No nausea – that was a start – and minimal achiness. Dry-mouthed and sore-headed, yes; broken, no. Suddenly the image of Hugo lying broken and bleeding by the side of the road, dangerously close to the icy stream, came thundering back to him. He rolled over, pissed off with himself for being so selfish. How could he sleep when Hugo might be . . .? No missed calls, no messages. Thank God. The hospital at least hadn't tried to get through. He checked the time on his phone and thought about waking Sally – she needed to be told, after all, and probably taken to see him – but then Angus caught sight of the empty bed next to him. No Max. He collapsed back onto the pillow as the rest of the night came back to him in waves of rather unwanted images. Max and Jenna in the hot tub, his fight with her . . . she'd said something about Max being in love with her. And Max wasn't here. He was with her. But why? Why had he gone for her after all these years? Angus raised himself gingerly up onto his elbows and swung his long legs out of bed. Pushing himself upright, he forced his eyes open wide, stretched his arms up and felt the roughly hewn wood of the beam above him. Slowly lowering his arms and feeling the burn as the toxins still swept around his body, he looked around for last night's jeans and pulled them on, before reaching into the wardrobe for what was at least a clean jumper. He didn't want to waste any more time showering when he knew he had to go and wake Sally, a task he was dreading.

Glancing up the corridor from his open door he could see Jenna's room, door firmly shut. Unless Max had told her about Hugo, she wouldn't know either, but he considered himself to be persona non grata in that neck of the woods at the moment and turned towards Sally and Hugo's room. Pausing at the top of the stairs to glance down and listen to see if Izzy was up and making breakfast, he found, much to his surprise, that hunger was replacing headache as the manifestation of his hangover. Ignoring the smell of freshly baked French bread, he took a couple more steps towards Sally's door and knocked smartly. There was no answer, but he persevered, knocking again. He had just begun to turn to the handle when he heard a sniffled 'hang on' from inside. Stopping, he waited until the door was opened by a big pair of eyes, set into a blotchy red face that seemed to have been varnished in tears and snot.

'Oh Angus, it's you,' she said, obviously trying to hide her disappointment.

'Sally, it's Hugo,' Angus started, not wanting to draw this out and unsure if the situation would call for the manly shoulder to be used to comfort Sally and, if so, if that much snot would be dry clean only. 'He's in hospital. I think he's OK, but we should go and see him. Like now. They haven't phoned, overnight or anything, so I guess he's going to be all right, but he was in a pretty bad state when we sent him off in the ambulance, and—'

He was not allowed to finish as the banshee wail of keening had kicked off at around the time he said the word 'hospital' and had really reached an un-ignorable pitch by the time 'ambulance' was uttered.

'Sally. SALLY!' He reached out to hold her by the tops of her shuddering arms and, as expected, her head careered towards his shoulder. With her hot little face already making its mark on his jumper, his usual English reserve dropped and he wrapped his long, strong arms about her. 'I'm sorry, Sal, I should have gone with him but the gendarme had so many questions at the time and the medics wanted him out of the cold and gone, so we couldn't jump in the ambulance.'

A final heave of a sob and Sally pulled away from Angus's hug. 'What happened?' She was professional journalist Sally again — except for the odd post-weep hiccup 'Why was he in such a bad state? What state? What's wrong? Why on earth didn't you wake me? Is he OK? I've got to go and see him.' Her eyes darted up to Angus's face and, as she released herself from his grip entirely, he saw the crying had now been replaced by the woman he recognised: the super organiser, the former head girl, the decisive features editor.

Ushering him away from her door she said she'd be down in a sec and then they must find the hospital, she must call Hugo's parents, her parents, the insurers, Daddy's friend on Harley Street, Daddy's friend at MI5 (that's a secret, kind of, she muttered, but he might help catch the bastards). The maelstrom that was occurring behind the bedroom door somehow made Angus relax a little. With Sally in coping rather than anguished-distraught-lover mode, he knew anything could be achieved and Hugo's fate and well-being were now out of his hands.

He went downstairs and raided the breakfast table, pressing slabs of cold butter onto the still-warm French bread. Squishing it down so that the butter softened into the stretchy dough, he took a big, satisfying bite and looked wistfully out of the window to the mountains where wispy white clouds were all that shielded the glistening white slopes from the spring sunshine. With reports of the weather again closing in by the end of the week he knew this would have been a fantastic day's skiing, and perhaps the last one with such glorious weather. Still, maybe he could get out there this afternoon, if he could convince Jenna to stay with Sally in the hospital. Although speaking to Jenna before he and Sal left the chalet was unlikely, and the thought of her soft little body entwined with Max just a few rooms away made swallowing the rest of his baguette very difficult indeed.

With his back turned to the room and still staring out of the window, he only heard the soft padding of feet coming down the stairs behind him. Assuming it was Sally, he briskly turned round, ready to jump to action. Instead he saw a very flushed Jenna, clutching an empty glass with one hand, and with the other pulling the front of her grey cashmere cardigan around her, as if it were a life vest and she'd recently been plunged into deep and unknown water. Her pyjama bottoms looked hastily pulled on and Angus was unsure, without looking too closely, whether there was anything under the cardigan. Without a word she nodded at him and indicated by the incline of her head and a wobble of the glass, the kitchen. Moments later when she came out to the dining area again with a full pint of water, Angus had composed himself, although the sight afresh of her dishabille almost made him lose his resolve.

'I assume Max has filled you in.' He looked appalled at his own accidental innuendo, but carried on, as gruff as before. 'I think you should take Sally to the hospital,' he said, matter-of-factly. 'Or do you have something better to do?'

'God, Angus, could you sound any more disapproving?' With a stare that pierced him through his heart and down his body, she turned and went back up the stairs. His eyes

156

followed her back up to the top landing where she turned towards Sally's room and not her own. Hearing her knock and enter, he knew he'd been a dick. Of course, Jenna wouldn't put sex before her best friend, especially in this sort of situation. What was it about her being with Max that, apart from the obvious, upset him so much?

27

'But JJ, how do you know all this? Were you up when the boys came home?' Sally asked Jenna as the two of them scurried along the de-iced pavements towards the rather swish clinic that Hugo had been taken to last night. Jenna was rather breathlessly filling in her friend with everything she had gleaned from Max's pillow talk this morning, thankful, finally, to be able to shed some light on Hugo's behaviour last night.

'No, it was a bit weird, actually. After I left you in your room I came downstairs and Angus was there, and we had this strange fight, well, you know, disagreement.'

'What was it about?'

'Max.'

'Max?'

'Yes. Oh Sally, I know you have far larger things on your mind at the moment, but please say you're happy for me, as Angus isn't, which is odd as he's his best friend.' She paused, as much to catch her breath as for the dramatic pause. 'Max and I got together last night.'

'What? But JJ, I — wow. This is big news.'

'Yes. I mean I think so. It was great.' Was it, though, she thought? Remembering the slightly awkward silences and lack of orgasm, which happened all over again just as dawn started peering in through the windows. Once was forgivable, but for bad sex to happen twice in one night . . . well, that was just depressing.

'I've been in love with him for years.'

'Don't I know it, sweetie,' Sally replied, not even breaking pace. Jenna paused, and looked across at her friend, before going on.

'Well, it's all right for you — Hugo's always been potty about you. Unrequited love is exhausting!' She threw her hands up in the air as if to prove her point and accidentally hit a passing ski that was being carried at shoulder height by some unsuspecting passer-by.

'I know, sweetie, I'm sorry.' Sally took Jenna's arm in hers, kissed her hand better, and leaned her head on her shoulder for a moment. 'God, I hope he's OK. I don't know why I flew off the handle so much last night. I guess it must have been Bertie rubbing me up the wrong way for the last couple of days.'

'Not to mention the vast amount of booze.'

'Yes. God, my head hurts this morning. If I wasn't so worried about Huggy I'd be checking myself in for a rehydration session! Anyway, so you and Max? Tell me more.'

'Well, last night, just before you found us all in the hot tub, he came on to me. Big time. It was bliss! But then, you know, "you" happened and Angus and I took you home, leaving Max to find Hugo. And that's when Angus and I had our set to. I saw him, after I'd said goodnight to you, and he was all judgemental about me and Max. "He's no good for you, Jenna" and all that shit. Who's he to tell me who's good for me or not? I'll tell you what's good for me: a hot guy — no, a hot, *successful* guy that I've lusted after for years, suddenly becoming my boyfriend. *That's* what's good for me.'

'Quite right, sweetie. And you told Angus that, I assume?'

'Sort of.'

Before the conversation could carry on they reached the sheltered portico of the smart clinic, its automatic glass doors swishing open and closed as efficient-looking porters and staff briskly went about their business. Jenna saw the colour drain from Sally's face and gave her hand a quick squeeze before leading her in and helping her find her poor, beaten-up Hugo.

Nothing quite prepared Jenna for the sight of Hugo lying there, heavily sedated, strapped to the bed by wires and tubes, and covered in bandages. And nothing quite prepared her for how Sally reacted when she saw him, either. Jenna had seen these two coo at each other, and knew they were deeply in love — of course they were, they were engaged — yet she was so used to seeing them both as the most ultimately practical people she knew. She had assumed that Sally would have been quizzing les docteurs about the ins and outs of Hugo's care and prognosis, but instead Sally had taken one look at Hugo and erupted into tears. Jenna threw her arms around her friend and held her tight until, true to form, Sally recovered herself and wiped away the hot, salty tears. Sweeping over to Hugo's bedside, she held his battered face gingerly in her hands as she whispered to him. Jenna felt slightly out of place, so she slipped out of the room to find coffees and a doctor able to translate enough of the medical jargon to keep them all fully informed. If, of course, Jenna wasn't involved with someone, as she assumed she was now, she would have noticed quite how handsome the young doctor was that came to their aid. Not tall exactly, but well built and smooth-faced, with kind grey eyes. His glasses added a much-needed few years to his face, but his voice was strong and deep. 'Hugo will be fine, in time,' he said in barely accented English. 'He has been badly hurt, very badly.' Sally's eyes implored him to tell her something positive, and luckily he continued with, 'But it is not lasting damage, not to his brain or his body.' Sally released a long sigh of relief.

The young doctor continued telling Sally and Jenna about Hugo's condition. A lot of the damage was superficial and he would need some dental work to replace the couple of teeth that had been dislodged; his arm was broken, but there was no more internal bleeding; and he hadn't suffered any hypothermia, thanks to his friends finding him so quickly and covering him in blankets. Jenna thought how heroic Max must have looked — the strong, darkness of him gently cradling the broken man he loved as a friend — but she couldn't quite help having Angus in her fantasy too, as the stalwart sentinel, standing guard over the scene and bringing the essential blankets. She was abruptly brought round from her reverie by Sally interrupting the kind doctor. Questions about travelling and getting him home, insurance and all that sort of thing.

Jenna tried to listen, just in case Sally missed anything and needed help later, but it was all she could do not to keep fantasising about her heroes. Hero. *Just one, Jenna. You can only have one.*

As it turned out, Sally was now in full Girl Scout mode and she'd ascertained that Hugo would be OK to fly out with them all at the end of the week, but that he really should stay in the hospital under sedation for the next couple of days to help his body heal as much as possible.

28

The snow glistened as Angus let the tips of his skis hover over the edge of the ridge before pushing his weight forward and letting gravity take him over the soft snow, its velvet-like friction hardly slowing him at all from the free-fall. Exhilarated, he descended at such speed that the agonising wait in queues and on the chairlifts seemed even more unfair, as what took twenty minutes to queue for and climb was taking him seconds to ski down. He began to slow himself by traversing in graceful arcs as the gradient of the piste lessened. As it met a blue run coming in from the right-hand side he slowed to a complete stop, a spray of snow coming off the back edge of his ski and decorating the compacted piste like a Victorian doily. Max wasn't far behind him. Banned from Hugo's bedside by an over-protective Sally who had insisted she would be fine with just Jenna, the two friends had rather sheepishly headed off to the slopes. Once out there though and enlivened by the crisp, chill air, they'd spent the morning egging each other on, increasing the speed and audacity of their skiing in what seemed like a macho bid to prove something to each other.

'Bête Noir in under a minute?' Max had taunted Angus, who had shrugged his shoulders and set his Go-Pro, then sped down it, moguls and all, in just under fifty-three seconds.

Angus had never been so determined and competitive. There had been few stops and even fewer of them had been filled with the usual banter.

Angus watched as Max slipped past a seemingly never-ending snake of tiny kids and almost took the last one out as his eyes were fixed on the rather nice bottom of their instructor. It was enough to prove Angus right in his own mind and he was determined to talk Max out of breaking Jenna's heart — if he hadn't gone too far down that road to stop the inevitable.

Max swooshed the snow up onto Angus's leg as he pulled into a perfect parallel stop next to him.

'Lunch?'

'Yup — La Feu d'Argent is that one over there. It's where we're meeting Jenna and Bertie if she got the message.' Angus was unsure, though, if Bertie would have even got up yet, let alone been back to the chalet and got his scribbled note. Jenna, he knew, would be there, having taken Sally to the clinic, if only to see Max.

'Last one there buys the first round,' shouted Max as he launched off, narrowly missing an elderly Frenchman in a shocking neon-green onesie ski suit. 'Zut alors, monsieur!' His cries of annoyance were lost on Max.

Angus followed, slowing his normal pace to accommodate the many skiers pouring down the mountain for their lunches at the Feu. Assuming he'd be heading straight to the bar, after Max's challenge, he headed for the racks of skis that stood nearest the door of the wooden chalet-style restaurant. In so doing he passed Max, who had skied straight towards the outside tables instead and had found Jenna, who was lying almost horizontal in a deckchair by the edge of the terrace. Forcing himself not to look, Angus clicked his boots out of the bindings, loosened the catches so he could walk a little easier, and headed in to get a couple of beers and, starting to get to know her really quite well now, a vin chaud for Jenna.

'Angus — your round, mate!' Max's voice was drowned out by the throng of Euroteens who dominated the dining tables around them. Assuming Angus would do the right thing and come out in a moment bearing a tray of beers and possibly even some frites, he surprised the snoozing Jenna with a ruffle of her hair.

'Hello, you,' he said, and then as if he'd just remembered, 'how was Hugo this morning, and Sally?'

Recovering herself from the excitement of being woken up by Max, Jenna answered as sedately as she could. 'He was fine, well not *fine* fine, but you know. Sally's staying with him this afternoon.'

'I should imagine so. Are you going back?'

'Not for an hour or two at least. I was feeling a bit of a third wheel, if you know what I mean. Sally's focus was either on Hugo or getting as much info from the doctors as possible.' Jenna paused. 'It means we only have to shake off Angus and we can have an afternoon to ourselves — fancy it?' Jenna held her breath, praying that Max would agree.

'Yeah, why not?'

Jenna's heart almost froze with excitement. With a newfound boldness she carried on, 'I'm exhausted, though, after last night.' She looked at him saucily, raising an eyebrow before putting on a more serious face and continuing, 'And seeing Hugo this morning. I may need a nap after some less-than-demanding runs.'

'Jenks, if you're asking me to escort you to your bedroom, you should know that I am more than willing to help. In any way you like. Anything that involves you and a mattress is fine by me.'

'Cheeky.'

Jenna was just wondering if she should lean in and kiss him when they heard the clatter of a metal tray being put down a little too heavily on a wooden table next to them. Jenna jumped and felt oddly shy about being caught with Max by Angus.

'Beers,' Angus said, then added, 'and a vin chaud for you, Jenna. You must be knackered after this morning. How's Hugo?'

Jenna gratefully accepted the steaming drink, served in a vintage jam jar, and held it in her hands, cupping the sides to get the warmth through to her fingers. She chose to ignore Angus's loaded statement about her energy levels, giving him the benefit of the doubt that he was only referring to her visiting Hugo's bedside, not Max visiting hers. Angus pulled up another deckchair and folded himself down into it, like a Transformer turning itself back into a car, and Jenna told them both in detail about Hugo's prognosis and what the doctor said about him being able to fly back with them all at the end of the week.

'He was still heavily sedated, though, and Sally was so upset — you could see how much she loves him in her face, and how utterly forgiven he was. Not that it was his fault anyway, by the sounds of it.'

'Would you look at me like that then?' joked Max, holding her hand and feigning death in his deckchair in a flamboyantly ridiculous way.

'Lord no,' replied Jenna. 'I'd feel more inclined to weep at Angus's deathbed, since he was the one who's just bought me a drink.'

No harm in a bit of teasing, thought Jenna, who was trying to analyse Max's words while being completely oblivious to Angus's widening smirk.

'Gus,' said Max, suddenly sounding serious, 'do you think one of us should spend the afternoon in the hospital? You know, give Sal some moral support and be there for Hugo when he wakes up?'

'Oh, that would be so lovely,' piped up Jenna, cottoning on to Max's tactics, thrilled that he really did want her to himself this afternoon. 'Sally really appreciated having me there this morning and it can't be fun for her to be there by herself — she loves skiing almost as much as you, Gus. Really, I should go back, but now I'm up here I'd like to get a few runs in. Where did you guys go this morning?' she said this pointedly turning to Max, who took the cue, saying, 'Just up the Soleil chairlift, over to Méribel, skied around up there, some ace runs, Bête Noir, I can show you if you like?'

'Oh please, but just some cruisey reds and blues would be perfect to blow last night's hangover fog away!'

'Guess I'll be going down to the town then?' said Angus, resigned to what had been skilfully engineered in front of him.

'If you don't mind, mate, that would be great.' Max put on his best concerned face, mixed with a soupçon of gratefulness.

Jenna would have chimed in with much more gratitude, but she was still smarting from last night's fight with Angus and felt there had been some definite change in their fledgling friendship because of it. She still wondered exactly what he'd meant when he'd said he 'cared about her too much'. And really, Max, stuff-of-dreams Max, had been very attentive just now with those lovely kisses. Although last night had been far from perfect in the McDreamy stakes, but then not every encounter has to be candles and Barry White, does it? And surely couples grow into each other and their needs, don't they?

The threesome chatted away a bit more and finished their drinks. It was decided that Bertie couldn't have got home in time to find the note and there wasn't much point in waiting for her to start lunch, so Max and Jenna headed inside to find some food while Angus found his skis and clicked his boots back into the bindings.

As he pushed himself off and back out onto the glinting piste, Angus's anger at the whole Max and Jenna situation welled up inside him again. He might be an architect, he thought to himself, but he sure as hell couldn't draw up a plan like Max just had. He knew Max didn't love Jenna, not in the way he did, and although the thought pained him that they'd most likely slept together, he knew that it would be his broad shoulder that comforted Jenna, as it had done to all the other girls who thought they could be the one to stop Max in his tracks. He just hoped that this particular case didn't take too long.

29

'Why is everything served in a Kilner jar these days? What's wrong with a plate?' exclaimed Jenna as the delicious Savoyarde dish of tartiflette, made with grated potatoes, smoked bacon and delicious Reblochon cheese was placed in front of her, along with a glass of rather nice red that Max had ordered. 'Oh, a glass, bliss! I was almost expecting another bloody jam jar!'

'Judging by your intake last night, I thought a glass wasn't strictly necessary — I could just leave you with a bottle and straw — or a horse's head?'

'Give me good wine from a glass over bad vodka from a stallion any day — honestly!' Jenna caught Max's expression — an eyebrow raise and smirk — and biffed him over the table with one of her ski mitts.

'I do feel bad, though,' she went on. 'Here's us joking about last night, while Hugo lies in a hospital bed, totally out of it, beaten to a pulp, by our host of all people! I'll never look at a Ferrero Rocher in the same way again.'

Max looked at her quizzically. 'There's nothing we can do to help him now, Jenks.' He put his fork down and reached out to touch her arm, something that should have made her heart melt and explode simultaneously. Jenna put the fact that her heart was still very much in one solid piece down to the stress and worry of seeing Hugo earlier.

Max continued, 'He's in the best place he can be and we won't help in any way at all by crowding round him. Let the doctors do their thing and we'll check in with Sally later.' Mollified by his words of seeming wisdom, Jenna carried on with her lunch, getting back into the swing of things and trying to enjoy this seminal moment in her new-found relationship.

Stomachs full, Max and Jenna clipped themselves back into their skis and headed for the nearest chairlift. The queue gave them plenty of time to discuss Hugo, the Russians, and that party all over again and, when that was done, muck about like any other couple enjoying the crisp blue skies and perfect snow that Val d'Argent had to offer. As their turn to get on the chairlift came about, Max fluffed about with his skis, losing their place on the row of six that were about to embark. Ignoring the protestations of the lift operator who gestured at the long queue, Max nudged Jenna into the centre of the waiting point, shooing away some French kids that had come up behind them. The massive six-seater swung around before any of the kids could edge themselves forward and, thanks to Max's arrogance, they may not have made a friend of the lift operator or the next fifty or so people in the queue, but they did have a vast, comfortable lift to themselves for what they both knew was at least a fifteen-minute journey high into the mountains.

'I love this lift,' said Jenna, spreading her arm out next to her over the white leatherette seating. 'It's like the way to heaven. I can imagine that, when you die it, could be like this: you're warm and cosy and all around is breathtaking beauty and a feeling of awe and a little excitement about what's to come.'

'I don't know what it is, Jenna, but everything you say sounds filthy to me at the moment.'

'What do you mean?' Jenna couldn't help but be a little thrilled with the direction this was going.

'Excitement about what's to come? On your way to heaven? I think I could help you with both of those, sweetheart.'

'Honestly, Max, it's not me with the dirty mind, it's y—'

But she couldn't finish her sentence, as Max had turned to face her and with his ski poles hanging loosely from his wrist, he'd clasped her face with his ice-cold mitt and kissed her firmly on the mouth. Moving in closer he kept kissing her while unzipping her ski jacket.

'Wait,' Jenna pulled away from him, not cross, but a little hesitant. 'I'll get cold.'

'I don't think so, darling,' Max growled as he pulled off his mitt and, with his much more dextrous fingers, began to feel his way into the layers under her jacket. 'Hmm, not exactly sexy, these thermals, are they?'

'And you mean you're not layered up too?' Jenna retorted, taking the chance to reciprocate and slide her hand, admittedly still fully gloved, across his ski jacket. Quite apart from having her gloves on, she was further inhibited from hugging and then kissing him, something she was fully prepared to do for the next ten minutes, by the fact that he took her hand and moved it slowly down the front of his ski jacket and onto his crotch.

'Not so many layers down there to contend with.'

Jenna looked up into Max's eyes, the dark brown turning almost to hazel in this perfect daylight.

'You're not shy, are you, Jenks? Not after last night? And I do like a girl with spirit — it's why Bertie and I always got on so well. You're game, aren't you?'

'Of course,' retorted Jenna, her ire piqued by the comparison to her arch-rival in Max's affections. 'But what if I lose my poles?' was the only thing she could think to say.

'More importantly, what if I lose this massive pole? You are giving me such a hard on. Why don't you nudge in closer, your poles can slide in between your thighs, just like I want to, and as long as you clench like a bastard, they'll be fine.'

With that he raised his arm up and pulled down on the overhead cover that sheltered the chair's occupants from blizzards. 'As you're so prim, some privacy?'

Why not? thought Jenna, YOLO and all that, and surely a blow job on a chairlift is one for the story vaults, to be used sparingly in social situations . . . or blurted out on Monday morning just after the low-down of what it's like to go to an oligarch's party and a French hospital all in the space of twelve hours.

Jenna pinned Max's gaze with hers and started to gently squeeze and rub his growing erection through his salopettes. As he was the only one with no cold, puffy gloves on, he reached down and started to undo his fly, pinging the couple of heavy-duty poppers at the top of his waistband and undoing the zip. Leaning back slightly to let his expanded shaft free of his jockeys and open to the air, he placed his hand on the back of Jenna's head and guided her down.

'Hurry up love, it's freezing,' and as Jenna did as she was told he could only murmur moans of encouragement.

Trying hard to remember all the pieces of advice she'd picked up from copies of *Cosmo* and some bored moments of Internet browsing, it was all Jenna could do to concentrate on the gentle sucking and licking, wary never to let any cold air get to the now quite impressive shaft of Max's cock. Her mittened hand was useless at helping stimulate him, so she relied on little flicks of her tongue and long, slow, licks to bring him on and, as she pressed her lips to the base of his shaft one last time, he juddered with pleasure.

'Oh baby, oh you are so the one, oh baby . . .'

Jenna felt the hot shot of salty cum shoot into the back of her mouth and tried not to gag as she swallowed it down. Spitting just wasn't ladylike, and anyway, who would want to find *that* icicle on their afternoon's ski? But she'd heard what he said: she was 'the one', the same thing he'd said in the hot tub. Sort of. He really did like her. Love her, possibly . . . *That* revelation was worth any amount of porn-star-style blow jobbing.

Max pulled his fingers through her tangled hair, encrusted as it was in places with tiny ice crystals and fresh snowflakes. He raised her head up and kissed her, sucking her lips into his. Then he let her go and used his still ungloved hand to push his now slightly diminished cock back into his pants and salopettes.

'That's my girl,' he murmured to Jenna as she raised herself away from him. 'Now I see what you mean about getting to heaven on a chairlift.'

'Was it amazing?'

'Yeah, yeah. Totally,' he said distractedly, concentrating on getting his poles back into position, ready to slide off the chairlift as soon as it docked. 'Awesome snow job, baby.'

30

Glowing-faced, and completely knackered from having tried to keep up with Max all afternoon, ski-wise and sex-wise, Jenna gratefully unclipped her boots from their bindings and hoisted her skis up and over her shoulder for the short walk to La Folie, the small bar that shouldered the bottom of the cable car. She could see Angus already there and waved at him, slightly hurt when he seemed to look right at her and not wave back. After yesterday's chivalry she'd grown to rather expect him to bound over, like some blond wolfhound, ready to help her, but today, after last night's argument, it seemed she would have to balance her skis, poles, and dignity all by herself. Max was no help, having whizzed down ahead of her in order to get to the ski wax shop before it closed for the day. For reasons unfathomable to Jenna he had to have his skis seen to so he could ski even more scarily fast tomorrow. Why he felt he needed to break Mach 1 on a blue piste was beyond Jenna, who had actually enjoyed her much more sedate descent into the resort after Max had pecked her on the cheek and said something about getting the beers in and he'd see her in the Folie. But she couldn't complain. They were on a ski trip, after all, and Max worked so hard, he deserved his time on the slopes to be just as he wanted them: fast, adrenalin-filled and something-else-fuelled too, it seemed. Perhaps when they got back to London he'd properly take her out, treat her to the Michelin-starred restaurants that she knew his squeezes got taken to when they whined about not seeing him enough. 'Whined, then dined' was how Hugo always joked about it. But she wasn't a whinger, so no doubt her relationship with Max would be a lot more low-key, but hopefully he'd love her for it and she wouldn't end up on that long list of Max's exes. Whined, dined and then declined . . .

Slotting her skis into the wooden rack, not bothering to separate them and hide one behind someone else's to prevent theft (who would want to nick one of these old rental planks?), she pulled off her sodden gloves and huffed over her fingers to warm them up.

Angus watched Jenna walk towards him with what he hoped was a dispassionate look on his face. Inside he was wondering where Max was: surely, as victor, he should be with his spoils, showing her off and not letting her almost trip over a child's sledge on her way into the bar, only to steady herself on an unimpressed Frenchman? He couldn't help it. Dispassion gave way to a wide grin and he locked eyes with her as soon as she had disentangled herself from the old guy's mittens that had been hanging from his belt loop.

'I was going to offer you a lady beer, Jenksy, but you're obviously two sheets already.'

With a sigh Jenna replied, 'Unfortunately for all of us, Angus, I need no alcohol whatsoever to be a complete klutz.'

'So Max wasn't showering you with champagne all afternoon, then?'

'No, not a drop. Skiing with him is worse than skiing with you — at least you pause occasionally to let me keep up. He was down a black run before I even had a chance to say no, so I had to follow him; it was a nightmare!' Angus beckoned over a waitress and asked for two more beers as Jenna continued, 'And then, at the end, he just whizzed off to go and get some sex wax, or whatever they call it, and I managed my only nice gentle run of the day! We may be compatible in some ways, but skiing hell ain't one of them!'

'Poor Jenks,' said Angus, softening towards her as he heard more about her traumas up the mountain, remembering how scared she'd been after her fall yesterday and secretly hoping that Max's less than gallant behaviour might signal that he wasn't as keen on Jenna as all that. As a couple of fresh beers were placed in front of them, Angus and Jenna's eyes met. A blast of cold wind made them both shiver and Angus noticed that little ice crystals of beer were forming up the side of their glass steins.

'"Thanks" is the usual word, Jenna,' he tried, hoping the small joke would break her concentration.

It worked as she drew in a deep breath and after thanking him for the beer quite quietly, said, 'About last night. I'm sorry I shouted at you. I don't want us to fall out and I know you were only thinking of me.' Angus opened his mouth to interrupt, but Jenna raised her hand a little, shushing him. 'I just want to check we're OK, you know, as friends? I know we've known each other a while really, but we were only really getting to know each other and then we . . . well, I don't want it to end like that.'

'Yes, Jenna, we're OK.' For what else could he say? 'I just don't want to see you get hurt, that's all. Cheers.' Raising his glass, he looked at her, her flushed cheeks showing not only the effect of an afternoon on the slopes but also the obvious effort it must have taken to bring up the subject of their recent argument.

A few minutes later the conversation had moved onto more neutral ground, if you can call discussing your beaten-up friend 'neutral'.

'How was Hugo? I've not heard a peep from Sally all afternoon.' Jenna's face was all concern, her hands clenched around the cold beer in front of her.

'I couldn't get past the front desk.' Angus pushed his half-empty beer glass out in front of him as he flexed his fingers, obviously frustrated at his failed mission. 'But Sally came out and saw me — God, she looked terrible, poor thing.'

'I don't think she's really stopped crying since this morning.' Jenna thought back to when she'd last seen Sally and felt chastened that she'd spent so much of their time together talking about herself.

'No, I can't blame her really. She said he was still heavily sedated, not unconscious as such, just out of it on morphine so he can heal as quickly as possible.'

Jenna nodded and tapped her phone screen to see if any other messages had come through. 'No news,' she said, as much to herself as to Angus.

'Speaking of no news, has anyone seen Bertie today?' Just as Angus spoke the pair saw Max and Bertie approach. 'Speak of the devil,' he murmured.

'. . . and she appears!' whispered Jenna back to him, meeting his eye and snorting out a little laugh into her beer.

'Look who I found,' said Max as he slipped himself into the bench seat next to Jenna, giving her a quick squeeze of the thigh with one hand while raising the other to the waitress.

'Hello, drones,' drawled Bertie. 'How was your day? Scintillating, I hope? I am *abso exhausto*. So much fun last night! Like, when you left, we stayed up playing this weird but, like, totally fun game involving a giant stuffed wallaby, a telephone directory and a semi-naked policeman!' As her words and snorts of laughter fell on silence, she finally remembered to ask, 'Oh, how's Hugo? Max has just filled me in.' She looked over at Max, sitting opposite her across the picnic-style table, pronouncing the word 'filled' as if she were Nigella squeezing cream into a choux pastry bun. 'But Jenna, you went there this morning, was he OK?'

'Well, no, not really, Bertie,' Jenna was incensed at Bertie's total lack of compassion. 'Do you know what your so-called friend did to him last night? He could have *died*, Bertie. I don't know about you, but I count that as a *bloody scintillating* start to the day.'

She was fuming now. How could Bertie just sit there and think that it was OK to be nonchalant about something so barbaric?

'Don't blame Berts, Jenna.' Max squeezed her thigh again in an effort to calm her down.

Angus was feeling less charitable towards Bertie. 'I think Jenna has every right to be pissed off, Max.' And then he said to a very pouty and sullen Bertie, 'That was a bit insensitive.'

'Bit insensitive?' said Jenna, her voice echoing the chill that was coming off the darkening mountains. 'My best friend almost lost the love of her life — we all almost lost our friend — and all she can talk about is some bloody stuffed wallaby!' Turning to Bertie, she continued, more quietly now as the initial fury had abated. 'I don't blame you, Bertie, for taking us to that party, it's not like it's your fault it actually happened or anything, but a bit of sensitivity wouldn't go amiss!'

'What could I have done?' Bertie flashed back at Jenna and Angus. 'I was in bed with the guy, everyone was bloody charging in, wrong ends of so many sticks were being grabbed by, like, everyone.' She paused to gather her thoughts. 'And as soon as Yuri realised what had happened, after you'd run off, Max, to go and find Hugo, well, he was really quite sorry.'

'Really quite sorry? *Really quite sorry.*' The sarcasm dripped off Jenna's words. 'He almost killed a man. Our friend. His guest!'

'Well, he didn't know who he was! Before Slavicka came in to say what a mix up it had been, for all he knew he was a sleazy friend of mine who should never have been welcomed in. I can tell you, it was a few very tricksy minutes for me when he thought that!'

'I'm sorry, I can't take any more of this. Max?' Jenna stood, gathering her gloves, goggles and bobble hat from the table.

Max looked up at her, a pause too long before replying. 'Look, Jenna, sit down. Bertie,' he looked from one girl to the other, 'we know it's not your fault and we don't expect an apology on behalf of Yuri from you.' Bertie rolled her eyes. 'But if you'd just apologise to Jenna for being a bit insensitive just now then I think we can get over this.' He paused for a moment before continuing, 'And Jenna, please stay. You know it's not Bertie's fault and Lord knows you've dropped some clangers in your time, so sit back down and apologise to each other.'

Jenna hung her head. She was desperate to run back to the chalet. Being told off by Max was awful, and what's more she knew he was right. If Bertie hadn't been so mean to Sally — and her — over the last few days she'd never have flown off the handle at her. Sitting herself down she carefully placed her gloves, hat and goggles back next to Angus's on the table and looked back up to meet Bertie's eyes.

'I'm sorry, Bertie, I overreacted.'

'I'm sorry too, Jenna, I hadn't realised how badly Hugo was injured. I made sure heaps of flowers were sent. And I think Yuri will cover all Hugo's medical expenses. That's what I was going to say before you blew up at me.' Recognising a truce when she saw one, Bertie decided not to over-oeuf the pudding on this one. 'I'll make sure he does and then I won't be seeing him again. I think his sort are a little more show pony than they're worth at times.'

The girls tried to smile at each other and Jenna raised her glass to Bertie, who looked a little aghast at actually having to pick up and drink the massive stein-like thing in front of her. But she shakily returned the gesture, even sipping a little froth off the top of her beer to seal the deal.

31

Piling back to the chalet, with the usual scuffle of boots and poles, skis and gloves in the basement boot room, the now rosy-cheeked foursome of Jenna, Max, Bertie and Angus caused enough noise to alert Sally, and a rather lazy Izzy, that they were home. Sally greeted them at the top of the stairs, her hands on her hips and her face still noticeably blotchy from the crying she'd been doing since the night before.

'Nice of you to stop by, you drunkards,' she said, sounding a little peeved and flouncing off.

'Sorry, Sal,' called up Jenna and then the boys chipped in with a chorus of sorrys too. Even Bertie murmured a half-hearted 'sorreee', proving that old grudges could be laid to rest for the moment.

Clattering up the stairs, Jenna found Sally curled up on the massive sofa, almost lost in among its cushions, flicking through the pages of *Hello!* magazine. She threw her arms around her.

'Sorry sorry sorry sorry sorry,' chirruped Jenna, a little bit tipsily, into her best friend's ear.

'I'm not sure you lushes even know what for,' sulked Sally, but accepted Jenna's massive hug gratefully and heaved a massive sigh before she began telling Jenna about Hugo's improvement this afternoon. The other three took it as a cue, as eager as they were to know about Hugo's recovery, to slip away upstairs and start showering.

'He opened his eyes, well, his good eye anyway, and saw me. I'd been holding his hand, well, the tips of his fingers really as the rest of his arm and wrist is in plaster, and when he saw me, he moved his fingers a little and it was all I could do not to burst into ruddy tears right in front of him, which Daddy always says is a perfectly useless female trait, but I was just so relieved that he obviously doesn't have any sort of brain damage.' She carried on telling Jenna about what the doctors had said and what had happened when so many white roses had arrived that she had to send some home with the nurses. 'They were from that bloody Russian of course. Which reminds me — *how* could you spend all afternoon drinking with Bertie?'

'Oh Sally, darling, it's not what you think at all. And I know you've had that line spun at you a bit too much these last twenty-four hours, but honestly you should have seen us.'

Sally raised her eyebrows, not able to hide her curiosity, while still trying to look serious and annoyed.

'I had a real go at her, like proper storming out of the bar. You would have been so impressed, sweetie.'

'Too right, honey, so what happened?'

'Well, Max happened.'

'Ooh yes, I want to know all about this afternoon's romantic hours on the piste.'

'Not so much romance as soft porn re-enactment.'

'What?'

'Oh, don't look at me like that, Sal.'

'Like what?! I'm just trying to picture you and Max doing some Swedish sauna beating thing by Le Feu d'Argent . . . No, actually, I'm trying *not* to picture that!'

The girls could have easily dissolved into giggles at this point if Sally hadn't managed to bring them both back on track. 'So, you and Max are very much an item? Noted and to be discussed later . . . And then you met up with Gus and Bertie?'

Jenna filled her in on the whole La Folie fight, ending with the revelation that Yuri was going to cover all the medical expenses as means of an apology.

'Gosh, that's good news.'

'Plus all those flowers.'

'I've brought some home: they were rather beautiful,' Sally thought for a bit. 'Although I don't like the thought of Bertie being totally blameless, or that Max should take her side over yours. I can see his point, though. I mean, apart from being totally railroaded, not to mention squeezed into the most uncomfortable dress ever, it was of our own free will that we went to that party.' Another pause. 'Did Bertie apologise to you, for not asking about Hugo, I mean?'

'Yes, she did in the end, I think she actually felt really bad about it. So we kissed and made up, as it were.'

'Now that really would be the sort of soft porn your new boyfriend would like to see.'

Jenna had no option but to throw a handily placed sheepskin cushion at Sally, who batted it off, but not without the giggles starting again.

Jenna went up to her room, her thick ski socks softening her tread on the wooden stairs and carpeted landing. Sally, who'd been holding back since she'd returned to the chalet after visiting hours ended, had finally helped herself to a large G & T and Jenna had left her flicking through another celebrity magazine, pretending not to ogle the stripped-down figures of the British Olympic male cycling team. Easing open her bedroom door, having knocked to check Bertie wasn't *in flagrante*, Jenna slipped inside. Bertie wasn't there at all, *in flagrante* or not, so she began to take off her ski jacket and salopettes.

The scalding heat of the shower's multiple jets eased the afternoon's — not to mention that chairlift's in particular — aches and Jenna moved her body from side to side, getting all the benefit she could from the pulsating water. She still couldn't quite believe she was together with

Max. Apart from his defence of Bertie earlier, which was probably just him being reasonable and playing devil's advocate, almost literally, he had been quite attentive really. Or at least as much as Max ever was.

She stopped mid thought as she heard the unmistakeable sound of a door slamming, and Jenna guessed correctly that her roomy was back. Turning off the jets and reaching for a towel, feeling finally fully defrosted, Jenna only took a few minutes to dry off and wrap her long hair up in another towel before opening the door of the en suite. She saw Bertie lying on her bed, eyes shut but screwed up tight. This was no power nap.

'Bertie, what is it?'

'Nothing. I'm tired.'

Still not feeling the most indulgent towards Bertie, Jenna didn't press her on the subject and walked across the room to her bed and started working out what to wear. But Bertie, ever the drama queen, let out a long sigh, making Jenna almost jump just as she was hoicking her knickers up.

'OK, come on, Bertie, what is it?' demanded Jenna.

'Oh, like nothing you'd understand,' she replied and turned over on her side, her back to where Jenna was now standing, drying herself. After a minute or two more of silence she turned over again and raised herself up on her elbow, flicked the lock screen on her bejewelled iPhone and silently moved her thumb across the screen, checking messages, tweets and emails before casually tossing it onto the bed.

By this point Jenna had slipped on a vest top and a pair of skinny jeans, relieved that she could still do them up even after all the beer, cheese and pasta so far this trip, and was brushing out her already drying hair.

'Really, Bertie, if you'd like to talk about something, I'm here.' And if you knew how much that took to say out loud, thought Jenna, then you'd be bloody grateful and take me up on the offer.

'Honestly, Jenna, you're the last person I can talk to about it.'

'Oh. Well then.' Jenna tossed the damp towel she'd been rough drying her locks with onto the bed and picked up her black jumper. The little sequins sewn on to it sparkled as she pulled it on over her head.

'Oh, I've got one like that at home,' said Bertie, perking up. 'But mine's from Versace and it's some amazing cashmere, you know, like actually knitted by Italian grannies or something cutesome like that.'

Jenna finished pulling the jumper down and shook her hair out. I'll never understand you, Roberta Mason-Hoare, she thought. Never.

Bertie looked at Jenna for a moment, studying her, before starting to strip off and head into the bathroom for her own shower.

32

'Of course, last time we went skiing he got in tangles all by himself,' said Sally with a hiccup, before she took another generous slug of the vin de table Izzy had been pouring into their glasses all night. Reminiscing to herself, as well as the others round the table, she continued. 'Silly Hugo, he managed to ski right into a half pipe where a competition was going on with all these *dudes*.' Sally pronounced it as if the word had suddenly acquired four 'o's, 'and they quite set on him, some of them. Said that he'd totally ruined their competition. They were very annoyed.'

'Jeez, how did he get out of that one?' Jenna was rapt, having never actually heard this story before.

'Oh, well, the "dudes" were only about seven years old or so and he looked a bit like the Hulk or something with small squirts of boys hanging off each limb.'

Jenna snorted and then tried to cover such an unladylike sound by coughing a bit, in the end giving up and just taking another sip of her wine.

'Well, at least we know that it definitely wasn't his fault this time, huh?' said Max, absent-mindedly spearing the last potato from Jenna's plate with his fork and scraping it around the red wine jus on his plate.

'Oi,' she started, before Bertie silenced her protestations by going on about carbs and how she had only managed to beat her addiction to them by going deep into hypnosis and demanding this Paul McKenna chap or whoever he was make her actually believe she hated them. 'I mean,' she continued, 'I told him in no uncertain terms, "Paul, my friend, if I ever eat another spud, chip or fry; spaghetti vongole or risotto primavera again, I will ask for my money back" and bless him, do you know it actually worked? Now when I see a carb my mind is programmed, literally programmed, to view it as a life-threatening poison, and to a certain extent we should all view them as that. Especially you, Sally.'

Jenna rolled her eyes and took another massive sip of her wine.

'I think Sally has enough to deal with at the moment, without worrying about her carbs,' said Angus, gently laying a hand on Sally's arm. To deflect Bertie's comment further, Jenna theatrically thanked Max for saving her from the deadly spud and while she locked his eyes into hers, slowly leaned over and deftly swiped his last bite of sausage from his plate.

'You can't say fairer than that,' she said after swallowing down the tasty morsel. 'I can take bread being radioactive or whatever, but I'm afraid this girl is always going to want a bit of sausage.'

Sally burst out laughing and even Bertie raised a smile, although it soon disappeared when she saw Max laugh out loud at Jenna's joke. Angus made an excuse about helping Izzy and started to collect the plates, as the chalet girl herself came into the dining room just in time to see the man of her dreams lean over and kiss the dumpy one she thought the tall one liked, and in her frustration slammed down the carafe of wine.

'Careful, chalet girl,' said Bertie, who just narrowly missed having her skintight white jeans sploshed with red. She had teamed them for tonight with fur-covered knee-high boots and a very low-cut, plunging, clinging black top, with a fur gilet to match the boots. Angus had attempted some joke about her looking 'a bit grizzly' but a withering look from the queen of fashion had put him back into his high-street-retailer place.

'My name's Izzy,' the poor chalet girl retorted.

'Whatever, Izzy, but just be a bit careful of my jeans, y'know? Merlot and Miu Miu do not mix, *capiche*?'

'Sorry, Roberta,' Izzy muttered before returning to the kitchen, making sure to give Max one of her dirtiest of looks, honed to perfection on the sports fields of Gloucestershire. It was, however, lost on Max as he leant over to kiss Jenna again, with one hand on her thigh and the other finger-crawling its way towards his wine glass to get another swig.

Izzy was not coping well with the double whammy of not only having her teenage heart broken but also being addressed as one of the serving classes in the space of sixty seconds. With astounding self-control she placed the dirty plates carefully down on the kitchen worktop — avoiding the urge to smash at least one over someone's head. She whipped her phone out of her back pocket and swiped and typed her frustration out to her friend Ginny.

'Message sent,' she muttered under her breath as she thought about how many cocktails she and Ginny could get through with her new-found cash bonus.

33

'Sally, you will come out for a few, won't you? Hugo will be sound asleep. You've been there all day and you deserve a break, honey.' Jenna was convincing her friend by degrees to come out with them. After all, with several carafes of the best vin plonk inside them (a 'good session wine', as Angus had pointed out just before he tripped over the sheepskin rug and pirouetted into Max's lap), everyone was desperate to relieve the day's tensions and go out for a bit of a boogie. Even Sally looked like she could be convinced. Her eyes had de-puffed and looked considerably less red and she'd drunk, for purely medicinal reasons, quite heavily all night and was just at the tipping point where the thought of Rick's Ski Bar actually seemed like a very good idea.

'But everyone will be younger than us in there,' Sally had half-heartedly pointed out . . . about thirty minutes before she half tripped through the door to that very same establishment.

'I'm really not sure I should be here, sweetie,' she shouted to Jenna, above the noise of the heart-busting beats and braying voices.

'Darling, we'll toast him with every drink. And I don't think the clinic would let you back in now anyway — the fumes from your breath would be enough to knock him out all over again!' Luckily for Jenna, Sally took this in the joshing way it was intended and started to settle herself down onto a bar stool. By this point, Jenna was in heaven. Her natural habitat: the cocktail bar. And she was, for once, the girl in the bar with the super-hot lover — plus her best friend, a not unattractive other guy and, unfortunately, Bertie too, who was at least a very expensive-looking bauble to add to the general decoration of the night.

Max bought a bottle of vintage champagne, much to the adoring looks of several young females who had stationed themselves around the bar. He poured generous glasses out to his friends and, just as Jenna had promised, they all loudly called out, 'To Hugo!' before taking their first swig. Even Bertie joined in with a gentle clink of the glass, although Jenna couldn't fail but notice how she sensuously caught the rising bubbly froth with her tongue while locking eyes with Max.

Sally nudged Jenna in the ribs at the sight of it. 'Doesn't it bother you, sweetie? I thought you were with Max now?' she half whispered, half shouted into Jenna's ear, hoping no one else would hear over the Whitney Houston mash up in the background.

'S'all right,' slurred Jenna back at her friend, swaying slightly and automatically catching hold of Angus's gilet as he stood behind her, solid as a rock. 'I know it's me he wants. He said he liked my twinkle in my eyes . . .' Jenna's hand grappled for more gilet and Angus gently put his arm around her waist, pulling her into him for just a moment before she lurched forward to the ice bucket and helped herself and the rest of them to more champagne.

'Let's go dancing!' suggested Bertie, who had been a little more abstemious than the others on the drinking front and still had the ability to walk in her heeled boots, fur covered and all, onto the dance floor. She grabbed Max's hand and a sub-second after reached back for Angus too.

'Whooo dancing!' Jenna pushed into the back of Max, wrapping her arms around him and goose-stepping with him onto the dance floor. 'Come on, Sal, it's exercise! You've been sitting down all day, you need it lovely!'

'Oh, do I now?' retorted Sally, a glint in her eye reminiscent of the university days when Sally would cause quite a stir with her 'how low can you go' antics and hilarious bump and grinding.

The five of them snaked onto the heaving dance floor, the crowd parting Red Sea-like for Bertie. Bodies rippled around them and bumped into them more often than not, but no one cared as they sploshed champagne around and sang loudly and boisterously to the well-known songs. Angus and Max buffeted the worst of the crowd away from the girls, but Jenna and Bertie both benefited more than once from a sudden unexpected push that would launch them towards either Max or Angus. Sally seemed oblivious, working off the stresses of the day, dancing with anyone who came within orbit of her and finding her own special rhythm, much to the amusement of those close enough to witness the strange cross between Shakira and Mr Bean. Jenna nestled her whole body against Max's and found his thigh a rather good gyrating spot. Putting on what she thought was an alluring smile, she made Max burst out laughing, but he pulled her close anyway and kissed the warmth of her neck while feeling his way down to her bottom and giving her rather excited rear a firm squeeze.

'Where's Angus?' Jenna mouthed to Sally as she peeled herself away from Max. Sally took about thirty seconds to refocus her eyes onto Jenna's face, and broke out into a grin. 'Drinks!' she shouted, raising an imaginary one to her lips a few times and waving her hand vaguely towards the bar to make sure Jenna got the message, before she closed her eyes and reached both arms up towards the ceiling, in all its glitterball glory, and continued her own private dance routine to the classic Take That anthem that was being mixed into the drum and bass beats of the last song. Jenna smiled to herself, almost tripped backwards but righted herself about halfway down Bertie's fur gilet.

'Ooopsh, sorry Bertie,' she slurred, with the room and the sticky, beery floor suddenly doing their own special dance too. 'Upsy-daisy,' said Max as he heaved her back up to standing, mouthing an apology on Jenna's behalf to the po-faced Bertie. Taking Jenna by the shoulders he looked her straight in the eye. A moment's decision-making and he pronounced her fit for service. 'Fit for a servicing more like,' she winked at him and wobbled off to find the loos, the feeling that a tactical chunder was about to rear its sickening head suddenly upon her.

With Jenna temporarily dismissed, Angus at the bar and Sally so completely oblivious to anyone except Gary Barlow's soaring tones, Bertie pressed herself in against Max. 'Now Maxie, darling,' she whisper-shouted into his ear. 'You can't tell me that you're seriously getting together with jelly-thighed Jenna, are you?'

'Getting it on . . . yes.' He moved his mouth to her ear, purposefully touching her skin with his lips as he continued. 'But getting together, no.'

Pulling her pout back into a triumphant mini-smile, Bertie ran her hand over his chest and pressed her lips up against his ear to make herself heard. 'Thank fuck for that, sweetie, I thought I was going to have to sleep all alone for the rest of the week.'

Pulling away in mock indignation, which did in fact have its roots in the real thing, he said, 'But you had Yuri all over you, what was I meant to do?'

'Leave her to Angus like every-bloody-one knows should happen!'

'Really?'

'Yes, Max, really!' Bertie was frustrated at his complete lack of second sight, but also rom-com happy that her ruthless jealousy-making had worked. He was hers for the taking and take him she would. Pressing her hands against his broad chest she slid them up towards his shoulders, flexing her fingers as she reached the crest of his strong, defined neck muscles. Moving her hands slowly up to the side of his face she pinioned him with her eyes and tilted her head up to kiss him. Not one to miss a trick, he returned her kiss enthusiastically, pulling her to him, his hands moving from her waist down to her butt. Squeezing her arse tight he moved his tongue deeper into her mouth, making it very clear that any sleepless nights on her part would be due to his ministrations and sleeping alone would not be an option.

Angus fought his way back to the dance floor, pushing his way past a group of students who were boat-racing shots along a high table, the poor guy at the end caught out by the final shot and administered with a half-dozen more as his punishment, accompanied by cheers and laughs. He noticed some older guys playing drinking games in the corner, no better than their student counterparts at making the poor girl in their group — someone old enough to know better — down the punishing gut-rotting shots for losing one round after another. He saw Max's head above the crowd and headed towards their spot. Not as tall as him, but still Max was useful to have as a dance floor sentinel. He disappeared, though, suddenly pulled down into the crowd. No matter, he saw his way through the dancing groups of friends, apologising and pushing in equal measure to get his bottle and five glasses through to party central. As the last group parted for him, he saw why Max's head had disappeared. He was kissing Bertie, full on, groping her on the dance floor, and Jenna was nowhere to be seen. As Angus approached, Max pulled away from Bertie, who hung on around his neck a little bit longer. When she turned her head and saw that Angus was back bearing gifts, she released herself from Max, gave a clap of delight and then took some glasses from Angus's hand while tapping Sally on the shoulder to bring her round from her dance trance. A few inches above their heads Angus's eyes drilled into Max's half-sheepish look. *You bastard*, they said. And then with his eyebrows slightly raised he mouthed 'Jenna?' to Max, wanting to see how Max would worm his way out of this one.

As if it was of no importance and just another run-of-the-mill night out, where Jenna's precious heart wasn't on the line, Max just emphatically rolled his eyes and mimed sticking two fingers down his throat, then thumbed in the direction of the loos. Mouthing 'Thanks buddy' as he helped himself to a fresh glass, Max was completely unaware that for the second time in twenty-four hours his best mate wanted to punch his lights out.

Jenna weaved her way back onto the dance floor, feeling much better for having a yak. Giving her hair a quick floof with her hand as she approached (she was very proud of herself for bringing a hair bobble out with her — and using it just in time to tie her frizzing locks back before she vommed), she took the proffered glass of champagne from Angus and beamed at him. She'd cleared her head a bit in the loo, but still took a wary sip of the bubbly before finding herself being scooped up by Max. Giggling, she wrapped her arms around his neck and rested her head on his big shoulder. Finding a soft patch of skin just below his jawline she inhaled deeply, his aftershave again flooding her drunken mind with memories of so many other nights out. She wondered how many girls in the bar were envious of her right now. Envious because she was with the most handsome guy here, perhaps; envious of her sophistication and self-control, no. To a more sober eye — and in Jenna's defence, sober eyes were few and far between — she looked a little bit all over place. Little Miss Fun mixed in with a fair dose of Little Miss Vodka

Shot. She didn't care though. Taking a final, long breath of eau de Max, thinking that this was an aroma that she would soon finally be getting used to, she peeled herself off him and pretended to play hard to get. Better stay off the bubbles, she thought, having a sudden moment of chaste clarity. I'm a lady. I mustn't let him think I can be fucked and chucked like all the others.

When Angus saw Jenna finally release herself from Max's embrace he'd made up his mind what he needed to do. He was livid. The vein in his forehead was throbbing and that only happened when something either very maddening or very exciting was going on. But he was controlling his anger because he'd known, in that instant when Max had so carelessly swatted the thought of Jenna away, that not only did his old friend not want to get together with her, he had barely any thought for her feelings. As if ten years of friendship didn't matter. As if Max hadn't stayed at Jenna's parents' place, met her gran, seen her drunk, walked her safely home, laughed at her jokes and bought her drinks for years; as if all of that just didn't matter as long as Max got his end away and taught Bertie a lesson. Angus had to talk to him. Had to make him understand what he was doing to Jenna. Had to tell him how *he*, Angus, was definitely beginning to feel something rather more than friendship for her.

With his hand about to grab Max's shoulder he felt a little tap on his back. Glancing behind him he saw Jenna, glass in hand, eyes closed, gently swaying to herself. He turned to face her, his back to Max and Bertie. Let them play around, he thought. Let them do what they want, but I won't let them hurt her. He put his hands on her shoulders and she opened her eyes, beamed again and moved towards him.

'Drunken make-up hug,' she muffled into his chest. He wrapped his long, strong arms around her too. Lowering his head he rested his lips on the crown of her head, gently kissing her hair. Worried, suddenly, that it might be construed exactly as it was meant, he turned it into a massive raspberry and delighted in the giggles that he felt against his chest. He gave her another squeeze and let her go. He saw Max look at him, head to one side, not exactly a smile on his lips, but a twist to the corner of his mouth. Angus just looked away, caught Sally's hand, and twirled her around to the final few songs before the house lights started to flash on and off and closing time was announced.

34

Walking home was the aim of the game, but for all anyone could tell Jenna and Sally had been replaced by bowling-alley skittles, constantly falling to a strike. Angus was still desperate to talk to Max, but keeping Jenna and Sally upright became the priority, and not a totally unrewarded one, as kisses were freely given to anyone offering a helping hand. The conversation wasn't up to the standard of the Oxford Union, but for now, at least, Sally was happy and Jenna was, too. Bertie, on the other hand, was only a little bit tipsy and recounted her days spent in Italy recently where a teetotal friend, whom she much admired as being so elegant and restrained, had said that when you drink, you are not a lady. 'And I totally agree. Natalia was such a dear.'

'She sounds quite dull if you ask me,' muttered Angus, as he lurched forward with Sally, managing just in time to capture her balance and rescue her from another icy encounter.

'I wish I was a lady,' slurred Jenna, wheeling her little going-out bag around by its wrist handle. 'I would be sooo happy, just sitting by a window waiting for my prince to come.'

'I think that requires an upgrade to princess, sweetie,' said Bertie. 'And we all know how many frogs they have to kiss . . .'

Angus punched in the code and pushed the heavy boot room door open. Sally and Jenna piled in after him like excited spaniels on the trail of a rabbit. Their quarry was the loo and they dashed upstairs, falling over each other with squeals of competition as to who could reach the nearest one first. Jenna was a clear winner, rounding the corner of the kitchen using the highly polished floor to capture an almost figure-skater-like elegance, before crashing full bodied into the door of the loo.

'A-ha! Wee-wee, oui oui!' she cried, before locking herself in. Sally, stalwart in defeat, double backed and headed up the slippery stairs, almost undoing all Angus's good safety work on the icy paths outside by slipping off every wooden stair in front of her. Summiting the top, she stood triumphant for a second before remembering the call of her bladder, grabbing her crotch in a most unladylike way and rushing into her room to the en suite.

Jenna held her head in her hands as she sat on the loo. With her jeans around her ankles, the warmth and closeness of the little WC seemed to overcome her. She opened her eyes, worried that she might fall asleep, but instantly regretted it as the walls closed in on her and started to spin. Desperately fighting back the urge to vomit, she concentrated, focused, on finding the loo roll. Must. Get. Back. Out. There. She needed to fight her way out of this evil castle of a lavatory and get back to the fun — who knew what they would all be getting up to? The walls loomed higher as she tried to focus on them. The loo roll turned into forest creeper and snared her in its deceptively white and innocent coils. A final tug and the long stream of paper came free from the holder and released her from the wall. Stumbling her way out of the little room, she double blinked and automatically headed for the kitchen, her body going into autopilot and searching out water.

Max took one look at Jenna and announced bedtime.

'Goody!'

'Up the stairs, sweetheart,' Max cajoled as Jenna stumbled over the first step.

'I am a sex gazelle from the African bush, leaping majestically up Mount Maximum-jaro!' she trilled.

'As much as I love discussing your bush, African or not, bedtime for you.' Max tried to guide her to her own bedroom, but like the sex gazelle she momentarily believed herself to be, Jenna leapt towards his and Angus's room. She missed the door handle with such shocking inaccuracy that Max had to laugh. And when they finally got into the bedroom she started to undress. Max knew she was putting her all into the shimmying dance-like thing she was doing as she tried to take her sparkly jumper off. But Moulin Rouge-style sexiness it was not. It was almost comical — and incredibly unsexy as far as Max was concerned. He watched as Jenna fumbled while pulling the thing off over her head, little vest top and all. The fact it got stuck made Max chuckle again and, watching her career blindly from wall to bed, eventually falling into the soft folds of his duvet with her arms released but her face still covered in clothing, made up Max's mind for him. This one, however willing, was going to be tucked in and left alone to sleep it off. And he was going to have to find another playmate tonight, and he knew exactly where he'd find her. Lifting Jenna's legs up and onto the bed he helped her free from her jumper prison and sat down next to her, tucking her into the duvet as he did so, so she couldn't fling an arm or leg out and over him, trapping him any longer than need be. He heard the tap-tap-tap of high heels on the wooden floor outside and guessed correctly that Bertie was on her way to bed. Jenna had tried to kiss him, but now she had closed her eyes and was drooling slightly, a sure sign she had accepted the lure of the alcoholic doze.

35

Max pulled himself off the bed. He walked over to the bathroom and splashed water on his face. He looked at himself in the mirror. What was he doing? What was *she* doing?

He turned around and looked at the sleeping girl in his bed. Quietly moving from the bathroom to the bedroom door, he eased it open. Listening out for sounds on the landing, he could hear nothing. Where was Angus? Fallen asleep on the sofa no doubt. He must have thought I'd be shagging Jenna. Max crept across the hallway and lightly knocked on the door of the girls' room. A couple of seconds passed before it was slowly opened. Greeting him was a girl the polar opposite of the one he'd left in his bed. Here was someone completely in control of herself. Bertie had removed her evening's outfit and replaced it with a black baby-doll negligee. Plunging down the front, the fine gauzy material barely disguised her nipples, which were making themselves very well known. Max dragged his eyes from them, taking in the flow of the thin, pretty material embroidered with silver bows every so often, one or two disappearing into the voluminous folds, his hands and eyes itching to discover where they had gone. Bertie looked at him, her level gaze waiting for his eyes to come back up to meet hers.

'Like what you see?' her voice husky with intent and anticipation.

'Very, very much.' And without further invitation he was in the room, wrapping his arms around her, and crushing her lips into a hard and demanding kiss.

She retaliated by pushing back into him, using the force of their bodies to slam the door shut, leaving them alone and private.

'Was Jenna a little bit too well-oiled for love-making tonight?' Bertie's eyes twinkled as she ran her hands down Max's shirt, fingering each button before deftly undoing it, releasing his chest inch by glorious inch.

'Hmm, very well oiled. Enough so I could slip right out of there, and thank fuck I did. You're so hot, baby,' Max was letting his hands do some exploring of their own, ruching up the fabric of the baby-doll as he found the pert cheeks of Bertie's bottom.

'You know I said, "When you drink, you are not a lady"? Well, turns out I can be quite unladylike too, and with barely any bubbles inside me at all.'

'Let's see what else we can get inside you, shall we?' growled Max and at that Bertie moved her hands up his now bare chest and slipped his shirt from his shoulders. She kissed the skin just above his flexed and muscled pecs. Fluttering little kisses brought her lips up his neck and as he leaned down to meet her, their lips met again.

Max's hands moved slowly up her body, feeling the soft skin under the diaphanous fabric of the negligee. Then, in one motion, he picked her up and stepped the few feet, through the minefield of knickers and make-up, to her bed, and gently placed her down on the duvet. As she watched, the look of expectant lust in her eyes, her chest heaving up and down in anticipation, he undid his fly and slipped off his jeans and boxers. Bertie's eyes widened in delight as she saw that an evening's worth of drinking had done nothing to dampen Max's ardour. He climbed on top of her, kneeling over her chest so that she could feel and touch his massive cock with tongue and lips.

'Thought you might like another bite of the cherry,' he said, winking at her, and then sucking in his breath in exquisite pain as she bared her teeth to the sensitive tip of his cock.

'You know I enjoy the fruits of my labour,' she replied, between long slow licks up and down his shaft. She ran her hands up from his hips to his torso as she continued to pleasure him with her tongue, and then gently started to push him down her, not wanting her own little cherry to be ignored too much. Max took the hint and slid himself down her body, running his hands over her taut stomach and then pushing the little lacy baby-doll up and over her breasts, whisking it over her head, but not letting her arms free. Stretching up to clasp both her wrists and most of the flimsy fabric in one of his large, strong hands, he used the other one to trace the line of her face, letting her suck his fingers before he trailed her hand down to her chest and felt her arousal in her beautifully flushed nipples. Letting her arms go, he continued moving down her body, kissing her skin, licking her, nibbling her thighs until she was pressing herself into him, desperate for him to reach her most private parts and make her come. She knew she wouldn't last long as his tongue began flicking in and out, swirling around her clit and penetrating her gently, but quickly. Max slid his hands under her butt and pulled her up towards his mouth as he licked and kissed her until, in several shuddering motions, she had yelled out his name and stretched out her toes and clenched the bed sheets to her in a thank-fuck-for-sex amazing orgasm. As she pulled away from him, so sensitive to any touch, he moved back up her body, kissing her stomach and sucking her nipples, moving his hands all over her, until with a slickness of movement he was inside her, enjoying her post-orgasmic clenching. He kissed her deeply, and pulled her onto her side, guiding one of her legs high up alongside his torso so he could get deeper and deeper into her with every thrust. Her moans of pleasure were timed with his thrusts and as he came inside her she bit down on his shoulder, making him seem to burst with pleasure and noise.

'Fuck, God, yeah, oh fuck,' he yelled as he clasped her to him, letting his cock pump into her.

'Oh baby,' she whispered. Bertie felt so completely satisfied. She felt so close to him now, in this vulnerable state he was in, depleted and knackered. She preferred it even to the macho guy who had just made her come so intensely. Stroking his back, his hair, his shoulders, she nuzzled into him, quietly confident of her own little victory.

36

Enough was enough. Being relegated to the sofa was not what it was about, thought Angus as he stretched his leg out and found it hemmed in by scatter cushions. He'd given Max and Jenna enough time — he'd painfully had to endure hearing some very obvious noises, which seemed to have now subsided, so surely by now one of them would have retreated back to their own room. Or maybe Bertie could be convinced to share with Sally if Jenna was still in with Max or vice versa. Angus couldn't imagine any outcome really being perfect, but anything to get him off this sofa and under a nice warm duvet so he could face whatever tomorrow would fling at them all.

He went softly up the stairs, making his tread as light as possible so he could peek into both the girls and his and Max's rooms without detection. The first door he came to was Jenna and Bertie's room. If Max had put Jenna to bed, like any decent man would have done when presented with a girl as drunk as Jenna had been, then he should see a couple of sleeping beauties when he popped his head round the door, and be all clear for lumbering into his own room and the blissfulness of his own bed. Not that he wouldn't rather have a certain someone in with him, but second place to that right now was just somewhere to be alone.

Gently pushing down the door handle, he felt the catch disconnect from the frame. Easing the door open just a crack he poked his head gingerly through the small space. A moonbeam from the almost-closed curtains illuminated the room, showing one very empty bed, the duvet pulled tight across and the area all around it moderately tidy. The light travelled then across a much more rugged landscape and Angus saw a tangle of legs and arms, duvet and clothing in the second bed. That it was Max was unmistakeable. That the other person was Jenna was less easy to ascertain but as he looked, his eyes adjusting to the silvery light, he noticed the slender arms and the small tattoo on the ankle of a dollar sign and knew at once who it was.

Gently pulling his head back around the door, and with the precision of a night-time ninja, Angus closed it and breathed again. Thoughts flooded his brain. It was beyond comprehension to him. Yes, very gentlemanly not to have taken Jenna to bed, but to cheat on her, so cruelly, with Bertie, in the next bloody room? At least one thing was certain. There was a spare bed available in his room, and if Jenna was in the one next to it, then he was sure she'd understand his need to sleep when they both woke up the next morning. How he'd explain to her that it was him five feet away, and not Max five inches away, was a bridge to be crossed come daylight . . .

He opened the door to his and Max's room. As he'd guessed, Jenna was fast asleep in Max's bed, tucked up like a small child swaddled in blankets. She hugged the spare pillow like a teddy bear, and didn't stir as Angus sat down on his bed and looked at her, her face so calm and still. Sleep made her look vulnerable. What he would give for the right, the privilege, to curl himself round next to her. But it was Max's bed she was lying in, and him that she imagined as she gripped his pillow to her. Angus gently brushed her cheek, her warm skin electrifying his hand, before he slowly got up and walked to the other side of the room. His fingers still tingling, he reached up and touched his own scarred cheek, the baldness of his skin still a novelty to him. No wonder she wanted his handsome friend and wouldn't look twice at him — and perhaps he didn't even deserve her; the violence and pain of that night flashing back as he touched his face. He'd given in to anger and fear that night — and perhaps losing Jenna now to his best mate was karma. He started to undress, glad at least of finding a bed for the night. What was left of it. He heard the church bells sound 3 a.m. as he brushed his teeth as quietly as possible and slipped into his empty single bed.

Wednesday

37

Jenna's first mistake the next morning was opening her eyes. Bright sunlight filled the room and blinded her, and her second mistake was to instinctively pull the duvet up and over her head. The sudden close stuffiness made her feel incredibly nauseous. *God, how much did I drink last night?* Memories flashed back through her now pounding head. Dancing. Embarrassing dancing. Oh, being a bit sick in the loos. Nice. More dancing and too much champagne. A Heidsieck headache . . . A Bollinger barf . . . No wonder she was feeling so dicey. Home after the club, singing, falling over? Call that a Veuve Clicquot cock-up . . . But there wasn't a Pol Roger-ing, was there? She gingerly flexed her ankles, checking for pain, half wishing for a proper excuse not to have to get up and hit the slopes this morning. These thoughts all ebbed away as she blinked again and worked out where she was. Too much male ski gear around to be her room so she must be in Max's, but there was no sign of him. She was very much alone. Oh dear, poor Angus, she thought, he must have been relegated to the sofa again. But Max, he must have slept opposite her all night, bless him. Such a gent. But not to wake her before he went, that was a bit rough. Speaking of rough, Jenna remembered she was due on the slopes at 10 a.m. with JP. If she knew where her phone was, or anticipated any sort of charge being left on the battery, she would seriously consider forfeiting her cash and cancelling last minute. But with ingrained politeness overcoming the waves of sickness and thumping headache, she got up and found her clothes. She'd slept all night in her bra — and her jeans — further proof that Max hadn't tried to ravish her, more's the pity.

Finding her jumper and little top in a tangled mess on the other side of the bed, Jenna stumbled into the bathroom. With slightly shaky hands she gripped the edge of the basin and braced herself for looking in the mirror. She drew in a deep breath, turned on the cold tap and winced at the stiffness of her neck as she leaned down and splashed handfuls of the icy water onto her face. She slowly lifted her head back up, water streaming off it, and opened her eyes. Looking back at her wasn't just a blotchy, red and very wet face, but also a ruggedly handsome one too.

'Max!' Jenna turned round to greet him, still holding onto the basin for support, unsure if she'd need it for something else too at any moment.

'Morning, Jenksy, how are you feeling?'

'Awful. Clinically awful. Sally might have to take me to the hospital with her — I'll check myself into the hangover ward.'

'That bad, eh? You did zonk as soon as I brought you up here. Thought it best to let you sleep it off.'

'Thanks. And sorry. You know, for not being sober enough for, well, you know . . .'

Max planted a quick kiss on her forehead. 'Don't worry, sausage, I don't need a bed-fellow every night, you know.' With a wink he ushered Jenna out of the small en suite, saying he needed a shower. 'And as much as I'd like to take you in with me, I think it might just about finish you off by the looks of it!'

'Hmm, we could try though?' Her valiant effort at a sexy pout was once again rejected by a laughing Max.

'No, no, Jenks. Really. Look, I think I heard Bertie in your room; go and get dressed and I'll walk you both down to the lifts. You've got another lesson, haven't you? Well,

Bertie and I will wait for you until the instructor comes and then we'll meet you again at lunch? OK?'

'OK Max, see you downstairs in a bit.' Jenna turned away from him, finding it hard to stay and plead for sexy shower time when it was obvious from his body language that he didn't want her. Stupid me, she thought, as she heard the bathroom door close behind her and the power shower whoosh into life. If I hadn't got so bloody drunk he'd have slept with me last night *and* I wouldn't look like such a swamp donkey this morning.

Knocking briefly on her own bedroom door, the sound reverberating through her arm and around her head, Jenna walked in and was instantly confronted by Bertie moisturising one long, tanned leg, its length extended elegantly as she balanced effortlessly with it up on her bed. Her silk kimono cascaded off her bony shoulders and its soft peach colour echoed the radiance in her face. She looked for all the world like a bloody supermodel. Bertie looked up at the intrusion, her honey-golden hair falling down in a glistening tumble over her shoulder.

'Jenna, darling, you're awake. Quick, quick sweetie, jump in the shower before Max uses all the hot water and we can have some *petit dejeuner* and get on the slopes. You look like someone who could do with one of my amazing acai berry smoothies. If I ever overindulge, which is, like, quite rare these days, then it just swooshes away all the nasties inside and makes one feel tip top in no time!'

'How do you know Max is in the shower?'

Only pausing for a moment, Bertie smoothly replied, 'Can't you hear it, darling? Clanky old plumbing round here. And it must be Max because Angus left ages ago and Sally, bless her, I assume from last night's attempt at dancing or whatever she was doing, is probably still drunk.'

'Oh.'

'Chop chop!'

'Right. It's just that I feel a bit unwell . . .'

'Nonsense, mind over matter, Jenna, get in the shower — it cures all ills.'

Jenna was too tired and hungover to argue with anyone, let alone an overly chirpy Bertie. You're a menace, though, she thought as she shuffled out of her jeans and pulled her jumper and strappy top off in one go — this time with much more success than last night. Stripping down to nothing she noticed some interesting bruises on her arms — Unidentified Drinking Injuries, she mused. Wonder how I picked them up?

Bertie was annoyingly right, and the shower did do its thing of reviving and perking Jenna up. Refreshed, marginally, she left the bathroom, dripping hair not towelled as the effort of tipping her head around to fit into a turban was just a little too much. Slowly moving around the room, she identified various pieces of her kit, glad that overly cheerful Bertie had left her to it. It must take a nanosecond for a well-moisturised Bertie to slip into one of her catsuit-like ski onesies, she thought. Making little grunts of pure jealousy to herself, Jenna donned salopettes and under-layers and pulled on the cosiest pair of socks she could find. If she was going to be forced up the mountain today then she sure as hell wasn't going to get cold while at it.

Jenna brushed her tangled knots out and gave her hair a quick blast with Bertie's super sub-ionic, frizz-busting hairdryer. She then followed her nose downstairs, where the smell of croissants and coffee was just too much for her empty tummy to refuse. Taking each stair rather gingerly, Jenna saw Bertie leaning over Max's shoulder as he sat at the table reading a local free paper. For a fleeting second she thought Angus was with them, but it was just Max's ski jacket flung over a chair. Bertie laughed at something she read in the paper, repeated it in French, and laughed again, each tinkling giggle causing her long hair to brush against Max's cheek. Jenna paused as she took in this intimate little tableau. Max himself wasn't really doing anything untoward, she told herself, and they are old friends. I can't really get jealous. I'm just not like that . . . am I? As she let out a rather audible sigh, Bertie turned round and released Max's shoulder from her territorial grip, but not before giving it a little squeeze.

'Come on, sweetie, no time for lingering. Brekkie!' Bertie fussed over Jenna and sat her down at a ready-laid place setting. A rather sour-faced Izzy was bidden to come and administer coffee to Jenna, before skulking back to the kitchen where she could be heard clattering pans.

'Lordy, could she be any louder?' Jenna moaned, covering her ears with her hands, her fingers clenched to her head, kneading her hair in anguish.

'Still feeling it, JJ?' Max reached over and patted her lightly on the shoulder before smothering a piece of baguette with Nutella and biting off a huge chunk.

'Honestly, sweetie, you're old enough to know better,' chastised Bertie, but Jenna wasn't listening, just thinking about what might have happened last night. Could she really be sure that Max had slept in his — their — room at all?

38

Twenty minutes later, an out-of-breath and generally a bit narky Jenna was at the meeting point where JP would whisk her off for a morning's lesson. Max and Bertie had been true to their word and walked her there, but ski-lovers that they were, they weren't about to waste piste time waiting with her. And although physical exertion of any kind was still feeling like complete anathema to her, it did rather cheer her to think of a few hours of ego massaging, as she hoped JP would be as incorrigible a flirt as before. She sat down on the bench, recently wiped clean of snow, and took in a few deep breaths. Time by herself had been in short supply recently, especially sober time. Looking up to the crisp blue sky that framed the mountains, both monumentally inviting and awesomely daunting, she thought about the men in her life. Darling Hugo, lying senseless in a hospital bed. Not exactly a man in *her* life but she did care about him and still smarted over her argument with Bertie the day before. And Max. Wow. Such public displays of affection, all that very sexy dancing that was going on last night, and him looking after her rather than shagging her when she was drunk: well, didn't that seem as if he was properly into her? But then this morning he'd not really wanted anything much to do with her . . . And Angus, the argument from the other night still bothered her. But why? He was lovely, that wasn't in doubt, but she was with the man of her dreams now — so why did Angus keep popping up in them too?

'Zhenna,' the deep French voice woke her from her reverie. 'You ees in anozzer world, oui?'

'Oui, Jean Paul, I'm sorry, je m'excuse.' Jenna blinked into the sunshine, looking up at the beautifully rugged face of her ski instructor. She noticed another equally sexy skier standing just behind him — dark skinned, tall, and holding onto JP's shoulder as he balanced on one leg trying to get his ski boot on.

'I will always forgeeve you, leetle Zhenna.' JP paused and held her gaze for an almost embarrassingly long time.

'Who's your friend?'

'Ah, zees is Jean-Claude — perhaps, as you zay, JC?' JP smiled, putting his hand on Jean-Claude's as it rested on his shoulder. 'We bang.'

Jenna raised her eyebrows — so JP/JC was more like AC/DC. Before she could open her mouth to say anything he had turned to face Jean-Claude, kissed him sensuously and whispered some French sweet nothings into his ear. He turned back to Jenna as if nothing could be more normal and continued. 'But now,' he looked longingly up into the mountains, 'we ski, ma cherie, we ski.' He turned back to her and held out his hand. With not so much as a blink of resistance, she took it and let him pull her up to standing.

'You are not so 'ot today, oui?'

It was that obvious, was it? 'Oui. I mean, non. Definitely not feeling super-hot, JP, but,' she took a deep breath, 'I will be. Lead on!' And with that she gratefully accepted his help with her skis and poles and, probably much like Jean-Claude had only moments earlier, admired his tight little French bottom all the way to the cable car.

The press of bodies in the cabin, the steam on the windows, the trickle of sweat down her back, all made Jenna's nausea raise its ugly head again. Luckily, as she stood propped up next to the window, she concentrated on the stunning scenery that she could see through a small patch of clean glass where she'd wiped the condensation with her mitten. How lucky were they that they got to come and play in these beautiful snowy slopes, each one now dotted with the wavy lines of skiers making their way quick, quick or slow, a waltz down the mountain? She craned her still stiff neck up to see blue sky that haloed the top of the highest peaks, but beyond it, grey clouds brewed.

'Do not worry about ze wezzer today, ma cherie.' JP had followed her gaze over the mountain tops to where the ominous-looking clouds billowed over the summits, making visibility on those peaks impossible. 'It will not be until, hmm, demain, I zink zat we get zat wezzer, and zen, peut etre, we try le spa, oui, le 'ot tub?'

'Too late, JP, I've already been ravaged in a hot tub, "JP'd in a Jacuzzi" as it were. Nice try though.' And she gave him a wink, suddenly feeling incredibly saucy, whereas ten seconds ago she'd been ready to vom. What was it about JP that brought out the Barbara Windsor in her?

Once the cable car had trundled its final ascent up to the top station and slowly disgorged all its occupants, JP helped Jenna with her skis and poles and, placing a mittened hand on her bottom guided her towards the edge of the slope.

'Maintenant, ma cherie. Today we squeesh ze bugs. Eet's a way of getting ze best parallel turns from zomeone, who, shall we zay, ees more creative zan technical.'

'JP, I hate bugs! What are you going to do to me?'

JP smiled, yet Jenna wasn't wholly convinced that the next two hours might not contain *I'm A Celebrity*-style mealy bugs and cockroaches.

'Ees zo easy, leetle one.' JP shuffled his skis up closer to Jenna's and put a comforting arm around her. She could smell his aftershave, a very French aroma of verbena, the greenness of the scent like an old-fashioned cologne reviving her still hungover body. The fact it *didn't* remind her of years and years of unrequited love, unlike a certain other person's, was quite frankly liberating. JP squeezed her a little tighter as he explained about skiing across the piste, imagining her most feared or hated creepy crawly in front of her. Using her uphill leg she was to force pressure down, creating a perfect parallel turn and, in her mind, squishing the dastardly bug all the way across the slope, only to do the exactly same thing on the next turn, and the next, until she was confidently down the hill and, in her mind's eye, the piste would look like a car windscreen after a particularly buggy drive up the M1.

'I get it, JP, I get it. That's amazing. It's so visual, so much easier to understand than "bend ze knees". You're a genius.'

'Ma cherie, I am not ze genius, well maybe a leetle beet. Alors, let's go. Squeesh le bug, mon petit choufleur, squeesh!'

Jenna chided herself that an image of Bertie's head popped up just as she was trying to imagine a long-legged stick insect, and she pressed down hard on her ski, squishing the Bertiebeetle right the way across the perfectly ploughed piste. Telling herself that Bertie really wasn't all that bad, Jenna tried very hard to just imagine bugs from then on, even if those bugs did have a St Tropez tan and wear Louboutins.

39

JP swished down past her and turned around to watch progress as Jenna completed her perfect parallel turns around the last few corners. Finishing her final one in perfect symmetry to JP, she stopped herself next to him. Even if she had wanted to, which she didn't, she couldn't hide her wide grin from him.

'I was amazing!' Jenna blurted out. 'I've never been that confident or felt like I was really, you know, skiing before! JP, whatever you say, you are a genius!'

'For you, Zhenna, I tell my best secrets. Now, tell me, ma cherie, who woz eet zat raveeshed you in ze 'ot tub. I want all ze details, you must, how you zay, paint me a picture of ze scene.'

'Certainly not, JP! Genius ski instructor you may be, but my confessor, oh no.'

'Confessor, what ees zis?'

'You know, like a priest. A confession.' She put her hands together in mock prayer. 'Forgive me, Father, for I *have* sinned.'

'Ah, I zee. Ma cherie, I would like verre much to hear your naughty stories, but I am too naughty to be a priest. I like ze ladies and ze boys and ze fun too much. Alors, we must ski on, and zen you can buy your JP a leetle vin chaud to zay merci pour le lesson genius, oui?'

'Oui, JP, oui.' And at that Jenna took off again, happily squidging bugs all over the piste until the mountain restaurant that she'd agreed to meet Max and Bertie in loomed into view. Confident in her new technique, she picked up speed and squished hell for leather down the mountain, slowing briefly to let a ski school of ankle-biters through, and finally only being overtaken at the last minute by JP, who effortlessly skied in front of her and blocked her path.

Jenna looked keenly over his shoulder, trying to spot Max in the crowd of tables on the large restaurant terrace, and before long heard Bertie's loud braying laugh. Jenna knew they were in there somewhere.

'JP, join us for a drink? Vin chaud on me!' Jenna looked up into the kind, handsome face of her ski instructor, trying not to visualise how much hair flicking and pouting would be going on in Max's direction as she wasted time standing around here.

'On you? Zen your JP would be made to take off all your cloze, oui? Zat ees what you want?'

'Oh JP, you are incorrigible. Come on in. Meet my friends. And my, well, my *new* boyfriend.'

'Oh Zhenna, you break my 'eart! A boyfriend?' But a wink told her that all was forgiven and his flirting could be reined in for the sake for a free drink.

As they clicked their boots out of their skis and found a suitable place for them on the wooden racks, they were ambushed by a snow-covered Angus.

'Good lord, Gus, what happened? Massive wipe out?'

'White out more like,' replied Angus, dusting flakes of snow from his shoulders and the creases in his ski jacket. 'It was like skiing through a milk churn up there. Weather's definitely closing in.' Then, 'Ah hello, JP, isn't it?' Angus pulled his hand, cold and red, from his glove and thrust it at JP.

'Oui, 'ello.' The Frenchman observed tradition and greeted Angus warmly before the three of them weaved their way through the lunching crowd to their friends.

Jenna veered off towards the loo, promising a full round of vin chauds on her return. As she found the steep, rickety stairs to the basement loos (honestly, are they trying to kill us all off with broken necks?) she glanced around, straining to see where Max and Bertie were sitting. Cursing her dratted bladder for its poor timing, and not wanting to miss a minute around the table, she almost skidded into the loos, narrowly avoiding crashing into a small child before managing to finish up and get back to the bar. Record timing for a salopette-hindered loo stop may have been broken. A few minutes — and a not totally unrewarding chat with a hot gap-year barman — later Jenna balanced five little steaming glasses (with their twee metal handles which were of no use at all) on a tray as she walked over the slippery wood of the terrace in her ski boots. She reached the table that her friends were sitting round with most of the steaming wine still in each glass, and happily accepted Angus's help to get each one safely down on the large wooden table. She busied herself doing this, while trying not to be seen gauging exactly how close Bertie was sitting to Max.

'Good spot, guys,' Jenna breezily said. Their table was on the edge of the large, sun-drenched terrace. A chest-high wooden fence, the slats decorated with alpine motifs of cut-out hearts and snowflakes, was the only thing separating them all from a sheer drop, and then a swoop of snow, valley, rock and air. It was breathtaking, and Jenna inhaled the mixed aromas of hot wine, fresh snow and French food. Looking up the mountain she could see what Angus must have skied through, and quite how fast he must have come down, as where they were, a good few kilometres away, there was still hot spring sunshine and unbroken blue sky. She looked over to him and saw the snowflakes that were all over him from the 'milk churn' only now starting to melt as he warmed up.

'Well, Maxie and I decided to stop early and put the world to rights, so we like totally beat the crowd.' Bertie took a small sip from the steaming glass in front of her before continuing, blithely, 'We just had so much to discuss and catch up on and Maxie and I have always seen eye to eye on so many things. So good to have a couple of hours one-on-one, y'know?'

'Right,' said Jenna, starting to bite the inside of her cheek. Thinking back on it now, imagining Bertie as the bug had actually been incredibly satisfying. Max leaned back against the post and rail fence that protected them from the edge of the terrace. He caught Jenna's eye and held her gaze, beckoning her to come and sit in the space opposite him, right by the fence. 'Here, Jenna, we saved the best place for you. Any news on Hugo, by the way? My phone's dead.'

'Shit. No. Let me check my phone.' Jenna pulled off her other glove and scrambled with the zip of her jacket to find the inner pocket and the phone within. Pressing the home button, a message was there, from Sally. Opening it up she read it aloud.

'Hi hun. Good news. Docs confirmed no sign of brain injury. Hurrah! Will be back at chalet later for celebratory drink! See you then S xx'

Jenna paused before repeating it back for JP, who had been caught on his way over to the table by a group of fellow instructors.

'Zat es great news Zhenna — I was wondering if eet might ave been leetle Russian bugs that you were squeeshing earlier. But, alors, et seems zings will be OK?'

'I do hope so. Oh, JP, I haven't introduced you.' Jenna, buoyed by the good news and the confidence that being around JP always seemed to give her continued, 'So we have my old friend Bertie . . .'

'Less of the old, sweetie,' Bertie said quickly as she placed her suede mitten on JP's shoulder and kissed him on the cheek. A lesser man might have blushed but instead JP just took her other hand, mitten-free and warmed from the hot wine, and pressed it to his lips.

'Enchanté, mademoiselle,' he murmured.

'And this is Max, my boyfr . . .' and yet Jenna could barely get the word out. It seemed unreal. 'Friend. A friend from uni too.'

Max looked at her quizzically, while Angus made a sort of throaty coughing sound and said he was going in to get menus.

'Oh, just a salad for me, Gus sweetie,' piped up Bertie.

Shaking his head, he carried on with his mission into the restaurant, keen to avoid having to witness Jenna with two men who were obviously both sniffing around for a shag.

With him gone, and with Bertie entertained by JP, Max turned to Jenna. 'How's the head?'

'Fine, thanks. JP cleared away the cobwebs.'

'I bet he did, the froggy devil,' leered Max, with a little too much 'that's-OK-I-don't-mind' in his voice.

'Nothing happened, Maxie.' Jenna instantly regretted using Bertie's pet name for him. The sound grated. She carried on quickly. 'He's a harmless flirt, all tongue and no action, as it were.'

'Honestly, Jenna, sometimes your choice of words astounds me!' Max smiled and leaned over and squeezed Jenna's hand.

Angus slipped back into the picnic-style table next to Jenna and put the menu clipboards down in front of them all. It was driving him mad seeing Max reach over and be all lovey with her when he knew what he'd got up to last night. He was resolved. He had to talk to Max after lunch.

On the other side of the table, Bertie was in heaven. To her right was Max, who she had one thigh very close up against, and on the other side, this delightful young Frenchman who Jenna had been quite selfishly keeping away from her. I can see why, thought Bertie, he's super cute. His eyes are like the sea in St Kitts and his rugged, unshaven jaw makes me want to scramble all over him. Bertie could have pounced, but she knew the long game she wanted to play, and now she'd ticked the 'making him jealous with another man' box with Max, she thought she'd better not play that one twice, having almost lost out to Jenna on the first round. Plus, gorgeous as this JP chap was, he was no oligarch. No, playing with this Frenchman might lead her right up the creek, sans le paddle. Still, while Max was carrying on this flirtation with Jenna for whatever reason, it wouldn't hurt to show off her excellent Lucy Clayton French, honed on the beaches and yachts of St Tropez and Cannes.

Jenna wasn't a bit fazed about Bertie seemingly muscling in on her territory. Why should she be, when Max was there, holding her hand, making plans for later? Jenna had texted Sally back, saying too right to a celebratory G & T (and that quite frankly she was impressed that Sal could even think about more alcohol after last night) and checked the boys were up for a few drinkies after chalet supper that night.

'I don't know, Jenksy, I might need a quiet one after last night,' said Angus, with a slight tone of resignation.

'Poor show, mate,' chipped in Max, who was still holding Jenna's hand in his, only letting go when the waiter came over to take their order. Four spaghetti bologneses and one 'green leaf with tofu, no dressing, and a dusting of turmeric' salad were ordered and the chat returned to what might happen that night.

'Why don't you come out with us, JP?' asked Jenna, missing the warmth of Max's hand now both of his had disappeared under the table. 'It'll be fun.' Jenna paused, following JP's gaze to Angus's face. 'Even if by the look on this one's face it won't be!' Jenna nudged Angus out of his sulk and carried on. 'We should try that other bar, the one with the lights all outside. Sal would love that, a bit of bright alpine fun and a world away from the hospital.'

'I would love to join you and your friends, Zhenna,' JP emphasised the word 'friends' as he shot a look at Max, 'but *malheureusement*, I 'ave anozzer plan. But maybe we come togezzer later, you know, in a bar, *peut etre*?'

Both girls would be forgiven for thinking something quite different at the term 'come together', especially when uttered by such a sex god, but they managed a straight face.

'Oui, bien sur, JP,' started Bertie in perfectly accented French, before continuing. 'I forget, JP, my friends here are not as good at le Français as me; I must speak in English for their benefit.' Eyebrows were raised from all three of the maligned party round the table. 'But we don't yet know our plans for after supper, so here's my number. If you'd like to call us, then we may be able to drag ourselves out to wherever you're hiding.'

Taking Bertie's card and pocketing it straight away without even looking at it, JP replied, 'Merci, tres gentil, but I have my leetle Zhenna's cell so I call on zat if I need to, oui?'

'Oui, of course JP, anytime,' said Jenna, trying hard to hide the big smile that came with a small victory.

Lunch arrived and all five tucked in. Four at least were under time pressure to eat the steaming hot pasta and sauce before it cooled tragically quickly in the brisk mountain air. Bertie picked at her salad, managing a few slices of lettuce before declaring it unfit even for animals and, pushing the plate away, amused herself with her iPhone instead.

Knives, forks and even spoons for the adventurous clattered onto plates, and with lunch over JP bade his farewells as he had to go to his next lesson.

'She is old, Zhenna, not as beeotiful as you, ma cherie. She will be ze bug that I 'av to squeesh, oui?'

'Oh JP, you're so naughty.'

'Only wiz you, eh? JP eez your favourite zing, oui?' He had eased himself out of the bench seat and had come over to hug her goodbye.

'Don't you mean guy?'

'Ah no, leetle Zhenna,' he leant down and whispered into her ear. 'Eet iz a zing wiz you I zink, JP.'

At that he gave her a quick peck on the cheek, nodded to the others around the table and left, swinging his gloves and helmet in such a camp fashion that suddenly made sense of the earlier JC revelation. Left in a total blush, Jenna tried to cover up by rolling her eyes and tutting about the French, but it hardly mattered.

'Another drink, guys, before we hit the slopes?' said Max as soon as JP had left. 'Now we can stick to one language that all of us idiots — thanks, Bertie — can understand, we can have a good old-fashioned English drink. Of Stella Artois.' Max laughed at the hole he'd dug for himself.

Bertie, made of stronger stuff than someone who would apologise, turned to flattery instead. 'Well, Maxie sweetie, how would I know if you can speak French? I've never heard you. I'm sure you're perfectly wonderful at French, practising your pillow talk every time you have to go to La Defense.' She looked over to Jenna, gauging to see how accurately her barb had hit home.

'Too right, ma cherie,' Max winked at her, purposefully mimicking JP's heavy accent. 'Trouble is, one flash of the black Amex to most girls in gay Paree and la defense is not an option, know what I mean?'

'Pant-wettingly funny, sweetie,' guffawed Bertie.

'Max, let's go to the bar,' insisted Angus. 'You two ladies stay here and save the table. Are you warm enough? He looked at Max and flicked his head in the direction of the bar.

'You can carry four beers, can't you, mate? I'm nice and warm here in my lady corner.'

With Jenna 'eewww'ing at him and Bertie giggling away he looked incredibly smug, so Angus shrugged and walked off in the direction of the bar, annoyed that he couldn't get Max by himself.

40

Although the terrace bar was starting to clear out, the afternoon drinkers — those not so eager to plunge down into what was now misty whiteness below them — were hanging on, and one large group had sat themselves down with all their paraphernalia right in Angus's way. He had to weave through the tables to get back to his friends, carefully holding the two large beers, one vin chaud, and a Perrier ('If someone suggests I have a "lady beer" one more time, I'll scream,' had been Bertie's exact words). He approached from behind where Max and Bertie were sitting, and to say that he wasn't shocked at what he saw was a telling sign. Unbeknown, he hoped, to Jenna, sitting opposite and happily chatting away with her hands flapping around as usual as she emphasised the fun parts of her story, Max had his hand on Bertie's thigh. He wasn't moving it, but it was there, all the same. As he got nearer he found the anger lessened at this latest show of complete nonchalance from Max. If he's that blasé about Jenna, and so into Bertie, then it really shouldn't take much convincing to get him to call it off with her. Although, of course, whatever happens, Jenna's heart will be broken, or bruised at least . . . and this thought made Angus furious.

Feigning a lack of balance, he brought the drinks down heavily on the table, slopping beer over Max.

'Oops,' said Max, hastily removing his hand from Bertie's nice warm thigh. 'Spillage, my friend. Drinking fine for that one!'

'I think Angus has paid his dues,' retaliated Jenna, in his defence. 'He has, after all, bought most of the drinks all lunch. Thank you, Gus!' She raised her little glass of vin chaud to him and clinked it with his larger stein.

'Oh yeah, thanks mate. My round next for sure.'

'Or even mine . . . again,' said Jenna quietly, taking a sip pretty quickly and smiling into the glass.

'Or even Bertie's?' replied Angus, playing along with Jenna's game.

Looking up from her phone, Bertie fixed Angus with that gaze, the one that minions run from and lesser folk tell stories about to warn their kids off night-time adventures. 'I,' she managed to let that one syllable stretch out for a couple of seconds, 'have totally contributed my share by inviting you all to the party the other night. Which,' she raised her hand, palm facing her friends in a gesture of defence, 'I understand may not have been the greatest of successes, but you did all drink yourselves stupid and I think I can be called the benefactrice of that evening.'

Jenna and Angus might have spontaneously raised their eyebrows, but the conversation moved on and soon enough the once-steaming drinks were finished and ice clawed its way up the inside of the glasses.

Jenna, still slightly wobbly on her pins from her morning lesson and the delayed hangover crawling all over her, decided that an afternoon's skiing wasn't for her — yet.

'You know what, guys,' she said, addressing the table as the empty plates and glasses were being cleared away and the others were starting to pull on gloves and zip up ski jackets, 'I think I might just stay a wee bit longer. I'm not totally sure I'm quite ready for the slopes yet, or them for me . . .'

'Are you sure, Jenks?' Angus looked concerned, while Max leaned over the table and placed a hand over her forehead.

'You'll be fine, JJ,' he pronounced, 'and the sooner you leave here, the sooner you can get back to the chalet for a kip or go and see Sally and Hugo.'

'Hmm, still, I just don't think I can cope with those red runs at the moment.' Jenna remembered yesterday afternoon's skiing with Max, where the world seemed to whiz past her just a little bit too fast in her effort to keep up. 'Honestly, guys, my hangover is shocking, you don't understand . . .'

'I think we do,' Max cut her trailing whine off. 'We did see you drink most of Val d'Argent last night.'

Jenna lowered her head into her mittened hands. Angus, who was still sitting next to her, put his arm around her shoulders.

'Come on, Jenks, we'll get you down in one piece. I promise I'll stay with you and not speed ahead. OK?'

Wondering if she really wished it was Max issuing promises and reassurances but pleased for a chaperone anyway, Jenna lifted her head and began to gather up her gear. 'Thanks, Gus, you're a star,' she mumbled, suddenly aware that Max and Bertie had already headed off to find their skis from the racks at the edge of the terrace.

'Come on, Jenks, you'll be fine I promise.'

'I just wish I hadn't drunk so much, Gus. This was meant to be a lovely afternoon of skiing and chat and fun and snowball fights and all sorts.' She looked up at him, trying to ascertain if there was a hint of 'I told you so' behind his kind face. But she so wanted to offload her feelings onto someone, so she continued, 'But I've ruined it. And now Max just wants to ski off with Bertie, even though he told me that it's me he likes. I don't understand.'

'I don't think any of us will ever understand Max. I don't and I've known him since prep school.'

Angus, of course, understood Max perfectly. Ushering Jenna towards the ski racks he saw Max and Bertie deep in conversation. She'd kept relatively quiet while Jenna was complaining of her hangover, in fact, silent, which must have been a first for Bertie. But now she was conversation central and, as Angus and Jenna approached, she finished what was obviously to her, and possibly to Max too, a hilarious story.

'What's that?' peeped up Jenna.

'Oh, nothing sweetie,' replied Bertie with the haughtiest of tones, 'just a little thing I heard on the grapevine recently about some fund managers Max and I know, no one you've heard of.' Glancing back towards Max and smiling, she then slipped her boots into the skis' bindings and slid away from the group, adding a gratuitous bottom shot to Max as she bent over elegantly from the waist to adjust her boot binding.

'Nice arse,' Max flashed back at her, then aware that he'd said that out loud added, 'if you like that sort of thing.' At that he patted Jenna on her bottom and continued, 'Look guys, you don't mind if I ski ahead with Bertie, do you? She'd like a bit of tutoring on how to get down moguls and I said I could do that black run with her. You're not really up for it, JJ, so if you and Gus do the easier way down, we'll see you back at the chalet sometime before supper.'

Sometime before supper seemed like an eternity away to Jenna, who forced out a smile and a 'guess so'. Angus knelt down and helped her into the ski binding that she had been struggling with for the past three or four minutes. An image flashed through Jenna's head: a man kneeling down for her, a glint as a box would be opened, the jewel's glistening facets as bright as the fresh, white snow glinting in the sunlight. She blinked a few times and shook her head to clear it: back to the real world.

'Thanks, Gus,' she murmured, realising quite how many thank yous she'd said to him over the last few hours. 'Are you sure you don't want to go with the others? I don't mind; I can ski at my own pace and I don't want you to ruin your day by having to babysit me'

'No, Jenks, I'll stick with you. Then, depending on what happens and how you feel at the bottom I'll see you home, or maybe we can go and visit Hugo?'

'I think if the nurses saw me they'd admit me straight away and put me on self-harm watch the way I look.' Jenna let out a snorty breath through her nose in derision at her own situation. But she was cheered by the prospect of being down at ground level and the possibility of seeing Sally, because she needed one hell of a big hug right now.

41

Angus watched as Jenna teetered on the edge of the slope. There were twenty metres or so of ice, quite steep, but after that it levelled off. Getting down this little bit first was the lesser of two evils: the only other way down from the mountain was a laborious semi-slope, so barely going downhill that the exertion needed to push or skate yourself along it would wipe out someone feeling like Jenna did at the moment. He'd explained this to her, as they surveyed the precipice in front of them, and she'd agreed in principle, knowing the pain of aching arms after kilometres of pushing yourself along, but still the prospect of just taking off into the icy unknown was scaring her just a little.

'You've done this piste before, I've seen you,' Angus coaxed.

'Yes, but I was feeling tip-top then. I feel more bummy-bottom now.' What she really meant was, 'I might turn that piste to pasta with my regurgitated spag bol all over it.'

'Come on.' Gently he pushed Jenna's back, and slowly she hovered nearer the edge of the run. Then suddenly, as if a rocket had flown up her arse, she skied off, the tips of her skis precariously wobbling and threatening to cross in what would be a disastrous move, but righted just as they hit the first ice patch. Digging her edges in she slipped a small amount sideways down the mountain, but found a mound of snow to squish her bug around, and made the arc-like turn almost perfectly — if you didn't count the scream, waving poles and bizarre posture. With encouragement being shouted down by Angus, and only one snowboarder vying for position over the snowy mounds that helped break the icy sliding, Jenna made it down the metres of peril. She could be forgiven this time, she thought, for imagining with increasing ferocity the image of Bertie's face every time she dug her uphill ski into the piste and squished.

Angus took barely a moment to join her. 'Well done, you! See? Easy!'

'Hmm. I suppose it wasn't as bad as all that.' Jenna looked up at Angus, his beaming smile buoying her up and encouraging her to go on. 'If that prick of a boarder hadn't cut me up on the last turn I think I might have almost enjoyed it. Almost. Not really.'

Angus laughed. Jenna carried on, 'And thank you, again, for helping me. I'm glad you let me keep my poles this time, though.'

'Oh, I don't know. Ending up with you between my legs again wouldn't be so bad, you know, Jenks.'

Before she could reply, Angus set off again. He stopped every hundred metres or so to wait for Jenna to catch up and catch her breath before pointing out the next rendez-vous point and skiing effortlessly down to it. Despite her hangover, she was, to her surprise, skiing with a smile on her face, and with a running nose and flushed cheeks, Jenna reached the bottom of the piste. The warmth of that day's early sunshine, and the hundreds of skiers now descending to avoid the mists, created a cesspool of slush rather than a nice snowy finish to her run. But the fact that it *was* the finish meant that even the trudge through the dirty, semi-frozen snow to the pavement and cable car office filled Jenna with joy.

'It looks like a Coke-flavoured Slush Puppie,' Jenna murmured to herself. Angus had stopped only a few yards in front of her, his own skis having drawn to a stop on the slush too.

'How are you feeling now, Jenks?' he asked, turning around to see if she could cope with the slippy release tab on her bindings. What he saw was someone pathetically trying to jab the end of her pole into the little dent in the tab to get some purchase and free herself from the debilitating skis she was attached to, without having to bend down. Angus shook his head, quickly released his own bindings and stepped away from his skis. Leaving them where they lay, he loped up the few yards back towards Jenna.

'Whoa there, cowgirl.' He stepped in front of her and held her shoulders. 'You just stay upright, I'll get these planks off you.'

'Thanks, Gus.' An exhausted Jenna leaned her head into Angus's shoulder as he reached with his ski pole behind her and one by one released the two skis from her boots. Jenna was so grateful to be out of her skis and only minutes from a nice hot shower and a nap that she stopped worrying about what Max and Bertie were up to and gave Angus a big hug. 'You're my ski saviour,' she said as she wrapped her arms around his chest, squeezing him, partly in gratitude and partly because standing upright was still a bit of a mission.

'Tell you what, Jenks, let's get you home and then we can perhaps go and catch up with Hugo and Sally?' Angus slowly released his own grip on Jenna and held her by the shoulders again.

'Are you sure you don't want to go up the mountain again? It's such a nice run — for people who can actually ski.' Jenna smiled as she ended her sentence, knowing full well that it would take at least three broken bones and a complete white-out to stop Angus from being able to shoosh down the slopes with ease.

'Nah, I'm good. Quite hungover too, if I'm honest. I wouldn't mind a chilled one.'

'Are you feeling all right?' Jenna brought her hand up to his forehead, mirroring Max's earlier attempt at a fake diagnosis. 'Hmm. No temperature but a sudden change in behaviour. I prescribe tea, cake, and a sit down immediately.'

'Rightio, doctor,' grinned Angus, before leaning down to pick up Jenna's skis, swinging them over his shoulder and then walking on to get his own.

Jenna couldn't help but wonder about Angus. From what Max had reported back over the years he was the type to run 20k races after three nights out on the trot and he'd even done the London marathon once with a broken wrist and an eyepatch, apparently. But now here he was, happy to succumb to a bit of a hangover just to walk her home.

Angus walked along next to her. Occasionally Jenna would point out something in a shop window, or say something about Hugo, until the pair reached the door to the chalet. Angus tapped in the code and buzzed them in. Pushing the door open, he stood back to let Jenna through. The warm air hit her like a jet engine and she became more tired than even she had thought she'd been.

'God, I'm knackered, Gus.' She slumped down on the soft-seated chair. 'Thanks so much for carting my skis around. I don't think I would have coped! I'd have been dropping them all over the place and causing a massive show!'

Angus nodded his head in agreement. 'For the sake of Anglo-French relations I thought it best to carry them for you.'

'Cheeky.'

'You started it, Jenks, I just don't like to disagree with you, gentleman that I am.'

Jenna bent over and, using up almost the last of her energy, unclipped her boots and prised her steaming feet out of them. Socks all ruched up, she couldn't even be bothered to put her boots away properly until the sensible part of her took over, knowing that it would be so much better tomorrow morning to ease herself into dry, warm boots than damp ones. She pulled open the ski boot cupboard and found the boot warmers — metal poles set an angle to the wall that had a warm element running through them — and heaved her boots up and over onto them. Finally feeling like the last ounce of energy had left her, she schlepped past Angus, who was rebinding his boots before hoisting them up onto the warmers as well, and pulled herself up the handrail of the stairs to the living area of the chalet.

Angus looked at her as she scuffled past, socks half hanging off and mittens trailing from her sleeve ends. His eyes rested on her bottom, tightly snuck into her white Roxy salopettes, and let his eyes follow its ascent up the stairs until she was gone.

42

The little resort clinic looked as clean and bright as usual, yet the sickly sweet smell that barely any hospital can avoid clung to the place and turned Jenna's still slightly fragile stomach. She and Angus had made themselves a cuppa and he'd had to physically pull her off the sofa and push her up the stairs to get her changed and ready to go and visit Sally and Hugo in the hospital. And now they were here, it brought home to Jenna again the brutality of the beating. Anger flared up inside her and she turned to Angus ready to vent, again, her hatred of Yuri and his men when she stopped, realising that Angus had paused, briefly, by the swing doors to the ward. Then it dawned on her. Angus hadn't seen Hugo since the beating, having failed to get past reception last time.

'He's just through here, Gus,' she said quietly, pushing open one of the swing doors and holding out her other hand to him.

Angus didn't take it, but he forced a weak smile from his rock-like face and followed her through the door. Jenna turned round to look at him again, but couldn't think of what to say. She didn't want to piss him off and make a fuss of the fact that he was as white as the face of the Eiger and about as immovable in his expression. She turned back and walked straight into a nurse, who after the initial apologies recognised Jenna and smiled, then almost immediately started talking in a fast French, almost completely unintelligible to Jenna's schoolgirl abilities. She got the gist though and she and Angus followed the sturdy little nurse down the corridor to a light brown wooden door with a little porthole window in it. The nurse rapped smartly on the door before opening it and ushering them in. Jenna caught something about the 'heure' being 'plus tard' and wished JP was there to translate.

Sally jumped up and rushed towards her friends, falling into Jenna's open arms.

'Oh, darling, thank God you're here!' she said, tears very near the surface.

'Had to come and see you, poppet,' replied Jenna, adding, 'plus Gus hasn't been here yet and I thought I'd better show him the way.'

Angus just nodded as Sally looked up at him from Jenna's shoulder. She let go of Jenna and in a second was holding onto Angus.

'Oh, darling Gus, thank you so much for coming,' and in a flash she was business mode again. 'Now, don't get upset when you see him. It really does look worse than it is. Poor H, he has been in the wars. He's still heavily sedated.'

Angus gently peeled Sally off him in order to go and stand by Hugo's bedside. Sally was right, he did look a state. A complete state. Angus swallowed quickly, worried that the bile that had been lurking somewhere down his windpipe would rise up. Last thing Hugo needed was sick chucked up on him. Angus took a few deep breaths then bent down to get a better look and remembered when he'd last seen Hugo, broken and bloodied by the river, and then being slipped into the ambulance under an all-too-red blanket. A similar scene from years ago flashed across his mind — ambulances in a dingy oriental alley, paramedics working on knife and glass wounds, chaos as heads were counted and everyone — no, not quite everyone — was accounted for. He shivered across his shoulder blades and stood up straight again, rubbing his hand over his chin and up his scarred cheek.

The girls were sitting at a little round table in the corner of the room. A large vase of white roses had been pushed to one side as Jenna stretched her hand across to her friend to comfort her, even as they just caught up on the day's news.

'So they skied all afternoon together — they're probably still out there now — and Gus saw me home. Honestly, if he hadn't I might have had to literally live on the mountain.'

'Oh darling,' Sally cocked her head and pursed her lips at Jenna, then burst out laughing. 'Although I am not one to judge you! Last night! Lordy, what did I do? I felt so utterly ghastly this morning I had to sit down at least three times on the way to the hospital. And the fact that one of those sit downs was in a coffee shop with a double espresso and a very swift word-to-self . . . Well, I was not best pleased with self today, I can tell you that!'

'You were magnificent on the dance floor last night, Sal,' Angus chipped in. 'All retro, yet futuristic . . .'

Jenna snorted and Sally threw an empty hospital-issue paper cup at him.

'Honestly, retro-futuristic! I'll tell you what it was, it was the Sally Shuffle, aided by champagne, gin and not enough spuds at supper!'

'Speaking of which, it's chocolate mousse tonight,' chipped in Jenna.

'Oh delish. My fave.' Sally sighed. 'But I mustn't come back with you, I've got to stay here.'

'Sally love, it'll do you the world of good. You haven't been out all day, you've missed the snow, you've missed lunch — please don't miss some evening fun too! Hugo wouldn't want it!' Jenna knew this last statement was a little below the belt, and certainly didn't want to turn the emotional screw too tightly on her friend, but she did feel that she was right — Hugo would hate to think of Sally missing out on all the fun, and he'd certainly be saying the same thing if he were in Jenna's position.

'But what if he woke up and I wasn't here? I'd feel so bad.'

'There are nurses,' Angus piped up, although his reassurance had little effect, as Jenna could see Sally not really liking the idea of her darling Hugo seeing the light and imagining all the pretty French nurses were his own personal angels.

'And they'd tell Hugo just how long you've sat in vigil by his side,' counteracted Jenna. 'And this is killing you — you need a drink. This place makes *me* need a drink and it was only about two hours ago I swore I'd never drink again!'

Sally sighed. 'Tell you what, you two stay here with Hugo and I'll go and tell the nurses that I'm done for the day. I really must get some fresh air, you're right.'

Sally left Angus and Jenna with the eerily still Hugo and busied herself for ten minutes finding nurses and doctors and leaving all her details again, just in case Hugo woke up in her absence. Bustling back in, she made a beeline for Hugo's bed, leaned in and kissed him gently, stroking back the strands of hair that had fallen over his forehead.

'Good bye darling,' she whispered to him. 'I've given them my BlackBerry number, my iPhone number, my Skype address and my email address — I'm going to pop home for supper and I'll see you later, my love.'

Jenna moved closer to Angus as the silence of Hugo's non-reply filled the room.

43

Half an hour later, Izzy was running Sally a hot bath as she tucked into a slice of the most delicious fruit cake.

'Izzy, darling, I know I said this before, but honestly, when you're back in town after this season you must stay in touch. I know an artisan bakery in Fulham that would go mental for this cake.' Izzy smiled wanly at her unsolicited benefactor and turned off the taps before leaving a fresh towel on the heated rack and retreating to the safety of the kitchen.

Jenna lay back on her friend's luxuriously large emperor-sized bed and realised how small Sally must feel in it now Hugo was no longer there to cuddle up to. Hearing the splashing noises from the bath, Jenna called through to Sally — letting her know that she was there, flicking through the pages of *Heat* magazine. Occasionally Jenna would give Sally a snippet of info about the latest *Made in Chelsea* crisis or who was doing who in Hollywood, and be gratified by the giggle she'd get in return from the other room.

'You don't have to be on suicide watch, you know, Jenksy,' Sally called through from the bathroom.

'I know, love, but it's nice to hang out with you — and check you're not hanging yourself. Sorry, rubbish pun.'

'Yes, you've had better, JJ.'

'Anyway, it might be me that chucks myself head first into a hot tub if Max is leading me on.'

'Oh darling, really? I thought you two were heading for 2.4 and a nice house in the country?'

'I thought so too until, well, something happened this morning, just over breakfast, and in fact all day. I'm sure he still fancies Bertie, but he says he fancies me. He likes my "twinkle", apparently.'

'Yes, you said that last night. I'm not sure I need to know what Max thinks of your, er, "twinkle", honey,' replied Sally before adding, 'Anyway, wouldn't someone like, say, Angus, be a much better bet, sweetie?'

Jenna raised her eyebrows. 'Really?' A small spark seemed to burn in her stomach at the very thought. 'Hasn't he got some amazing Amazonian or African girlfriend or something?' She frowned and carried on. 'I know Max has never been interested before, and it's a broken record me trying to work out if *this* gesture or *that* word means anything. I mean, it's like for the last ten years I've been standing there waving at him with a big flag saying, "Shag me, shag me!" And now finally he has! But it was just, well, a bit "meh".' Jenna flipped the magazine closed in disgust.

Sally replied from the other room, pausing slightly as she rubbed a flannel down her arm. 'The problem is, darling, he's just a man, and unless that flag was actually a flag and you perhaps went up to him and stapled it to his head, he wouldn't notice. You should have jumped him years ago!'

'And risk years of embarrassment from then on as we still tried to be friends? Not likely.'

'Oh, the pride of the young!' Sally made a theatrical sigh. 'You've got to strike while the iron's hot, sweetie. And I have a sneaking suspicion that your and Max's iron is so cold, it's back in the cupboard with its power cord wrapped round it, hence the "meh" sex, as you so eloquently put it. Hugo and I would never have got together if I hadn't thrown myself at him almost straight away, you know, in a classy way, at that hunt ball. I'd heard rumours he was seeing someone else, but no one there really knew her and if I'd let a silly thing like that get in the way . . . Well, let's just say he wasn't very into her as he rallied to my hullabaloo almost instantly!'

'But you're so confident, Sal.' Jenna was finding the whole conversation a little exasperating now.

'Bloody am not! Or at least I wasn't then, I just couldn't let that hot potato get away. Speaking of which, Max is very handsome, honey, but don't you think Angus is just as hot in his own way? That scar . . . ooh, it's so mysterious.'

'You'll probably have your own scarred hero now, Sal,' Jenna retorted, not yet sure if she wanted to openly discuss the hotness of Angus as a replacement for Max.

'Too soon!'

'Oh God, I know, I know. Sorry Sal.'

'You haven't known Angus all that long really, not properly anyway. And none of us know this girlfriend of his, if she even exists. This could be your fresh start, your very own Hugo . . .'

'But, finally, I'm with Max! Why would I want Angus?'

'Are you though? Really?'

Jenna buried her head in the pillows of the massive bed and kicked her legs up and down in frustration, sending Kim Kardashian's bottom, and the rest of *Heat*, flying.

Sally's voice echoed through from the bathroom and demanded a 'rather large glass of plonk please, darling' and so Jenna pulled her aching muscles off the bed and scurried downstairs to the kitchen to fetch her friend the medicine they all knew made everything, if not better, then slightly rosé-er.

44

Bertie was finding it hard not to look like the cat who'd got the Crème de La Mer. She and Max had skied all afternoon in a happy tandem, both equally as fast and skilled as each other. The clouds of wet mist had done nothing to dampen their spirits as they vied for pole position on each end-of-piste finish. They'd stopped for a quick drink at the bottom of the piste, but not at La Folie, where so many others were celebrating the end of another great day on the slopes. Max had scooped up her skis for her and led her by the hand, bypassing the swarms of skiers outside that particular bar.

'I know somewhere much more your style, Berts,' he'd whispered as he pulled her closer behind him and guided her down a side road. A small ski rack was positioned next to a nondescript wooden door. Max placed both of their pairs of skis in it, along with their poles, and then punched in a code on the pad next to the door. An audible click, and then he pushed it open to reveal a narrow staircase.

'After you, my dear,' he said as Bertie looked at him, a quizzical eyebrow raised. 'You'll see,' was his answer to her silent question. Bertie had climbed the stairs and emerged in a beautifully decorated drawing room. The tall ceilings were more Parisian town house than chalet, with large sash windows framed by lush velvet drapes. The walls were decorated in a shabby-chic grey colour, with sophisticated oil paintings of aristocrats and horses hung artfully around them, giving the whole place a Regency splendour, or like something out of Versailles.

Max nodded at an obsequious waiter who appeared and then disappeared into nowhere it seemed, and then guided Bertie to a sumptuous chaise longue.

'I feel so . . . so at home!' Bertie trilled, clasping her hands together with glee as the waiter reappeared with an ice bucket and a bottle of vintage champagne.

'It's only what I promised you before we left, sweetheart.' Max took the bottle from the waiter and almost silently popped the cork in a well-rehearsed manner.

'I almost thought my luck was out.' Bertie demurely took a proffered glass and waited until Max had filled his own before raising it to eye level and saluting him with it. 'But perhaps my luck is very, very in?'

'I can't see why not . . .'

'Well, Max,' Bertie leaned forward and put her glass down as she unzipped her fur-lined jacket to reveal the barest of under layers. Removing her jacket altogether and reclining back on the chaise longue, glass back in hand, she continued. 'There's a little something, or rather semi-hefty something, called Jenna who seems to be standing in my way.'

Max moved from his seat and came and sat next to Bertie on the chaise. 'Is she here now?'

'No . . .'

'Is she sipping Taittinger Comtes de Champagne 2005 from a crystal flute in the resort's most expensive bar?'

'No, but she has been in your bed.'

'She's just an old friend who wanted some fun — and it seemed, dare I say it, that you were looking beyond moi to more eastern charms earlier this week anyway. What's a man to do?'

'Oh Maxie,' Bertie leaned in close to him. 'Let's not do this anymore. Let's let it just be us from now on . . .' Bertie didn't complete her plea, as Max's lips had met hers before she could utter another sound.

As Jenna skidded in socked feet round the corner to the kitchen, she saw Max and Bertie come upstairs from the boot room. Her heart gave a little skip as she saw Max's tanned face break out into a smile — but the little skip was all it was as she realised he was laughing at something Bertie had said. Catching her eye, though, he winked at Jenna and caught her hand as he rounded the top of the stairs.

'Hello, old pal,' he said as he kissed her chastely on the cheek.

'Oh hi, you.' Jenna tried to ignore the platonic term and lean in a little closer to the kiss, expecting to find the same familiar smell of his aftershave. Instead she caught the distinct whiff of booze and her mind was filled with jealous thoughts.

'Hi, Jenna,' Bertie chipped in, cementing Jenna's jealousy. 'Sorry Maxie and I are a little late, we just had to stop for a quick refreshment on the way home.'

Jenna's jealousy was not only cemented, it was quick-dry concreting itself to her. She pulled away from Max and headed for the kitchen, still on a mission to get Sally her much-needed glass of wine. While Bertie went upstairs she heard Max's footsteps behind her as she opened the door of the fridge. Without thinking, she tensed.

'What's up, Jenksy? How was your afternoon with Mr Linklater? Did he get you between his legs again?' So Angus had told Max about that, then, Jenna noted.

'Are you drunk?' Her non-sequitur caught him off guard. 'Hugo's fine by the way, thanks for asking.'

'Don't be cross with me, mate.' Again the platonic. 'Bertie just needed a little cheering up.'

'Fine.' Jenna closed the fridge and found a clean glass on the draining board. Pouring wine in silence, thoughts ran through her mind as Max filled her in on most of his afternoon's activities. He wasn't dumping her, was he? No, this would be the most banal dumping in history if it involved telling her about which ski lift he took to the glacier and how fast he skied down it. But those platonic terms — mate, pal — why had they replaced the 'babe' and 'sweetheart'? Jenna convinced herself that Max was just being a bloke and forced a few smiles and 'oohs' for him as he continued to describe his jumps and how much 'air' he'd got. Excusing herself finally from his monologue, she took the glass (having refilled it once, or maybe twice already) to the expectant Sally.

Later, wandering out of Sal's room, she hovered in the corridor and saw Bertie through the gap in the door, parading around in her underwear again, obviously about to have a shower. Angus and Max's door was closed. She guessed Angus was still out getting some beers and bits and bobs, as he'd popped out just after he, Jenna and Sally had got back from the hospital. But there was no sound of Max from their room. Weird, thought Jenna, but turned and headed down the stairs for a bit of a chill-out before supper, looking forward to her own very large glass of wine. Hearing the noise of a door open just as she reached the bottom of the stairs, she quickly turned and looked back up to the landing, but didn't see anything. She just heard the closing click of the boys' room door and the sound of water draining from a bathtub.

45

Wine had never been something that Jenna was much of a connoisseur about, though she'd been told she had a good palate. There were the fine wines Jenna knew the names of, Château Lafites and Margaux and things, but they were never in her price range. And there were 'session' wines, the nice easy-drinking merlots and stuff that she and her less affluent friends would pick off the Co-op shelves for a girls' night in, but to call her a buff, no, you could not. However, she knew what she liked, and this rather nice Gevrey Chambertin that Sally had picked up on one of her little 'shops for essentials, darling' was going down a treat in light of her earlier conversation with Max. Swirling the tawny, delicious liquid around the inside of the glass, Jenna inhaled the mellow aroma of a rather nice wine.

'A definite lingerer on the palate,' she said to herself in a comic old man's voice, 'with the finest of legs and the smoothest of bodies. Just like Bertie-fucking-Mason-Hoare. A lovely, hmm, I'd say *wine* taste . . .' Jenna took a large swig gulping it down, 'with a wine-like finish and definitely *whiney*.'

'Jenna, you're a vintner in the making,' said Angus as he entered the sitting room, having carted a couple of crates of beer up the stairs from the boot room.

Jenna put down her glass with a slight wobble and jumped up off the sofa, giving her upper lip a quick wipe with her wrist in case of Ribena-tache, before bounding over to Angus to try and cope with the embarrassment.

She followed him into the kitchen, where Izzy was muttering into the mobile phone that was clenched between her cheek and shoulder. The concentration she was giving the phone call, and the determination needed to not let her phone slip and possibly land on the floor, not to mention the odd evil look thrown Jenna's way, meant Izzy was paying next to no attention to the six-inch knife she was wielding as she crudely chopped onions. If Jenna wasn't still slightly pissed off with her after Max-gate, she'd have been seriously worried about the life-expectancy of Izzy's fingertips. So as not to disturb her, Angus gently placed the two crates of beer down as far away from the chalet girl as possible and motioned Jenna out of the room with a comically emphasised shoving motion and finger to the lips.

Jenna couldn't help but feel bad for Izzy, though. She'd caught enough of the conversation to realise she was bitching to one of her friends about how the 'sexy older guy' had 'shat on her from a massive height' and was now out of the picture. And Jenna knew it was because he was now with her instead. Or at least she hoped that was the reason.

'I'm off to have a shower and prepare myself for the night ahead,' she said to Gus.

'Good plan, Stan,' he replied. 'Suppose I better do the same, if Maxie baby, as you ladies seem to like to call him, hasn't used all the hot water or intoxicated the room with poof juice.' At that, Jenna snorted, and they headed upstairs, each to their own rooms, agreeing to be downstairs in time for another pre-supper cheeky drinky.

Unsurprisingly, about twenty minutes later, it was the boys who were downstairs first, showered and ready. Angus flicked the tops off from a couple of bottles of biere d'Alsace and carried them through from the kitchen, narrowly avoiding Izzy brandishing another knife, this time cutting up potatoes. He sat down next to Max, who was sprawled on the sofa over a few cushions, lazily flicking through one of the girls' magazines. Angus passed him a beer and told him to shove up.

'Cheers, mate. You wouldn't think, after the amount we've drunk this holiday, I'd need it, but I really do.'

'No worries.' Angus turned his face away from his friend and stared out of the window at the gently falling snow, watching the dance-like movements of the flakes before steeling himself to begin the conversation. 'Yeah, it's been quite a week so far, hasn't it?' Angus turned back to face Max, who gulped down a gullet-full of his beer. He looked tired, dark circles under his eyes showing how little sleep he'd been getting, one way or the other.

'Hugo will be OK though, won't he? I've spoken to the guys back in the office.'

'Oh right, that's good of you. What did they say?'

'Usual gumpf, you know, hope he's OK, anything they can do, don't rush back, etc., but I think they mean it. Everyone loves Hugo at work. And he might seem like a total ass to us when he's out and pissed, but he gets the job done and wins the business. He'll get support when he gets back and I wanted them to know it wasn't the devil of all hangovers and a last-minute excuse when he doesn't show up on Monday morning.'

'God yeah.' Angus was impressed at Max's thoughtfulness and forward thinking. Remembering that Max really was a good bloke deep down made this all the harder. 'Mate, look. I've got something I need to say.'

'Yeah?' Max raised his eyebrows.

'It's about Jenna.' Angus wanted to let Max fill in the gaps, using that analytical brain of his for all it was worth, but he pressed on. 'I'm worried that this thing that's kicked off between you. Well, it might not be the best thing for her. I mean . . .' and he stopped again, mid speech, trying to find the best words to say, in the nicest possible way, that his friend was a dick when it came to women.

'What do you mean, mate?'

'Well, you know how you can be with girls. You have a fling and they fall in love with you, God knows why.' Angus nudged him, raising a smile from Max. 'And then you get bored and dump them. And this is Jenna we're talking about.' He almost added 'my Jenna' but stopped himself, not wanting this to sound like a jealous rant, just a friendly warning.

Max took a long sip of his beer and sat back in the sofa, turning at more of an angle to face Angus. 'But that's the beauty of it, mate. Jenna understands exactly how it is. She knows my MO. She knows this is just a bit of fun. I mean, she should do — she's seen me do it countless times and the poor girl might not earn much, but she isn't stupid.'

'That's just it. I think she does think that you mean to carry this on, at home, you know as a couple. A "this is it", sort of thing.'

'What? Mate, you're talking out of your arse. Why on earth would she think that?' Max looked genuinely shocked.

Angus shrugged his big shoulders and mirrored Max's nonchalance by sitting back in the sofa and resting his feet on the coffee table. Although 'relaxed' was far from how he felt inside.

'It's just something she said. And I mean the way you've been acting — y'know, a bit *couply* and all that. Holding hands over lunch? I know it's how you are with all of them, but I'm guessing Jenna is a bit of a hopeless romantic and I think she might have fallen for you.'

'Well, love her as I do, and I mean as a friend, she's being an idiot! Can't she see I've got Bertie on one hand, literally, I mean that girl can . . . well, you know, and,' Max lowered his voice into a conspiratorial whisper, 'you know I've had Izzy too. Now *she* was hot.'

'Yeah, I noticed I had our room to myself a bit, and Jenna in it too.'

'Yeah, and Jenna's different, you see. She's not my usual type, but you've got to admit, now she's lost the puppy fat she's quite fine. Not like super-hot, but definitely shaggable, plus, as she knows the ropes, it's perfect, no awkwardness.'

Angus put his beer bottle down, taking an inordinate amount of care to put it centrally on one of the brown leather coasters, before resting his elbows on his knees and rubbing his face with his hands. He tried desperately to find the words to express how he felt without looking like a total idiot.

'I don't think she's like that, though, Max. Shagging around, etc. She doesn't strike me as a player. And I think she's always been beautiful. Ever since I met her, before I went away—'

'Whoa, whoa. Hang on a minute. Do I detect the Great Unattainable Angus falling for someone?'

Christ, thought Angus. 'Look, mate, if I honestly thought you two were going to get together and all that, I'd wish you well as I'm sure she's not interested in me. But I can't see her get hurt. Especially not by my best mate.'

'Fuck. Gus, look, I'm sorry. I had no idea. I mean, I think you could have said something earlier.' Max looked Angus in the eye. 'But fine, I'll call it off and with any luck she'll fall into your massive gangly arms and all will be well.'

'I don't think it'll be that easy, but thanks, mate.'

Max paused. 'You really care about her, don't you?'

'And you don't? She's been one of your best friends for years.'

'Of course I do. I love her to bits. She's a hoot. Pure comedy value. But I'd never go out with her. God, could you imagine the chaos you'd live in?'

Whether he was trying to lighten the mood with jest, or rub in how far from his idyll she was, Angus had taken enough.

'Yeah, well I'd like to give that chaos a try one day.'

'Fair enough, mate. Hands off and all that.' Max raised his palms skyward to illustrate he knew exactly what Angus wanted. 'Frees me up for more Bertie-banging, which is fine by me. She was on my case earlier about us giving it a proper go again. And do you know what? I might just try it with her. She's the whole package, you know?'

Angus took a sip of his beer and nodded, but his mind was as far from Bertie and her package as could be imagined.

Bertie, banged or not, had caught most of the conversation as she teetered on the top step of the stairs. At first galled by the whole thing, she had listened in growing fascination to what Max had said. Fine, he'd had a thing with Izzy. She knew that. But thank God the thing with Jenna was as frivolous as she had hoped. Never a long-term thing. And although she felt a twinge of guilt for poor Jenna, who was about to face the chop, she felt more of a twinge elsewhere, as she silently stepped back into the corridor and towards her room to rethink her outfit, suddenly remembering a rather fetching lacy top she'd brought that would go oh-so-well with her skinny jeans and death-defying heels.

Jenna, on the other hand, was bent over holding the hair-dryer, desperately brushing out knots as she tried to inject what the magazines would call 'body' into her hair. Frizz was the usual outcome of such an experiment, but just for once she'd like it if something even vaguely close to Elle McPherson's mane framed her face when she righted herself. And if that little bit of very expensive-looking serum she'd found in Bertie's washbag helped, then she was sure the love gods would look kindly on her, and put in a good word with the less forgiving gods of theft and retribution. Bertie had, after all, left it out right next to Jenna. Just a little bit hidden, perhaps, but really only one zip away from being right next to Jenna. One zip and maybe a vanity case clasp or two. And a piece of Velcro. And the trunk lid. But otherwise, totally in front of her.

Jenna flipped her head back and looked in surprise as her hair was indeed a damn sight glossier than usual. Definitely less frizzy. Damn, she thought. Bertie will never believe I mastered this on my own. Brazen, be brazen. Pep talking herself thus, she jumped slightly when Bertie re-entered the room.

'Oh, thought you were ready and down there?' stammered Jenna, running a guilty hand through her tamed locks and thinking that having taken over an hour in the bathroom earlier and at least forty-five minutes deciding what to wear afterwards, Bertie should damn well be ready.

'Oh, I remembered a top I just love and thought since we might be out on the town later, I'd like to give it a go. I might have exhausted the town of its one and only billionaire but you never know who else you might meet.' Bertie winked at Jenna in an amazingly friendly manner, which left Jenna slightly open-mouthed and seeking divine inspiration. 'Oh, and your hair looks nice tonight, did you finally work out how to tame it? Clever you.'

Speechless, by the sheer pleasantness of Bertie's comments, and by the fact that surely she had been rumbled, it was all Jenna could do to squeeze out a thank you, before having to turn round as Bertie stripped bare in front of her, tits out for all to see – or at least for Jenna to see, if she'd still been looking. Jenna was instead contemplating the snowflakes through the window, falling faster every minute it seemed.

'Dashing down now, sweetie, mwah.' Bertie air-kissed the fragrant Chanel cloud behind her, vaguely in Jenna's direction, and even held the door open for Sally, freshly bathed and clad in towels, who'd come in to see what all the chat was about.

'Blimey, she's in a good mood.' Sally breathed in the Nº5 and shook her head in wonder at it all. 'You look lovely though, darling, impressing someone?'

'Hope to.' Although Jenna felt sure her considerably less skinny legs and lack of lace might leave something to be desired in Max's mind. Her own skinny jeans were tucked into black suede boots — flats, of course, had Bertie seen the snow and ice out there? And a soft silky camisole floated over her ample bosom, covered modestly with her one good cashmere cardigan. 'I know it's not high fashion,' said Jenna pulling at a sleeve as she adjusted the cardie around her shoulders, 'but it'll have to do. And hopefully Max will appreciate the, er, vintage quality.'

'Is that your gran's cardigan again, Jenna?' Sally looked sternly at her friend. 'Isn't it about time you spent just a little bit of money on clothes, sweetie?'

'If I had, Little Miss Bond Street, then I couldn't afford to be here now!' Jenna picked up her phone from the bed and gave her hair a last flick before heading towards her friend and the doorway. 'Now, go get dressed and I'll see you down there in a sec.'

46

Supper had been laid out on the long, refectory-style table by Izzy, possibly by now the moodiest chalet girl in the whole of the Alps. She couldn't work out which of the other girls Max was supposedly getting together with, she just knew that after the fondue night she'd seen neither hide nor hair of him. He'd sent a few lame texts in reply to her answerphone messages, so to her mind that was it. Finito. The final straw had come when Ginny had called earlier to say that she'd spotted Max and 'some It girl' going into La Parisienne.

'I mean, Iz, it's not just the sort of place you go for lols. It's top end. Like pulling serious strings top end.' Ginny's words had unwittingly crushed any of Izzy's hopes of snaring him long-term. Still, better know now and if, accidentally, a bogey ended up in his bowl of soup tonight, then who could blame her?

Angus, however, was in a much better mood as he generously filled the glasses on the table and called everyone over. Bertie sashayed through, having languorously removed herself from the sofa. She posted herself at the head of the table, and demurely patted one of the seats next to her when Max sauntered in from the sitting room. Angus shook his head in disbelief, knowing exactly what Bertie was up to, and noticed Bertie's slight annoyance when Jenna, instead of sitting on the other side of Max, came around the table and plonked herself opposite him. Angus, not usually one for playing this type of game, took the opportunity to sit next to Jenna, and Sally scurried through, carrying a magazine with her, to sit down next to Max. Izzy brought out steaming bowls of carrot and coriander soup (clever Mummy had read out the New Covent Garden Soup Company's version's ingredients over the phone, and once Izzy had worked out what coriander was in French, she was up and running) and everyone tucked in, except for Sally who was waving the magazine she'd brought through in everyone's direction.

'Did you see this article? Did you?' Angus and Max stared blankly at her, shaking their heads. Jenna had a mouth full of soup so could only raise her eyebrows in interest, while Bertie had taken only the slightest sip from her spoon, and so came to be the first to answer Sally's open question.

'No, Sal, what can be so stimulating,' she eyed Max, 'that you feel the need to furnish us with its contents over supper?'

'Well, that's just it.' Sally hastily sipped a spoonful of soup before finding the relevant passage that had caught her eye and, after she'd swallowed, began to read.

'"It's snow joke that the fresh mountain air can make for fresh behaviour", writes our correspondent in the Alps, Jessica Turner." Shall I continue?'

Sally waited for at least two approving nods before just going ahead anyway. '"The snow might be white, but consciences aren't, as a cold, calculating blast from the East brings more chills than any Alpine winter."' Sally looked up to check that she still had everyone's attention. Noticing the general lack of chatter and gentle slurping, she carried on. '"Never before have so many resorts seen the influx of Russians. It's not just Courcheval 1850 now, other more typically British strongholds are starting to feel the Siberian chills, such as Val Thorens and Val d'Argent."'

Sally paused again and looked up to find Bertie staring at her, almost accusingly. Max gently laid a hand on her knee, which Jenna saw. Only Angus noticed her flinch. He asked Sally to carry on, hoping it would save Jenna from seeing any more of Max's over-friendly 'friendly' support.

'"The resorts that once boasted nothing more sinister than the odd drunken rugby club and Hooray Henry on the piste, are now suffering from the effects of post-communism partying. Our insider tells of chalet girls reduced to cleaning out hot tubs full of condoms and cigarette ends as rich Russians party into the small hours with prostitutes brought up from the nearest towns, while hired chefs and butlers take away the normal chalet-girl duties."' Sally stopped, thinking to herself for a moment, before saying, 'Don't you see what this means? Poor Hugo, he's one of those darling old Hooray Henrys that Val d'Argent obviously misses so much. He was just a victim.'

'He's a pretty serious victim, honey,' said Jenna, remembering in time the handshake that had ended her and Bertie's previous conversation on this matter. 'But I'm sure not all Russians are like that, are they, Bertie?'

'Well, I think it's pretty rotten you both bringing this up again. You know I had no idea what would happen at that party and—'

'No, Bertie, you don't understand,' Sally interrupted her mid-speech. 'That's just the point. It's them, the pesky Russkies and their partying ways. How were you to know about this sort of thing? It's evident that Hugo was a mere pawn, a . . .' she waved her spoon around, luckily drained of soup, as she thought of the word, '. . . a nonentity, just the wrong man at the wrong time, and he's not to blame for these crazy Russians and their crazy behaviour!'

With a victorious nosedive back into the soup, Sally's spoon came to rest and she beamed at the others. Bertie looked skyward, but seemed to take Sally's last few sentences to heart and sighed, lowering her eyes.

After the soup came a delicious main course of chicken pot pie ('do avoid the pastry, ladies — goes straight to the thighs!') and then a decadent pudding of rich chocolate mousse and lots of fresh strawberries and raspberries. Izzy may have built up a grudge against almost every guest in the chalet, but you had to hand it to her, she was still a professional. Jenna got up, having left some of her chocolate mousse for Miss Manners, as her mother had always taught her — and also because, compared to Bertie, it had looked like she'd wolfed down the European surplus food mountain and would be brought up in front of a Brussels tribunal, ready to repay the subsidies for the poor French farmers. She squeezed past Bertie's chair, breathing in the perfume that she wore, and wondered how she, herself, could ever carry off such a presence. Lingering behind Max's chair, she put her hands on his shoulders, and was only slightly put off when he didn't raise his own up to touch hers. Undeterred, she leaned down and popped a little kiss on his cheek.

'What's that for, Jenksy?'

'Just saying hello.'

'Ah. Great.' Max seemed awkward and Jenna assumed it was because Bertie was staring right him — those gimlet eyes were enough to put anyone off their stride.

'I'm going to put some lippy on and then I'll be ready for a few lady beers. You both are coming out tonight, aren't you?'

'I don't know, Jenks, it's been a pretty full-on few days. We thought we might chill tonight.'

'We?'

'Yeah, Bertie and I were just saying earlier that we were pooped. Do you mind if we stay? You go for it though, Jenksy,' Max smiled at her, in the same old way he always did, and always had. *And always will*, sighed Jenna.

'We,' Bertie emphasised the *we* a little too much for Jenna's liking, 'had such a great session on the mountain today, it was just so . . . I can't think of the word . . .'

'Knackering?' chipped in Jenna. Bertie laughed and sat back in her dining chair, exposing her décolletage and running her fingers through her perfectly bouffed hair. Jenna could feel Max's head turn to look at her, mostly because, like a big fat limpet, Jenna was still rigidly holding on to his shoulders. She only slackened her grip as he almost shrugged her off; even Jenna could detect something that unsubtle.

'We saw some fun guys on the piste earlier.' Max directed his comment at Jenna, who by now had sunk into Sally's vacated chair next to him, aware that for some reason Max's ardour had vanished, and yet, like a teenager in the full throes of a celebrity crush, she couldn't bring herself to take her eyes off him. 'Vets, we reckoned, huh, Bertie?'

'Ya, like because the girls that were there were wearing these hoodies with dogs on them and it said something about "bitches on heat" and this one guy, they called him "Sick Puppy", which is just odd if you ask me.'

'Oh, right.' Jenna was slightly perplexed, not so much at the news itself, but why Max and Bertie were almost encouraging her to go. A vet would be a catch to most girls, but not to Bertie and, as far as she still knew, Max was taken — by her.

The penny dropped. 'Thought you and Sal might like to do a bit of hunting.' Max sounded like his old self, the old self who was just her friend. Who'd always laughed at her attempts to find a man and had egged her on and been there as a nice, almost too nice, hug when the latest soldier, doctor, banker, heck, even window washer, had turned into nothing.

'Well, Sally won't be interested,' Jenna mumbled before Sally's voice preceded her into the room.

'Interested in what?' Sally looked quizzically at the three.

Bertie piped up, 'There are some dishy vets out tonight and Maxie and I thought you two might like some, um, eye candy. I overheard a couple in the gondola; they're on a conference and have some free ski time each day when they're not, like, discussing cats and stuff.'

'Oh, well, sounds thrilling, doesn't it, Jenna?' Sally might be like a social steamroller at times, but she picked up Bertie's meaning only too clearly. 'Shame I've got to go back to the hospital, though.' She glared at Max, and softened it only when Jenna raised her head, and hand, reaching out to hold Sally's as she got up off the chair. Rousing herself from her thoughts, and self-recriminations, she ushered Sally out of the dining room in front of her, before the hot spikes of tears could find their way out of the corners of her eyes.

47

Jenna followed Sally up to her room, and once the door was closed, she let the first sob rack through her body as she crumpled into her friend's hug.

'Now forget Mr Idiot-pants down there, you're better off out of that.'

'Oh, but Sal, it's so, it's so . . .'

'Embarrassing? Yes I know, sweetie. What you always feared — awkwardness, embarrassment, rejection . . .'

'You're not helping!' Jenna took a massive snort in as a stream of snot threatened to fall off her chin.

'Let me finish. Jenna, look at me.' Sally held her friend at arm's length as she looked her in the eye. 'The world is still turning. These people, here in this chalet, are still your friends. Well, maybe not Bertie, but anyway, Max will always love you as you have done nothing wrong in his eyes. In fact, he'll probably cherish the memory of having a lovely bounce on top of you . . .'

'Oh, stop it, Sal,' Jenna tried not to laugh as she hiccoughed back another stream of snot. Then, slightly more considered, 'Thank God I never told him I loved him.'

'There you go, silver lining — he comes out of this looking like the one with the decade-long crush. He did all the running — smooth bastard that we know and love.'

'S'pose so.' Jenna hiccoughed again but the tears had started to dry up. 'It's just that, finally, finally I thought I'd got my man.' The tears were back with a vengeance. 'I should have known he was too good-looking for me . . .'

'Now look here. I'm your best friend, so I think you're hot enough to pull Prince Harry if you want to.'

'But I wasn't pretty enough for Max.'

'Rubbish. What did you expect, hooking up with Max Finch, ladykiller extraordinaire? He was always going to be onto the next one as soon as your back was turned.'

'But he said he loved me!'

'Did he? Really? And of course he loves you — as a *friend*.'

'Well, maybe not in those actual words, but he said he always thought we'd end up together.'

'Not quite the same thing, is it? Look — dry your eyes, pop on a coat, and let's go and see Hugo. I could do with a friend with me and your terrible, monstrous, hideous love life is just about the level of distraction I need to stop bursting into tears myself at the state of poor Hugo.' At that Sally gave her friend another massive hug and ushered her into the en suite so she could splash her face.

Angus didn't quite know what to do with himself. Having left the table just after pudding to check if his skis needing waxing downstairs, he'd come back up to what seemed like a partially deserted chalet. Max and Bertie had taken over the massive L-shaped sofa and were discussing which film they might download from the home cinema system. Feeling like a third wheel to their love bicycle, he pottered into the kitchen to see if Izzy needed any help, back-tracking almost as soon as he saw her wielding yet another knife, this time chopping dates for tomorrow's afternoon tea cake. He mooched back into the sitting room.

'Did you see where Sal and Jenna went?' he asked Max, studying his friend's face for any sign of guilt, remorse or responsibility for so quickly replacing the object of his affections.

'I think they went upstairs, you know, *girl talk*.' Max widened his eyes as if he'd said 'human sacrifice' instead. Bertie was studiously ignoring Angus altogether.

Angus climbed the stairs and pondered knocking on Sally's door. He raised his arm, then thought that the last thing Jenna needed was another bloke, telling her how to feel or asking anything of her. He lowered his hand, and instead crossed the landing to his and Max's room. Fetching his ski jacket from behind the door he pulled it on and went back downstairs. To their credit, Max and Bertie hadn't formed a human shagfest yet; in fact Bertie was once again idly flicking through emails or texts on her iPhone as Max surfed the channels trying to find something to watch.

'I'm off to see Hugo,' Angus said roughly in their direction, as he opened the door to the boot room. He disappeared off down the stairs and seconds later Sally and Jenna emerged from her room, as fresh-faced as it was possible to be. Coats on and zipped up, they too descended the stairs into the sitting room. Max and Bertie were still flicking through their respective devices, although Max did have the courtesy this time to get up when the girls walked past and see them to the door.

'Off to see Hugo?' he said as he held the boot room door open for them.

'I'll make sure to tell him *all* about your latest escapades,' said Sally, as she gave him what only could be described as a Paddington Hard Stare, and ushered a quiet and cast-down Jenna through the door and down the stairs in front of her.

48

Angus reached the clinic in pretty quick time. Without a tipsy Sally or Jenna on his arm it was actually remarkably easy to walk along the warmed pavements without slip-ups or icy skids. He punched the late-night entry code into the key pad by the sliding doors and was greeted by a wall of warm air as he stepped inside. The night receptionist looked up and furrowed her brow, but said nothing as Angus confidently strode towards the private wing of the hospital where he knew Hugo was recovering. He found the door to Hugo's room and flexed his fingers a couple of times before balling up his fist and knocking on the door. He hadn't noticed that it wasn't properly on its catch, and it swung open under the slight force of this knock.

'Angus!'

He looked through the low-lit gloom to see not just Hugo, lying in bed, softly snoring, but a stunning redhead sitting next to him, the book she'd been reading now lowered as she got up from the chair by Hugo's bedside.

'Sonia,' he recognised her instantly. 'What are you doing here?'

'I thought I should come and see how he was doing. He seems so much better already since last night.'

'Last night?'

'Da, yes, I mean, I came last night too. Look, Angus, it was a terrible thing that happened to your friend, terrible. And Yuri regrets it, believe me. He knows that reputations are won and lost on gossip and hearsay, but he has a quick temper and when he thought that brat of his had been, well, compromised, he reacted — bosh — he's like that.'

'Did he send you here?' Angus was still standing in the doorway, unsure of how he felt seeing Sonia again.

'He sent me yesterday, with a chequebook.' She laughed in a derisory sort of way. 'I had to fill in all the forms and while I waited for the clinic to process things, I came in here to read. It's very peaceful you know. It's nice to . . .' Sonia paused. Angus took a step further into the room, closed the door behind him and could feel that Sonia wanted to offload something.

'Go on,' he encouraged.

'Well, you know what it's like.' She used her now closed book as an extension of her hand as she pointed towards his scar. 'You hang around with violent people and you get hurt. Sometimes it's nice to just sit down for a bit, dress conservatively,' she gestured towards her modest jeans and jumper combo, 'and be alone.'

'Sonia,' Angus was worried about her now, 'does Yuri . . . hurt you?'

'Ah, you know,' she got up from the chair and posted the slim volume into her handbag, 'it's not so bad. I have a plane to catch in the morning, we're leaving early, back to Moscow.' She took her coat off the back of the chair and slipped it on over her plain jumper, releasing the long auburn locks of her hair from under the collar as she did it up. 'It was very, very nice to meet you, Angus,' she said as she crossed the few steps of the floor towards him. 'If you are ever in Russia and need anything. Anything at all.' She looked up at him and gently bit her lip before carrying on. 'And I'm sorry again about your friend. Please forgive us. We're not all bad, really.' At that she raised herself up on tiptoes and kissed him, reaching up to caress his scarred cheek as she did so.

Jenna opened the door to Hugo's room, having accepted Sally's offer to get her a hot chocolate from the machine down the hallway.

264

'Oh!' her eyes adjusted to the low light in the room and she stopped still as she saw Angus, with his back to her, kissing . . . who was that? She squinted in the darkness as her eyes adjusted to it. 'Oh . . .' Jenna didn't quite know how to feel. Sally had just been telling her, as they'd been walking arm in arm from the chalet to the hospital, how she thought Angus would really be a much better bet for Jenna to set her hat at: his steadfastness of character, his integrity. 'He's really quite funny, too, darling, not to mention the family pot, and, of course, his A-grade brain.'

'Jenna!' Angus turned at the sound of her first exclamation. By Jenna's second 'oh' he had extricated himself from Sonia's embrace and was standing awkwardly, staring at Jenna just as Sally popped her head round the door.

'What's going on?' It wasn't Sally that asked the question, but a groggy Hugo. Sally bustled over to his bed, giving a hot chocolate to Jenna and an accusatory stare to Angus and Sonia.

'I should go,' Sonia whispered to herself and to the room in general. Hearing the Russian accent, Sally looked up from stroking Hugo's bandaged and bruised head, and opened her mouth, about to launch into a tirade.

'Sally,' Angus interjected, 'Jenna . . . Hugo? Anyway, guys, it's not what you think. This is Sonia. Yes, she's a friend of Yuri's, but she's OK.'

'And she's leaving,' the redhead muttered as she slung her handbag over her shoulder and tangoed with Jenna to get out of the door.

'But she's . . . she's . . . responsible!' gasped Sally, waving one hand in the direction of the parting auburn beauty, the other one still clasping Hugo's hospital gown. Angus, who had instinctively taken a few steps towards Jenna, a thousand thoughts going through his mind as to what it must have looked like to her when she walked in on them, now turned to Sally. He had a sudden pity for

Sonia and her lot in life. Clearing up the mess that Yuri left in his wake, a diplomatic mission almost everywhere they went, no doubt.

'Yes, she's responsible,' he said, quietly, so as not to rouse the nurses from the nearest desk, who by now must be wondering why so many visitors were here after hours. 'She's responsible for paying for all of Hugo's treatment. She's responsible for sitting by Hugo's bedside while we were all out last night . . .'

He'd gone too far, and as Jenna saw Sally struggle to put into words how under the belt that was, she countered, 'And she's responsible for giving you one hell of a hand job too, isn't she, Angus?' At that she turned and left through the now open door to Hugo's room, not quite sure where she was going to go, but just wanting to be away from him, from men in general, from memories of that hot tub.

Angus mouthed a massive 'I'm sorry' to Sally, who was for once rather lost for words, though no doubt starting to question her views on Angus's 'integrity' and general niceness. He dashed out of the room and caught sight of Jenna as she turned the corner at the end of the corridor. Catching up with her in a waiting area filled with low-slung, upholstered blue chairs and pale wooden coffee tables liberally scattered with magazines, he realised she'd found a dead end.

'Jenna,' he started, 'I'm sorry, I didn't mean to make Sally feel bad, it just came out.'

'Like your cock did in that hot tub, I assume?'

Angus was taken aback. Why was Jenna bringing that up now? 'Sonia's not really like that. In fact, we didn't really talk about that at all just now.'

'Too busy kissing her?' Jenna looked around her, saw that the only way out of the waiting room was past Angus and sighed, plumping herself down on one of the chairs.

Angus came closer to her and sat down opposite, his hands resting on his knees as he tried to explain further.

'I didn't kiss her. I mean, she kissed me.'

'That's what they all say.'

'Jenna,' Angus looked closely at her and saw that her eyes were already red, although not from the small tear that was now just appearing in the corner of her eye. 'What's wrong?'

Jenna sighed. She closed her eyes for what seemed like an age and Angus was about to lean over and nudge her when she opened them and said, 'It's Max. You were right. He was no good for me. He's with Bertie now.'

Angus was lost for words. Yes, he'd seen them flirt a bit over supper, but he'd actually gone through with it and dumped her? 'Oh Jenna, I'm sorry.'

'No, you're not,' her words struck him. *Did she know how he felt?* 'You're just waiting to say: "I told you so", aren't you?'

'No, Jenna, I just want you to be happy.'

'Do you?' She looked up at him, and a picture of a sadder girl he had never seen. The temptation to kiss her now was monumental, but he knew he couldn't take advantage like that, plus she was probably still yearning for Max's lousy touch, not his. Angus couldn't help it though, he pushed himself off his seat and knelt down in front of her. Taking her into his arms, he held her as she let the tears of hurt and frustration come.

Thursday

49

Morning broke and once again Jenna found herself waking up in a room that wasn't hers. Mustn't make this too much of a habit, she thought to herself, though lord knows my love life couldn't get any more tragic. Stretching her arm out she soon realised that she was in a much larger bed than her normal single and the sleeping body next to her was definitely not taut, toned and masculine, but instead pyjama-clad, soft and fluffy of hair.

'Gerroff,' Sally muttered as Jenna accidentally hit her in the face with her exploratory hand.

'Sorry, Sals,' she whispered and quietly got out of the bed, remembering now that after the evening at the hospital she'd decided it was better not to play bedroom roulette and be faced with either seeing Max in her room, but with Bertie, or two empty beds, meaning they were in his room. Instead, she'd climbed into bed with her best friend and left Angus to fend for himself. Angus, though . . . he'd been so sweet last night. Well, apart from insulting Sally. And obviously having it off with that bloody Russian by his desperately ill friend's bedside. But after that, and after he had properly apologised to Sally (who was upset once more as Hugo had been sedated again only a few minutes after waking up), he'd walked them both home and Sal's words from earlier were ringing true. He had made them laugh on the way back to the chalet, had told them stories about his work and how Singapore had changed in the years he'd been there, how London had changed too, but how happy he was to be back, and how he hoped to be seeing a lot more of them, of her, now he was in the country full-time.

'My family have got a little place by the sea in Cornwall,' he'd said as he held the door open for them into the boot room. 'I'd love to show you it, Jenna, and Sal, you'd love the view and the walks, and there's a gin distillery only about ten minutes away . . .'

'We'd love to come, wouldn't we, JJ?' Sally had winked in the most exaggerated way possible at her and Jenna had felt, really felt, that yes, perhaps spending some more time with this rather nice man might not be a bad idea at all.

Jenna hopped across the corridor and opened the door to her room, safe in the knowledge that Bertie was at least up, if not dressed, as the sound of the supersonic subwoofer of a hair dryer was going off. As she opened the door, Bertie switched it off.

'Another morning, another hangover, eh? You know what I always say about drinking?'

Jenna for once could take the high ground.

'No, actually. Sober as a judge. And, actually, as judge-mental as a judge too. Where did you sleep last night?' She wanted Bertie to say it, to admit that she'd been sleeping with Max.

'Here, silly. Honestly, you really are taking this whole Max thing a bit too seriously.'

'Well, excuse me, Miss Frivolous, but Max did say he thought we should always be together. I mean,' Jenna took stock of her drunken memories from that night again, 'that it's surprising that we hadn't got together. Anyway, of course I took it seriously.'

'Whatevs.'

'No, not "whatevs", you . . .' she stopped short. 'I just can't believe he'd lead me on so much. He's my friend. He's meant to be my friend!'

'Calm down, for God's sake,' Bertie snapped. 'And who knows what Max's intentions were really. None of us know what men think. But I know Angus told him to cool it with you.'

'He what? Angus did what?' Jenna was furious. She stared at the smirking Bertie as she crossed the room to the en suite and, once inside, slammed the door before Bertie could tell her any more soul-destroying truths and slumped down on the loo seat, hanging her head in her hands, her throat aching with the tears that quickly followed, wondering if she'd ever survive this godawful trip with her dignity intact and a scrap of self-esteem left.

50

'Jenna! Jenna!' Sally ran out of her room, hair all over the place and a towel loosely clutched over her. 'Hugo's properly awake!' Sally pounded on Jenna's door, bursting in just as Bertie was leaving. The look on the latter's face was one of shock and slight disgust at the barely attired woman flinging herself through the door, but also relief, as whatever she felt about Hugo and Sally, she had never wished that sort of pain on the poor chap.

'Oh Sally, that's great!' Jenna was almost dressed now, having washed her face umpteen times to try and undo the damage caused by hysterical crying. 'I'll come back to the clinic with you.' Jenna was as happy to support her friend as she was to have some distraction from her own traumas. 'Just let me get dressed.'

'Yes, dressing. Gosh.' Sally seemed scatty and confused. 'Right. Yes, I'll get dressed and we'll go there and he'll be fine. Oh Jenna, I'm so bloody relieved. Bloody. Relieved.'

'I know, sweetie, I know. Me too. Now come on, let's eat on the way and we'll be there in ten.' And five minutes later the two girls were zipping up their jackets and hot-footing it through the cold wind to the hospital. Angus had been at the breakfast table as they left. He had nodded at them both and Jenna had scowled back at him, but only for a moment, as it was hard not to stay jolly with Sally in such an infectiously good mood.

It might have only been a few hours since Sally had last left his bedside, but the way she now flung her arms around Hugo made it look as if she was greeting him again after years apart. Hugo, blinking in surprise, tried his best to move his weak and punctured arms up to hold her to him. The feeding tube and drip had been taken away and the wounds to his face had healed faster than Sally could have hoped. He was still the colour of chopped liver in places and certainly looked like he'd come off the worse in the fight, but he was awake, on the mend, and back in his darling Sally's arms.

Jenna backed off to let Sally smother him in peace. Too many high-pitched screams might have sent him right back under, as even a strong man, blessed with all his working faculties, can barely cope with a room of screeching women. She headed down the corridor to the vending machine and scrabbled around in her pocket for loose euros to get herself a coffee. Thankful at last for her morning's caffeine fix, she slumped down on a soft waiting-room chair and took quick little sips until the steaming coffee cooled enough for her to slurp it down properly. The waiting room smelled faintly of disinfectant and feet, but the chair was comfortable and Jenna was grateful for it. With an eye on the door of Hugo's room, and an ear that was still being accosted with Sally's excited ramblings and chatter from within, she leaned her head back against the whitewashed wall behind the chair and finally had time to try and work out what had happened this week. Why had Angus been so intent on splitting her and Max up? Not that Max had needed much persuading, she presumed, if he was going to go off with someone else anyway. It just didn't make sense. I mean, she thought, he could just have been being very protective. Annoyingly protective. But why bother? It would all make sense if Angus fancied her. But didn't; last night, with that Russian again, proves that he doesn't want me like that, Jenna thought as she gulped down the coffee in order to stop the bulky feeling in her throat lead to that fizzing of the nose that would mean tears again. Why was thinking of Angus in that way making her well up? Jenna let out a long, slow breath and tipped her head back. Wasn't it just last night, in this very same waiting area, that he'd wrapped her up in his arms? As upset and confused as she'd been, she couldn't help but relive that moment over and over again in her head.

She continued her musings as she finished the coffee and decided that action, rather than tears, was needed. She pulled herself up, found a bin for the cardboard cup and wandered back into Hugo's room, tentatively knocking on the door just in case his recovery had been so rapid that Sally had decided to take her almost-matrimonial rights to another level. There was no need, however, as she went in to find Sally staring at Hugo and crying a little bit as he held her hand and told her over and again that he was OK, and all would be well.

'Sorry to interrupt . . .' Jenna edged towards the bed, putting a hand on Sally's shoulder as she leaned in to give Hugo a squeeze. 'So good to have you back with us, Hugs.'

'Bloody nice to be back, I can tell you.' Hugo sounded almost his old self, but for the odd wince.

'You gave us quite a fright. Poor Sally here has been beside herself.'

'Not terribly clever of me, was it, I mean letting that funny little Russian kid jump on me like that? Thing is, Sals,' and at this he gingerly turned his stiff neck so he could face Sally better, 'they never gave me the chance to explain.' He coughed a few times, the effort of speaking making his dry throat rasp. Sally reached up instinctively for the water jug and poured him a tiny mouthful into a paper cup.

'Here, drink this, slowly.' She continued to nurse him until he gently pushed the cup away. 'You know I would never cheat on you Sal. She really did launch herself at me.'

'I know, Hugsie, I know. Bertie told us all about it. Yuri apologised, apparently, plus he's covering all the bills here.' Sally was stroking his hand as Hugo, reacting slightly to the mention of the Russian's name, laid his head back down on the pillow.

'Too right he should cover the bills. I don't really remember anything, but it was his blokes, wasn't it? That did this?' Sally nodded. 'I wondered, you see,' Hugo continued, 'as to whether it might be Bertie getting her revenge after all these years.'

Sally looked startled at her darling fiancé's suggestion.

'What on earth do you mean, Hugo?' Jenna said, pulling up a chair on the opposite side of the bed to Sally.

'Revenge. Sally, how long have we been together? Eight, nine years?'

'Almost ten.'

'Yes, almost ten. It must be. Met you back at that Suffolk Hunt ball mid Lent term in the first year. But you know the table I was meant to be on that night had so many empty spaces that they just plumped the four of us that turned up on all the other tables.'

'Yes, I never thought why. It's how we met, you were squeezed in between me and Lucie Ayres-Cobb.'

'God, yeah, she was wild that night.' Hugo closed his eyes and smiled to himself.

Jenna, frustrated at the time it was taking to reach the essential info, nudged Hugo.

'Ouch, watch it Jenks, sore ribs and all. Anyway, yes, that's when we really got to know each other, Sal, but the reason there were so few of us was that most of the hunt had got an awful flu, too many falls on the Boxing Day outing, we thought. But anyway, I was going out with one of the unlucky fluers, and that was Bertie.'

Sally gasped whereas Jenna just opened and closed her mouth a few times, unable quite to process the information.

'You. Went out. Slept with? Bertie?' Sally could hardly get the final word out, the name of the girl who had been so cruel to her under the guise of friendship for so many years. 'No wonder she hates me! Oh Hugo, if you weren't so bloody damaged I'd throw this catheter bag at you! Why on earth didn't you tell me?'

'Well, I thought I had. But I suppose I didn't really think about it. We called her Robbie back then. Sorry, Sal.' Hugo could see that he couldn't really explain away this one with his usual bluffing and bravado. Sally was taking it all on board and mentally adding up all the pieces of the story, nodding to herself as she recalled 'the exes' chat with Hugo all those years ago.

Jenna chipped in, to complete the story. 'So you went home, after that ball I mean, and dumped Bertie? And you thought she'd organised this,' Jenna waved her hand over Hugo's broken body, 'as a means to get back at you? Ten years later!'

'Well, it crossed my mind, but only because I had no other idea how I'd come to be like this, not knowing about the wrath of the oligarch and all that,' Hugo justified himself.

'Robbie. Of course. I feel like such an idiot.' Sally was now staring out of the window.

'Come on, Sal, it's not that bad,' Jenna urged her friend to engage in eye contact again. 'It was years ago, I'm sure Bertie can't really hold it against you. And she doesn't hate you. She's just, you know, bitchy in general. She loved telling me this morning that I was taking this Max thing "far too seriously".'

'Oh,' Sally made a mental note to go back to that conversation when she'd quite finished raking over her own past. 'But that year we got together, Hugs, that was the year I bested her at the horse trials. I got the final place in the county team and it meant she never got a shot at Team

GB, even though she was much better than the others and possibly, I hate to say it, probably better than me.'

'You mean me dumping her, and you beating her in one year? Well, I mean, yes it would have been a shitter for her, but why would she still hang out with us if she hated us, except so she could plan this devious revenge?' Hugo's eyes twinkled at his own joke as he in turn waved a hand over his immobile body.

'Well,' said Jenna, 'I don't think she'd hold a grudge for that long. But I know what I now have reason to blame you two for . . .'

Sally and Hugo turned to her, horrified to think that their best friend could have a reason to dislike them, too. Jenna laughed at their inquisitive and apprehensive faces. 'I mean, it's blatantly your fault that she's turned into the rampant man-eating city chick that she is, as what with your philandering, Hugo, and Sal showing her up at the trials, well, she probably packed up her spotted handkerchief and tossed it over her shoulder and made for the big city all because of you two. And now look what she is!'

'You can't blame us for the stupidly massive trust fund she happened to inherit a year or two afterwards,' Hugo implored Jenna. 'Although just think, if I'd never met you, Sal, I'd be in the lap of luxury now, and not relying on my morphine fix every ten minutes.'

Sally stroked his head, then lightly biffed him on his still swollen nose.

'Ouch!'

'Serves you right, you big buffoon.'

'Hang on a minute!' Hugo looked towards Jenna. 'I missed that. What's all this about you and Max taking things seriously?'

'No need to sound so surprised.' Jenna felt a bit miffed. Why was it everyone had had a problem believing hunky Max would have gone for her?

'Well, I am a bit surprised. Max isn't the man for you, Jenks, anyone could tell you that. You need a much nicer bloke, someone with integrity, a nice safe pair of hands, someone like—'

'If you're going to say Angus,' Jenna interrupted him, 'then don't bother.' Jenna pushed herself into the back of the chair and crossed her arms. 'I saw him last night kissing that Russian floozy again and he practically sobbed *with* me when I burst into tears on him about the Max situ.'

'I don't know, JJ.' Hugo gave another little cough and nurse Sal was back in action. 'I may have just had a rather severe bump to the head, but it doesn't take a mind reader to see that he likes you.'

'But what about his girlfriend?' Jenna was sure that would put the kybosh on Hugo's matchmaking and end this whole awkward conversation.

'Old news. Didn't you hear? They broke up just before he came back to London. I think these model types can be a bit high-maintenance, really.'

'See, sweetie?' Sally implored. 'Just like I was trying to say last night. And apart from his little blip, I still think that a) he'd be a great match for you, and b) he's like a lost puppy the way he looks at you sometimes! Plus, now that awful beard has gone, well he's quite handsome, isn't he?'

'Careful old girl,' Hugo chipped in, '*I'll* be getting jealous next . . .'

As Sally and Hugo gently bickered with each other and she administered more healing strokes and kisses, Jenna sat back in her chair and ran everything through in her head again. As far as she could see it was all a huge mess. Maybe Angus wouldn't want her now anyway, not now she was Max's sloppy seconds. And why was she even thinking about Angus like that? It's true, he had been popping into her thoughts quite a lot, and he had been the inspiration for her own bathroom climax the other day, and, *hello*, had

Hugo just said he was single? A smile crept across her lips all too briefly before old habits brought her mind back to the subject of Max. It was him, Max, that she had always wanted, Max that she was upset about losing, *wasn't it*? Jenna roused herself from her thoughts and started to make her excuses. She had to go back and confront Angus and, if her already bruised heart was strong enough, ask him how he felt about her.

'Darling?' Sally queried as Jenna started to pull on her coat.

Hugo, for once in his life showing a modicum of emotional intelligence, piped up. 'Sally, why don't you and Jenna go and enjoy the snow? I'm fine here, and probably need "ze rest" as the Frenchies keep telling me.'

'Are you sure, darling?' Sally's eyes darted from fiancé to best friend as she tried to work out who was in the most desperate situation.

'Absolutely. Jenna,' he looked up at her, 'just go easy on her — I know you'll ply her with gin at lunch, but try and keep the self-pity to just you.' He winked at her, and she took it in the spirit it was intended, grateful to be given Sally as a support, as she knew she had to go out there and face the others with varying degrees of embarrassment.

'Darling, thank you.' Sally leaned in and kissed him.

'Don't be silly. Great snow up there, I reckon, given this sudden dump. I'd be begging for you to release me into it if it was you lying here!'

'Oh Hugo, honestly darling, if you weren't already battered half to death I really would have a good go at it myself!' But she chuckled and kissed him again and made to leave, pausing just once again to lean down and nuzzle her nose against his cheek.

Jenna gratefully held out her hand to her friend.

'Now then, darling, what will we do with you?' Sally said as the girls walked off down the corridor.

51

Bertie slunk into Max's room as soon as the coast was clear. Sally and Jenna had left for the hospital and Angus was devouring baguettes at pace down in the dining room. Quietly clicking the door closed, she crossed over to the rumpled sheets, still warm from his hot body. She stroked her manicured hand over the pillows, remembering how their faces had touched, almost kissing, breathing into each other for hours, lying there with his hand gently caressing her, running it down the length of her body, murmuring sweet nothings as he gradually moved in towards her most private area.

The shower stopped and Bertie knew he'd be dripping wet, steamy, and hot as anything. She sat down on the bed and then lay back suggestively, her little silky baby-doll riding up her thighs, leaving it all too clear that the matching French knickers were still folded up in the Louis Vuitton trunk.

She remembered how his practised fingers had made her reach orgasm in an almost embarrassingly short time. And she'd wanted more and more, until he'd filled her with himself, clutching her to him as he thrust inside her again and again.

Now she waited and fantasised about how right now he was towelling himself down, the soft fabric soaking up the beads of water from his hard abs and muscled arms. Lying back on the pillow she closed her eyes and visualised his naked body, and what she would do with it as soon as she had it within her reach again. Raking imaginary fingers through his hair she thought about how good it felt when he kissed her, softly, gently, and also passionate and hard. Her hands clenched the duvet as suddenly fantasy merged into real life and he was there, on top of her, his naked body covering hers, his mouth on her mouth, his hands framing her face as he peppered her with feather-light kisses. Putting a finger to her lips as he pulled himself back, he motioned her to stay quiet, then he gradually drifted his hand down, over her chin and along the graceful curve of her neck. He ran his hand down her collarbone and slipped it under the silky negligée she was wearing. Her heart beat faster and faster as she closed her eyes and breathed in deeply, filling his hand with her breast. He pushed aside the soft silk, letting the fine strap fall over her shoulder and reveal her pert, pink nipple. Lowering his head, he kissed it, nipped it, and licked it until Bertie couldn't help but let out a small whimper of pleasure. Far from admonishing her, Max let his hand wander to her other breast and started to pleasure her all over again, only letting himself slowly move down her body when he knew she was at the breaking point of arousal. His hands slid the delicate ivory fabric away from her toned body, pushing it up and out of his way as he continued kissing her, further and further down until his lips were caressing her almost to orgasm. Without needing to be encouraged, Bertie opened her legs. Raising her hips, her stomach knotted in anticipation of the heavenly delight she was about to receive. Oh God, yes, she thought as his tongue licked and flicked at her aroused clit, as his thumb pushed inside her.

'You're so hot,' he breathed as he kissed her again, this time letting his tongue feel its way deep inside her, tickling her and caressing her until she was begging him to be inside her, to satisfy her. He pulled her body down the bed towards him, and she wrapped her legs around him. Gripping her buttocks, he pulled her up towards him and drove himself inside her, all gentleness gone as he thrust and thrust until they were both gripping each other with force and delight. Bertie's voice caught in her throat as Max's final jackhammer-like drive made her mind explode into blissful orgasm. Her thighs quivered as they released their grip around him, and he slumped on top of her, nuzzling her neck as he breathed heavily in and out, released and relaxed.

Bertie was in heaven. This feeling was better than diving off a yacht into the crystal waters near Cannes, better than preview night at the Harrods sale, better even than the thought of marrying an oligarch. Much better, really, than the last of those thoughts, but as Bertie lay in Max's bed, wrapped in his arms, listening to his breathing, she knew she had one very important chore to do and it certainly wasn't a *From Russia with Love* moment. Bertie had to go and see Yuri again and make sure that, if not justice, something was done to him. She'd heard nothing from him since she'd left his bed the morning after the party. He'd been reticent in his apologies, but she'd seen him send a minion off to the hospital with what was, effectively, a blank cheque. At the time, she'd agreed that that had been his apology, his comeuppance, and his duty fulfilled. But as she lay there she realised that now Hugo was awake Sally would channel her relief and energy into bringing Yuri to justice. Bertie wasn't a fan of Sally's, but she needed to stop her from doing anything stupid. Sally just didn't understand these people or how they worked. What happened to Hugo was just a taster of how someone who crossed them would be treated.

Bertie stretched and nudged Max out of his post-coital slumber.

'Wake. Up. Darling,' she said, kissing his chest in between words.

'Hmm, rumphy,' Max rolled over and pushed his face harder into the pillow, ignoring Bertie.

'Oh really, Maxie, come on. Don't be a layabout. I think Angus has gone up the mountain already. You should catch him up; he shouldn't be alone up there in this weather. And I think the girls have gone.'

Max rolled over again to face her. 'Are you going?'

'Yes, obvs. But I need to run a few errands first. I seem to have run out of my hair serum and the French pharmacies are *so* much better than ours. I won't be long, though. I'll catch you up.'

'Tell you what, sugar, you pop off and find your more-super-than-Superdrug and I'll stay here.' Max saw Bertie calculating the risk of leaving him alone, naked, in the chalet with Izzy at his beck and call and added, 'I just need to catch up on some zees, and I promise, darling, I'll be ready to go as soon as you come back.'

Bertie thought for a bit. As little as the enterprise ahead of her attracted her, and as little as leaving Max, let alone leaving him alone with the little chalet temptress, inspired her, she knew she had to trot off and find Yuri.

She leant over and kissed Max, biting and sucking his lip as a naughty reminder of the pleasure, and pain, she could cause him, and then quickly got up, found her peignoir and negligee and floated off in a vision of peach silk to her own room.

52

A little while later a fully made-up and hair-floofed Bertie buzzed the intercom at the über chalet where the party had been. A shiver passed through her as she remembered the cool and unemotional farewell she'd had from Yuri when she left a couple of mornings ago.

'*Da?*' a disembodied voice crackled through the intercom. A maid, she thought, although telling if the voice was actually female or not was no easy thing. Bertie used her rusty Russian to introduce herself and demand to see Yuri. She knew there was no point pussying around with these people; they only responded to hard words and shows of strength. After a minute or two, the door was buzzed open and Bertie stepped out of the cold wind and snow and into the raised ground-floor lobby. She remembered the layout of the place well from the party. Below her was the underground car park with the sports cars and skidoos, and above her the bedrooms, living room and terrace that held the hot tub. On this floor there was a hallway and she followed it through to the main kitchen. It was pristine and perfect, already cleaned by the maids after breakfast had been served. But she wasn't prepared for it to look so hollow, so empty. Where was everyone? The voice on the intercom?

Bertie was running her hand over the smooth granite work surface of the island unit, gazing out of the bifold doors that overlooked another terrace and from there the mountains, when a noise behind her made her jump. She turned round and saw silhouetted in the doorway the beefy form of one of Yuri's personal bodyguards.

'*Da?*' he questioned.

Bertie wanted to say something about common manners being free and all that, but knew that wasn't the path to go down with this one. She raised her chin a little and looked him right in the eye as she advanced forward a few steps. In slow but authoritative tones, she again demanded to see Yuri.

'*Niet.*' Bertie almost became wistful for the '*da*' of a few moments ago. Again, as forcefully as she could, and walking right up to him, she asked to see Yuri. She realised she'd pushed it just a bit too far when the thug stuck his arm out and grabbed her around the neck, at the same time wheeling her around and forcing her up against the frame of the kitchen door. Terrified, Bertie couldn't scream, she could barely breathe as his massive hand pushed her jaw higher and higher. Pain shot through her temples as he said in Russian: 'Yuri has gone. You will never see him again and you will never speak of him again. In deference to your father he has been most generous to you and your friends and he asks for your respectful silence in return. If you decide that this magnanimous offer is not to your taste, you will find that it is not just your friends that turn up in ditches. You understand?'

'*Da* . . .' whispered Bertie, fighting for breath as she forced out the single word.

'*Da*,' he replied in confirmation, and slowly let go, releasing Bertie from her tiptoes and his iron grip.

She found the inner strength to regain her posture, shoulder the ghastly lump of a man out of her way and stalk down the lobby corridor to the front door. Buzzing her way out of the door she managed a dignified exit for about five paces into the snow until she bolted, running faster than even her personal trainer made her, back to the happy comfort of the chalet. Her mind was ablaze. If that's how she felt after a bit of mild intimidation, then what Hugo must have gone through? She couldn't bear it. For the first time in years Bertie felt like she might cry. Most situations could be flirted, schemed, paid, or whined out of, but this one had caught her out. All the old feelings of friendship and camaraderie that she'd had at university with Jenna and the boys returned. How could she have let their friendships get so battered? As battered as poor old Hugo, her first love. And Sally. Sally never knew she'd nicked her man. She'd been a bitch to her ever since, and Bertie suddenly hated herself for it. She realised now that it wasn't some misplaced sense of justice that had driven her to confront Yuri this morning, it was a deep need she only now recognised: to get her friends back.

53

Angus, at that moment, was himself wondering what he was going to do. Not with Jenna, or Max, but with the thirty-foot wall of ice he'd got himself lined up on top of. Having left the chalet when Jenna and Sally did, he'd decided not to wait for Max, worried that what with the way he was feeling, their friendship might take a thorough tooting if he was to see him now. To 'cool it off' with Jenna was one thing, but to flirt so callously with Bertie right in front of her was cruel, and had created exactly what he hadn't wanted: a broken-hearted Jenna. He chucked himself down the slope, catching his edges on the icy gradient just as he wanted to, making a lightning-quick turn just before the slope became a drop to certain death. Finding powder again, his pace slowed slightly, but he carried on down the mountain, knowing he'd hook up with a good, fast red run before the off-piste route got any more dangerous. What wasn't great though was the visibility. The snow was falling, massive great flakes hitting his goggles every second. Pausing for a moment to wipe another huge clump of snow from his face, he saw a figure coming down behind him, following the fresh tracks he'd made and narrowly avoiding the sudden drop on the far side of the piste as he had. As the skier got closer Angus recognised the vibrant red uniform of the French ski school. Waiting for the guy to pass him, Angus realised it was JP. Great, he thought, yet another reminder of someone who wanted Jenna, and if he wasn't careful, might just pick up where Max had left off.

*

Jenna huddled up close to Sally on the chairlift, relieved that at least with your best mate there was no chance of having to give her a blowjob to get a cuddle.

'So sweet of Hugo to tell me to enjoy the snow,' Sally said, 'but to be fair, I might have rather stayed in the nice warm hospital rather than face this, well, this *squall*. It's bloody Baltic out here!' Sally clenched her arms around herself to battle off the cold.

'I know,' shivered Jenna from behind her goggles, fleecy snood and hood.

Leaning in even closer to her friend, Sally said, 'JJ, are you OK? I mean about Max and stuff. Sorry, I've been a bit, well, distracted due to Hugs, but I am here if you want to talk.'

Jenna lifted her chin out of the fleecy snood so she could reply properly. 'Sal, don't be silly. Of *course* Hugo is more important than my stupid old love life. I suppose it has sort of imploded this week, but it's fine. I'm just really disappointed in Max. I need to go home and lick my wounds.'

'Well, at least you don't have to go home and lick something else, which is what I'm sure Max would be having you do, as some sort of sex slave.'

'Sally! Urgh.' Jenna paused, rubbing her lips together to try and warm them against the driving wind. 'Thing is,' she piped up over the rattle of the cables as the chair passed another pylon, 'once I'd got used to the fact that he liked me, for what? Twenty-four hours? Well, I think it's just hard to get un-used to it.'

With the snow getting heavier, the girls decided to call it a day, and although the sun had barely shone, let alone shown whether it was past the yardarm or not, Sally decided that the nearest chalet-style restaurant was to be their sanctuary for a few hours. They skied the last few metres towards the restaurant, and found it hard to see where snowy piste stopped and snowy terrace started. Jenna was sure she might have just skied over something wooden, but unclipped her bindings anyway and found a wall to hoick her skis up against. Motioning to Sally that she needed a pee, she clattered her way into the airlock-style entry hall and let most of the loose snowflakes fall off her before stomping slowly down the nearby stairs to the basement loos. Sally, in the meantime, went through the same snow-decontamination process then found a table before ordering them both a vin chaud and some French fries and plumping herself down on the banquette seat of a booth, close to the crackling logs of a real fire. She carefully laid out her snood, gloves, hat and goggles on the brickwork edge of the fireplace and watched as the steam rose off them. Jenna slid into the booth a few minutes later and seemed to almost physically collapse. Luckily, before she could cry, sleep, or even think about anything else, the little French waiter brought over the two steaming glasses of hot wine and smiled at them both benignly.

'I'm sure we'll bump into the others here,' Sally said authoritatively, having taken her first much-needed sip of vin chaud. 'It's so ghastly out there, no one would ski much further today.'

'It's only eleven thirty,' Jenna said, though she gratefully took a sip from the steaming little glass of wine. 'Hey ho.' She paused, and then asked Sal, 'Do you think Max is with Bertie? Or Gus?'

'Who knows, love. Will you be OK when you see him?' Sally stirred a sugar lump into her wine and tasted the hot, sweet mixture again.

'I know what's coming from Max,' Jenna finally said, as she too stared into her wine and slowly stirred it with a long teaspoon. 'Bertie as good as told me earlier. I just need to work out what to say and how to maintain my dignity without letting him get away scot free.'

'No histrionics, then?' Sally asked, with a slightly hopeful gleam in her eye.

'No, Sal. Not even for your enjoyment, I'm afraid!' Jenna smiled at her friend.

Twenty minutes or so of companionable drinking and eating passed before Jenna noticed the entrance of Max and Bertie.

'Wish me luck,' she whispered under her breath to Sally, as she then called over, 'Maxie — over here, sweets!'

Sally looked her, slightly confused, but then caught on. 'So you've worked out your game plan then?' she whispered. 'Nice one, sweetie.'

Jenna just winked at her, as she shuffled up to let Max and Bertie dump damp ski gear near the fireplace next to her. Steam came off them, as if they were racehorses after the Grand National. Jenna beamed up at Max. 'Hello little sausage,' she said, scrunching up her face in an approximation of a cutesy greeting.

'Er, hi JJ,' Max responded, not looking her in the eye.

'You guys go get some drinkies and come and join us, Sal and I are well settled in and we'd love to hear all about your morning, sweets.' She emphasised the last word, letting it hang as he bashfully turned away and headed to the bar. Bertie caught his arm and asked for a mineral water before sitting down with the girls, without a hint of awkwardness.

'I hear Hugo has woken up?' she said, sounding reasonably genuine for a change.

'Yes, he has. And bless him, the first thing he said was that I should get up here and stop worrying.' Sally felt the need to justify her place at the table, rather than at her fiancé's side. She picked at a chip, fiddling with it in mid-air before tentatively popping it into her mouth, glancing at Bertie first to check if she was about to be verbally lashed for daring to go near a carb.

'Oh God, yah, of course,' Bertie again sounded totally supportive. 'I mean the snow is a-mazing, even if visibility is a little tricksy.' Bertie played with her hair. Jenna, seeing this entente cordiale between the two girls, almost decided to recant on her plan to tease Max into submission, as this was a show in itself.

Max came back, putting the drinks down on the table for the girls before hastily, if a little clumsily, sliding into the booth next to Jenna.

'Have you guys seen Gus this morning?' Sally asked.

'No, he'd gone before we had, er, got our stuff together,' replied Max.

'What a lovely coincidence that you two were both up at the same time!' A kilo of sugar couldn't have sweetened Jenna's tone any more. Bertie caught on and finally deigned to look sheepishly at her, but Max still seemed to have no idea. 'We must all promise to see more of each other when we get back to London,' Jenna continued, reaching over and playing with the stem of Max's beer glass. 'It's been so fun jumping in and out of each other's beds' — at this she pointedly stared at Max before continuing — 'and I don't see why we should leave the alpine horn behind.' She paused, while Max opened and closed his mouth a few times without saying anything and Bertie found the bubbles in her Perrier intensely interesting. 'But I guess when we tell everyone what we were doing — you know, sort of sharing each other — which I personally am fine with, I guess people will talk and reputations will—'

Max reached out and touched Jenna's arm. 'I get it. I'm sorry. I've been an arse, Jenna. Look—'

'No, you look.' The sugar had turned to hardball. Jenna thrust her finger at Max, jabbing him in the chest. 'We've been friends since I first drunkenly bumped into you at college. We've been through every milestone together since, as *friends*, and I thought that perhaps I meant a little bit more to you than I evidently did.'

'I'm sorry.' Max hardly dared to look her in the eye.

'You're sorry? You're an arse. And you and Bertie are supremely welcome to each other.' Jenna folded her arms and looked across at Bertie for confirmation.

'I'm sorry, Jenna,' she said quietly. 'I couldn't help leading him on, even when I thought he'd actually chosen you.'

'Bertie, I never thought I'd hear myself say this, but it *isn't your fault*.'

'No, it's definitely mine. And if Gus hadn't told me that you were, well, um, believing in me . . .' Max struggled, actually looking fairly bashful as he tried to sound as modest as possible, a rarity for Maximilian Finch, 'well then I guess I would have thought it was fair play and that you were up for a bit of fun. I should have known better. I'm sorry, Jenna.'

'You should be, Max, you've been a complete dick. Literally.' As Jenna said this, she heard a snorty giggle from Sally next to her, which in turn made her start to purse her lips and find it incredibly hard to keep a straight face. She regained her composure, however, and carried on. 'But I'm not broken or devastated. I'm just embarrassed and bloody annoyed that this week has been the week that I was made an utter fool out of. By you. So forgive me if I feel the need to drive my point home, and do not consider yourself off the hook yet, Max Finch.'

'Sorry, Jenks,' Max resumed the hangdog expression that seemed so greatly gratifying to Jenna.

54

Angus hiked higher and higher, using his hands to pull himself up the compacted snow, his poles and skis slung over his back in their makeshift harness. Just one more metre or so and he'd be good. He needed the escape, the pure adrenalin of flying down untouched snow. And he was tired, God, was he tired. His arms stung with the build-up of lactic acid and the muscles ached in his calves and shoulders. How blissful the release would be when he made it one, two, three metres further onto that plateau.

Hauling his lanky frame over the last of the ledges, he slumped down, pressing his sweating face into the icy powder before quickly tearing it away as the pinprick crystals burnt him with their fiery coldness. He wished he had his beard back; it would have been damn useful now. Looking beneath him he could barely make out the route he'd planned as the snow pelted down, making fiddling with his bindings all the harder. He knew he had to embrace his challenge now, before the heat of his climb turned to numbing iciness and he was immobilised by cramp or cold. Clipping his boots in, he dusted the clumps of snow from his gloves and picked up the poles he'd wrestled off his back when he'd first got onto the ledge. Using them to steady himself, he looked again, eyes straining through the dark of his goggles, at the way below him. He remembered the rocks to the right: he'd noted them as he climbed up. And he knew below that it was ice with nasty little drops, mini caves almost, as snow had carved its way with the wind around outcrops and boulders. Stay to the left, he told himself as he pushed off over the edge and instantly fell about five feet before his skis hit soft, fresh snow. Bouncing with the energy of it, he stayed upright and took off again, using the momentum from the jump to keep him from sinking further into the already knee-deep snow. Picking up speed, he concentrated on the few metres he could see in front of him, knowing he couldn't make a sudden turn or stop in this fresh powder. Suddenly a flash of light illuminated the scene with a ghastly fluorescence. Lightning. So there was a storm up there, high in the peaks. Thunder followed moments later and Angus prayed he was far enough down the mountain for his poles not to attract the attention of the lightning gods. As the snow evened out he cannoned down a half-pipe, naturally formed out of a mountain crevasse. He was hurtling through the snow at an awesome speed. If only it were bright sunshine and if only Jenna were below and could see how daring and heroic he looked, like one of those adrenalin junkies you see on the TVs in the village bars, but there was no way anyone could see through this blizzard. And any sensible person would either be holed up in a warm and safe restaurant, or taking it easy down at the resort, playing table football and nursing a few beers through the afternoon. He hoped Jenna was. But Angus didn't feel like taking it easy. Angus wanted to test himself, prove he wasn't a coward. Feel the adrenalin and the fear, at least in this one aspect of his life. Flinging himself over one more jump, he finally landed, catching the tip of a ski on an unseen rock several inches below the surface of the snow. He catapulted forward, his skis pinging off from his boots so his legs weren't twisted and broken in the force of the fall, but his body was flung in a somersault, and he landed with a sickening thump on his back, inches deep into snow, and only a couple of feet from the edge of the red run he'd wanted to join. Angus felt nothing, neither cold nor pain, as the darkness crept over him.

55

'Don't you think it's strange that Gus hasn't come in from the cold yet?' Sally asked Jenna as they ordered a hot chocolate. 'I would go for another vin chaud, sweetie, but I'm not sure my liver can take it!' Having made her peace with Max and Bertie, Jenna had sent them on their way, but the effort of it all had made the prospect of that last ski down in that blizzard as hellish a thought as there could be.

'He might be sulking,' mused Jenna, 'or knowing him he packed a whole baguette of cheese and ham down his trousers and is sitting on some rocky outcrop somewhere, chowing down, oblivious to the cold — no, actually *enjoying* the cold!'

'I've never known someone so happily masochistic. I reckon he'd sleep out there if it meant he was first on the piste in the morning!'

A blurred sort of vortex of grey light stirred Angus's consciousness. There was nothing else, no other stimulation. No movement, no sound, no feeling, just a swirling mist of silvery will-o'-the-wisps, and then deepest black again.

'You know, I think we'd better get a move on,' Jenna suggested to Sally as she drained the last of her hot chocolate. 'I don't think it's getting any better out there and I'm going to be a liability for you anyway, let alone if we stay here for another hot choc or two.'

'Yes, and if sitting around's all I'm doing, I should really be doing it at Huggy's bedside,' agreed Sally, slowly starting to pull on her thermal layers and jacket. Jenna did the same and soon the girls were muffled- and gloved-up, thankful for the warmth the fireside had given their clothes, ready to face the icy wind and blizzarding snow outside.

Jenna felt incredibly uneasy. It wasn't that she couldn't ski perfectly competently, but in these conditions even someone like JP would struggle. She kept Sally in her sights — all five metres or so of it — and followed her turns, thankful that for once Sally wasn't whizzing on ahead. Broken pieces of speech came to Jenna occasionally through the wind, Sally guiding her on, encouraging her to make the turns and stay in her tracks. A thicker flurry of snow hit the pair just as they crossed a now almost impossible red run, traversing it to get over to what should be a cruisey blue. Sally stopped at the edge of the piste and let Jenna catch up. A quick nod of the head was all they needed as reassurance to each other to carry on. Almost home now, Jenna thought, as she painstakingly followed Sally's tracks across the squalls of windblown powder. Then blam! From behind, a total idiot, heedless of the conditions or the laws of the piste, cut Jenna up, making her lose her balance and skid crazily out of control into who knows what. She buckled her knees, preparing to fall and bracing herself for the crunch of arm and leg against mountain. Crying out with shock and fear, she hoped Sally would hear, although by now, even at her slower-than-usual pace, Jenna knew Sally would be metres away, too far to see her, and above and beyond the call of friendship to side step back up the inhospitable mountain to find her. Slumped in a pile of skis and poles and not at all happy, Jenna wanted to cry. Again. Skiing was meant to be fun and this was not. She gingerly tested her legs and tried her knees to see if she was hurt. Just bruises, she thought, and a bloody nose for that arrogant twat if she could ever identify him at the bottom. Poles now, where were they?

As soon as she spotted one, a few feet away, it was tossed down the slope by a sudden gust of wind, which also blew through her body, chilling her through her thermals and ski wear. Determined not to lose her deposit on the bloody things, Jenna knew she had to clip her skis back on and, wobbly as hell, ski over to where the pole now lay, slightly off piste and in danger of becoming totally irretrievable. God, Sally would be waiting too, in this cold. Hurry up, Jenna, she told herself. Man up. Woman up, more like. She managed to stand and slipped only a few inches before finding her balance, helped hugely by the one pole she did have on her, and maybe by the practice Angus had made her do the other day. Realising she'd have to make a turn in practically no space at all, she plucked up her courage and went for it, sliding erratically over an unseen ice patch before using all her weight and strength to force the outside ski around and into a turn. She was almost at her pole when she spotted a lone ski, gently sliding down the mountain a few feet away from her. Reaching down to pick up her pole, she managed to grab it and use it to halt the progress of the errant ski at the same time. She looked up the piste behind her, wondering who the owner was. Surely they'd be immobile, yelling for help, but she could hear nothing in the blizzarding sleet all around her.

'Hello!' she yelled up the mountain, 'Hello!'

There was no reply. What should she do? What could she do! Feeling bad for making Sally wait, she was about to try and gingerly set herself off down the mountain. As she rammed the lost ski firmly into the unpacked snow (she must be at the very side of the official piste, she thought to herself), a sudden light shone through the snow and for a brief second the sun seemed to break through a few layers of the cloud. Instead of being a smog-like yellow all around her, the light had changed and she could suddenly see each individual flake falling as the wind dropped and the sheets of sleet-like snow subsided. Looking back up the side of the piste she saw it then, the body lying there, half covered in snow. The wind picked up again and Jenna knew she'd lose track of where she'd seen that poor helpless stranger unless she started to hike in that direction right now. Unclipping her bindings as quickly as she could, she set her own skis into the snow in a cross shape, hoping that it might alert another, bolder skier to help her. She started the hike up to where she'd seen the body lying. Walking up the mountain was hard enough on a normal day, but now, with the wind pushing against her, willing her to go down, down, down the hill, it took all her strength to climb up, digging the toe of each clunky ski boot deep into the loose snow to keep her grip. Had she gone too far? She felt like she'd been climbing for hours, when really it was probably just a few minutes. She wiped the build-up of snowflakes from her goggles and through the smeary lens she saw the body. Yelling at it, she struggled on faster and practically launched herself the last few feet towards him. To her absolute horror, lying there was Angus.

'Gus! Gus!' she yelled, brushing the built-up snow from his face with her mittened hand. 'No no no no no . . .' she repeated to herself as she leant down into him to see if he was breathing. His poles were still caught up around his wrists, so she carefully unwound the straps and removed them so she could fold his arms into his chest, hoping that the warmth in them would help keep him from hypothermia.

'Gus, oh Gus!' Her words fell from her mouth. All thoughts of being annoyed at him for telling Max to leave her alone were forgotten. She climbed on top of him, trying to shield him from the snow, but careful not to touch him too much in case his back or neck were broken. Oh God, she pleaded, please let him be OK!

Jenna had absolutely no idea what to do. Save putting the skis into a cross thing, which she'd already done, and checking to see if he was alive and trying her best to keep him warm, she was at a loss. In a moment of clarity she checked her phone, but found to her dismay that it had no signal at all.

'Shit, shit, shit. Oh, come on, Angus, wake up! Help me . . .' she implored him, although her cries for help gradually got louder and without really realising she was shouting at him, at the mountain, at the thundering blizzard all around her. She straddled him — oh, how different this was to two days ago, she thought — and pressed her full body against him, desperately trying to keep them both warm. She pulled her woollen snood down from covering her face and rested her chilled cheek against his even colder one.

'Oh Angus, Angus . . . I've been such an idiot,' she confessed to his unhearing ear, nuzzling her face in closer to his, convinced she'd warm him somehow. 'I know I used to cry on your shoulder about your shitty old best mate. But Gus, I don't love him, not really. I keep thinking about you. I can't stop. You have to be OK, you have to be!' Reaching her arms around him she let herself cover him totally as he lay there, holding onto him, like a raft from a shipwreck, not letting go as the wind and biting snowflakes danced around them, threatening to cover them completely in a deathly soft blanket.

301

56

Sally swore under her breath. She loved her friend, and lord knows this was quite literally the worst snowstorm ever, but really, how long was she taking? She'd been waiting by the edge of the funicular station, almost at the bottom of the slope, for ages now. It was clearer down here — the worst of the fog-like cloud that was so aggressively full of snow was above her — and she squinted back up the slope, eyeing up every skier, trying to recognise the familiar white salopettes, blue jacket and ridiculous bobble hat.

'Jenna!' she called, back up the slope, letting the 'n' linger longest in the air. *'Jenna!'*

''Allo?' An incredibly attractive Frenchman skied over to Sally as she stood yelling her friend's name.

'Yes?' Sally looked inquisitively at the ruggedly handsome although somewhat windswept man who seemed to have no sense of what 'personal space' meant.

'I 'ear you calling a name.'

'Yes, it's Jenna, she's my friend,' Sally was about to ask why he cared when he carried on.

'I zink I know 'er. Eet is leetle Zhenna, oo I ave been so lucky as to 'ave been, shall we zay, piste-ing about wiz zees week.'

'Oh!' Sally's expression changed from being slightly cautious stranger-danger to really quite intrigued. Forgetting her current ire at her friend (and almost her trussed-up fiancé too), she introduced herself. 'You must be the one-and-only JP? I'm Sally Jones, her best friend.' She stuck out a mittened hand and shook his proffered one.

'Ah, you are not ze, how you zay, beetch, zat I met ze ozzer day.'

'I should hope not!' Sally flustered a bit, before taking the compliment as it was intended. 'She is our other friend, Bertie. I'm the non-beetchy one. I hope!' Sally felt a little disloyal to Hugo; was she flustered or flirting?

JP, however, seemed as oblivious to his charms as ever and carried on. 'You 'ave, ow you zay, perdue, eh, lose her?'

'Yes, it's that dratted storm up there. She was only a few metres behind me I'm sure, but now . . . I've been here for ages and I'm worried about her and *peesed orf* with her too in equal measure!'

'Ah, I remember, Zhenna tells me about your affiance, he is in ze 'ospital, oui?'

'Yes, and I feel terrible not being there, but then I'll feel equally terrible if I don't wait for Jenna.' Sally's true and honest confusion was clear for even a trouser-brained Frenchman to see and he placed a hand on her shoulder, pausing before speaking to let a gusting howl of wind pass down the slope.

'Eet is OK, Sally, I will keep ze eye out for leetle Zhenna, and you can go and zee your man.'

'Really?' Sally was by now feeling every icy gust as her ski wear seemed to be doing nothing to keep out the cutting wind. 'Oh JP, you are every bit as wonderful as Jenna said you were, a true gent, oh, an absolute darling, thank you.'

'No offence, but I zink she will not mind eet being me zat greets er, oui?' JP winked at Sally and then nodded towards the piste, with its ever fewer skiers streaming down it. 'I will stay 'ere. Now you go, ma cherie, JP does not like to stand in ze way of true love.'

Thanking him again, Sally bustled away, turning back again and again to check that he really was true to his word and waiting for Jenna to make her way down.

Jenna was nowhere near making her way down. For who knows how long she had half hovered, half crouched over Angus's prone body, protecting him from the ever-increasing flurries of snow that swirled around them. Her own back must have been covered in at least an inch of snow now, she thought — the bright Smurf-blue of her jacket blending uselessly into the off-white dunes beside her. She whispered to Angus, coaxing him to stir. Shifting her weight from one arm to another, she took the opportunity to dust the snow from his goggles, having decided to keep them on to protect as much of his face as possible. As her mitten made its swipe she saw a flicker — an eyelid — it moved!

'Angus, Angus!' She crouched lower and huffed on the Perspex of the goggles. Wiping it clear again and then clasping his face between her hands, she repeated his name over and over again.

'Jenks . . .' he croaked.

'Oh Angus!' She could feel his whole body tense as he came to. Moving her hands down from his face she clasped his hands in hers and held them tight against her. 'How do you feel? What hurts?'

'Cold. And everything.' But his voice was stronger and his dry sense of humour still there. He moved his hands within hers and she slowly began to move herself off him, wary of her own cold limbs and heavy ski boots. She could barely feel her own feet now, although the adrenalin that his waking had caused inside her was spurring her on and getting the little grey cells working too.

'Angus, can you walk, do you think?'

'I don't know, Jenks. Perhaps. I can barely feel anything.'

'Oh God,' Jenna remembered her initial fear that his back might be broken. But staying out here in this pelting snow and thrashing wind was suicide. 'We have to try and move, Gus, else we'll freeze. There's a restaurant by these pistes, I'm sure of it. I remember thinking it would make a good pit stop if I needed it on the way down with Sal. Oh Sal!' Jenna blinked away tears as she thought of her poor friend, still on the edge of a piste somewhere, perhaps, patiently waiting. But needs must, she thought, and the cold wind made her an unnaturally speedy decision maker. 'Angus, you've got to get up!'

Steady as she could, she helped him roll over and slowly move his legs so he could get some sort of grip on the snow. As he fumbled a bit, Jenna searched inside her ski jacket pocket and found her barely used piste map. Hardly daring to open it in case the wind had it out of her numbed grip in moments, she found the piste she knew they were on and hoped against all odds that the restaurant was nearby. Deciding one direction was better than nothing and that down was the easiest, she slipped the map back into her pocket, sealed her jacket up as high around her neck as she could and turned to find Angus standing upright, at last, next to her.

'Fuck me,' he sighed, not knowing how Jenna right now in her head was saying 'oh God, yes', as he leaned against Jenna's shoulder, testing his weight on each leg in turn.

Gradually the awkwardly moving pair slid, slipped and skidded down the snow, using the rougher, uneven ground next to the piste to gain purchase whenever they could. Jenna's heart was pumping faster than she could ever remember. The physical exertion was one reason, but realising that she was falling hopelessly in love was probably the real cause.

57

Steam suffused the little en-suite bathroom, filling Sally's nostrils with the herbal spa-like scent of whatever luxury gel Bertie had made the mistake of leaving by her shower. Well, near the shower. If you could count 'zipped into the back pocket of her vanity case' as 'near the shower'. Still, thought Sally, she could afford it and after everything that had happened, Bertie owed her a few expensive bubbles, and not just of the champagne variety. Easing herself around in the warm water, she wondered where everyone was. Jenna, she assumed, had finally got herself down the mountain and probably collapsed into the not-too-shabby arms of that rather dishy instructor of hers, and why not? Poor old Jenks had had a miserable time of it this week. Still, the chalet did seem eerily quiet. Bertie and Max were no doubt making hay while the snow fell, as it were, but surely Angus should be back by now? Sally worked out that she'd been at least an hour or two after lunch with Hugo in the hospital, giving them all plenty of time to get down the mountain, surely? Dripping wet all over the bathroom floor, she got out of the bath, deciding that a relaxing soak it was *not* while her brain was working overtime.

Prayers may or may not have been answered, but there, looming out of the swirling fog, was a low, dark shape — a corner of the roof of the alpine restaurant.

'Angus, look!' Jenna wiped her goggles with her mittened hand to check. Sure enough, it was there and thankfully just below them. Taking the side path, which in better weather would have been a perfectly kept little swoosh into the main entrance from the piste, they slid down on their bums, impossibly relieved that their trudging was over. Angus almost fell against the doors and to their absolute delight it gently swung open on its heavy hinge, ushering them both into the airlock-style porch. Confident of success again, Angus pushed against the next set of double doors, the ones that would let them into the rather inviting little restaurant within, and was stopped in his tracks.

'Shit.' Jenna said it for both of them, but before she could get that adrenalin-fuelled brain working again on the next plan she heard a shattering explosion as Angus's ski boot was hurled through the plate glass of the door. 'Shit.'

'Executive decision, Jenna,' Angus stated as he leaned in and flicked the internal lock so they could push their way in. Half expecting an alarm to start blaring out or for angry French chefs to run from the kitchen waving comically massive cleavers, Jenna was caught off guard by the silence. And then again as Angus leaned down and kissed her.

Washed and floofed, Sally traipsed downstairs just as Max walked in. Awkwardness from today's lunch put aside, she questioned him over his recent whereabouts.

'I thought — I thought it was OK now?' he said rather sheepishly, having recounted an afternoon of bar hopping with Bertie.

'Oh, I don't care about your love life, Maximilian; well, at least not now Jenna is out of it,' she said. 'I just wondered where she was. I thought perhaps you and her and Angus, and of course Bertie, had all been together this afternoon?'

''Fraid not. In fact I haven't seen Angus all day. Sort of thought you guys would hook up with him.'

'No . . .' Sally bit her lip. This was not good. 'Izzy!' she shouted to the chalet girl.

'Yah?' she monotoned as she languidly walked out of the kitchen, wiping her hands on a tea towel and causing Max to put that sheepish look back on his face again.

'Did Gus come in for tea earlier?'

'Nope. I wasn't here, but only one slice of cake had gone, which I reckon must have been one of you girls, as you pigs,' she looked pointedly at Max, 'always eat at least two or three slices and raid the fridge at teatime, and much to my happy surprise, I won't have to go and buy more bread for supper today!' With that she turned on her heel back into the kitchen and opened and slammed the fridge door a couple of times.

Sally looked at Max accusatorily. He shrugged.

'They're probably having a few beers,' he said, while he fished his phone out of his pocket. 'I'll text him. How's Hugo, by the way?'

Sally, back on familiar territory, filled him in while he tapped out a quick message.

'There. If they're not here by supper, we'll go for a trail of the bars. But believe me, we know Gus and Jenks — those two boozehounds won't miss the free drinks, not to mention the free supper.'

At that Max gave her shoulder a squeeze and lolloped upstairs to get changed.

'And of course they might have gone to see Hugo?' Sally called after him, with no answer from his departing back.

58

Jenna's mind fizzed. Her heart was beating so fast at the intensity of Angus's kiss that her hitherto frozen fingers and toes were getting their feeling back in all sorts of glorious ways. As he pulled away from her she let her face linger, longing for the kiss to carry on. Ever the practical one, though, Angus had limped to the maître d's desk and picked up the phone. Jenna didn't quite know how to feel when he slowly replaced the receiver and shook his head. The lines were down. Holding out her hand to help him limp back over she saw him wince as he bent over and tried to get his second boot off — clumsily handling the clasps, concentrating hard on each one as they got the better of him.

'Oh, your hands, Angus, they're red raw!' Jenna left her boots undone and crawled on her knees as close to him as she could.

'I — I just can't get any strength in them now,' he grunted as he pulled hard again at the iced-up metal clasp.

'No wonder — your hands are probably numb as anything and this boot's got so much snow and ice packed in under the fittings. Here . . .' Jenna took her mittens off and, with her slightly more dextrous fingers, she started to dig out the caked-in, hard ice that was stopping Angus from undoing his more troublesome boot.

'Wait, Jenks.' He indicated towards the far wall of the restaurant, where the embers of a dying fire were still glowing. 'They must have bailed when the storm got bad, but no more than an hour or two ago, I guess.' Unsteadily, they both got themselves to their feet, scooping up the gloves and hats and goggles that had fallen just as they had when they'd first collapsed into the room. Jenna noticed Angus limp, the heavy ski boot seeming to weigh down that leg more than it should.

'Are you OK, Gus? Your leg?'

'Hurts like buggery,' he replied as he sat down by the fire. This part of the restaurant was a more casual corner, with a low coffee table between two saggy but genteel old sofas. A candle surrounded by pine cones decorated the rustic table, but it soon became obscured by the damp hats, goggles and gloves that got dumped on, around and next to it. Angus raised his legs up onto the table and Jenna sat next to them, working out the compacted ice from the boot clasps, aided now by the thawing warmth of the fire. Finally Jenna managed to ping them open. Easing his ankle out, Angus clenched his teeth, and Jenna could see why as the bruise and swelling was already coursing up his shin from the sickeningly blue and yellow joint.

'Ouch,' she sympathised. 'I would offer to kiss it better . . .'

'But you don't love me that much?'

'Oh Angus!' Jenna looked up at him. He reached his arms towards her and she gratefully made the swift movement from the table to the comfortable sofa cushion next to him. Wrapped up in his arms, she rested her head on his chest. Even through the layers of ski jacket and doubtless many thermals, she could hear his heart beating.

'Angus, I—' she looked up at him, but he stopped her with another kiss.

Sally sat on the sofa of the chalet, hugging her knees to her chest. Max was pacing up and down and Bertie was there too, sitting very still, but white-knuckled as she gripped the edge of the cushion next to her on the sofa. They could hear Izzy speaking in fast, fluent French on the phone in the kitchen. Various words were recognisable to even the most basic French speaker: *neige, aide, montaigne, morte* . . .

Sally gulped and looked up at Max, who in turn looked imploringly at Bertie, who got up from the sofa and went to stand near the kitchen so she could eavesdrop and translate.

'It's mountain rescue. They found skis on the piste on their last run down . . . Crossed as an SOS sign, and one loose sliding down the piste. Well, the chairlift operators had, and they contacted Mountain Rescue when there was no sign of the other ski . . . or the skier.'

'But why are they calling here?' Sally asked, dreading the answer. Max shuffled along the sofa and put his arm around her, sensing the growing panic in her voice.

'It's the skis, Sally. Every ski has a bar code – you know how they zap them when you hire them? They took them back to one of the shops, and all the machines are linked as so many skis go missing and mixed up; anyway, so they traced them back to Angus . . . and Jenna . . .'

'What?' Sally was as worried about her friends as she was confused. 'But Jenna can't be up with Angus? She was only a run or two behind me, I'm sure, and well, I assumed her ski instructor brought her down . . .' Sally was about to start gabbling on as Max pointed out of window.

'Sally, they're all up there. Look,' and he held her steady as he pointed out of the large picture window that in daylight had the most amazing view up the mountain, past the nursery slopes to the valleys beyond. Now, she could just about make out through the falling snow fuzzy light high up on the pistes: headlights of piste bashers, or skidoos perhaps? 'They're looking for them and we're under strict instructions to stay by the phone and await information.'

Izzy walked into the room, carrying a tray on which sat three steaming mugs of hot sweet tea and a few rounds of sandwiches. Max looked up at her and smiled, and she ignored him completely, as she put the tray down on the coffee table in front of the shell-shocked Sally and explained that she needed sugar and food. Bertie reached for a mug of tea. 'Sally, you should have one too,' she said, 'though I warn you: refined sugar is only going to make you feel worse in the long run.'

'I thought you might all be off supper, so I made these,' Izzy explained, 'but I'll keep supper warming for a bit anyway, just in case. I've spoken to Mountain Rescue, and it looks like it could be a long night. They can't stay up past 9 p.m., for their own health and safety, plus the dogs will get lost, and it would be of little use anyway, they say. Sorry,' she looked down at Sally, 'but they did say not to give up hope. If they've found shelter then perhaps they won't be able to find them, but they'll be safe. And they'll send a crew up first thing in the morning, at first light, with a chopper, to search the bits that are just too dangerous now.' Izzy reached down and picked up the plate of sandwiches, passing it to Sally. 'Please, do eat something. You'll feel much better for it.'

Sally took the plate off the young hostess. She could barely digest the news, let alone ham and cheese sarnies, and rolled her eyes as Max dived on them as soon as she lifted her hand away.

'What?' he muffled through a mouthful of bread. Sally just shook her head and even Bertie drew her mouth into a thin line of dismissal.

59

Angus threw another log on the now roaring fire and unzipped his jacket. Jenna had pulled herself away from his warm arms and had gone to investigate the kitchen. He saw her try the light switch on the way, and caught her backward glance to him as she toggled it up and down to no avail — the storm must have cut the power. Thank God for the fire, he thought, and for Jenna finding him before . . . well, it didn't bear thinking about.

'Here you go.' Jenna approached him, bearing a plate of cold meats and cheeses, plus the end of a baguette. 'It's so bloody dark in there, I could barely see — and lord knows how to operate one of those industrial gas hobs, especially with no power, so I'm afraid it's just this.'

Angus didn't mind if it was 'just this' for evermore, as long as it was Jenna serving it to him.

Jenna had stood in front of the massive industrial fridge and pondered over what to make for her first-date supper with Angus. A fillet steak with a béarnaise sauce, that would be fitting, but no can do on that front. So she'd made the best cheese board she could and raided the refrigerator shelves for various pâtés, cornichons, cold meats. 'Spicy sausage for my spicy sausage,' she giggled to herself. And indeed painkillers — she raided the First Aid box that was helpfully kept just next to the fridge. Mentally noting what she'd taken so she could reimburse the restaurant tomorrow, she suddenly baulked as she realised the bill for the smashed front door was going to be considerably more. But oh, Angus had been so manly doing that! And while in pain! No wonder he had crept into her thoughts over the last few days. Max-schmax! She should never have wasted so much time over *him*! Bringing the plate of food over to Angus, she saw him stoke the fire and take off his jacket. As he slid it off over his figure-clinging, ultra-sporty thermal layers, she saw the definition of his back muscles, the shadows thrown off from the fire showing the contours of his well-defined body.

The wind outside howled around the chimney stack as they began to eat, both offering the choicest looking pieces to the other first.

'Chef's perks,' said Angus, refusing a particularly oozy bit of Camembert that Jenna almost had to spoon onto the bread.

'Hardly chefing,' she retorted, forcing him to take the delicious morsel from her, along with a couple of horse-pill sized painkillers. She enjoyed watching him eat it: the movement of his jaw seemed to mesmerise her. If only she could see his other cheek, the one now turned to face the fire. Jenna was desperate to know how he'd got that scar — but if asking him about it led to another abrupt conversation about her minding her own business, well, she definitely didn't want that. No, nothing to break this perfect — well, as perfect as a trespassing-slightly-injured-in-someone-else's-restau-rant-while-a-wild-storm-rages-outside-and-you're-not-sure-if-they'll-forgive-you-for-smashing-their-door-in perfect moment could be. As if Angus read her mind, he turned to face her.

'Jenna . . .' She could see the raised, pale mark across his face now and her eyes couldn't help but flick along its length. She raised her hand up to caress it, but Angus flinched.

'Sorry, sorry!' She quickly lowered her hand and her eyes and stared at the back of the sofa very intently.

'No, I'm sorry . . . Here.' He gently took her hand and guided it along his cheek.

'It was in Singapore, a few years ago . . .' He began to tell her the full story. 'We were set on one night after a team night out. The project we'd been working on . . . we didn't realise but it fell right in the middle of gangland. The "triads" are as busy there as they are in Honkers.'

'So they attacked you? For building on their land?'

'Sort of.' Angus held her hand to his cheek. 'They thought we must be working for a rival gang, when really we were just architects commissioned by the government. We hadn't even started the build; I mean, no tenders had even been sent out to builders, but they'd got wind of it. Wrong end of the stick, though.'

'So how did it happen?' Jenna was hooked by the story. Perhaps Angus wasn't the quiet, well-behaved man she'd pegged him as after all?

'They ambushed us. Bottles, knives, furniture — it was all being thrown.' Jenna's eyes widened as he said 'knives'. 'I was petrified. I had to find a way out but it was chaos. I saw a get-out through the carnage in the room — a table had been overturned, a natural barricade that I could crawl behind, then one short sprint to the fire exit. I can't really remember what happened but something made me look back . . .'

'And they got you then?'

'No, it was then I saw Pei Ling.' Jenna's eyes furrowed, a flicker of jealousy as she imagined a Lucy Liu type with seductively dark hair and exquisite figure. Angus smiled as he saw Jenna's crestfallen face. 'Ha, nothing like that, Jenna. She was like a mentor to me, Pei Ling. I worked at Stafford Ling Architects. She's, like,' he waved his hand in exaggeration, 'a hundred and two and has been designing buildings since the Second World War.' Jenna tried to contain her relief, but her trying-to-be-sage-and-understanding nod couldn't belie the smile underneath.

'What was happening to her?' she asked, relief giving way to curiosity again.

'She was stranded. As a people, the Malay may respect the elderly, but the gangs respect no one. I had to take her with me. She's like a cultural legend. I doubled back and caught her attention — but in so doing, I caught someone else's. A bottle came flying across the room at me — lucky, I guess, it wasn't a knife, or a bullet. I couldn't think, just knew I had to grab Pei Ling's hand and get her out of there. But on our way we were confronted by one of the gang members.' Angus paused, closing his eyes in order to piece together the fractured memory. 'God, he was a nasty piece of work. Tattoos on his face, up his arms, a jagged blade in his hand. He swiped at me, making this,' he held Jenna's hand to his cheek again. 'I lashed out at him after that with a chair leg I'd picked up in the wreckage. I went for him — and it wasn't a fair fight as he'd just been knocked to the side by something else flying through the air. I just hit him and hit him, his blood, my blood — there came a point where I couldn't tell the difference,' Angus flexed his fingers at the memory, as if he was trying to rid himself of the guilt. 'I've always felt so ashamed of attacking him, when I should have just been defending myself and Ms Ling.'

Quietly Jenna said, 'But it sounds like it was defence. You were terrified — I mean, who wouldn't lash out if someone was attacking you?'

'I just wanted to get us both out. I just . . .'

'So she was unhurt?'

'Yeah, miraculously. She came to visit me in the clinic afterwards to thank me.'

'But, Angus, that's . . . well, that's heroic!'

Jenna was feeling so incredibly close to Angus — his story only heightening the rush of feelings she was experiencing. His hand was still holding hers, although it was no longer up by his face. Now their fingers interlaced and he brought his other hand up to her cheek, holding her so gently as he leaned in to kiss her.

'What was that again?' he whispered, as he gently kissed the lobe of her ear.

Deep breath and a little gasp. 'Heroic. Angus, you're a hero . . .' Before she could even finish the sentence she was kissed so passionately that she forgot all about Singapore and bar brawls and rescue attempts and fell hopelessly into the moment, kissing him back with equal passion and fervour. He pulled her in closer to him and slipped his arms fully around her so she was entirely his. Jenna moved her face to one side, nuzzling his cheek. She pulled her arm up and out of his embrace so she could touch his face again before kissing him again and again.

As the clock ticked on and it got closer to 9 p.m., the more fidgety and filled with angst the friends became. Max wouldn't stop pacing, the three sandwiches he'd had sitting uneasily in his stomach. Bertie was crouched in the corner of the sofa, her legs tucked up under her and her chin resting on her knees. She checked her iPhone occasionally for the weather report, while Sally had texted Hugo down at the hospital and explained that she couldn't come and see him tonight. At about eight-ish she had broken down in sobs, saying this was the worst ski trip ever and if anything happened to Jenna she'd never want to ski again.

60

Jenna let Angus kiss her and kiss her, and it felt so right. She regretted her affair with Max so much now, and in this very moment all those years of hurt, of never being the one who he wanted, always being the also-ran, always getting drunk and weeping on Angus's shoulder — they were wiped clean by this deeply wonderful, amazingly sexy man, who happened to be pulling her onto his lap.

'You know, you saved my life, Jenksy,' he murmured into her neck as he continued to kiss her, 'so technically you're the hero.'

'And do I get a ticker-tape parade on our return to the big smoke?'

'No, but you do get this . . .' At that Angus kissed her again and slowly began to caress her neck, moving his hands down her body. Slowly they began to undress each other, the pile of hats and gloves on the coffee table gradually being joined by under layers, salopettes and long johns.

'Definitely much, much sexier without those on,' Jenna said as she carefully pulled off his thermal leg wear over his now desperately swollen ankle. Noticing his wince, she made him lie back, moving his sore leg from resting on the table to the arm of the sofa.

'I promise I'll be gentle.' Jenna carefully climbed on top of him and pulled her polo shirt off and over her head. She reached around behind her back and released her bra fastening. She barely had a moment to sensuously flick her bra around or tease her hair down around her breasts before Angus had exerted quite some strength and put those abdominal muscles to good use raising himself up and pulling her down on top of him. Jenna felt his skin on hers, the hairs on his chest brushing against her. The fire cossetted them both in its warmth and its gentle golden light guided Jenna's hands as they reached down for Angus's cock that rose, proudly, from his boxers, begging to be touched, licked and caressed. Jenna turned herself around, letting Angus get a full and glorious view of her wonderfully peachy bottom. Taking his cock in her hands she gently, then firmly, stroked and kissed it, making it rise larger and larger until his moans of pleasure told her it was time to stop teasing him. Turning around she saw the massive grin on his face, his eyes shining in the glow of the fire, eyes she now knew she wanted to gaze into for ever and ever. Jenna gently lowered herself onto him, rhythmically starting to ride him, the motion bringing them both to exquisite pleasure in a matter of moments. Jenna raked her fingernails across his chest, now glistening with perspiration, as she came in a shuddering climax, electric pulses careering through her body as she gasped in pleasure.

'Oh Angus . . .!' she collapsed onto him as he wrapped his arms around her and held her close to him. It had all felt so completely right, so wonderfully perfect. Angus held her, the moments turning into minutes as they lay in each other's arms, both gently stroking each other and murmuring sweet nothings as the fire burned down in the grate and the warm embers crackled, the only sound now against the howling of the blizzard outside.

319

Friday

61

'Darling, words fail me. Honestly!' Sally fussed over her best friend, alternately scolding her and hugging her in the waiting room of the clinic where Angus was now holed up as well as Hugo. Jenna, sparing some details, had filled Sally in on last's night's adventures: finding Angus, limping to the restaurant, their rather unorthodox way of getting in, and then the rescue, early that morning, once the snowstorm had subsided. Angus, although he'd said he was loath to end their joyous coupling, had done the sensible thing and tried the phone again — and was just a little bit disgruntled that the line was now reconnected to the outside world. It had only been a matter of minutes after that that they'd heard skidoos roaring up the piste outside, blood wagons attached, the rescue team primed to deal with victims of the storm. To find two remarkably happy-looking 'victims', both looking rather satisfied and healthy, except a terribly swollen ankle on one of them, had been almost a disappointment, or so it seemed to Jenna. They'd been whisked to the little hospital nonetheless, with Jenna released to the waiting area almost right away as Angus was taken in to have an X-ray.

'So I phoned you as soon as I could really,' Jenna explained to Sally. 'We only got here at about 7 a.m. and I didn't want to wake you then.'

'Wake me? Wake me! Like we, any of us, had a wink of sleep last night! We thought you were *dead*!'

'Sorry, Sal, I'm so, so sorry.' Jenna did genuinely feel bad for not letting her friend know sooner, but couldn't hide the smile from her face as she almost blurted out, 'But it was all so exciting and so, so perfect. Although I think I might have left my knickers down the side of the sofa. Oh well, never mind, I'll swap knick-knocks for nookie with Angus anytime!' She clasped Sally in her arms, her friend returning the joyous hug, forgiving her instantly for any lack of comms.

'Oh, sweetie,' she admonished playfully as she drew away, 'I always knew Max wasn't the one for you and Angus is so much the better choice. He's loaded too, you know, you lucky minx.'

'Sals, I wouldn't care if he was the poorest man in the world. Or at least, middle-lower-middle . . .' she teased her friend. 'He's just sublime. And my word, even with a poorly leg he was a-maze-ing last night. Everything that Max wasn't — so caring and selfless — I've never been so, so . . .'

Raising her hand to stem the flow of Jenna's enthused — and edging towards downright dirty — chat, Sally interrupted her, 'Yes, we get the idea darling!'

Laughing and hugging, the two caught up some more on the night's events.

'Even Bertie was quite worried about you two, you know,' Sally carried on.

'Blimey, how the mighty have fallen,' Jenna mused. 'I didn't think she'd care a jot about anyone else, ever.'

'Well, I suppose she got the cream.'

'Max's cream.'

'Eew . . . darling, please.' The girls giggled until a rather handsome doctor came out and asked Sally to come in and sign a few forms for the broken-wristed Hugo. As she got up, Jenna really noticed how the usually bonny and rosy-cheeked Sally looked ashen-faced and gaunt, this week's 'adventures' peaking with last night's worry over her friends having taken their toll on her pretty features.

Sally turned back to Jenna before following the doctor into his office and clocked Jenna's concerned expression before saying with a wry smile, 'I don't know about you sweetie, but I think I need a holiday!'

Epilogue

The train crawled into the platform at Clapham South, packed as usual with the Monday morning commuters. Jenna was jostled on each side — a man in a cheap, shiny suit pressed against one of her shoulders while a large woman with a huge multi-coloured poncho braced herself against the other one. Jenna barely noticed, though, and with an almost mechanical automation found herself stepping up into the carriage and seeking out a bit of breathing space as the rest of her fellow south London commuters pushed in around her. Not much different to the packed cable cars I was in only a few days ago, she thought. But oh, how different life is now. Ahead of her, beyond the commute to Waterloo (change for the Jubilee to Green Park), she was going to relish the morning coffees with her colleagues. The gallery intern was never going to believe her stories, and who could blame her? Jenna still played the week's events over and over in her mind, the ups and downs and final days. Angus had had to stay in the little French hospital overnight on the Friday too, but had been discharged, along with Hugo, on Saturday morning, in time to get the Ice Bus back to Geneva. Without two of her Sherpas, Bertie had been in a tricky position trying to get her trunk into the back of the van, but with relations warming between her and Sally, they'd managed it, three girls and one Max finally pushing the thing in. A slightly recalcitrant Bertie did admit that for St Barts she might just about manage with just a sturdy Louis Vuitton suitcase, or three, much to the applause of her fellow travellers.

Max was a changed man. The emotion he'd felt when he heard that Angus and Jenna were rescued had overwhelmed him, and he'd made sure he apologised properly for being an utter twat all week. He'd promised he'd do anything to make it up to his two best friends and, true to his word, he'd organised first-class seats for them on the plane, along with ones for Hugo and Sally too. For all his trying, though, he and Bertie were stuck in economy. Bertie, to give her her due, hadn't complained too much, but had sworn never to leave the travel arrangements to anyone else ever again.

Angus, though, darling, darling Angus, Jenna thought. They had spent all afternoon on the day after the accident together, he with his ankle up in the clinic bed, her sitting next to him, or cuddling him through the hospital blankets. It had all come out — how he realised that he was falling in love with her and that he wasn't sure at all that he'd have any chance of winning her — plus he was certain she'd still be too emotionally raw from Max. Jenna had listened to all of this and held him even tighter, realising quite what a special guy — especially compared to Max — he was. And that she was, actually, possibly, as hopelessly in love with him as he seemed to be with her.

As the train doors opened at Green Park, Jenna couldn't help but smile to herself. Although still limping, Angus was home with her. She'd left him tucked up in her bed, resting his sprained ankle and nursing his almost-frostbitten hands. But, like their new-found relationship, his ankle was getting stronger with every kiss she'd given him (or with the painkillers from the French doctors, but she preferred the romantic view). It would only be a few hours before she could slide back into bed next to him and rest her head on his chest in the knowledge that finally, finally, she was loved.

Acknowledgements

Firstly, my thanks to my agent Emily Sweet for taking me from nought to sixty and plucking me out of writing obscurity; and to Anna Simpson for pointing me in the direction of Justine Taylor and her editorial help, without whom this book would have languished on my laptop for ever more. Thank you to Clare Hey at Orion for taking a chance on a manuscript that wasn't exactly what she was looking for but made her laugh anyway. And thank you to my friend Tracy Staines who was the most alpha of beta readers and gave me the confidence to keep writing — as well as accompanying me on a few of those inspirational ski trips. Talking of ski buddies — you all know who you are — and to Martin Hemsley, the ski instructor who taught me to squish the bugs.

Thank you to John Adair — mentor in chief — you said I could, and I did! And to Ardella Jones from Chalk The Sun — your creative writing classes got me over my fear of reading my work out loud to an audience, even if you did all laugh at me (sometimes for the right reasons!) — and Vanessa Richmond; I think you always knew I was more of a writer than a sub-editor!

And to my family — all of you, you lovely lot — but especially my amazing Mumsles who once said, 'Anything but dull, darling' — I hope this fits the bill . . . And last, but never my least, my darling husband Rupert — thank you for all your support, your love and for making me smile every day (and for bringing Toby, our fleabag, into my life).

**If you enjoyed *Snowballs!* then get ready for
Corkscrew! Summer Fun at the Vineyard
Out Summer 2018**

Jenna Jenkins is in trouble. She's lost her job and it's make or
break time with Angus. Frustrated at his lack of commitment – and
desperately short of funds – she accepts a flirtatious friend's offer of
work for at the prestigious Carstairs & Co of Piccadilly, the oldest
wine merchant in London and from there a summer secondment at
the beautiful Chateau Montmorency.

Organising the party of the century, dining out with suave
Frenchmen and getting tempted among the vines seem all part of
a day's work . . . but is there a secret lurking in the cellars of the
glamorous chateau?

Caught in a trap she can't talk – or drink – herself out of she's
well and truly corkscrewed. Angus is nowhere to be found when
she needs him, but a mysterious benefactor helps her out of her
jam. Funny how he seems so familiar though?